I0613000

THE 13th POWER
JOURNEY

Terry Wright

2016, TWB Press
www.twbpress.com

The 13th Power Journey

Published by TWB Press

ISBN: 978-1-944045-24-1

In the second book of The 13th Power Trilogy, Ray Crawford, having failed to achieve fame, has formulated a new plan: reprogram the Supercomputers, build a bigger gravity chamber, and degenerate NASA's prototype Inter Space Station Transporter into the 13th Power. He will discover that fame carries a terrible price.

Since the undercover operation in Simi Valley failed, *The Ark* is under more pressure from the President to fulfill Directive 119, the Strategic Defense Initiative, and deploy at network of proton laser beams in orbit. He captures the fugitive murderer Dr. Curtis, aka Melvin Anderson, and offers him a deal he can't refuse.

Just when Janis Mackey is settled into a peaceful life with Tracy in Boulder, the CIA calls on him to help them steal the 13th Power technology for Star Wars. Of course, he refuses, so acting on orders from *The Ark*, they take Tracy into custody and threaten to kill her if Janis doesn't deliver the goods.

Janis's return to Simi Valley is not the joyous reunion Lisa expected. She's heartbroken over his devotion to Tracy, but she's determined to win him back. And Lisa has a new problem: her mother. Kate returns after her release from prison. She's looking for forgiveness from a daughter she'd abandoned and a husband she'd betrayed. Good luck with that.

In this stunning sequel to The 13th Power Quest, humanity is at the mercy of technology, and a family's love for each other is put to a brutal test.

Chapter One

THREE DAYS AFTER the explosion and fire at Tech-Com Control, the Fire Chief and building inspectors deemed the labs safe to reenter. Ray Crawford got the call first. “I’ll be right there.”

With excitement thrumming in his chest, he jumped into his staff car and sped toward the twin stainless steel and plate glass buildings of the Solartech Labs complex, which was nestled in the rocky hills above Simi Valley, California. He drove with one hand, cell phone in the other.

“Hello,” Janis Mackey’s voice groaned from the safety of his quiet university life in Boulder, Colorado. “What do you want, Ray?”

“We’re going back in.”

“Just give it up, will you?”

“I can’t.” Ray understood his obsession with the 13th Power. It was an addiction no different from an alcoholic’s thirst for another drink, or a junkie’s craving for a fix that would destroy him.

“It nearly killed us all,” Janis shouted.

“Your formula was the reason—”

“My formula got us to the 13th Power.”

“But it negated the MIGGS.” The Mass Imitation Gravity Generating Simulator was supposed to keep the experiment safe. “Admit it, Janis. You blew the experiment.”

“We shouldn’t have done it in the first place. Negative

and positive are never equal."

"You mathematicians are all alike—"

"Shut up, Ray. We've been friends too long to start blaming each other for what happened...what almost happened."

"You almost destroyed the world, Janis."

"Go back to Nevada. Take Lisa with you. Forget about the project."

Like a voracious monster, that urge for discovery gnawed at his guts. He had to complete what he'd started. The 13th Power could be achieved. The Higgs boson was there somewhere. He had to find it before CERN or Fermilabs beat him to the prize. There was no other way to satisfy the monster within.

"Sorry, Janis. I have to—"

"Then don't call me to bail your ass out of trouble." Janis hung up.

"Damn it." Ray folded the phone closed and jammed it into his jacket pocket. Janis Mackey was one stubborn son of a bitch. Ray gunned the engine toward Tech-Com Control. Anticipation made his heart pound and his palms sweat.

He careened the car onto the ramp between the two buildings. A big man in blue coveralls held up a stop sign. Ray hit the brakes. Sunshine pierced the morning haze and reflected off a towering crane to which workers had attached the twisted steel arch that once spanned the entryway.

Cables strained and steel creaked. The crane lurched, and the mangled arch rose into the air. Ray could barely make out the words inscribed on its crumpled facing.

Welcome to Solartech Labs, Gateway to the Atomic Universe.

"Are you going to fix that thing?" he asked the man with the stop sign.

"We're going to fix everything, Mr. Crawford."

Settling back in his seat, he ran a finger over his mustache and looked around at the damage left in the wake of the 13th Power experiment. Broken glass and busted office fixtures littered the ramp, and all the way down the side of the five-story building on his right, curtains flapped from glassless windows. And most of the windows in the adjacent building on his left were cracked and broken, too. Above, catwalks between the buildings were buckled, and one had fallen.

Ray shivered when he thought about how close they'd come to destroying the world. All he wanted was the 13th Power and the recognition it would bring him for discovering the Higgs boson: the Nobel Prize and his name synonymous with the likes of Einstein, Cockcroft, and Oppenheimer. However, his entire career, all twenty-six years, had been plagued with failure and obscurity. This time he'd come so close to achieving his fame, but what had it left him with?

This mess.

Drumming his fingers on the steering wheel, he thought about the one good thing that had come out of the 13th Power experiments: Lisa. He'd finally told his daughter the truth about Kate. Lisa was twenty-five years old already—the past nineteen of them wasted because of her mother. Ray was thankful Kate was still in prison and not around to do any more damage to their lives. At least now, Lisa didn't blame him for her problems anymore.

The crane swiveled the mass of twisted steel to a flatbed trailer where a crew went to work with chains and tie-downs. A few minutes later, the ramp was cleared, and the big man waved him on.

Inside the lab, Ray made his way through the shambles of Tech-Com Control. The huge windows that once overlooked the supercomputer room were blown out. Jagged shards of glass dangled from a splintered wooden framework. A ceiling fixture flickered, and above the busted window frame, the countdown clock's red digits displayed all zeros, still flashing. He looked over the rows of supercomputers below. Green lights twinkled on the main control panel indicating the Supers had survived.

He smelled smoke. It had taken firefighters several hours to extinguish the blaze in the maintenance galley. The concussion in the accelerator had thundered back through the tunnel and into Tech-Com Control, upturning consoles, smashing terminals, and showering the place in glass and debris. The team was lucky they got out alive.

Kicking aside a tumbled chair, he made his way to the blackened window of the MIGGS. Its foot-thick glass was cracked in a pattern much like a garden spider's web, almost beautifully broken. Peering into the window, he saw that the gravity chamber was cluttered with a tangle of twisted piping and buckled steel ribs. The shiny titanium cylinder still hung from the ceiling by its mechanical arm. Its polished surface was scorched blue where the particle beam had struck it on the side.

Across the room, he spotted the monitor at his station, canted and dusty. *CHANGES LOCKED OUT* still flashed in the status window. He shuffled past a tangle of wires, meters, and dials that once were part of the power distribution console and stepped over the remains of the laser control terminal smashed on the floor.

He remembered how Tracy had worked that keyboard in a frantic attempt to calculate the damage Janis's formula had done to the MIGGS. *When* $13P = (10^{-12})^{-13}$ *then* $(- = +)$ had nearly destroyed the world. Yet in spite of his failure, Ray had to give Janis credit for one thing. If he hadn't rotated the titanium cylinder when he did, nothing would have been left.

A door creaked. Ray spun around.

Stan Burton, wearing a white lab coat, entered with his team of engineers, welders, and electricians. They wore gray jumpsuits and white hardhats. Stan stood about five-foot-four. Brown hair hung down to his shoulders. He looked more like a hippie than a mechanical engineer. "Where do we start?"

"I'm glad you guys made it out all right."

"Janis sounded the alarm just in time."

Ray went back to rummaging through the debris.

Stan lit a cigarette. "The 13th Power experiment sure made a mess of things."

"We made some mistakes. We'll get it right next time."

"Why bother?" Stan asked. His men stood behind him. "This company has made huge strides in medical equipment research and development. This quest for the Higgs boson is a waste of our time."

Ray brushed his hands together. One look at Stan told him the man was no scientist. His pea brain couldn't imagine the possibilities of the 13th Power, to control the Higgs boson...to have the Higgs Field in mankind's grasp. "What if I were to tell you that the Higgs boson is just the tiniest part of an immense field that saturates the universe around us in the same way a magnetic field saturates the area round a magnet?"

"So? Is it going to build a better toaster? What's the average joe going to gain?"

"It's going to give us the means to travel great distances across space in seconds."

"Go blow your nose," a man said. He wore dark goggles parked on his forehead.

Ray shot him a how-should-you-know look. "The 12th power negative is the diameter of the atom's nucleus, and that diameter to the 13th power negative is where we believe the Higgs boson can be found. But to the positive, the 13th Power is equal to the diameter of the Milky Way Galaxy."

"Jeeze," was all the man could say.

"And because the Higgs Field saturates the universe,

understanding how the Higgs works can make travel around the galaxy commonplace. No toaster, mind you, but one hell of a ride."

"So have you seen this Higgs thingy?" another man asked.

Ray felt a chill. "In one experiment, a particle appeared just before we reached the 13th Power. It was so intense, that the supercomputers couldn't keep up with the flow of data coming from the MIGGS. When the particle disappeared, it took the titanium cylinder with it, somewhere into the void. It was the Higgs boson's doing, I'm sure."

"It disintegrated," one man said.

"Degenerated," Ray corrected him.

"What's the difference?"

"Degenerate an object, it will move from one place to another. Its atomic structure remains intact. Disintegrate an object and the atomic structure is destroyed."

Ray cringed a bit at the significance of being wrong about that. Janis's ominous words echoed in Ray's brain: *"We shouldn't be messing with this."*

Stan exhaled smoke. "I can think of the possibilities."

Ray blinked. That's what scientific research was all about: exploring the possibilities. He wondered if he should heed the mathematician's words but thought how Janis didn't believe in the 13th Power anyway. He too considered the experiments a waste of time. And where was he now? Back at the University of Colorado, showing Tracy around campus, taking her out to dinner, and who knows what else? Whatever happened around here from now on was of no concern to him. The future was in Ray's hands now. He'd made mistakes in the past, but he'd learned a lot. With a little fix up, Tech-Com Control could be back in operation. The Supers were in good shape. He only needed to take out Janis's formula and start over. Surely he could find another mathematician, though probably not one as good as Janis Mackey.

Tingling with excitement, Ray thought he still had a chance to make his mark in history and become one of the greatest physicists in the world. The 13th Power could still be his claim to fame. All he had to do was trap the Higgs boson and find out where the titanium cylinder went. He turned to Stan. “Can you fix the MIGGS?”

“We can fix anything. I’ve already got a crew repairing the accelerator.”

“What about a new laser?”

“We have a backup. It’s still in the crate.”

“Can you mount a camera on the titanium cylinder, or some kind of tracking device?”

Stan frowned. “What for?”

“So next time, when the cylinder degenerates into the 13th Power, we can find out where it went.”

“Come on, Ray, you know we can’t transmit that far: 100,000 light years away? Hell, the dinosaurs will be back before the signal reached earth. There’s gotta be another way.”

A young engineer whispered into Stan’s ear. Stan’s eyebrows tweaked. He nodded and turned to Ray. “Why not go see for yourself?”

Ray’s breath hitched in his throat. “What do you mean?”

“Take a journey into the 13th Power.”

“Are you nuts?”

“Come on, we’ll show you how you can do it.”

Flooded with doubt, Ray followed Stan and his men out of Tech-Com Control and through a set of swinging doors that opened into a long hallway. He wondered what they were going to show him. Solartech Labs had always been on the cutting edge of research and development. It seemed as if nothing was technically impossible for these guys, after all, they were the best engineers in the world. But a journey into the 13th Power... how did they think that was possible?

Transitioning another hallway, Stan motioned a turn down a corridor to the left. At the end, a set of double doors blocked their way. A sign posted a warning: *No Admittance without Pass Key.* Ray patted his pockets, but Stan had already stepped up to the computer terminal and inserted his card into the slot.

A buzzer sounded.

The doors opened.

"After you," Stan said.

Ray took a breath as if he was about to plunge into a deep pool. Inside the cavernous maintenance galley, men wearing gray jumpsuits and white hardhats moved about on electric carts. Some hauled work crews, while others towed trailers piled high with supplies they needed to make repairs to the synchrotron, the accelerator, and the other equipment damaged by the blast. Welding torches glowed and popped and spit molten slag as noisy machinery and echoing voices filled the room. The whole place smelled like wet cement.

Ray followed Stan through another security door and into a dark room. "Get a load of this," Stan said and worked the light switch.

Ray had never expected to see anything like the sight that spilled into his brain. The air in his lungs felt heavy as mud. "What is it?"

Stan put his hands on his hips. "A project Dr. Curtis mothballed when he took over Solartech Labs, before he hired you and Janis Mackey. The 13th Power project took priority."

Ray's throat went dry. "Dr. Curtis turned out to be a big disappointment."

"He duped us all." Stan crushed out his cigarette on the heel of his boot. "He had us believing the 13th Power was a scientific project. Instead, he really wanted the Higgs boson so he could turn lead into gold. Imagine that."

"It's not impossible..." Ray fixed his gaze on the marvel Stan had brought him to see.

"I wonder where Curtis is now," somebody said.

Ray grumped. "Probably hiding out in Mexico with his tail tucked between his legs. Turns out he'd escaped through the maze of synchrotron maintenance tunnels. The authorities are still looking for him. I say good riddance." With his heart drumming, Ray made his way around the room, studying the sight before him. "It's beautiful."

"We're proud of it," Stan said.

His men nodded.

Walking all around the vehicle, Ray thought it looked like a jet of some kind, silver skinned and pointy in the nose. It was a good forty feet long and as tall as a bus with swept-back delta wings and wingtips that angled ninety degrees straight up, forming twin vertical stabilizers. It had no landing gear or wheels but rested on three skinny tripods.

Huge panels lined the back of the craft. He counted six of them, but they didn't look like any kind of engine component he'd ever seen before. These were rectangular, about ten feet high, four feet wide, and shiny as polished mirrors. The fuselage had no markings of any kind, not a single warning sticker or sign that usually cluttered the skins of jet aircraft. Thick cockpit windows, black as mica, glistened under the ceiling lights. He saw no door, only something that looked like a space shuttle hatch on its belly. Ray took two more turns around it. "What is it?"

"Ain't she a beauty?" Stan stood next to him now, his arms folded over his chest, his long hair a mop on his shoulders. "It's an I.S.S.T."

"I should know what that is?"

"An Inter-Space-Station-Transporter. She has no means of launch or reentry because she was designed only for use in orbit, you know, to ferry men and supplies between space stations, whenever NASA gets around to building another one, that is. She fits in the cargo bay of NASA's newest Aerospace Shuttle, Odyssey. Once she's deployed in orbit, she can't come back down without burning up in the atmosphere."

"Then why does it have wings if it's not meant to reenter?"

"This design can also be fitted with a heat shield and wheels to be used as an emergency escape craft for the space station."

Ray rubbed his chin. "It can't hold much fuel."

"No fuel," Stan said. "She's equipped with pulse light engines. NASA gave us the design, and Lockheed's boys showed us how to make them work. It wasn't long before we made some modifications of our own." He pointed to the mirror-like exhaust ports. "They run on starlight by trapping photons then magnifying and reflecting them out the rear refractors. In the vacuum of space, the transporter is thrust forward. Of course, the closer she is to a star, the brighter the light and the faster she goes."

"How fast?"

"Light speed. But we can add refractory angles that could conceivably boost that ten times."

"Christ! At that speed, this thing would weigh a gazillion tons."

"In earth orbit, yes, but if the 13th Power breaks the rules of physics, what then?"

Ray shuddered. That was only a theory. This hypothesis went way beyond any sense of reason.

"Confidence is high as we say in this business."

Ray blinked. "*Why not see for yourself?*" Stan's words rolled around in his brain. "Are you saying we should put this I.S.S.T. inside the MIGGS...in place of the titanium cylinder?"

Stan shrugged. "Why not? It's made of the same stuff."

"But the gravity field in the MIGGS will crush it and

anyone inside."

"We'll reinforce the transporter with additional ribs and install an ion shield in the MIGGS. You'll be quite safe."

Ray's heart started racing as his mind considered things he had never thought possible: space flight without liftoff, interstellar transition without fuel. He'd be more famous than Einstein. And what would he discover in the 13th Power—other solar systems, other civilizations? The Nobel Prize was as good as sitting on his fireplace mantle...if he lived to tell anyone. With that thought stuck in his throat, he looked at the spacecraft with no heat shield or wheels. "How will I get back?"

"We'll build a mini MIGGS inside the I.S.S.T. so it will regenerate right back inside the MIGGS where it degenerated from." Stan slapped Ray's shoulder.

"Are you sure about that?"

"You leave the engineering up to us and concentrate on finding the 13th Power without getting us all killed."

Ray gulped. He wasn't only thinking of the Higgs, he was also thinking of his daughter. Lisa would never go for him risking his life for the science he believed in. She'd never understand how a journey into the 13th Power would be an opportunity of a lifetime. He feared she'd only see it as an excuse for her father to leave her again. His hands went damp and his stomach turned upside down. Maybe he shouldn't tell Lisa anything.

He looked at Stan. "All right. Let's do it."

Chapter Two

THE BELL WENT OFF, just as it had every morning for the last three and a half years. Kate didn't have to look at the clock to know it was 7am and time to get up. She'd stand in for breakfast at the commissary and then get on with the chores of the day, which included sessions with drug counselors and classes on anger management and relationships. Therapy had helped Kate deal with her addictions and, finally, the nightmares of her father had stopped haunting her.

As usual, today she'd spend two hours in the gym and run around the track a few times. Keeping in shape was a never-ending battle. However, one thing made this day different from all the others: freedom. The Southern Nevada Women's Correctional Facility would be less one inmate by sunset.

She kicked off the bed sheet and stretched. At forty-four, her body felt stronger than ever. Her mind was clear, and that craving for another line of cocaine seemed under control. Still, she didn't trust herself. She'd been free of the stuff in the past, only to take it up again for no better reason than to get high and damn the rest of the world. Then the cycle started all over again: drugs for sex, sex for drugs, sleazy motels and sweaty men with more money than time.

"Let's go, Crawford," the guard said through the bars.

"Yeah. Yeah." Kate sat up, rubbed her eyes, and tousled her hair, which she kept short for ease of maintenance: a little over the ears, a little on the collar and fluffy bangs. She used to keep it long, back when it flowed shiny and black. Now the only sparkle came from streaks of gray, which seemed to fit with the little wrinkles around her eyes and the thin lines on her forehead. Even her lips had lost their fullness. Years of partying and doing hard time in prison had robbed her of her youth. She sighed and thanked God for makeup.

Sarah Beth stirred in her bed on the other side of the cell. She was a cumbersome woman in her late thirties with thinning blond hair and broken teeth. Someone said she was drunk when she busted up the Desert Lagoon Bar after some old geezer declined her invitation for a night of uninhibited bliss. Kate chuckled. She couldn't blame him much, though he didn't deserve the beating he got. Sarah Beth got three-to-five.

Having a roommate was nice, though. Sometimes late at night they'd tell stories to each other. Sarah Beth talked about her family a lot, her mother and father and three sisters. She'd even hung pictures on the wall over her bed—a handsome young man she called Riley, her son, Mom and Dad, and one of her sisters, as well. Once she asked Kate why there were no pictures on the wall over her bed. That was a hard question to answer.

Everything about Kate's past seemed lost. Her husband and daughter were only fuzzy memories. She didn't have any family stories to tell, so all she could do was talk about the wild parties and the rich men she'd catered to. She saw no sense in talking about the smelly ones, or the reality of her lifestyle before this place—the pits she woke up in and the sickness in her stomach.

Sarah Beth had always seemed entranced as she listened to Kate's tales, but Sarah Beth didn't realize that the family stories she'd told Kate had affected her in the same way. Now that the nightmares of her father were gone, she thought she could handle sobriety well enough to deserve having a family again. She'd made such a mess of things the last time.

"Get up," she said to Sarah Beth.

"Easy for you to say," she mumbled. "You've got something good to do today."

"I've done my time." Kate lifted the nightgown over her head and climbed into her prison uniform. Pressed with too much starch, the stiff cotton grated against her skin. It felt as if she were crawling into a cardboard box. As her fingers wrestled with stubborn buttons, she swore she'd never again wear anything navy blue.

"What's the first thing you're gonna do when you get out of here?" Sarah Beth sat upright. Her hair hung over her eyes, and some of it stuck to the side of her face. "Get laid, I bet."

"Not likely." Kate tied her shoes.

Sarah Beth pushed back her hair, revealing big round eyes. "Maybe you'll pull a trick for some rich guy on his yacht."

"No."

"Are you gonna get drunk?"

Kate lit a cigarette. She really wanted to pack her nose full of cocaine and forget that any of this ever happened, but the drugs and the prostitution had gotten her into this god-awful place. And Willy. The bastard had ruined her life.

Blowing smoke, she thought about going back to Las Vegas to find him and get her money, the money he'd been holding for her, for safekeeping, he'd said. But did she dare? She knew that being anywhere near Willy was dangerous. He wielded cocaine like candy, his instrument of control. With it, he could make her do unspeakable things. Then the cycle would start over again. She shivered at the thought and pushed it out of her mind.

"I wish I was you," Sarah Beth said. "You're pretty and smart."

"Look what it got me."

"At least I stayed away from the drugs," Sarah Beth proclaimed. "The booze was tough enough."

"I see where it got you."

Sarah Beth sighed. "You'll be back, too."

"Don't count on it."

"My brother was a junkie. He couldn't stay away from the stuff, and it killed him."

"I'll be all right." She crushed out her unfinished cigarette.

"Staying clean will be the hardest thing you'll ever do, Kate. Most addicts fail, like my brother."

"I can do it," Kate said with determination in her heart.

"You can't do it alone."

"I won't be alone."

"Where're you gonna go, back to Willy?"

Kate feared Sarah Beth was right. Staying away from the drugs and booze was imperative. Facing Willy was out of the question. The money wasn't worth the risk. He'd just tempt her with cocaine, convince her to stay, and pull her back down into the sewer. Counseling had taught her some things: like asking for help was not a sign of weakness, and solid family ties offered strength in numbers. To keep from slipping back into that seedy lifestyle and ending up in prison again, she needed her family's support, the husband she'd betrayed and the daughter she'd abandoned. But could they ever forgive her?

She gave Sarah Beth a half-hearted smile. "I'm going home."

Chapter Three

AGENT CRAIG STEVENS DUCKED behind a squad car, his Glock .45 in hand. The rattle of machinegun fire echoed from an old farmhouse across the road. Bullets pinged off the trunk lid and ricocheted over his head. Instantly, pistol shots banged all around him as his team of CIA agents returned fire. Wearing dark suits, white shirts, and thin ties, his men looked out of place in this gun battle.

Glancing down the line of squad cars that barricaded the gravel road, he saw twenty ATF boys from the Bureau of Alcohol, Tobacco, and Firearms and about as many drug enforcement agents, all dressed in black fatigues, bulletproof vests, and helmets. They looked right at home, popping rounds from their weapons like well-trained soldiers. A shotgun boomed. M-16 assault rifles rattled, and farmhouse windows exploded. Stevens grabbed a quick breath, swung the Glock over the bumper, and squeezed off six rounds into the screen door. All this could have been avoided, but the bad guys refused to surrender.

Today, Herrera and his drug gang were going out of business. The DEA could have handled this case themselves if Herrera had been just a regular drug lord, but he happened to be a Mexican diplomat with immunity status.

A few weeks ago, a team of CIA agents had uncovered a family cartel operating out of Central America, headed up by their patriarch, Miguel Herrera. Agents traced the flow of drugs to his oldest son, Carlos, now holed up in the farmhouse, and rumor had it his youngest son was dealing drugs out of Las Vegas. CIA Chief Lawrence had pulled Stevens off the 13th Power case in California and reassigned him to this task force. After discovering the gang had stockpiled munitions and explosives, Stevens called in the ATF. Herrera became top priority.

"They've got us pinned down," Cisco said.

Stevens shifted his eyes to the young agent kneeling beside him. Cisco Mendez hailed from San Francisco. He got his dark complexion and wavy black hair from his father and his appetite from his mother, or so he'd told the men. Right now he was a wide-eyed and sweaty-faced rookie. The Atlanta Bureau was no place for this snot-nosed kid unless he was looking to get himself killed. Stevens pumped another six rounds into the farmhouse. A fierce barrage of bullets came back.

Cisco ducked. "How we gonna rush 'em?"

Ejecting the empty clip from the Glock, Stevens looked at Cisco again and shouted over all the gunfire. "What's the hurry, boy?"

"I'm hungry. There's a Burger King back down the road a bit."

Bullets exploded the squad car's windows. A shower of glass rained down. Stevens spit. "Quit worrying about your stomach and shoot at the bastards." He slapped in a full clip and held his breath, thinking the rookie might be right. They should rush the farmhouse and end this siege. If they didn't, it could easily end up like Waco or Ruby Ridge and drag on for weeks. The press would sell a lot of papers, and the government would somehow get blamed for it all.

Peering around the fender, Stevens scanned the bullet-splintered old farmhouse with its curled and peeling whitewash. The roof had shed most of its gray shingles a long time ago, exposing wood planks to the sun like the ribs of a rotted corpse. Some of the redbrick chimney lay in crumbles on the ground. A rickety front porch wrapped around the right side of the house, which was surrounded by weeds and dry brush. Dusty and decaying, this secluded hideout Herrera and his band of thugs had chosen for their last stand looked much too fragile for the barrage the agents were laying down.

However, Stevens knew that Herrera wasn't stupid. The place was probably a fortress in disguise, possibly steel-plated on the inside, or perhaps sandbagged and reinforced. And Herrera may have stored enough ammo to make this a long-winded media event; after all, he had been quoted as saying he'd never be taken alive. He'd rather go out in a blaze of glory.

A bullet pinged off the bumper, sending Stevens back behind the fender. He began to wonder where Herrera might have stored that much ammo. The safest place would be the center of the house, maybe against a strong wall or, better yet, in the brick fireplace. Stevens looked again at the broken down chimney and grinned. *A blaze of glory, huh?*

As Cisco emptied a clip into the place, Stevens tapped him on the shoulder. "We're going in."

"Are you crazy?"

"You want to eat, don't you?" He looked left. "Robins...Baker," he called out to the agents crouched behind the front fender. "Spread out and cover us." He waved the Glock. "We're taking the car."

At that, he pulled open the rear door, unlatched the back seat, and yanked it out. "Here, Cisco. Cut a peephole in this thing and shove it up on the dash against the windshield. Then wedge a couple of bulletproof vests up there with it. It'll be kind of like making a tank."

"Cool." Cisco got out his pocketknife.

Turning his attention to the trunk access, Stevens felt around for the spare gas can and the roadside emergency kit. He stuck a flare in his back pocket and pulled off his tie. After knotting it around the gas can handle, he slung it over his shoulder. "Let's go."

"Burger King?"

"Not yet," Stevens said. "The side porch. Go!"

Cisco cranked up the squad car, and after ducking down on the front seat, Stevens grabbed the radio mike. "Cover fire, boys. Lay it down heavy." He clutched the Glock and the gas can. The tires threw gravel.

Agents laid down a barrage of fire designed to keep the suspects' heads down. With the engine roaring and firearms blazing all around him, Stevens gritted his teeth. The windshield cracked and spit glass. A bullet clanked through the door. Fishtailing, the car bounced and lunged as Cisco wrestled the steering wheel and aimed for the side porch. Seconds later, he slammed on the brakes. "We're here, you crazy bastard."

Stevens grabbed a determined breath and pulled himself out of the car, leaped on the fender and then the roof. Out the corner of his eye, he caught sight of a muzzle protruding from a bedroom window. His reaction was instant. The Glock banged, and the suspect fell out the window and landed in the bushes. Stevens didn't give the killing a second thought and climbed onto the porch roof.

As he scrambled toward the broken-down chimney, bullets started spitting up through the sun-dried roof planks. The suspects were shooting through the ceiling, probably aiming at the sound of his footsteps. When a round ripped through his coat sleeve, he held his breath, and like a drunkard, stagger-stepped the rest of the way to the chimney.

With hot adrenaline surging through his body, he removed the gas can lid and drained the fuel down the black flue. All the gas gurgled out in a few seconds. Noxious fumes stung his eyes. After tossing the empty can aside, he stepped back, grabbed the flare from his pocket, and ripped off the cap. A hissing flame came to life.

"Blaze of glory, asshole!"

He dropped the flare down the chimney, igniting the gas fumes into an instant pillar of fire that shot straight up into the air. Stevens ducked the plume of heat and flame, hurled himself off the porch and onto the squad car's roof. Clinging to the light bar, he started banging on the roof with the flat of his hand. "Go! Go! Go!"

Gunfire went silent as the car lurched forward. A scream or two could be heard inside the farmhouse. Then men shouted and cursed. A second later, a horrendous explosion blew the old farmhouse apart. Debris flew in every direction. Fire rained down around the speeding squad car. Dry brush swirled into flames and pumped black smoke into the Georgia afternoon sky. The explosion rolled away in the distance. Ammunition popped and banged within the inferno. Hanging onto the light bar for dear life, Stevens kept his head down and managed a grin. There would be no siege, no big news event, and no blame taken today.

Back on the road with the rest of the agents, Stevens accepted all the "atta boys" from his men. Being a hero was everything it was cracked up to be.

As fire trucks were allowed through the barricade, television crews came closer. Stevens thought they were like vultures, profiting from death, but this was all they were going to get. It was over. Tomorrow it would be old news, replaced by someone else's misfortune.

He watched the farmhouse burn and firemen battle the blaze with their hoses. The air stunk of gunpowder and burned flesh. Soon, the ATF boys would go in and scrape up the gang's remains. The CIA was finished here. Carlos Herrera's diplomatic immunity was now null and void.

Satisfied, Stevens kicked at gravel on the road. He was itching to get back to Simi Valley where he'd left his partner, Alex Gibson, on an undercover assignment for *The Ark.* The 13th Power case was the kind of mission Stevens liked most: covert and dangerous. He patted dust and soot from his suit coat and fingered the bullet hole in his sleeve. But first, a little vacation would be nice.

Cisco approached. “That wraps things up for us. Let’s eat.”

“What do you say we take a week off and head up to Canada?” Stevens suggested. “You know, fly into one of those little lost lakes and catch fish as big as your leg?”

It must have been the melting of Cisco’s ear-to-ear smile that sent a chill down Stevens’ spine. He followed the San Franciscan’s gaze to the ATF team leader who was now pacing toward them, his brown eyes ringed in white.

“What is it?” Stevens asked, his heart rate up a notch.

“We just got a message on the ComLink,” the officer said. “*The Ark* wants you back in Washington. Tonight.”

Chapter Four

JOHN NATHAN RODE THE ELEVATOR down to the first floor. It had been another long day at CIA headquarters, and the strain of it all weighed heavy on him. His blue eyes ached. At fifty-six years old, the long hours seemed harder to endure. He ran his fingers through his neatly trimmed salt and pepper hair then checked his watch: *11:05pm.*

The elevator doors slid open, and he headed down the corridor, the clicking of his heels on the marble floor echoing around him. The building seemed as cold and hard as the services the CIA supplied: espionage and covert operations, some of which didn't always turn out very well. In spite of all his efforts to protect the 13th Power project in Simi Valley, California, security was breached, and the experiments failed. The particle beam technology had eluded him, and Directive Number 119 was no closer to being fulfilled than when the President gave him the assignment: "You'll be a national hero," he had said.

Nathan agreed.

At the front doors, he spotted Craig Stevens and his rookie partner, Cisco, standing next to each other with their hands in their pockets. Neither had removed their sunglasses. Stevens stood an inch over Cisco and combed his blond hair down over his forehead. Cisco's black hair, combed in a wave on top of his head, shined greasily under the hallway lamps. They looked like an odd pair: Stevens with his boyish freckles and Cisco, dark-skinned as if he had been vacationing in Florida.

Up close, the two looked dusty and frazzled. "You boys have a nice flight?" Nathan asked, offering Stevens a handshake and nodding to Cisco.

"Rushed as usual," Stevens replied. "What's so important that it couldn't wait until tomorrow?"

Nathan thought bad news was harder to break than to bear. "It's Alex Gibson." He put a hand on Stevens' shoulder. "He's dead."

"Alex?" Stevens took a step back, his face ashen. "My God. What happened?"

"The 13th Power case went haywire. He was murdered."

"I should've stayed with him," Stevens growled.

"We pulled out our team just as the Air Force came in. The experiments are over."

"Who killed him?"

"Melvin Anderson..." Nathan wished he'd never let the bastard stay in the country. "...aka, Dr. Frank Curtis."

Stevens bared his teeth. "Is he in custody?"

"Now don't go getting any big ideas. He got away, probably in Mexico by now."

"So you want us to go down there and get him?"

"No."

"Then why are we here?" Stevens sounded appalled.

"Mexico's a big place. You'll never find him down there. However, I do have a plan."

Stevens glanced at Cisco and then back to Nathan. "Let's hear it."

Motioning toward the doors, Nathan said, "I'll tell you on the way to Andrews."

"Where are we going, now?"

"Back to Simi Valley."

"What for?" Stevens followed Nathan outside to a black Lincoln idling at the curb. "Alex is dead. The experiments are over. You said so yourself."

"Damage control." Nathan nodded as the driver opened the rear door. "Colonel Fallon will fill you in when you get there."

"Who the hell is he?"

"You'll see."

Cisco got in the car, but Nathans held Stevens back. "It's not my fault the Air Force is involved."

"And you want me to get in the middle of it?"

"We have to cover our tracks."

"What about you?"

"I've got a date tonight."

Stevens huffed and got in the car. "A date? What a waste of time."

"It's not what you think." Nathan got in.

The driver shut the car door.

"Why don't you just drop this case?" Stevens spat. "Let the military handle it."

"I'm not giving up on Directive Number 119. We need that particle beam. It's a matter of national security."

"Then you should go with us. Make your case to the Colonel. What's so damned important about your date, anyway?"

"Let's just say I have a little undercover work to do."

"Sure."

The Lincoln squealed away from the curb as a northerly wind swirled leaves and litter into the air, and the engine roared when the car sped through a yellow light.

Cisco asked, "Who's Colonel Fallon?"

Nathan settled back. "He's the Air Force Security Police Commander stationed at Indian Springs, Nevada. Somehow, he got wind of the 13th Power Project and stuck his nose in it."

"The 13th Power?" Cisco frowned. "What's that?"

"Some scientific technical term." Nathan shrugged. "But Dr. Tracy McClarence thought the technology could help fulfill the President's Strategic Defense Initiative."

"Star Wars?"

"Reagan may be gone from the White House, but his Directive Number 119 has not yet been fulfilled. His dream of a space-bound defense grid is still to be achieved."

"Congress cut the funding," Cisco said. "I remember the uproar from the Department of Defense."

"General Brigham was furious," Steven's added.

Nathan crossed his arms. "The President still believes the particle beam is our future defense against nuclear attack."

Cisco chuckled. "With ray guns and proton lasers? Give me a break."

"I'm backing him on it," Nathan said." I expect the same from you two."

Stevens cleared his throat. "Just think of it, Cisco. If we had one of those things, we could've just zapped Herrera and his gang from space."

"Cool." Cisco smiled.

Nathan took in a breath as the Lincoln cleared the main gate at Andrews Air Force Base and sped toward the tarmac where a Falcon jet sat gleaming chalk-white under the floodlights. Two silver stripes ran the length of the fuselage, and up on the tail, the silver seal of the CIA glimmered. Strobe lights pulsed on the wingtips, and a flight attendant stood in the open cabin door. The wind tugged at her blue skirt and fluttered the lapels of her matching jacket.

"Listen up." Nathan looked at Stevens as the car came to a stop alongside the jet. "You'll find a Global Positioning System tracker in your travel case. When you get to Solartech Labs, plant the GPS on the Learjet parked on the tarmac. When Colonel Fallon releases it to the pilots, we'll track it from our center in Houston. I'm betting it'll lead us straight to Melvin Anderson."

The driver opened the door, and the air came alive

with the whine of turbine engines. "What then?" Stevens asked.

"Wherever he goes, we'll be waiting."

"You want him dead?" Cisco asked.

Nathan grinned. "I've got bigger plans for him."

As Stevens started to get out of the car, Nathan grabbed the agent's arm. "One more thing, boys. Find Dr. Tracy McClarence. Bring her to me in handcuffs. If she won't cooperate, kill her."

Chapter Five

STEVENS PULLED HIS SEATBELT tight as the flight attendant swung the door shut, and the cabin pressurized with a thump. Two fresh travel cases, courtesy of the CIA, were strapped down next to the galley. He relished the thought of taking a shower once the plane reached cruising altitude. The executive Falcon jet was equipped with hot water, a television, and a well-stocked bar. There were four sleepers in the back, four plush leather seats up front and, in the galley, some of the finest food to be found anywhere. Cisco would appreciate that.

A chime rang through the cabin. The flight attendant buckled herself into the jump seat next to the cockpit curtain. Engines whining, the jet began to roll.

"Welcome aboard, gentlemen," the intercom squawked. *"I'm Captain Wilfred Baines. First officer Patti Duncan is my copilot. The winds are going to give us a bumpy ride on the way up to our cruising altitude of 37,000 feet. After that, we expect smooth air into St. Louis where we'll refuel before heading on to California. If you need anything, feel free to ask."*

Stevens cast a glance at Cisco. He seemed a little nervous in this small jet, more so than the big commercial aircraft they usually traveled on. "What's the matter, Cisco? Afraid of flying?"

He shook his head. "Afraid of dying."

"You don't say." Stevens remembered Nathan's last

words: *"Kill her."*

He couldn't imagine pulling the trigger on Tracy. She was smart. She knew all about laser physics, and she was surprisingly attractive. Under different circumstances, he'd have tried to get to know her better, more intimately perhaps. Putting those feelings aside would be difficult, he knew, especially if he had to kill her, a true test of his loyalty to *The Ark*. He hoped it wouldn't come to that.

On the runway threshold now, the jet stopped, and Stevens turned his attention out the window. Green lights lined the concrete, and the wingtip strobes flashed into the darkness beyond. Gusty winds buffeted the wings as the jet inched forward and stopped again. A chime dinged three times, and the cabin lights dimmed. As the engines revved to a thunderous roar, the jet screamed down the runway and sliced into the night sky. The landing gears banged into their compartments.

Cisco turned to Stevens. "I don't get it. One minute we're blowing Herrera to bits in Atlanta, and five hours later, we're on our way to California to kill some chick. And it's Sunday, for Christ's sake. What happened to Canada and them big fish?"

"They'll have to wait."

"Then tell me what's going on."

The jet banked left and pitched into a steep climb. Stevens looked away from the sinking city lights. "It's a long story."

Cisco shrugged. "So? It's a long flight."

***

At dawn, the Falcon broke through fifteen thousand feet on its descent into the L.A. basin. "Call it," Captain Baines said to his copilot.

"SoCal Approach. Falcon Six-Seven-Whiskey at fifteen thousand," Patti reported to Air Traffic Control.

The Captain double-checked his compass heading. It had been a long night with only one thirty-minute refueling stop in St. Louis. Between course corrections and with the help of the autopilot, he and Patti had managed to relieve each other for a couple hours rest.

During the stretch over Nevada, he couldn't sleep, so he'd struck up a conversation with her, told her about his flying career, the missions in Bosnia and Desert Storm, and before that, in Vietnam, where he'd flown C-130 transports, and how working for the CIA was gravy compared to the other stuff.

The radio crackled. *"Falcon, Six-Seven-Whiskey. Welcome to Southern California. Turn to heading three-two-zero."*

Patti repeated her clearance and gave Captain Baines a nod. He banked the Falcon to the right. Ten thousand feet below, the LA Basin lay under a blanket of clouds that had drifted in from the sea. The morning sunshine streaked the landscape with long shadows and painted the San Bernardino Mountain peaks with a yellow hue.

He gave the scene a fleeting glance. It all looked the same two weeks ago, when he flew a C-130 Hercules transport into Simi Valley with a band of mercenary soldiers onboard. Under the command of James "Red" Colburn, they were on a mission for *The Ark*. The target was the Atomtech compound in Desert Rock, Nevada. It was a top-secret nuclear research and development facility that had to be put out of operation. A lot of men died in that battle, he remembered, a bloodletting of Americans, by Americans. Sworn to secrecy under the threat of death, he hadn't told Patti or anyone about that flight, but now he felt as though he were returning to the scene of the crime.

The radio squawked. *"Falcon Six-Seven-Whiskey, clear for your approach to Solartech Field."*

Captain Baines gave the Falcon a small course correction as Patti scanned her instruments and set the dials for landing. From the flight-plan folder, she dug out the approach chart for Solartech Field and handed it to the Captain.

He clipped it to his yoke and pulled back on the throttles. The jet began to sink in the air. After a quick check of his instruments, he pitched the Falcon's nose down toward Simi Valley.

Patti switched on the intercom. "Flight attendant. Prepare for landing."

Chapter Six

A TINNY VOICE IN THE SPEAKER interrupted Stevens' sleep, and he suddenly became aware of the gentle roll of the jet. Everything seemed tilted forward, and the engines sounded eerily quiet.

"Gentlemen, it's time to get up and buckle in," the flight attendant said.

His heartbeat jumped. They were almost there: Simi Valley, California, and Solartech Labs.

He gave Cisco a swat in the sleeper next to him. "You heard the lady. Let's go."

Dressed and buckled in his seat at the window now, Stevens watched the wingtips glide through misty puffs of clouds glowing white from reflected sunshine, a bright white that made his eyeballs ache. He set his sunglasses on.

Below, roads and rivers cut across the landscape and merged into subdivisions that soon became the city of Pasadena. The jet flew on toward Glendale and then over Burbank. Los Angeles, with its clumps of skyscrapers and endless maze of streets and highways, sprawled out in the distance, dotted by shadows cast down from the clouds.

"What's for breakfast?" Cisco fixed his tie.

The jet hit a bump of air, yawed, and sent Stevens' stomach crooked. He wondered how Cisco could think of food after all he'd eaten last night.

A low ridge of hills went by, and the Falcon dropped down into Simi Valley. Stevens watched the jet's shadow race along the ground, rippling over grasslands and rocky boulder fields. As the Falcon dropped lower, he could see the remains of an old ghost town. Rugged landscape gave way to industrial parks, condos, approach light towers, and finally the runway. Tires squawked, reverse thrusters roared, and the jet slowed to taxi speed.

Out the window, he saw Melvin Anderson's gold and white Learjet parked on the tarmac. Military jeeps and soldiers wearing helmets and blue armbands surrounded the jet. Several Apache assault helicopters were lined up behind it, all bearing Air Force Security Police insignias. In the distance, the twin stainless steel buildings of Solartech Labs' main research complex gleamed in the California sunshine. Stevens felt humbled by the show of technology.

As the Falcon turned off the runway, an army-green C-130 transport on the tarmac came into view, its four huge propellers motionless. The cargo ramp was extended, and at the foot of it, two flag-draped coffins were cradled in the arms of a yellow forklift. A full-bird colonel in combat fatigues stood next to the coffins, along with some other officers whose eyes were on the Falcon as it whined to a stop twenty yards away.

Stevens checked the clip in his Glock, strapped the holster over his shoulder, and threw on his black suit coat. A chime dinged three times. The flight attendant pushed open the door, flooding the plane with sunshine. Cisco squinted, put his sunglasses on, and led the way out into the muggy morning air.

With some kind of fancy walking stick in hand, the Colonel approached the plane. Stevens noticed he didn't carry a holstered gun, but a ring of keys dangled from his belt. He wore sunglasses and sported a silver mustache that he kept trimmed short. His bald head, stocky six-foot frame, and professional military posture made Stevens feel a little overpowered.

"Craig Stevens, CIA," he said, offering a handshake.

The big man took Stevens' hand with a firm grip. "Colonel Bruce Fallon, Air Force Security Police."

Stevens cocked his head toward Cisco. "My partner, Agent Cisco Mendez." Stevens eyed the peculiar walking stick the Colonel held in his left hand. It looked as if it was made of pure gold. A carved eagle's head adorned the handle, gold with emerald green eyes. It seemed an odd thing for a colonel to possess. "That staff. I've never seen anything like it."

Fallon huffed. "It's heavy and cumbersome."

"Bad knees?"

The Colonel frowned. "Bait."

"I use worms," Cisco said.

"Not to catch a killer, you wouldn't."

"Melvin Anderson?" Stevens asked.

"Better known around these parts as Dr. Frank Curtis. He killed my best friend, Walter Devin, and your agent Alex Gibson, as well as thirty seven employees of Atomtech."

Stevens shook his head. "Sounds like he's a dangerous man."

"I suspect Curtis had a hand in downing the FBI's Hawker Jet in Washington DC."

"I heard it was an accident."

Fallon grunted. "He sabotaged the jet and killed the entire task force assigned to shut down his experiments here."

Wincing, Stevens said, "He couldn't have done that all by himself. He must have had connections in high places."

"Yeah, you think? Where's the GPS tracker?"

Stevens pulled the device from his coat pocket.

"Let's get it on the plane."

"What about the pilots?" Stevens asked as he walked with the Colonel toward a gold and white Learjet gleaming in the sunshine. It was parked on the other side of the C-

130.

"They work for Dallas-Air Leasing," Fallon explained. "I ordered them to take the Learjet back to their headquarters, but I know they won't do it."

"Why not?"

"We found a contingency plan on the flight data log transmitted directly from their corporate office. It's a mandate for client retrieval in case of separation. The only problem is we don't know where that will happen."

"So enter the GPS tracker."

The Colonel didn't say anything.

"Where are the pilots now?" Stevens asked.

"In the cafeteria having breakfast." The Colonel tapped the golden staff on the tarmac as he walked.

"I'll go check on them," Cisco interjected eagerly.

"Forget it," Stevens snapped, his attention on the flag-draped coffins and the forklift lumbering up the C-130's cargo ramp. Using hand signals, the loadmaster was guiding the operator aboard. "Is Alex Gibson under one of those flags?"

Fallon acknowledged with a dip of his head.

"And the other?"

"Walter Devin. If it weren't for him, I wouldn't have known what Dr. Curtis was doing here at Solartech Labs." Fallon shook his head. "But we arrived too late."

Stevens didn't comment as he walked past the C-130 and its cargo of death. He felt bad over the loss of his old partner. The dead man in the second coffin, Walter Devin, must've been the loose cog in the wheel that derailed *The Ark's* mission to steal the particle beam technology for Star Wars. Stevens couldn't help but wonder how many other loose ends might pop up on *The Ark.* At that thought, the hairs on the back of his neck prickled. "Why did Dr. Curtis kill Walter Devin?"

"Those two hated each other," Fallon said as they kept moving. "Devin knew Dr. Curtis's real name was Melvin

Anderson. When he found out the imposter was after the 13th Power, he came to me for help." The Colonel's face creased. "But by then, Anderson had already orchestrated the attack against Atomtech."

"An attack?" Stevens stretched his gait to match the Colonel's long strides. "I read about that in the papers, a government-funded research and development company in Nevada exploded. It was an accident."

"Not so," Fallon said. "Atomtech was attacked by a military contingency. Thirty-seven employees were murdered, ninety-two wounded. Walter Devin barely got out alive."

Stevens felt a chill. "If it was military, then why did Devin think Curtis had anything to do with it?"

"Because Devin was trying to stop the 13th Power experiments. Curtis struck back."

"You're saying Curtis had military connections? That's not possible."

Fallon frowned. "If he can sabotage a jet, he can do just about anything." He stopped at the Learjet's boarding steps. "When I catch the bastard, I'm going to find out who his connection was." Turning sharply, he stepped up into the plane.

Stevens couldn't move. He knew *The Ark* had issued strict orders to protect the 13th Power project "at all costs," but he doubted *The Ark* would have gone so far as to use military force against Americans. On top of that, Stevens couldn't imagine where *The Ark* had found the soldiers who would have done such a thing. Stevens' stomach knotted. He wondered if there was any way Melvin Anderson knew the CIA was involved in the raid, or maybe even the sabotaged jet. If he did, Colonel Fallon would get it out of him. *The Ark* would go down. Stevens couldn't let that happen. He had to get to Melvin Anderson first, to kill him before Colonel Fallon got a chance to interrogate him. It was the only way to protect *The Ark*.

"Let's go." Cisco gave Stevens a nudge up the steps. "We gotta eat sometime today."

Stevens shook his head and looked down at the GPS tracker in his hand. This thing would lead them to Melvin Anderson. *The Ark* was sure of it, but did he realize how dangerous that would be to his own secrecy?

Chapter Seven

DEEP IN A JUNGLE IN MEXICO, flames danced in a fire pit, and yellow embers swirled into the night air. A greasy monkey was skewered head-to-tail over the flames. Choking down impatience, Melvin Anderson gave the fire a poke with a stick. He was stuck here waiting for Jonathan Kyles to return from town.

Clear down to the bottom of his belly, he hated Mexico. He hated the jungle. Everything was black under the sky, the air thick and clammy and still as death. The whole place stunk of rotting vegetation, sappy leaves, and wormy tree trunks. And the damn bugs. He slapped a mosquito that was feeding on his arm. Two days ago, he'd ripped the sleeves off his white shirt and shed his tie. He'd lost his cell phone when it fell into a river just south of Mexico City. But he still had the black coat, he was sitting on it, the only thing left of his Dr. Curtis facade.

Stewing over his misfortunes, he gave the monkey a turn over the fire. Bright flames reminded him of his golden Pharaoh's staff, his most prized possession. Since leaving Jakarta, he'd never gone anywhere without it, and now, he missed the feel of its carved and polished gold: the eagle-head handle, the smooth shaft, and the finely cut edges of the eagle's green emerald eyes. But mostly he missed the way it made him feel when he held it, the prestige and the power it gave him, and the deadly secret it possessed.

The last time he saw it, bullets were flying. He'd dropped the staff and had to leave it behind. Now, someone else had it. The thought of who it could be soured his stomach. Was it Janis Mackey, or perhaps Colonel Fallon? Whoever it was had no idea how much trouble it was going to cause them.

Melvin licked his teeth. Fire crackled, and the monkey sizzled. His mind replayed the escape from Simi Valley. Of all the things that went wrong, Jonathan Kyles, his aide and confidant, took the prize. He'd driven the Rolls Royce into a mud bog and sunk it to the fenders. Some shortcut that turned out to be. They'd been on foot ever since, sticking to the back trails and away from the main flow of traffic to southern Mexico.

Legs tingling, Melvin realized he'd been crouched on his haunches in front of the fire too long. Standing, he stretched. Even though he was sixty, his years as a digger had kept him trim and strong. He likened himself to his favorite movie hero, Indiana Jones; only Melvin was a lot tougher and prone to take bigger risks. "Risk nothing, gain nothing," his father had taught him. That's what life was all about.

He scanned the shadowy jungle around him. Jonathan was taking too damn long. He'd headed off for a cantina in Juchitan, a little town just over the hill and to the north, about two miles down the trail. Supplies and a phone call were on his list of things to do there. It was too risky for both of them to go. Two gringos walking into town this time of night would draw unwanted attention, but one of them could get by without notice. "Just don't burn the monkey," he'd said before he slipped into the darkness.

"Well the monkey's almost done," Melvin shouted at the jungle.

The rattle of an engine and grinding gears suddenly came from somewhere to his right, by the river where a jeep trail dogged the muddy bank. A sharp glow of headlights penetrated the foliage, bouncing and jerking along. Melvin's throat went dry. At first he thought Jonathan had stolen a jeep, but then realized it was coming from the wrong direction.

Heart racing, he flung on his black coat and fingered the gun under his belt, the gun that once belonged to Alex Gibson. The memory of the CIA agent flashed through Melvin's mind as the glow of the headlights came closer. Anger flared up inside him again. Gibson had weaseled his way into Solartech Labs and became Chief Security Officer, but he turned out to be a government spy. The charade had cost him his life, and Melvin relished the memory of how he'd killed the CIA agent with a dagger through the throat. Just thinking about it got his adrenaline pumping.

Squealing brakes sent roosting birds aflutter through the forest canopy. The vehicle stopped just beyond a clump of jungle brush, its headlights now silhouetting thick tree trunks and hanging leafy branches.

Two doors slammed. *"Hola campamento."*

Melvin said nothing, his finger tightening on the trigger of his gun. Sweat trickled down his forehead. He hoped he wouldn't have to get into a shooting match with these guys. Since the gunfight at Solartech Labs, there were only four bullets left in his clip.

The jungle moved, and two helmeted soldiers appeared, their features broken by shadows. They pushed through the bushes with their rifles. *"¿Que haces?"* one of them said as they walked into the light of the campfire, uninvited.

Melvin stood tall against the young Mexican nationals. They had high cheekbones, hard eyes, and sported the black stubble of new beards. They might have been brothers. Their jungle fatigues were sweat-stained, and Melvin couldn't see any insignia of rank on their sleeves. But the smell of booze was on them, and one soldier had a bandage around his hand, a filthy thing, torn and ragged.

Swallowing hard, Melvin gauged their intentions, shifting his eyes between them. He presumed they were on a regular patrol through this area, or perhaps, from the look of them, they might have been renegades with robbery or murder on their minds. Though Melvin itched to pull the gun, he figured a more casual approach would be better. "Welcome."

Their yellow teeth showed. "Ah, gringo," one said and then cast a glance to the monkey on the fire.

Melvin bent over slowly and gave the meal a turn.

"*El mono*," the other said, grinning.

"It's almost ready." Melvin stepped back and motioned toward the fireside. "Sit. We will eat soon."

They both looked warily around the campsite, still holding their rifles. Melvin thought they were ignoring him, or perhaps they didn't know English. But they looked strong as they sized up the camp. Perhaps they had done this kind of thing before, or maybe they were being cautious of traps. Melvin checked his urge to panic, to start firing off his four rounds, and wondered where the hell Jonathan was. "Please, have a seat."

Slowly, the soldiers started moving away from each other, one to the left of the fire, the other to the right. Melvin took one step backward, then another, keeping both of them in his field of vision. He cleared his throat. "Help yourself."

"*No me gusta el mono*," the one with the bandaged hand said and kicked the monkey into the fire. It started burning like a ball of grease, and they laughed.

Melvin seethed. The bastards had just ruined his dinner. He'd killed a man for less than that. Without further hesitation, he yanked out his gun.

At the same time, the soldiers spun around with their rifles leveled on him.

Melvin dropped to the grass and went flat on his back, the gun now clasped in both hands. He squeezed off two rounds to the left and two to the right. Muzzle flashes lit up the jungle like strobe lights.

The soldier on the left keeled over. The other soldier's rifle flashed and boomed, and a round zipped into the grass not an inch from Melvin's head. As he rolled right, the night came alive with gunfire. Not just one or two more shots, but four, five, then six of them banged. He tightened his stomach muscles and winced against the pain he thought would soon rip into his insides.

But as quickly as it all began, it was over. He heard the chatter of irate monkeys and the cawing and screeching of birds. Rolling his gaze toward the fire, he saw both soldiers slumped on the ground by the flaming monkey. He'd shot them after all, he thought, the second soldier taking longer to fall than the first. Everything had happened so fast.

Suddenly, the jungle went dark. Someone had turned off the jeep's headlights. From his position on the ground, Melvin heard rustling leaves and footsteps in the grass. He gulped. More renegades? That would be a bad thing. He was out of bullets and defenseless against any more intruders. All he could do was hug the ground, stay low and out of sight.

A tall, lanky man emerged from the darkness, the firelight revealing a familiar face. Sweat glistened on Jonathan's forehead and under his black eyes. Razor stubble made his cheeks look sooty, and his thick hair hung sloppily over his ears. He shoved his Colt revolver under his belt. "I told you not to burn the monkey," he said and held up a key pinched in his fingers. "At least we don't have to walk anymore, boss."

Melvin sat up, his heart hammering. Speechless, he watched Jonathan drop his fat backpack by the fire and begin rummaging through the dead soldiers' stuff.

"Hey, look here," Jonathan said. "Forty caliber shells—oh wow, check the bayonet." He kicked aside their M1 carbines. "Look at this old junk."

Wiping sweat from his forehead, Melvin let out a sigh of relief. Jonathan reminded him of the shoppers who frequented the street markets in Jakarta, fumbling through all the goods and making a mess of the place. Melvin got to his feet. "Took you long enough to get here."

Jonathan thumbed the bayonet's sharp blade, his six-foot-six frame silhouetted by the fire. "I'd say my timing was impeccable, boss."

Melvin nodded, shed his coat, and ejected the empty clip from his gun. "Any luck in Juchitan?"

"Yup." Jonathan stuck the bayonet behind his belt and lifted the backpack from the ground. The fire lit up his smile. "And I bet it's still cold." He unzipped the pack and pulled out a bottle of beer, a Mexican brand named Tequize. After prying the cap off with his teeth, he offered it to Melvin.

Sitting on the ground Indian style, Melvin's eyes went to the fire and the smoldering monkey. "So much for dinner." He sucked beer from the bottle.

"I bought some apples." Jonathan reached inside the backpack. "We won't starve." He tossed one into Melvin's lap. "Eat up."

Melvin just sat there, drank his beer, and stared into the fire. A pesky bug buzzed his ear. Simi Valley, California, came to mind. He was convinced that if Janis Mackey, the so-called hotshot mathematician, hadn't blown his calculations, things would have worked out differently. Instead of sweltering in this jungle, they'd be basking in the wealth of the 13th Power. He wondered if Janis Mackey had tipped off the CIA, and if the son-of-a-bitch was in on it with Alex Gibson. Or maybe it was that bitch Tracy McClarence, the laser tech from Cambridge. He didn't trust her from the beginning. He spit into the fire as the Russian scientist, Boris Dagloskoff, came to mind. It could have been him; after all, he talked too much whenever he was drinking.

"Don't worry, boss," Jonathan said, interrupting Melvin's thoughts. "I spoke with Señor Carbone on the phone. He's waiting for us in Belize City. The bank vouchers are ready for you." He zipped the backpack and bit into an apple.

"And the plane?"

"The way he tells it, some big-shot Colonel will release the Learjet on Monday. The pilots have orders to fly directly to Dallas." Jonathan took a swig of beer. "But they won't let us down."

Melvin swallowed. "Contingency plans are expensive but well worth the insurance."

The fire, now dwindling, crackled with less ferocity. The monkey was charred beyond recognition. In the waning firelight, mosquitoes began attacking with a vengeance. Melvin smacked one that had landed on the side of his face.

Jonathan was waging a battle of his own not three feet away. "Damn bugs!"

Melvin shrugged. "The jungle never changes. It was just like this some thirty years ago when I was here with my father, digging through the Altun Ha ruins. The Mayans had built a formidable civilization here two thousand years ago, but in the end, the jungle reclaimed it."

"Probably wasn't any different back then, either," Jonathan said. "The heat, the decay, bugs and death everywhere you look." He kicked the dead renegade, the one with the bandaged hand. "And idiots like him."

Melvin regarded the dead soldiers, and for a moment, he saw his father lying there dead on the ground: the campfire lighting his pain-wracked face, the poisoned dart sticking in his neck. "Did I ever tell you about my father?"

"Only that he was an archeologist."

"A struggling archeologist, at best. He died poor as dirt." Melvin took a swallow of beer. "He was brave and honest and played by all the rules. It got him nowhere."

"What happened to him?"

"The Zambos killed him."

"The Indians of the rainforest?" Jonathan said with a frown. "They're a peaceful lot. Something must have really pissed them off."

"Yeah—my father. The Zambos had warned him not to dig up their ancient burial grounds, but he wouldn't stop the excavation. He even showed them his permit. They just spit on it. I told him that we should leave, but he said he wasn't running from no savages...so we stayed and dug up their stuff."

Jonathan whacked a bug. "And the Zambos attacked?"

"Like you said, they didn't want to fight, but they set out to make things miserable for us and drive our expedition away. Night after night they went whooping all around the camp. They were everywhere: in the trees, the underbrush, and the tall grass. "*Whoop, Whoop, Whoop*," like monkeys all night, and they banged their hollow drums so loud that none of us could get any sleep. Scared me half to death...but not my father. He got mad as hell. One night, he said he'd had enough and tried to scare them away. He stood in the middle of the camp, yelling, calling them savages and shooting his gun into the air." Melvin gulped the last of his beer. "One of them killed him, but we never found out which one."

"Sorry, boss."

"It's an old wound, scarred over hard."

Jonathan passed him another beer.

"My father was a well respected archeologist," Melvin went on. "But the whole business drove him crazy, not just the Zambos. In the end, I came to believe my father was right. They were savages, all of them: from the self-righteous Pharaohs of Egypt, to the industrious Mayans of

Altun Ha, and even the wealthy Kediri of Malaysia. Savages, I tell you, just like the ones that killed my father."

Jonathan poked at the dying fire. "Is that why you gave up archeology?"

"I never gave it up—not really. I dug where I wanted, and I kept what I found. I sold most of the stuff on the black market and pissed off a lot of people. They called me a grave robber because I wouldn't play by their rules."

"What rules?"

"The scavengers' rules."

Jonathan squinted. "Scavengers?"

"The freeloading government officials who idolized the savages. They glorified their own past and lined their pockets along the way. Their museums became fat and full of the stuff I dug out of the ground with my sweat and blood. So I took it from them, and they set out to kill me for it."

"Do they still think you're dead?"

"I wonder. The CIA probably let the word out that I didn't die in that croc-infested swamp back in Borneo."

"If so, that makes the Malaysian Federation, the CIA, and Colonel Fallon after us." He counted them on his fingers with wide-open eyes. "Maybe we should just forget the whole thing, slip down into Brazil, and live it up in Rio for a while."

"No. We're going back to get my golden staff. And don't forget, Janis Mackey still owes me the 13th Power for the million dollars I paid him."

Jonathan shook his head. "What if he refuses to help you this time?"

Melvin sneered. "I'll kill him."

Chapter Eight

BACK AT THE UNIVERSITY OF COLORADO, Janis approached the blackboard with a stick of chalk in his hand. The mathematics class was seated behind him. Their professor was out sick, and they wanted to know about the 13th Power, so he volunteered to stand in for them. His administrative duties could wait. "So you want to know about the Higgs boson?" He wrote the formula: $10^{-12}cm$ on the blackboard. "Who can tell me what this is?"

"The nucleus of the atom," one boy answered.

"Right. And somewhere inside that nucleus hides the Higgs."

"So?" one girl asked.

Leaning on his desk, Janis explained, "The Higgs boson has been the object of a multi-billion dollar world-wide scientific investigation since 1964 when Peter Higgs, a Scottish physicist, mathematically predicted its existence as a way to explain why atoms have mass even though they are mostly empty space, like the universe itself. He theorized these bosons were somehow connected, which eventually became known as the Higgs Field Theory."

Another girl threw up her hand. "They hold everything together like some kind of subatomic glue, right?"

"Correct," Janis said. "And one would think that something that fills the universe would be easy to find, but it's not. Thousands of American and European scientists built enormous machines at Fermilab and CERN in hopes of finding the Higgs boson. It's a race. Even the Russians were in the game for a while, until they lost the Troitska accelerator."

"Why is finding the Higgs so important?"

"A theory is just that, a theory. Using Peter Higgs' formula, the mathematics of the atom and universe proves out, but proof based on a theory is no proof at all. And therein lies the problem. No one has ever seen the Higgs boson, much less knew where to look for it, but scientists need to find it in order to substantiate the theory. If they fail to find it, that means the mathematics of the universe and the atom is wrong. They'll have to start over from scratch."

The door squeaked open. "Please excuse the interruption." Dean Billings walked in.

Janis pinched the corner of his glasses. "Can I help you?"

The dean approached, stone-faced. "I'm sorry, Dr. Mackey," he whispered. "The nursing home just called. It's your mother."

Chapter Nine

HILLCREST NURSING HOME SEEMED cellar-like and cold today. Janis had never noticed it like this before. The place was usually warm and sunny and smelled of food from the kitchen, with all the cooking and baking they did around here. Janis didn't notice any of those things as he followed Nurse Henderson into his mother's room.

In the dim light, the air was heavy with the aura of death. She lay on a bed in the center of the room. A white sheet covered her up to her neck. No IV tubes dripped drugs into her arms, nor were there any machines hooked up to her body. She looked peaceful and dignified. On the nightstand, her ticking clock made the only sound.

"How long has she been like this?" he asked the nurse and took hold of his mother's clammy hand, yellowed with sickness.

"Three hours."

"You should have called me sooner."

"Dr. Penny was late." She adjusted the window blinds, letting in more sunshine. "I'm glad you're back from California."

"What did the doctor say?"

"Her liver has failed. That's why she looks so yellow. Her kidneys can't handle the strain, and dialysis isn't an option. It would kill her outright. Her body has finally given up, Dr. Mackey."

Janis leaned forward and brushed a thin lock of gray

hair from his mother's face. The years had not been kind to her. Her beauty had long ago been replaced by a maze of wrinkles and sagging skin, spotted with age. Now, her eyes were closed. It was just as well. She wouldn't have recognized him anyway. He could count on his fingers the number of times during the last year that she'd even said his name. Alzheimer's had taken her away a long time ago.

Nurse Henderson pushed a chair up to the bedside, and Janis sat, his eyes still on his mother. He caressed her doughy hand, small and frail and streaked with wormy blood vessels. It didn't seem all that long ago that he'd held onto her hand and taken his first steps. On his first day at school, he was terrified to let go of that hand. He'd cried and clung to her and said the school bus was a big yellow monster that would swallow him up. She'd glow whenever she talked about those times he couldn't remember: when he was young, and she was too.

The memories faded into the ticking of Mother's clock. She'd once told him how much she liked that sound. It had lulled her to sleep at night and greeted her every morning, a little thing that gave her great joy.

Closing his eyes, Janis listened to the clock ticking away. He wondered how mankind could ever begin to understand time, eternity, and the universe. How did it all begin? Where did it all end? What lies beyond the grave? There had to be something. If not, then there really was such a thing as *nothing*.

Janis popped open his eyes, a little dizzy from the thought of nothingness. He knew how these things worked on the minds of scientists striving to find the answers. He'd seen how it had plagued Ray Crawford, how it had obsessed him, and how it drove him to risk the very existence of the world. Janis wondered if Ray had learned his lesson: the size of the universe and the length of eternity did not matter. The experiments in Simi Valley had gone beyond the limits of mathematics and physics. Negative and positive, big and small, at the 13th Power, they were all the same thing...

His mother moved a little, giving his heart a quick beat. She took in a raspy breath as her mouth came open slightly and her tongue touched her upper lip. She opened her eyes and looked at him with that same blank stare.

He rubbed her arm. "Hello, Mother. Do you know who I am?"

Her eyes widened and gave off a little sparkle. "Of course...Janis," she said hoarsely and looked away, the blank stare returning immediately.

It had only lasted a fleeting moment, that glimmer of hope that came over him. How badly he wanted to believe his mother would get well, but he knew she wouldn't. Alzheimer's was cruel in that way, deceptive. She had forgotten him as quickly as she'd recognized him. All he could do was give her a pat on the hand.

Nurse Henderson left the room, quietly closing the door behind her. Janis was left alone to say goodbye to his mother.

***

The funeral was on Tuesday. Tracy held Janis's arm as he stood at his mother's graveside. The casket had already been lowered into the ground. She detected a tremble in his body as he tossed a white rose down on the coffin. It was his final tribute to his mother, a last goodbye, the way he wanted the service conducted. His sorrow seeped into Tracy's heart.

Making a sign of the cross, the preacher said, "Ashes to ashes, dust to dust, I commend you to the house of the Lord." He turned and walked away.

"I'm sorry," she said softly, looking into Janis's eyes. They were watery around the rims, but he wasn't crying. She thought he probably held back his tears because of all the people who were here today. They wore dark suits and gowns and sad faces, faculty and students from the University of Colorado. Janis Mackey had a lot of friends willing to share in his grief.

He didn't take his eyes away from the grave. She thought he was handsome, sharply dressed in a three-piece suit and shiny black shoes. His pepper-gray hair was combed straight back. Silver-framed glasses rode low on the bridge of his nose. He patted her hand. "She's gone, Tracy. I wish you could have known her."

Tracy blinked, thinking they could have been close friends and done things together, like cooked for a family gathering, or gone shopping for things like baby furniture and outfits. The thought made her sigh. She'd always been too busy to start a family. Besides, she was forty-two and hadn't found the right man, until now, maybe. She looked at Janis and wondered if he could read the desire in her eyes. Her imagination had drawn a picture of them together, a picture she yearned to share with him, but she feared he might not be receptive to the commitment. After all, at forty-eight, he'd never been married, except to his work, an anomaly much like her own. Taking in a slow breath, she put her lips to his ear. "Your mother was a wonderful person."

"How do you know?"

"I see it in her son."

Janis put his head down and closed his eyes. "I don't deserve that."

"Of course you do, Janis."

He looked up to a clear blue sky, his lower lip trembling. "Nothing's gone right lately."

"What do you mean?"

"I should have been here with her, instead of California."

"Then we wouldn't have met."

"But she needed me."

“You couldn’t have known.”

“I should have...I mean...I was too busy chasing Dr. Curtis’s fantasy, the 13th Power, and for what? It wasn’t my mother’s fault her care cost so much...that there was never enough money to cover it all.”

Tracy rubbed his shoulder. “Is that why you agreed to help Dr. Curtis, for the money?”

“For my mother.”

“You gave her the best of everything.”

“It was the least I could do for her.” Janis took a deep breath. “My father died when I was nine. After that, my mother took good care of me, scraped and saved every dollar she could live without, for my education, for my future.” He toed the graveside dirt. “When she fell ill, it was my turn to take care of her.”

“Like I said, you’re a good son.”

“You think?” He sighed, his eyes again turned up to the sky. “I once thought I was a good mathematician, too, maybe even a great one.”

She couldn’t believe he’d said that. “What makes you think you’re not?”

“The 13th Power project, Tracy...I really screwed it up.”

She frowned. “You can’t blame yourself for that.”

“My formula was wrong. I damn near destroyed the world.”

“We figured it out in time.”

Janis shook his head. “Still, I failed.”

Tracy turned to face him and put her hands on his cheeks. “You hung in there. I wish you were at Troitska...in Russia. You might have saved my brother’s life. He was their chief mechanical engineer when the accelerator imploded.”

Janis frowned. “It wasn’t a meteor strike?”

“I have a reliable source who disputes the official version. They were after the Higgs boson.”

His jaw muscles flexed. “The 13th Power is too dangerous.”

“You saved the world this time, Janis.”

“Dumb luck.” A wan smile formed on his lips.

“Humility to the end, huh? Well, I’ll have you know, mister, you’re the smartest and bravest man I’ve ever known.”

“Brave?” Janis looked at the dirt. “You’re kidding.”

“The way you stood up to Dr. Curtis, you didn’t flinch.”

“I was scared to death.”

“You got us out safely.” She hugged him, inhaled the scent of his cologne, felt his smoothly shaven cheek on hers. “You’re my hero, Janis. Like it or not.”

“I’ve never been a hero before.”

“And I’ve never had one.”

Janis smiled lightly and looked around at his friends. They were wandering toward the recreation center for the reception, as if they knew it was a good time to leave Janis alone. What they didn’t know was that Janis would never be alone again, not if she had anything to say about it.

She remembered, back at Solartech Labs, when he’d said he was going home to Colorado, she didn’t want him to go without her. She’d just started to get to know him. The attraction was strong and undeniable. She was happy he wanted her to come along. During the past week, he’d showed her around Boulder: the university campus, dinner at the Broker Inn, a drive up Flagstaff Mountain in his new Camry. She was falling in love with him...and Colorado.

She took in a deep breath of pine-scented air. This would be her new home. After all, she couldn’t go back to Washington. The CIA had no use for her anymore, in fact, they probably had her pegged as a liability with what all she knew about *The Ark* and the President’s Star Wars conspiracy. A sudden chill rippled down her neck. The CIA might come looking for her. They might even want her dead. Janis could be in danger, too.

“Goodbye, Mother,” he said and turned from the grave. “Let’s go home.”

She hooked his elbow with her arm. “What’s next?”

“Whatever we want. The 13th Power is behind us now.”

Tracy hoped he was right about that.

Chapter Ten

IN THE COLDEST HOUR BEFORE DAWN, Melvin listened to the dew dripping from the trees. He curled himself into his black coat and looked up at the stars glinting through slits in the jungle canopy. They didn't twinkle in the hazy tropical sky but glowed with small haloes. He remembered Janis Mackey telling him to look up at the night sky and be thankful he was still around to see the stars. The mathematician actually believed the 13th Power could have destroyed the world. He was a traitor, as far as Melvin was concerned. He had no sense of adventure, no lust for discovery.

Closing his eyes, Melvin let his mind work in that place between drowsiness and dreams. Janis appeared to be a great thinker, a man of vision, but he'd had a negative attitude toward the 13th Power from the very beginning. And on top of that, his incorrect formula had doomed the project. He'd turned out to be an expensive disappointment.

But that wasn't the case with Ray Crawford. Ray had spent his whole career touting the possibilities of the 13th Power. It made him an easy recruit for the project. Blinded by his lust for fame, he'd signed on without even questioning the real purpose for the experiments. And in spite of Ray's failure to harness the power of the Higgs boson, Melvin knew he was the kind of scientist who would take a step back, look at it from another angle, work out the problems, and find a way to succeed. Ray Crawford would never give up on the 13th Power. Melvin was sure of that.

From somewhere in the grass nearby, Jonathan let out a snort in his sleep.

Melvin opened his eyes and saw the smoldering fire pit three feet away. The charred monkey protruded from the ashes like a ghostly sentinel. Last night, as the conversation dwindled, Jonathan had reloaded the gun, and after the beers were gone, he tossed the dead renegades into the river. Crocodiles lurking in the muddy waters were in for a treat. There'd be nothing left of the bodies by dawn. He let that thought comfort him and closed his eyes again.

A couple hours later, the gunning of an engine yanked him from his sleep. He leaped up from the ground. Gun in hand, his heart beating hard, he saw shafts of sunlight knifing down through the trees and glisten off water cascading down from the canopy where dew-laden leaves dripped. Monkeys started hollering.

He spun around, looking for Jonathan. He was gone, and so was his backpack. The irritating engine popped and wheezed. A cloud of blue smoke drifted in the air, stinking of oil. Melvin pulled his coat from the ground, gave it a shake, and cautiously headed toward all the noise.

Peering through a crotch of leafy branches, he saw Jonathan bent over the fender of the renegade's jeep, the open hood above his head. He gunned the throttle a couple of times, put a tool to its innards, and gunned it again.

The man was always tinkering, even out here in the middle of nowhere. Melvin pushed his way through the sweating foliage. "Is this going to take all day?"

"I about got her, boss." Jonathan backed out from under the hood. His face was smudged with grease and a knuckle leaked blood. "She's got a half tank of gas. The cans strapped on the back are full, though. We should get quite a ways."

Melvin examined the jeep. It had no roof. If it rained,

which it did at least four times a day around here, they'd be drenched. The windshield was busted out, black spray paint covered the previous military markings, and the seat upholstery was torn. There wasn't any carpeting on the floor, just a bunch of loose ammo, scattered tools, rags and trash. She was a beautiful thing.

Jonathan slammed the hood. "Let's load up. Belize City or bust."

Mile after mile of rutted road went by. The jeep trail weaved its way through thick jungle choked with sapodillas, bamboo, and tangles of clinging vines. The air was wet and hot and filled with the whistling and screeching of birds and the *"gagoon gagoon"* of monkeys. Low gray clouds hung in smoky rolls, bumped the treetops, and swirled. Melvin thought the bone-jarring ride would never end.

Clutching the windshield frame, he held his breath as the trail narrowed and crept along the edge of a deep ravine. The tires bounced over broken rocks and exposed roots that dangled into the abyss. He cast a worried look at Jonathan. "Are you sure we're going the right way?"

Jonathan bobbed his head. "Villahermosa's on the other side of that ridge, boss." He wrestled the steering wheel and clenched his jaw. "I just don't remember this trail being so bad."

Then the rain came down in torrents, soaking the jungle and misting in the heat. It banged on the tinny hood and stung Melvin's face. He pulled his black coat over his head and cast an irritated glance at Jonathan. Rain dripped from his nose as he squinted against the onslaught. His cheeks and wide chin were covered with a crop of new beard that shed water like the fur of a dog.

Melvin chuckled at the sight of him. Jonathan was certainly no prize for the ladies. He was tall and wiry but smart as a fox. The marines had made him jungle wise, and after Vietnam, he'd spent a lot of time in Central America, supervising teams of Peace Corp volunteers. They'd built roads, water and sewer systems, and generally tried to improve the quality of life for the people of these parts. What a waste of time.

As the jeep rambled through the sopping jungle, Melvin remembered the night he met Jonathan. It was at the Mayan ruins of Uxmal in Champeche. Melvin had traveled there all the way from Jakarta for the festival of Chac, the rain God. During a street party, some drunk Amuzgo Indians picked a fight with Jonathan, talking trash about how ugly he was. Melvin couldn't resist jumping into the middle of the brawl. They'd fought side by side and spent the rest of the night in jail together.

Thunder cracked overhead and rumbled away. Chac was working overtime now, pelting the jeep with drops the size of quarters. By the time they made Villahermosa, the rain had ended. The town, cut from the jungle, looked every bit as poor as the slums of rural Jakarta. The only evidence of modern-day luxury was the array of TV antennas sticking up from the roofs of wooden shacks. Power lines sagged from crooked poles and crisscrossed the town in total chaos.

Jonathan drove on, passing naked children playing in puddles left by the last cloudburst. He headed down the mud-rutted main street. It was lined with open-air markets piled high with mangos and coconuts and brightly colored fruits with strange shapes. Long stems of bananas hung from rickety green awnings that shaded bushels of nuts and bins of spices. Flies buzzed around fish skewered to nails on a post. Wearing colorful dresses, fat brown women sat on wooden crates next to their stores. Dogs roamed about the place, sniffing and panting.

At a hand-painted petro sign, Jonathan stopped the jeep and got out. Melvin watched over the crowd, his gun close at hand.

From a squeaky barrel pump, Jonathan cranked fuel

into the tanks.

Meanwhile, a street vender hobbled up on crutches. He was selling burritos wrapped in foil. The smell of chilies and beans made Melvin's mouth water. He bought two burritos from the cripple while Jonathan bartered with a leather-skinned old woman nearby. A little parrot perched on her shoulder cocked its head up at the tall stranger. He came away with a bunch of bananas, two apples, and a broad smile. The jeep teetered as he got in.

Halfway through eating his burrito, Melvin saw a convoy coming up the road, swerving and weaving through the mud. He counted three military jeeps and one truck with a white cross on the door. Emergency lights flashed from its roof. Heart racing, he put a hand on his gun, but they sped by and disappeared down the jeep trail that went toward Juchitan.

"I wonder what that was all about." Melvin returned his attention to his burrito.

Jonathan shrugged, fired up the engine, and they drove off into the jungle.

***

After two more days of rain showers and little towns like Villahermosa, the jeep finally rattled into the bustle of Belize City. Melvin scratched his beard, nearly an inch long now and as gray as his hair. He glanced at Jonathan's scruffy face and chuckled at the way the two of them looked. They could easily have been mistaken for a couple of archeologists returning from a dig hidden deep in the bush. Right now, Melvin was looking forward to taking a shower.

Belize City was a welcome sight, sprawled out along Haulover Creek at the mouth of the Belize River. The Caribbean Sea sparkled beyond a white coral shoreline.

As the jeep sputtered down into the city, Melvin

noticed how different the place looked from the way he remembered it. Newer colonial style buildings were intermixed with the broken shells of roofless, windowless buildings, remnants of hurricanes long gone. He wondered if the old hotel was still standing, the one he and his father had stayed at before setting off on their expedition into the Mayan ruins...before the savages killed him.

Along the bricked streets of the inner city, the heavy beat of brukdon music filled the air. "*Yo bon day, Yo bon day*." Drums pounded, guitars strummed, and tambourines rattled to the rhythm and the words, "*Yo bon day, Yo bon day*." And sidewalks teemed with tourists wearing colorful clothing and dark sunglasses. Hawkers of everything imaginable swooped down on them, pushing their goods relentlessly. The jeep chugged through the throng, drawing curious expressions from those who took the time to notice. Finally, they came to the Quarter B Bar. Jonathan shut off the engine. It backfired.

Unnerved, Melvin pulled on his black coat and stuck the gun under his belt. Combing his fingers through his tousled hair, he felt just as ratty as he looked.

Inside, clones of the tourists on the sidewalks occupied every table and stood in the aisles and along the walls. Brukdon music filled the barroom, the drone of conversation rarely peaking the beat. As Melvin followed Jonathan toward the bartender, he observed a big mahogany bar, its intricate framed mirror, and pillars in the corners and ceiling beams overhead, all made of mahogany, too. A staircase went up to a balcony that overlooked the barroom. From the ceiling, a line of brass fans hung on black chains, twirling and circulating the smoky air. The whole place smelled of roasted chilies and popcorn.

Jonathan got the bartender's attention. "Señor Carbone, *por favor*."

Frowning, the bartender inspected the haggard men asking for his boss. He set a foaming beer on the bar and wiped his porky hands on his apron. His eyes narrowed, his black mustache twitched, and his nose wrinkled as if it detected a bad smell. "*¿Cual es su nombre?*" he asked in a voice like sandpaper.

"Kyles, Jonathan Kyles," he shouted over all the noise.

The bartender curled a finger toward the end of the bar where a baldheaded bouncer in a sleeveless gray shirt stood with his thick and tattooed arms folded over his chest. His brows drew together as he acknowledged the page and made his way toward the bartender.

Melvin gulped. Jonathan took a step back.

The burly man and the bartender whispered back and forth. A moment later, the goon turned and puffed out his chest. "Get the hell out of here."

Jonathan stepped up to him. "You don't understand. Señor Carbone is expecting us."

"No." The goon poked Jonathan in the chest with a stiff finger. "You don't understand, beanpole. Get out of here or die."

Every muscle in Melvin's body tightened. Jonathan had never backed down from a fight, and this time would be no different. Though both men were the same height, the man with the tattoos was twice Jonathan's bulk.

The goon grunted, bared his teeth, and balled his fists. "What are you waiting for, creampuff?"

Jonathan sneered back at him. "Feelin' froggy, mister? Go ahead. Leap."

The goon came at him hard and fast. Jonathan gave him a quick sidestep left and tripped his feet. The oaf went down with a thud. In that split second, Jonathan jumped on him, the renegade's bayonet now poking the goon's Adam's apple, drawing a thin line of blood. "Say ribbit."

"What?"

"Say ribbit or die." He shoved the bayonet in a little deeper.

The music stopped. A woman screamed. Tourists scrambled for the door, chairs scraping on the floor and beer bottles breaking.

"Say it," Jonathan shouted.

The brute gritted his teeth, his neck muscles taut as steel cables. "Screw you."

"I don't like frogs." Jonathan stuck the blade tip into the goon's throat just enough to prove he wasn't fucking around.

Wincing, "R-ribbit," he said hoarsely.

"Ribbit, ribbit, ribbit," Jonathan taunted him.

"Kyles!" A voice boomed from the top of the staircase. "You have made your point."

Jonathan held the bayonet where he had it. "Your goon is a frog, Señor Carbone. Wanna hear him croak?"

Melvin took his hand out from under his black coat, leaving the gun in its hiding place. Hot adrenaline lingered in his bloodstream. "Let him go, Jonathan." He looked up to the man who saved the frog's life. Señor Carbone, a pudgy and balding man with fat cheeks and a thin mustache, wore a white shirt and gray slacks. A cigarette smoldered between his fingers as he stood there with his thumbs hooked under the straps of his overloaded suspenders. His black eyes stared down on them, hard and cold. With an uneasy feeling in his guts, Melvin walked toward the staircase. "Please excuse our appearance, Señor Carbone. We've had a rough week."

"So I see."

"Let's get down to business," Melvin pressed. "I want to clean up and get the hell out of this piss hole."

Jonathan let the frog up from the floor.

He hastily hobbled from the bar, holding his throat.

"Ribbit," Jonathan said and laughed.

Chapter Eleven

IN HOUSTON, AT THE Orbital Operations Center, the controller reported his Global Positioning System status into the ComLink. "GPS telemetry is true. We're getting a good signal from the Learjet, Colonel Fallon."

"I want a report every fifteen minutes."

"Yes, sir."

"Don't let it out of your sight."

"No problem, sir." He flipped the *TRANSMISSION TERMINATE* switch.

General Brigham looked over the controller's shoulder at the OPS monitor with its pulsing dot of light. It wasn't moving yet, but stationary in Simi Valley. He pulled a hard drag on his cigar. At sixty-four, Brigham stood six-foot-two and felt as comfortable in his dress uniform and polished shoes as he did in combat fatigues and boots. The army had been his whole life. The four stars on his collar were hard-fought to get, and at one time, hard-fought to keep, no thanks to the President and *The Ark* and their *Star Wars* conspiracy. "What are they up to now?" he growled to the controller.

"The CIA has us tracking a Learjet out of California. They're after Melvin Anderson again."

The General huffed. "What about my satellite?"

"We're working on it," the controller said. "It's not easy to commandeer a spy satellite."

"The damn thing belongs to the Department of

Defense, for Christsake."

"Atomtech changed the transmission codes. They were lost in the explosion. We're sending up random codes, one right after the other. It'll take some time, but we'll lock-on to it eventually, sir."

Brigham grinned, his cigar now clenched between his teeth. "I knew I could count on you boys."

"General, look," the controller said, suddenly pointing to his monitor. "The GPS tracker is moving. The Learjet has left Simi Valley."

***

The sun over Belize City seemed hotter, more intense than yesterday. Melvin tossed his coat over the balcony railing and looked down on the noisy street below. As he watched the procession of tourists and hawkers flow by, he ran his hand over his smoothly shaven face. He felt human again, the shower long overdue. Señor Carbone had scrounged up a clean blue shirt and tan trousers, and a porter at the hotel had polished his boots. He felt rested. Last night he'd savored the crisp sheets and soft blankets of a real bed. It seemed to him like a year had passed since he'd slept in one. However, it had only been a week since they escaped Simi Valley...a week since the 13th Power slipped from his grasp. The whole thing sat in the pit of his stomach like a rock.

He patted the pocket of his vest. In it were the bank vouchers he needed to finance his return trip to Solartech Labs, thanks to Señor Carbone and his connections.

The aroma of roasted chilies, ham hocks, and corn bread floating on the breeze put his mind on lunch. He wished he had time for a meal at the El Pedro Café, a favorite haunt of the locals, according to Jonathan, but they needed to get to the airport. The Learjet had already left Simi Valley and would arrive at 11:30. Melvin checked his watch: It was *11:10.*

Jonathan stepped onto the balcony. He looked like a new man. His hair was slicked back, and the length of it lay over the top of his ears and hung down above the collar of his white shirt. He'd loosely tied a black bow tie under his broad chin. The brown sport coat he wore was a little short in the sleeves. Señor Carbone had a hard time finding clothes to fit Jonathan's tall and lanky frame. But his boots glistened in the sunshine, and he wore a big smile. "Mornin', boss. A driver is bringing the car around."

"What arrangements did you make for us in Dallas?"

"We're booked into the Marriott as Blue Ridge Construction, a really nice room..."

"I told you I wanted the penthouse. Spare no expense."

Jonathan shook his head. "Now, boss, take it easy. We gotta keep this thing low key. You can't expect to march back into America ahead of a brass band. Too many people want a piece of your ass."

Melvin was thinking about that when a commotion on the street caught his attention. Three soldiers with rifles slung across their shoulders approached the renegade's jeep and started looking through the junk in the back. One of them opened the glove box and rummaged through it, while another studied the black spray paint that covered the military markings that once identified the vehicle.

Melvin's heartbeat jumped. He wondered if it was just curiosity that drew the soldiers' attention to the jeep, or perhaps they were looking for its previous owners. The probabilities went from bad to worse when one of them started yapping Spanish into his radio while the others scanned the crowd as if they were looking for someone in particular.

Jonathan nudged Melvin. "This don't look good, boss."

A military jeep careened around the corner with four

soldiers clinging to the roll cage and another manning a machinegun mounted to the crossbar. They started yelling.

The crowd scattered.

Carbone appeared in the doorway. “Trouble. Follow me.”

Melvin grabbed his black coat and followed Carbone down a hallway. Jonathan’s heavy footfalls clunked behind him. “What the hell’s going on?”

“Two of Herrera’s sons were found floating in the river outside of Juchitan,” Carbone explained as they hurried down the hall to a flight of stairs. “They had stolen the jeep you drove into town.”

“So what’s the big deal?” Melvin asked while running down a dark stairwell. “The army should be glad they got it back.”

Carbone led the way through another hallway with creaking floorboards. “It is not that. They believe the killers are nearby, and now I am wondering how you came about that jeep.”

Melvin’s chest tightened. “Those thugs ambushed our camp. It was self defense.”

Carbone pushed open a big door. “Miguel Herrera won’t give a damn about that. You messed with the wrong family. He’ll stop at nothing to catch his son’s killers.”

“Who is he, the governor?”

“The Herrera clan is powerful. They deal in drugs and extortion.”

“Then how do the soldiers figure into this?”

Carbone bounded up another staircase. “Miguel Herrera controls everything around here, including the army.”

“Sounds like my kind of guy,” Melvin said as he followed Carbone into a parking garage. A white Ford LTD roared up and skidded to a stop. The driver got out, wide-eyed. Señor Carbone said something to him in Spanish. The man dashed away.

"Hurry," he said to Jonathan and handed him a two-way radio. "Use this to communicate with your plane. It should be landing soon."

Jonathan slid in behind the wheel as Melvin jumped into the passenger seat. The garage door was already going up. Another jeep raced by outside. The soldiers looked angry, their cold eyes fixed on the crowd.

Carbone bent to the window. "We are even now, Jonathan."

"Gracias." He threw the transmission into drive.

"What did he mean by that?" Melvin asked as the tires squealed.

"It's a long story."

"Must be a doozy."

The car lurched through the door and careened onto the sun-baked street. Melvin squinted and wiped sweat from his forehead. In the rearview mirror, he spotted two jeeps and an MPC, a Military Personnel Carrier, gaining rapidly. He saw about twenty soldiers riding in back with their rifles at the ready. "They're after us."

Jonathan made an evasive maneuver around a donkey-drawn cart, which bolted and took down the awning over a street market, but the jeeps kept coming. Then the soldiers in the MPC started firing their rifles.

Melvin pulled the gun out from under his belt. "How'd they spot us so fast?"

Jonathan swerved around a slow-moving bus. "Señor Carbone is in a difficult position here. He has to play on both sides of the fence, so don't take it personal, boss. After all, he gave us a head start."

"How thoughtful of him." A bullet shattered the back window. He ducked the shower of glass. "Remind me to send him a thank you card."

Bullets pinged off the roof as Jonathan weaved in and out of traffic, driving like mad.

Through the busted back window, Melvin squeezed

off a couple shots. The turn for the airport was just up ahead on the other side of the intersection, but the traffic light switched to yellow. Two cars in front of them blew the light, but a third car stopped in the left lane. "Go right."

Jonathan jerked the wheel and floored the accelerator. The engine roared. Just then, from the curb, an inattentive local coaxed his donkey cart into the right lane.

Melvin gasped.

Jonathan careened onto the sidewalk with a bone-jarring bang. Parking meters exploded on impact, sending pesos flying like tinkling rain. A shoe repair vendor dove for cover just before the Ford demolished his little cobbler stand. Nails and tacks flew everywhere.

"Sorry," Jonathan shouted over his shoulder as he drove off the curb and through the intersection.

The light turned red. Cross traffic lurched forward, cars and trucks and a bus. Tires screeched as both jeeps collided with the bus. Horns honked and voices cursed.

Melvin grinned.

Gritting his teeth, Jonathan aimed the battered Ford onto Northern Highway, and barreling toward the airport eight miles away, he weaved in and out of traffic.

At first, Melvin felt confident they were going to make it, but what he saw after Jonathan turned left onto International Airport Road suddenly changed all that. A big green tank was tracking down the opposite side of the street, headed straight toward them. It looked like an ancient relic from World War II, probably an old Sherman tank, Melvin surmised. But old or not, its turret swiveled around, and the black-barreled cannon suddenly boomed and spit fire.

"Look out."

Jonathan clutched the steering wheel. There was nothing he could do.

Feeling like a sitting duck, Melvin bared his teeth, every muscle tensing for the explosion. Whistling overhead, the shell hit a light pole, toppling it to the street. Tires squealed as cars veered to miss it and crashed into each other.

Jonathan threaded the Ford through the mayhem. The tank fired again. This time the round exploded twenty yards ahead of them. It quickly became obvious to Melvin that the tank crew was not very experienced.

"Take a shortcut through the fence." Melvin braced himself against the dash as the car left the road, flew over the ditch, and hit the chain-link fence. It tore from its footing, which allowed the car to barrel under it. When Melvin turned to look out the glassless back window, he saw the tank crash into the fence and crush it to the ground. It fired again, but the shell fell short.

With sweat trickling down his face, Jonathan drove a zigzag course across the airfield and careened the battered Ford onto the runway. The tank, flinging dirt in the air, bounced along behind and fired another shell. About twenty yards on the left, a plume of smoke and fire spewed into the air with a boom.

Jonathan veered right.

"They'll never hit us like that," Melvin said. "Not while they're moving."

"They could get lucky." Jonathan veered left. He flipped Melvin the radio Carbone had given him. "Call the plane. I'm a little busy right now."

***

In the sky over Belize, the Learjet descended to one thousand feet above the lush rainforest canopy. First officer Jerry Daniels pressed the transmitter button on the yoke. "Goldson International tower. Lear November-Alpha-three-seven-Xray, inbound for landing."

"*Alpha-three-seven-Xray. Radar contact, two-zero miles north of Belize City. Winds light and variable. Make left traffic. Clear to land, runway two-five."*

"I see the field," Captain Richards said.

Daniels took a moment to look over the jungle gliding by below. The wide and muddy Belize River cut through the carpet of green like an ugly gash in the skin of the earth. It always looked the same down there: inhospitable.

He and Captain Richards had been in and out of Belize City's nearest International airport many times. Their Learjet 60 was equipped with long-range fuel tanks, giving them two extra hours flying time. They were supposed to fly directly to their corporate headquarters in Dallas, but Captain Richards had ordered the tanks filled at Solartech Field because he had other plans. Dr. Frank Curtis was in Belize City, and they were going in to get him out.

Captain Richards made left downwind traffic over Belize City, turned base over the water, and turned to final approach at one thousand feet and cut the engine power.

At the inner marker, Daniels started calling out approach altitudes for the Captain. "Four hundred feet...three fifty...three hundred." The Learjet was gliding in at one hundred fifty knots and dropping five hundred feet per minute. They'd be on the ground in twenty seconds.

Suddenly the radio squawked. *"Alpha-three-seven-Xray, go around,"* the controller in the tower ordered. "*The runway is unsafe. Go around."*

Captain Richards reached for the throttle levers to execute a go-around just as another transmission came over the radio. *"Hey! Where the hell are you guys? We're in deep shit down here!"*

"Who's on this frequency?" the controller shouted.

"I'm looking for my airplane," the voice came back.

Daniels checked the altimeter. "Two hundred." He looked out over the nose of the jet. On the field below, he saw a white sedan driving like a drunkard down runway two-five. A plume of fire and smoke suddenly erupted alongside the car. Then he saw an old tank careening across the beltway and heading toward the runway threshold. Everything became very clear. "Is that you, Dr. Curtis?" Daniels said into the radio. "One-fifty," he told the Captain.

"Hell yeah! Where are you guys?"

"Right on your bumper."

"Go around Alpha-three-seven-Xray," the controller ordered again. *"Go around."*

"One hundred," Daniels reported to the Captain. "What should we do?"

"We're going in." The Captain pushed his mike button. "Negative on the go-around, Alpha-three-seven-Xray. Dr. Curtis, we'll meet you at the end of the runway. Prepare to board immediately."

"Fifty feet."

The jet over flew the tank, and one second later, the tires hit the runway. Captain Richards kept the power on and did not hit the reverse thrusters. Quickly, the Learjet overtook the speeding Ford. The right wing barely cleared the car's roof as it passed. Only then did he hit the reverse thrusters. The engines roared, slowing the jet to taxi speed. At the end of the runway, he turned the Learjet around one-hundred-eighty degrees.

Daniels blew out a sigh and retracted the flaps as the Ford raced toward them. In the distance, through rippling heat waves rising from the sun-bleached concrete, he saw the tank lumber onto the runway threshold, way down at the other end of the field. Unbelievably, its cannon belched smoke and flame. Daniels gasped. "My God. They're going to kill us."

Whistling, the shell exploded about thirty yards from the left wingtip. The concussion rocked the jet. Daniels leaped out of his seat, scrambled for the cabin door, and swung it open just as the Ford skidded to a stop.

Dr. Curtis and Jonathan Kyles climbed in. They were sweating and breathing hard.

"Welcome aboard," the Captain said evenly over the intercom.

Daniels latched the door. "Please buckle your seatbelts for takeoff."

Back in the right seat in front of his instruments and controls, Daniels thought he'd rather be somewhere else, like Dallas or New York or even Las Vegas. The tank was getting closer. Its black barrel was aimed right at them. "Okay. Let's roll."

The cannon came alive again.

Captain Richards pushed the throttles forward. The jet engines revved, but much too slowly for Daniels' liking. He clenched his jaw and held his breath as the whistling shell flew over the left wing and slammed into the Ford with horrendous force, sending shattered and burning fragments of the car in every direction. Debris slammed against the fuselage, and a swirling cloud of yellow fire engulfed the jet as it accelerated down the runway.

Daniels gulped what he thought would be his last breath, but the accelerating jet shot out of the fireball and roared toward the tank. It was still coming toward them from the other end of the runway. The tank's tracks threw sparks from the concrete, and the cannon was still smoking.

The Learjet accelerated faster and faster as the tank came closer and closer.

Daniels grimaced as he watched the airspeed indicator finally reach rotation speed. Captain Richards pulled back on the yoke. At the same time, the tank's cannon fired. With engines screaming at full power, the Learjet sliced into the Belize City sky.

"Set a course for Dallas," the Captain said coolly.

Daniels blew out the air he'd been holding onto so dearly and thought Las Vegas might be a better destination. After all, he was feeling pretty lucky right about now.

Chapter Twelve

AT CIA HEADQUARTERS, John Nathan listened into the telephone as the controller at Houston's Orbital Operations Center reported the Learjet's flight path. The signal from the GPS tracker had been coming in strong for the last four hours.

"At first we thought the Learjet was headed for Mexico City," the controller said. "But it turned east."

"What does Air Traffic Control know about it?" Nathan asked.

"ATC reported Alpha-three-seven-Xray was en route to Puerto Rico. However, the Learjet doesn't have enough fuel to go that far."

"They've got to refuel somewhere," Nathan said. "Where's the best place?"

"Wait a minute." The line went silent. A moment later, "They're descending to Belize City right now," the controller said, excitement edging his words.

Nathan grinned. "My money says Melvin Anderson is there."

"Should we send a team to Puerto Rico?"

"It's our only shot. Do it." Nathan hung up, his head buzzing. He wondered if they could make it to Puerto Rico before the Learjet, and he wondered why Melvin Anderson was going to Puerto Rico, anyway.

The door came open. Chief Bret Lawrence stormed in with a rank cigar clenched between his teeth. The CIA

Chief of Internal Affairs was a stocky man and bald as an ostrich egg. He stood about five-foot-ten, wore a gray suit and a red tie that hung loosely around an unbuttoned collar. "What the hell are you up to now, John?"

"I got a handle on this thing, sir."

The Chief huffed. "Like last time?"

"Look, goddamnit." Nathan stood and pointed at Lawrence. "Your men blew it. Security was breached and Colonel Fallon pounced on Solartech Labs. Why didn't we know about him?"

Lawrence sneered. The veins on his forehead swelled. "You shouldn't have authorized the assault on Atomtech. Now all our asses are in hot water. Walter Devin escaped because your boys did a shit job. I've got Agent Stevens' report right here." He reached into his suit coat and pulled out a folded paper. "Walter Devin went to Colonel Fallon after the assault and told him about Melvin Anderson and the 13th Power project." He slammed the paper on the desk. "Who the hell botched this thing?"

Nathan leaned forward. "Alex Gibson was in charge of the raid on Atomtech. He recruited the mercenary soldiers, and they're the ones who were supposed to kill Devin before he could interfere with the experiments in Simi Valley."

"Then why didn't our bug in their supercomputers get the particle beam data?"

"The techs found *The Worm*. They worked around it somehow. It's useless to us now."

"So what are we going to do about it?"

Nathan shook his head. "We're going to do things differently...ruthlessly, if need be."

"And that's something new?"

"Hey!" Nathan went face to face with Lawrence. "Sabotaging the FBI's jet was your idea, Bret. I told you to do it somewhere over the Colorado mountains. But no, you wanted to watch Agent Marston and his boys go down right here in Washington. A confirmed kill, I remember you saying."

"I warned him to leave the 13th Power project alone." Lawrence grabbed the cigar out of his mouth. "He wouldn't listen. He'd have had us both on death row by now. I handled it my way. Now, nobody knows anything. It's covert all the way. I saved your ass, John."

"You know the FBI is still investigating the crash."

"And what are you doing about that?"

Nathan grinned, his undercover operation in mind. "I'm on top of it."

"How?"

"Don't worry, Lawrence. My connection is very close to the investigation."

Lawrence's face reddened. "I've covered everything else. There's no evidence left: all the computer files were erased, and even the Hawker's black box was dumped in the ocean." He stuck out his chin and took another drag on his cigar. "It's a clean sweep, I tell yah."

"What about the Russian scientist, Boris Dagloskoff? He knows everything. You know how he brags when he's been drinking."

"Don't worry, I've got a team on his trail right now."

"I don't want any witnesses." Nathan poked a finger at Lawrence. "Don't take any chances, you got that?"

Lawrence's eyes glared. "Look who's talking about taking chances. Hell, instead of getting the CIA out of this mess, you're digging us in deeper. What's this I hear about a team going to Puerto Rico?"

Nathan sneered. "We're going in to get Melvin Anderson."

"What the hell for? He's caused us enough trouble already."

"We went about this thing all wrong." Nathan retreated behind his desk. "The covert operation at Solartech Labs failed. The way I see it, if we're going to fulfill Directive Number 119, we'll need to be upfront with Melvin Anderson and Tracy McClarence. We're going to offer them money and incentives to do the experiments."

Lawrence's brows arched. "I see." He puffed on his cigar. "Bring them into our little game and let them think we're all on the same team. But when they find out Congress cut the funding for *Star Wars* and there's no money to pay them, what's going to keep them from blabbing to the press?"

"We'll make them think they're just as guilty as we are."

At that Lawrence scowled. "That's pretty damn guilty, John."

The phone rang.

Nathan picked up the call. "Yes?"

"Don't send a team to Puerto Rico, sir," the controller said. He sounded frantic.

"Why not?"

"The Learjet didn't refuel in Belize City. It landed and took off again. Now it's headed north...towards Dallas, we suspect."

Nathan took a deep breath and wondered what the hell was going on around here. Every time he thought he had a grip on the situation, something went haywire; nothing ever went according to plan. It was as if the 13th Power had a will of its own, deliberately screwing up everything and making fools of those who would try to possess it. But Nathan wasn't about to give up now. "Send the team to Dallas instead," he told the controller. "And contact Agent Stevens on the ComLink. I want him there too."

***

Departing Belize, First Officer Daniels checked the altimeter. They were flying at 6,000 feet. The airspeed meter read 485 knots. He'd rather be cruising at 35,000 feet, but the Captain didn't want to file a flight plan, as it would alert ATC to their destination. This way, the Learjet was just an unidentified blip on ATC's radar screens, same as any other light aircraft flying under visual flight rules.

Up ahead, rain fell from a patch of gray clouds, and Captain Richards adjusted his course five degrees left. Turbulence buffeted the aircraft as they flew around the rain shower. A few seconds later, the air calmed, and the Learjet went on toward Dallas.

Daniels made himself busy reading charts and scanning his instruments. He noticed the fuel gauge needles quivering near the warning band. In his mind, trained by years of aviation schooling and thousands of hours flying time, he did the math. By calculating speed, time, and distance, and factoring in the rate at which the engines consumed fuel at this low altitude, he knew that Dallas was just beyond the Learjet's range. He glanced at Captain Richards and noticed his jaw muscles twitching.

***

Back in the passenger cabin, Melvin watched the jungle streak by under the Learjet. The engines made a soft droning sound as the jet cruised along. The jungle looked like an immense expanse of green carpet. From up here, he could only see beauty. The bugs, heat, decay, and death were all but fading memories.

The wings tipped, and the jet rolled right. Melvin clutched the armrests of his seat. At least his heartbeat was beginning to recover from their encounter with the tank and their narrow escape from Belize City.

He looked at Jonathan sitting across the aisle. Sweat still beaded his face and neck, yet he sat stoically as if unaware of how close they had come to dying. There was something almost magical about Jonathan. He had an uncanny knack of getting out of trouble. Because of him, they were safe on the Learjet, heading for Dallas and eventually back to Solartech Labs. It seemed as if nothing could stop them. They had survived it all: Colonel Fallon, the renegades, the backstabbing Señor Carbone, and even the soldiers of Belize City, thanks to an old tank and its inept crew. Melvin was sure that the rest of this trip would be a cakewalk.

"How about a margarita?" he asked Jonathan.

***

Craig Stevens made his way through the crowded concourse at Dallas – Fort Worth. The humid Texas night stuck to his skin like a fungus. Cisco followed behind him. Lately, it seemed as though they'd spent more time in the air than on the ground, flying from Atlanta to Washington, then Washington to Solartech Field, and then to Denver and now Dallas. It was a rat race, and now, this assignment had taken them off Tracy McClarence's trail. They were getting close to her. Rumor had it she was hanging around with Dr. Janis Mackey at the University of Colorado, in Boulder. But now, Melvin Anderson was more important. *The Ark* wanted him taken alive, but Stevens had other plans. He wanted Melvin Anderson dead so Colonel Fallon wouldn't get the chance to interrogate him.

A clutch of agents and airport security personnel had gathered by the door to a corporate gate. Stevens greeted the Lieutenant in charge.

"Ground controllers are going to direct the Learjet here," the Lieutenant said. "Our team is in position. Some of us are disguised as ground personnel and others as luggage handlers. The gate attendants are ours, also. Anderson won't get away this time."

"He won't show up here," Cisco said with an edge to his words.

The Lieutenant shot the rookie a frown. "Houston is

tracking them in this direction. They're staying under instrument minimums, and Air Traffic Control hasn't had any radio contact with them. Their fuel is critical but not impossible. They'll be here."

Cisco put his nose in the air. "It's not going to work. Remember, nothing ever goes right with this thing. You'd better have a backup plan."

"Leave it to us," the Lieutenant growled, poking a finger into Cisco's chest. "We'll get the bastard. The rest is up to you guys."

Cisco looked like he was going to pop. Stevens grabbed his partner's arm and pulled him toward seats in the waiting area. "Jet lag," Stevens explained to the Lieutenant and pushed Cisco into a chair. "What are you trying to do, start a war?"

"I'm sick of this crap. These guys are going to blow it, just like all the others."

Stevens thought about that as he glared into Cisco's eyes. Melvin Anderson had been underestimated all along. Alex Gibson made that mistake and paid with his life. From the Malaysian Federation to Walter Devin and Colonel Fallon, they all failed to stop Melvin Anderson. Stevens glanced at the team now huddled together again. They too were destined to fail, he surmised. The jet would pull up to the gate, and Melvin Anderson wouldn't be on it. At that, Stevens sat in a chair next to Cisco. "I think you're right. He's going to get away again."

Cisco shook his head. "The Lieutenant presumes too much."

"What do you think?"

"He'll bail out on the tarmac, in fact, he's probably got a car waiting to pick him up. Why would he risk coming to the terminal?"

Stevens rubbed his jaw. Cisco may have a lot of idiosyncrasies, but he wasn't stupid. In fact, right about now he was the only one making any sense around here. A backup plan couldn't hurt. He patted Cisco's shoulder. "I'll talk to them."

He stood and moved to the group of agents and airport security personnel standing around. "How much time do we have?" he asked the Lieutenant who checked his watch.

"Fifty-nine minutes."

"We need to cover the runways and taxiways," Stevens said. "Just in case Anderson decides to jump the plane."

"How do you propose we do that, in taxicabs?"

"We need something a little more practical."

A thin man dressed in a blue uniform approached with his finger in the air. He wore Airport Security patches on his shirtsleeves and a grin on his face, as if he knew something but was reluctant to jump right in with it. Maybe all this CIA brass was a bit overwhelming for the little guy.

Stevens nodded to him. "You've got something to say?"

His face lit up with a smile that reached his eyes. "Norm. You can call me Norm." He offered an exuberant handshake.

"What's on your mind, Norm?"

"Fire trucks," he said, his eyes now darting back and forth between Stevens and the Lieutenant. "We got a bunch of 'em."

"Fire trucks?" Stevens rubbed his neck. "Of course. Fire trucks."

***

In the Learjet's cockpit, a red light started flashing over the fuel gauges. First Officer Daniels tapped them with his index finger, but the needles didn't budge off empty. The fuel pressure gauges held firm. Nervously, he looked out over the nose of the jet. Up ahead and to the right, the lights of Dallas illuminated the darkness, and Fort

Worth glowed as brilliantly on the left and Arlington under the nose. They lit up the night with three domes of light. The airport's rotating green and white beacon was clearly visible in the distance.

Daniels dialed up ATIS on the radio as the Learjet descended to five thousand feet. The Automatic Terminal Information Service gave him a prerecorded report on the current weather and runway conditions for the field. It ended with, *"On initial contact, advise you have information Sierra."* Daniels keyed the mike. "Dallas Approach, Learjet Alpha-three-seven-Xray, inbound for landing with Sierra."

As he awaited his clearance into Dallas, Daniels looked to the left seat where Captain Richards was pulling his safety belt tighter. Fear shot through Daniels' brain. He gave his seatbelt an extra tug and then activated the intercom. "Gentlemen. Buckle your seatbelts for landing."

The radio crackled. *"Alpha-three-seven-Xray, squawk two-two-four-zero and ident."*

"Roger." He set the transponder and pushed the *IDENT* button, which identified the Learjet on the air traffic control radar screens.

Suddenly, an alarm rang out in the cockpit. The blood in Daniels' veins turned cold. He knew it wasn't any ordinary alarm. The engines surged. He glanced at the Captain who was clutching the steering yoke with both hands. His eyes shifted to the fuel pressure gauges, which had both suddenly dropped into the red. The tanks were empty, just as Daniels had calculated.

"Alpha-three-seven-Xray," the radio crackled. *"Radar contact, twenty miles south of Dallas - Fort Worth. Fly heading 360. Clear for your approach."*

The jet shuddered as the right engine flamed out and quit. Another clanging alarm went off. Losing the engine caused the altimeter to start dropping down from four thousand feet. Daniels shut off the fuel to the right engine and sent all the remaining to the left engine.

"Work the rudder," the Captain said as he added more throttle to the only remaining engine in an effort to slow the jet's unwanted descent.

Daniels pushed on the left rudder pedal, counteracting the right turn produced by the thrust of the left engine, thus keeping the jet's nose pointed toward the airport beacon. The lights of Dallas and Fort Worth drew closer. The altimeter wound down below three thousand feet.

"We'll go in at two hundred knots without flaps," Richards said in a very businesslike tone. "Keep the landing gear up until we make the field."

Daniels nodded his understanding, though he thought the tires might blow if they hit the ground at that speed. The runway lights were now discernable from the city lights. He felt a little better about their chances of making the field.

The radio squelched. *"Alpha-three-seven-Xray, Dallas-Fort Worth tower. Clear to land, Three-Six Left.*"

"That's Three-Six-Left for Alpha-three-seven-Xray," Daniels replied. His heart was pounding now. They were cleared to land, but the runway was still ten miles away. The jet was dropping at five hundred feet per minute. They only need three more minutes.

The left engine flamed out.

***

"They're on final," the Lieutenant's voice came over the radio.

Stevens clutched the fire truck's handrail as they raced down the taxiway toward runway Three-Six-Left. The diesel engine roared, and huge knobby tires whined on the concrete as the fire truck bounced and rocked across the airfield. A fireman wrestled the steering wheel with both hands. He wore a bulky orange fire suit, brown rubber boots, and a yellow helmet. Texas sweat rolled down his cheeks.

Stevens glanced at two CIA agents sitting in the jump seats behind the driver. They wore black suits and frowns. Cisco, on the other hand, had climbed on top of the pumper with two firemen manning the giant turreted nozzle. They'd bragged about how it could spray foam two hundred ninety feet. Cisco had told them he always wanted to ride on a fire truck, ever since he was a kid. Stevens chuckled to himself: Cisco was still a kid, and now he was playing with the big toys, probably driving the firemen crazy with questions.

Looking out the front windows, Stevens saw several other fire trucks converging on the runway at different positions. Others were parked on the taxiways, and some were blocking access ramps and exits. The runway was completely sealed.

***

With no engine power, the crippled Learjet was coming down at one thousand feet per minute. Daniels shut off the alarms. He didn't need to listen to them anyway. He already knew they were in trouble. Now he noticed how quiet the Learjet had become with only the sound of air rushing over the airframe. The flight deck was dark because the electricity had shut off when the generators lost engine power. His electronic instruments were dead, but the altimeter, which worked on barometric pressure, was still functioning. A battery supplied power to the backup hydraulic control system, but it wouldn't last long. The Learjet had become a heavy glider, steadily working its way down toward a runway that was much too far away.

Grabbing the emergency flashlight, he shined it on the altimeter. "Two thousand feet," he said to the Captain. "I'd better radio an emergency."

"No. I don't want that kind of attention. We'll make

the field using a little trick I learned in the military."

"What's that?"

"It's called the porpoise."

Daniels had heard of that gut-wrenching maneuver and immediately spoke into the intercom mike. "Get ready, Dr. Curtis. It's going to be a rough ride." Then he wiped sweat from his palms and looked at the Captain. "Ready when you are."

Richards pulled back on the yoke, and the Learjet pitched upward and climbed rapidly.

"Twenty five hundred feet," Daniels announced, his stomach feeling heavy as a rock. "Three thousand."

The airspeed dropped until the jet began to shudder, a clear warning of an imminent stall, then Richards pushed the yoke forward, sending the Learjet into steep dive. The airspeed climbed as the jet plummeted. "Twenty five hundred," Daniels said, his insides floating. "Nineteen hundred."

Using this excess airspeed, the Captain pitched the nose up and climbed as high as he dared before the jet would stall, then began a slow glide rate until the altitude became critical again.

"Eighteen thousand feet," Daniels announced.

Richards pushed the nose over, and using the increased speed, he pulled back on the yoke, again putting the Learjet into a steep climb, and then another slow glide.

"Twenty-five hundred."

The Captain worked the controls in this manner for the next two minutes, sacrificing altitude for airspeed, and then in turn, airspeed for altitude in order to sustain another long slow glide path. Like a porpoise, the Learjet worked its way toward Dallas – Fort Worth.

At the airport's outer marker, Daniels reported their altitude at one thousand feet. Richards trimmed the jet for landing. Everything was set for the touchdown—in less than one minute. The jet was lined up with runway three-six-left, a two-mile stretch of concrete edged with green lights. Blue lights marked the taxiways, and yellow fire trucks were everywhere. Daniels' throat clutched. They hadn't declared an emergency. Why were all those fire trucks deployed?

His mind racing, Daniels called out the altimeter readings for the Captain. "Five hundred feet...four hundred...three hundred." There would only be one attempt at this landing. No second chance; no go-around. It was all up to Captain Richards. "Two hundred."

"Landing gear down," the Captain ordered.

Daniels held his breath and worked the lever that dropped the wheels. Backup hydraulics whined, and the sudden drag took hold of the aircraft and shook it. The nose pitched down, and with no engine power to counteract the landing gear drag, only brute strength on the controls kept the jet from nose-diving into the ground. "One hundred feet."

As the jet flew over the runway threshold, the Captain fought the yoke with both hands, his knuckles white and his teeth bared. Below, fire trucks took to the chase, their overheads flashing chaotically.

Suddenly, the cabin curtain flew open. "It's a trap," Curtis yelled.

"Get back in your seat, sir." Daniels ordered.

"You've got to find another airport."

"We're out of fuel, doctor."

"You have to do something."

"We'll die if we don't get on the ground...fifty feet, Captain...take your seat, Dr. Curtis."

***

"Come to papa," Agent Stevens said under his breath as he watched the dark Learjet fly over the runway threshold without its navigation or landing lights on. Fire trucks sped after it. Sirens and horns pierced the muggy Texas night. They were ready to spring the trap.

With a puff of smoke, the jet touched down, rolling along the runway at breakneck speed. But there was no roar from the engines and reverse thrusters. Stevens snapped his fingers. They had to be out of fuel...there was no other explanation.

A screech from the tires told him the pilots were applying the brakes hard. But the jet came closer and closer, and the squealing tires started spewing smoke that swirled in the air. Careening down the runway, the speeding jet looked dangerously out of control.

The fire truck driver threw the transmission into reverse and backed off the runway. Several other trucks followed his lead.

Suddenly, fire erupted from the Learjet's brake casings, igniting the tires, twirling flames like a circus act.

"Fire on the runway," came over the emergency radio.

The driver spun the fire truck around. "Get ready," he said to his men on the roof. They were poised to hit the jet with a spray of foam. More fire trucks barreled down the runway with sirens wailing. As the jet screamed past throwing sparks like a grinder, the fire truck raced after it. Foam sprayed from the rooftop nozzle doused the fire quickly. Finally, the crippled jet creaked to a stop just before the end of the runway.

Stevens didn't waste any time. Just as the fire truck stopped, he leaped out and drew his Glock. Other agents surrounded the jet. The cabin door swung open. Gunfire erupted through the door. He dove to the ground and rolled. Bullets zinged through the air. When he came back up on his knees, he couldn't believe his eyes. A thick spray of foam was streaming into the Learjet's open door. The cabin was filling quickly. A scream of joy came from the fire truck's roof, and when Stevens looked up, he saw Cisco holding onto the turreted nozzle and aiming the spray at the Learjet. He was yelling and carrying on like a kid with the biggest squirt gun on the block. As the firemen finally shut it off, Stevens looked again at the jet's open cabin door. Rivers of foam poured out. There was no sign of Melvin Anderson.

A team of agents stormed the plane. Moments later and dripping foam, they emerged with Melvin Anderson and Jonathan Kyles in handcuffs.

"Nice work," the Lieutenant said to Cisco who was standing with his legs spread on top of the fire truck like Superman.

Stevens holstered the Glock and shook his head. The rookie had his first collar: Melvin Anderson. *The Ark* would probably give him a medal.

Chapter Thirteen

IN BELIZE CITY, THE Quarter B Bar was quiet. A ray of morning sunshine knifed through a slit in the window shade and streaked across the wood-planked floor. Last night, chairs had been set upside down on the tables, and sparkling beer mugs were stacked pyramid-style along the back of the bar. A sharp scent of wood polish lingered in the air.

Señor Carbone shuffled to the refrigerator, his eyelids heavy with fatigue from a restless night. A cigarette dangled from his lower lip as he poured himself a glass of tomato juice. Drink in hand, he plopped into a stool at the end of the bar and flicked away the gray ash from his smoke.

Now, his mind replayed the endless recordings that had robbed him of his sleep. Seeing Jonathan Kyles had stirred up the memories again: the nightmare of that fire, the searing heat, the flames lapping up the bedroom walls, and the air choked with smoke. It wasn't the crackling roar of the inferno that had terrorized him that night, but the screams of his children trapped in their bedroom and the sobs of his wife lying next to him on the floor. He tried to forget the gut-wrenching agony that had sliced through him when his children went suddenly quiet.

Carbone threw down a swallow of his drink and wiped sweat from his forehead as the memory of smoke and flames swirled in his mind. None of it had seemed real, not even the tall, lanky shadow that appeared over him. At the time, he thought the devil was carrying him through hell. They were floating together, drifting without weight or form until the air was suddenly clear and the ground was cool. Little arms went around him. "Daddy, daddy," he could hear his children calling, and his wife was there too. It was a miracle. Jonathan Kyles had saved them all.

As risky as it was double-crossing Miguel Herrera, Carbone had repaid his long-standing debt to Jonathan. Now, his wife and children were alive and well at his estate in Cancun, and Jonathan was safely away from Belize City. The debt had gone full circle. Carbone slammed the rest of his drink, hoping the nightmares would finally end.

Squealing brakes came from the street, and suddenly alarmed, he crushed out his cigarette and rushed to the window. Pushing aside the shade, he saw an MPC teeter as soldiers with rifles spilled out and lined the street in front of his bar. They were yelling "*traidor*" with a look of murder on their faces. When a black Cadillac pulled up to the curb, he realized the nightmare was just beginning.

Carbone wasted no more time watching the forces gather. He ran for the stairs, thinking that if he could make it up to the balcony and into his suite, he had a chance to get out alive. The fire escape there led down to a tunnel under the street. He had designed it himself and spared no expense. Now perhaps it would save him from the soldiers.

But before he reached the stairs, bullets exploded the front door, splintering the wood and sending the locks flying. The door burst open, chairs toppled to the floor, and gunshots echoed through the barroom. He ducked low as he ran, but suddenly, his right leg went out from under him. He hit the floor hard. A burning pain raced up his body. The room began to spin.

Soldiers crowded around him quickly, all shouting and now dragging him along the floor by his arms. He tried to cry out, but fear choked his words. The soldiers set a chair upright and lifted him into it. Ropes went around his chest, his wrists, and his ankles. He struggled to get free. They pulled the knots tighter. As if satisfied, they backed away and stood to the side.

The place went deathly quiet.

Fighting against the ropes, he shifted his eyes from the soldiers to the man who had stepped through the busted door. He wore all black: a shirt, a vest, sharply pressed slacks, and pointy boots. A big silver bear hung from a silver chain around his neck. His thin face was olive-skinned. His slicked-back hair and well-groomed mustache were as silver as his necklace. Carbone shuddered with an instinctive fear.

It was Miguel Herrera.

Boot heels thudded on the wooden floor as Miguel walked across the barroom. The old man's hawkish eyes speared Carbone with a vengeance, a look that told him Herrera had found out how his sons' killers had gotten away. He probably wanted the names: Jonathan's and Melvin's, though that would never happen. A debt was owed; a debt was paid. Herrera would soon learn he was wasting his time.

"I had seven sons." Herrera pinched the silver bear on his necklace as he stood in front of Carbone. "Did you know Carlos, my oldest? He was killed by the Americans in Atlanta, USA."

Carbone shook his head. "My condolences, Miguel."

He scowled. "Now, two more of my sons are dead...Ricardo and Philip. They were shot down like pigs outside Juchitan."

"A dreadful loss, sir. Could you call a doctor to look at my leg? It hurts something awful."

"We shall attend to that later."

"What do you want?"

"You know who did the killing."

"I know nothing," Carbone said with conviction.

"Who killed my boys?" Herrera shouted, his cheeks mottled with rage.

Carbone jutted his chin forward. This was no time to be timid. Tied up or not, he had to be tough. Maybe this bullet in his leg would be the worst of it. "How should I know who killed your boys?"

"You know," Miguel bellowed and struck him across the face with the back of his hand.

Carbone's head flew back; his face erupted in pain. Lights blinked in his brain. *Don't panic. Make up lies.* "I don't know what you're talking about."

Herrera leaned forward and went nose-to-nose with Carbone. "Don't play stupid with me. The jeep was found in front of your place. The killers were here."

"A lot of people were here, Miguel."

Herrera stood upright and stroked the silver bear. "Tell me then, where is your car?"

"My car...it's...it's in the garage."

"Wrong!" Herrera slugged Carbone in the mouth. "It is at the airport in a million pieces."

Carbone spit blood. "What?"

"They got away in your car, you stupid man."

"But how...?" Carbone shook off the fog in his battered mind. He wasn't going to give Herrera any information because he knew that they would hunt Jonathan down like a wild dog. Nowhere would he be safe from their wrath. "My car must have been stolen, Miguel. I didn't know."

"Liar! You knew!" Herrera balled a fist again but held it back. "I should beat you right now, but you won't talk. I know this already...some say you are pretty tough. I say you are not tough enough."

"Go to hell, Miguel!" Carbone's lips were swollen and bleeding. "Beat me if you like, shoot me if you must, but go to hell, just the same."

A smile came across the old man's face. "I've

something else in mind for you, stupid man." He signaled the sergeant standing guard at the door. "Now we shall see how tough you really are."

Soldiers appeared in the doorway, dragging three prisoners, bound head to toe and gagged. Two of them were very small, their hair tousled and ratty and their wide eyes ringed in white. The third prisoner had flowing black hair and eyes that glittered with sparks of recognition. Carbone stiffened. "God! No!"

Herrera shoved Carbone's wife and children to the floor in front of him. They struggled against the ropes that bound them, squirming and squealing.

A rage came over Carbone like none he'd ever known. He cursed himself for not resisting Miguel's influence over them in the past. He had accepted it as a way of life, in favor of peace rather than conflict. Now he realized that long ago he should have done something to stop the Herreras' reign of terror as Miguel and his bully sons walked among them with impunity. Suddenly, the consequences of that complacency were laid out at his feet. His family was now at the mercy of this madman. Carbone choked. He had been such a stupid man.

"So let us see," Herrera said with a cackle in his throat. "How tough are you now?"

"Damn you, Miguel, let them go."

"Give me the names of the killers. It is all I ask."

Carbone held his breath. It was too simple: Jonathan for his family. They looked so helpless lying on the floor, tied up and struggling. Surely Jonathan would risk his life for them one more time.

"I'm growing impatient with you," Herrera said.

"I know nothing."

"Petro," he ordered the sergeant.

Soldiers rushed in carrying gas cans and immediately went to pouring fuel on the floor, moving through the barroom, dousing the walls and tables and even splashing some on his children and his wife.

Terror sliced through Carbone's guts like the blade of a knife. "All right," he shouted. "I'll tell you the name." Gas vapors burned his eyes. "Please get my family out of here."

Herrera scowled. "First tell me who killed my boys?"

"Melvin Anderson did it. He told me it was self-defense."

"Where is he now?"

"In Simi Valley, California, Solartech Labs. There he is known as Dr. Frank Curtis. Now please take my family from this place."

"Not so fast, stupid man. There were two killers. Why do you protect the other?"

"Only one of them killed your sons," Carbone said, hoping to save Jonathan.

"You lie." Herrera shook his fist. "My sons died of bullets from two guns." He waved the soldiers from the barroom and pulled a book of matches from his vest pocket. After peeling back the cover, he bent several matches over the striker. His eyes narrowed. "Who was the other man?"

Carbone's blood went cold as the nightmare raced through his mind once more. He knew Miguel wouldn't hesitate to torch his family. There was no choice, no other way out. "Jonathan Kyles," Carbone said and slumped his shoulders. His heart felt empty for his betrayal of Jonathan. "Now go, and leave my family in peace."

With a flick of his thumb, Herrera struck the matches. The whole pack burst into flame. "I will give you all peace in hell."

"No!"

Herrera tossed the fiery mass into the corner and headed for the door. The place went ablaze with a horrendous whoosh.

"Take my family out of here."

Herrera was gone. Thick black smoke began to fill the barroom. Fighting panic, Carbone hopped the chair closer to his wife and children who were now squirming wildly on the floor. High-pitched squeals came from their throats. Their eyes were wide with terror.

Carbone gasped a breath of acrid air. Wildly, he pulled and tugged on the ropes around his wrists. “Damn you, Miguel Herrera. Help. Somebody help us.”

A wall of fire sprang up around them, now feeding on the mahogany pillars and beams, the wooden floor and furniture. The intricate mirror behind the bar creaked and busted. Beer mugs crashed to the floor. Booze bottles exploded into blue flames that danced on the bar.

The rippling curtain of fire crackled and glowed bright as the sun. Heat seared his face. His sweat began to sizzle, but the pain was nothing compared to the agony in his heart, the anguish he felt for his wife and his children. They had managed to wiggle close to each other, and coughing, now lay trembling together on the floor. He worked the ropes with a renewed fury now, pulling on the knots and stretching the loops. A part of it came loose, and that gave him hope. He strained against the knots as hard as he could with no regard for the way the ropes were cutting into his wrists. But before either arm came free, his lungs started convulsing from the cloud of thick smoke.

“Help!” The word came out raspy and weak.

A flaming ceiling fan crashed down onto a table, which was already ablaze. The heat in the barroom was like a blast furnace, causing his hair to smolder and blisters to appear on his skin. His throat and lungs burned. He hacked and coughed uncontrollably.

Suddenly, pain rifled up his leg. Fire took hold of his shoes. The ropes around his ankles started burning...and his pant-leg too. He kicked and flailed, but the fire bit into his flesh like the fangs of a dog.

Then flames leaped onto his writhing children and his

wife. A scream stuck in his throat. He tipped over the chair and tried to cover his children with his body in hopes of smothering the flames, but his shirt caught fire. Searing pain overcame him. He couldn't move. It was surreal. His mind swirled everything into one chaotic blur. The roaring inferno seemed to drift away as the intense brightness slowly faded to black.

Chapter Fourteen

A STIFF WIND BLEW SWIRLING SAND down the gully just off Interstate 70 out of Green River, Utah. Under the highway bridge, Pico covered his mouth with his coat collar. He'd barely made it back from town when this storm came up. Now squatting, he worked his way up toward the girders as blowing sand went everywhere, down the front of his coat and into holes in his jeans and ragged tennis shoes. Thunder rumbled in the distance, but no rain came down.

Huddled around him, other migrant workers sought cover from the sandstorm. His plight was similar to theirs: hitching rides on trucks, hopping freight cars, and even a lot of walking. From the Colorado melon fields to the California vineyards, orchards, and strawberry fields, work rotated with the seasons. One year he broke his leg jumping off a truck and nearly starved to death. But this had been a good year. He had money tucked in his socks and a new bottle of Old Crow stuffed in a brown paper sack under his coat. He couldn't wait to get at it.

An eastbound diesel rig rattled over the bridge. Air brakes hissed and tires squawked. The workers hurried out and were gone in the dust. Now that he was alone, the Old Crow came out. He twisted off the cap and put the bottle to his lips. The liquor heated his insides, and welcoming the sensation, he took another swallow before recapping the bottle. Vapors burned his nostrils, and he closed his eyes in ecstasy.

The diesel engine revved as the truck pulled away, leaving him with only the sound of the wind and the traffic rumbling across the bridge overhead. A few moments passed before he opened his eyes again and was suddenly confronted with an unexpected sight. Out of the storm, an old man had appeared. He wore a brown suit coat with torn pockets that flapped in the wind. Lean in the face, he was a wiry old coot, with bushy gray hair that matched his eyebrows, sideburns, and thick mustache.

The old stranger squinted against the wind and blowing sand. "Looks like some mighty fine whiskey you got there," he said and ambled up the slope to the girders. His smile showed a mouthful of perfect teeth.

Pico quickly tucked the bottle under his coat and wondered how he could have been so careless. Not wanting to share his booze with this bum, Pico chose to ignore him, but the old man crouched down next to him and smiled. "It was long ride on truck. I sure could use drink of yours."

Pico stared at the stranger, not recognizing the old man's accent. He wasn't from anywhere around here, that was for sure. "Go get your own bottle."

"But there is a storm, and I am thirsty."

The wind whipped up a barrage of sand and sent it stinging into Pico's face. He closed his eyes, hoping the sand and the stranger would be gone when he opened them again.

"I have money," the old man said. "Ten dollars, American."

Pico opened one eye and looked at the money pinched between the old man's fingers as it fluttered to the rhythm of the wind. Now both eyes went to the money and then to the old man's face and back and forth a few times. Pico had never sold a drink to anyone before, and ten dollars seemed a bit overpriced, but he wasn't one to turn his back on a good deal. Snatching the bill from the old man's hand, he said, “Name’s Pico.”

“Boris. Boris Dagloskoff.” His eyes went to the bulge in Pico’s coat where the bottle was stashed. “Comrades, yes?”

Pico took out the Old Crow and handed it to Boris who drank ten dollars worth in a gulp. Pico put the money in his sock. “Aren’t you a bit old for pickin’?”

Boris licked his lips and handed the bottle back to Pico. “I nuclear physicist.”

Pico tweaked his eyebrows. “I’m a brain surgeon on my regular days off.” He took another swig of Old Crow and looked the old man in the eyes. “You talk kind of funny, mister.”

“Boris. You can call me Boris, okay?”

“Where’re you from?” He handed Boris the bottle.

“Russia.” Boris took a drink. “I was once a scientist there and did many experiments.”

Wind whipped under the bridge with the force of a hurricane.

“I was President once.” Pico grabbed the bottle from Boris. He put the sand-laden thing to his lips, took a drink, and spit.

“I was once a prominent Russian citizen. I drank vodka and ate caviar, went to fancy restaurants, and I owned a big home and a small car.”

“Then what are you doing here?”

“Long story.” He held out his hand for the bottle. “But you I will tell.”

Pico passed him the bottle. “I’m not interested.” In fact, he wished he hadn’t asked.

Boris took a long slug and smacked his lips. “After my wife died, I traveled to Ukraine to do experiments with my colleagues at remote laboratory. But something went wrong and a big hole was left in the ground. Moscow sent in soldiers to arrest us, but I ran away, and for two years I hid in the jungles of Borneo.”

"Borneo? Jesus. You're shittin' me."

"Then I came to America to do the same experiments."

Pico grabbed the bottle from Boris. "You're just a crazy old man."

Boris furrowed his brows. "The experiments were very dangerous."

"Why are you telling me about this?"

"We are comrades, yes?"

Pico had to laugh. "Only because I have the booze."

"I have no one else to talk to, only my comrade."

Pico didn't care to be the old man's comrade, and he didn't care about any experiments. He wouldn't know one from another anyway. However, it was windy, and there wasn't anything better to do but humor the old guy. "Okay, Boris. Tell me about your experiments." He took another drink of Old Crow, thinking the old man's story had to be good for a laugh or two.

Boris's face soured. "The 13th Power is very dangerous," he said, his voice low in the wind.

"Like I'm supposed to know what that means."

"It could destroy the world."

"Yeah, right."

"This time, American soldiers came with helicopters to stop us."

"You mean the men in white coats?" Pico laughed. This was getting better by the minute.

"Go ahead. Make a joke. I ran again, I kept moving from town-to-town, because I knew they are looking for me."

"The helicopters?"

"The CIA."

Now Pico roared. "You're full of shit, old man."

"It is true. They are after me." Boris snatched the bottle from Pico's hand. "Why don't you believe me?"

"Give me back my bottle," Pico shouted.

Suddenly, a gunshot rang out. The bottle exploded. Old Crow flew everywhere.

Pico jumped. His eyes went to the gully just beyond the bridge where three men stood in the sandstorm, their black suit coats whipping in the wind. He gasped and wondered where they had come from. He hadn't heard a car stop, but he knew they must've followed the old man...and they had guns.

A muzzle flashed. Pain sliced through his chest like a hurled spear.

#

Boris leaped down the embankment and rolled into the gully on the other side of the bridge.

"Stop," the CIA agents ordered.

Boris didn't listen. He ran. His head spun from Old Crow, and adrenaline lit fires in his bloodstream. He slammed through a thatch of prickly bushes.

Gunfire popped and bullets zinged through the air.

He ran headlong, his eyes smarting from the bite of the wind, and stumbling over jagged rocks, his heart raced and his lungs burned. Busting out of a cloud of dust, he came upon a train trestle that spanned the gully. It was made of thick wooden beams with splinters the size of Russian swords. They tore at his hands as he climbed. Bullets were cracking all around him. He thought they were warning shots, otherwise he'd have been dead by now. Perplexed and pumped with fear, he made his way up the trestle to a slanted beam that took him up to the tracks above. The wind howled in his face.

With every bit of strength he could muster, he clung to a railroad tie and finally pulled himself up onto the tracks.

Below, the agents had spread out: one was climbing the trestle, and two others were trying to claw their way up the rocky embankment. One slipped and tumbled back down into the gully, cursing.

Boris felt a moment of hope. As long as they were busy climbing they couldn’t shoot at him. Running low and ducking into the wind, he scrambled along the trestle, which suddenly began shaking, vibrating, and rumbling. He whipped his head around. The bright light of a speeding express train was barreling down on him at incredible speed. Panic-stricken, he turned and ran as fast as he could. Quick-stepping tie-to-tie, he almost made it to the end of the trestle when the sound of the locomotive hammered up right behind him: the rumble and the roar and the blaring horn.

He jumped.

Chapter Fifteen

HIGH-PITCHED BEEPING SOUNDS echoed through the cavernous maintenance galley down in the basement of Solartech Labs. Yellow lights rotated and flashed overhead as a ceiling crane rolled along greasy tracks eight stories above the concrete floor. The contraption had square corners, a thick yellow frame, and hung from the tracks on grooved wheels. Behind cooling vents on its boxy belly, gears turned and levers moved as steel cables rolled off huge spools restrained by thick brake bands. Fat chains hung from the giant crane's hook and strained from the weight of a massive black iron casing, bigger than a railroad car.

Wearing a white lab coat, Ray stood on the third floor observation deck, his heart pounding with trepidation as he watched the goings-on below. On the floor some thirty feet down, a dozen men dressed in gray jumpsuits and white hard hats worked guide-ropes that were tied to the casing. The assembly moved along at the pace of a snail.

Lisa stepped out onto the deck and stood beside him. She wore blue jeans and a pink pullover blouse. "Is this crazy or what?" She set her hand on his shoulder.

Glancing at his daughter, he detected the fragrance of *Enjoli*. Shuddering, he remembered how her mother had worn the same perfume. Kate used lots of it to mask the smell of her smoking, but as hard as she'd tried, she couldn't hide her addiction to cocaine and the lifestyle that came with it: the all-night benders and the tricks she pulled to finance her habit. He was thankful she was out of their lives forever.

"I've seen crazier," Ray said, thinking of the time he and Kate were together and the misery she'd brought with her. "How are you feeling?"

"Better...but getting over Janis is going to take some time."

"You weren't meant for each other."

"That's what I keep telling myself, Dad. But still..."

"We're together now. That's all that matters." Finally Lisa was home after nineteen years abroad. And she seemed happy now, with fewer outbursts, thanks to the medications. Doctors believed her mood swings had a lot to do with suppressed memories of her mother, memories that affected her behavior subconsciously. They admitted they had little experience with *Abandoned Child Syndrome*, but they figured she was better off not remembering what had happened to her when she was six years old.

Standing next to him, Lisa shook her head, her blond hair swaying, her eyes fixed on the crane and its heavy load. She was a lovely woman, like her mother. He could see why Janis Mackey had fallen for Lisa. It may have been love at first sight, but luckily he'd come to his senses and realized he was too old for her.

She leaned against the railing. "What is that thing?"

"The new MIGGS," he said and left it at that. If she knew what he was up to, she would have a fit.

"It must be ten times bigger than the old one."

"Impressive, huh?"

She frowned. "Why?"

He wasn't about to tell her the truth, at least not until he was sure it was going to work. Stan Burton's men had labored day and night to build the new MIGGS, welding and grinding, fitting and bolting. They had tests to run, computer programs to write, and lots of things to calculate, but to make it all work, Ray needed a mathematician. He hadn't found one yet. A shiver crept up his spine as he thought about asking Janis to come back. He was going to have a fit, too.

"Dad, what's it for?"

Ray grimaced. He'd have to tell her something or she'd harp on him forever. He came up with a good one. "An experiment in gravity and the birth of stars. The old MIGGS was too small to put the Gindrich Phenomenon to the test."

She gave him a funny look.

"Hypothetically, celestial gasses subjected to massive gravitational forces cause fusion of atoms and the ignition of a star." He chuckled at the blank look that came across her face. Because he couldn't dazzle her with brilliance, he had to baffle her with bullshit. Besides, what she didn't know wouldn't hurt her. He knew he was beginning to sound like an overprotective father again.

"If you say so," she said with a wan smile. "Just as long as it has nothing to do with the 13th Power."

"Not a chance," Ray said with a smirk. "It's too dangerous. I learned my lesson."

Lisa's blue eyes glared at him now, as if she didn't believed him.

Double doors to the observation deck banged open. Stan rushed out followed by three MIGGS team supervisors. They all wore white lab coats with Solartech insignias on the pockets, and ID tags flapped from their lapels. Stan held a two-way radio to his lips. "Keep it moving...and watch that strain gauge."

"What is it?" Ray asked, feeling like the last one to know when things were going wrong.

"The lift winch is overheating."

Ray flinched. "Why?"

"The MIGGS is too damn big."

"You overloaded the crane's capacity? How could

you...?"

"We're trying to make do with what we have," Stan said sharply. "We're pushing the envelope on everything around here."

Ray looked up at the crane crawling across the ceiling and saw wisps of smoke swirling from the cooling vents. His stomach knotted. He knew that stopping the crane wouldn't help. The weight of the MIGGS would still be on the lift winch. And the brake bands would burn up if they tried to lower the MIGGS down to the floor. It would certainly fall. The MIGGS would be destroyed and men would die. He looked to his left at the concrete emplacement that the new MIGGS was to be lowered into. It suddenly seemed like a long way from the assembly room. "How much time do we need?" he asked Stan.

Checking his watch, Stan replied, "Seven minutes..."

"The gauges are in the red," an urgent voice crackled over the two-way.

"Shut it down," Stan ordered into the radio. "Get out of there."

"No!" Ray shouted. "Keep it moving. It's our only shot."

"But it's too hot."

"Then cool it down with water," Ray said. "Tell them to use the fire hoses." He pointed to the crane. "We only need seven minutes."

Stan shook his head. "We don't have thirty seconds."

"Then don't waste them."

"Break out the fire hoses, men," Stan barked into the radio. "Train the spray on the cable spools and brake bands."

A moment later, wide-eyed men on the floor below wrestled with fat fire hoses. Thick streams of water, five in all, arced up to the eight-story high ceiling, soaking the crane as it crept along its track. Steaming water cascaded down to the floor and drenched the men on the ropes.

Ray held his breath and winced against the noisy spray of water and shouting men. Lisa put her hands over her ears and blinked away the mist landing on her eyelashes.

"Six minutes," a technician said.

The beeping crane's flashing yellow lights reflected eerily through the spray and continued to move slowly toward the concrete emplacement. Chains creaked and men cursed.

Lisa shook Ray's arm. "Stop it, Dad." She looked down at the men sopping on the floor, the ones working the ropes and the ones manning the hoses. "Someone's going to get killed."

"It would take months to install a heavier crane in this building. Don't you see? We have to take our chances right now." Ray shot a glance at Stan, hoping to detect some hint of optimism in his eyes, but his face had turned white as he held his radio.

"Four minutes."

Ray put his arm around Lisa as he watched the new MIGGS edge closer to the end of its journey. The spray of water was more intense, the beeping much louder.

Lisa trembled in the crook of his arm. "Please make it stop."

Holding his breath, every muscle in Ray's body tensed. He wouldn't stop it now. Success was only four minutes away.

Somewhere up on the girders, a rivet popped. Steel creaked like the sour note of a violin, but the crane rolled onward.

Chapter Sixteen

JANIS OPENED THE PASSENGER DOOR of his new Camry, stood in front of Tracy, and gazed into her eyes. She wore a sleeveless yellow blouse and blue shorts, and her red hair sparkled in the Colorado sunshine. As she gave him a kiss on the cheek then slid into the seat, he still found it hard to believe she was with him here in Boulder.

After closing the door, he looked up at his old apartment building. The moving van's diesel engine rattled to life. He waved to the driver, gave the place a last look, and climbed into the car.

Tracy put her hand on his knee as he drove out of the parking lot. "Are you glad to be moving?" she asked as her dangling gold earrings swayed to the motion of the car.

Janis sighed. "It's been a long time coming."

"I can't wait to see your new place."

"I can't wait to show it to you." Checking his rearview mirror, he saw the moving van lag behind, puffing black smoke from its exhaust. A few miles down Baseline road, he swung the Camry into a subdivision where new homes sported freshly sodded lawns, and small saplings lined the streets. His new house was only two blocks away.

Janis glanced at Tracy and wondered if she was the woman he'd been looking for all his life. He'd wasted a lot of time going from one dead-end relationship to another, like with Donna. She was a nice gal but always complained that he didn't have enough time for her. He'd explained how important his students were and how much his position at the university meant to him. She wasn't mad when she left; she just left. And then there was Jill. Her cats stunk up the apartment, so he'd told her she had to make a choice: him or the cats. She *was* mad when she left. Then Lisa came along and stirred up a lot of emotions inside, but she wasn't the right woman either. After all, she was Ray's daughter. She was too young for him. It seemed as though nothing ever computed when it came to love, until now, until Tracy.

He parked in the driveway, shut off the engine, and looked at the front of his house: a split-level ranch with a two-car garage and a large front porch. Blond brick and beige trim gave it an earthy look. "This is it." He climbed out of the car. The smell of moist sod filled the air. "Come on."

Tracy joined him at the front door. He keyed the lock and let her go inside first. Standing in the foyer, Janis took in the scent of fresh paint. To him, it smelled like French perfume.

Sunshine, beaming down through a skylight, glistened off the white marble floor in the hallway. A doublewide staircase went up on the left, and the hall opened up into a kitchen and breakfast nook. Gold fixtures hung from the ceiling, and off to the right, an arched doorway lead into a living room with a vaulted ceiling made of thick wood beams that shined with varnish.

Tracy's eyes glistened. "This is beautiful." She walked into the kitchen. "It must have cost you a fortune."

Janis followed her, thinking she was right. He'd had his eye on this place as it was being built and, when it was finished, he'd walked through it several times, wishing he could afford it on what was left of his university salary after his mother's expenses. Every time he came here, he feared the developer would tell him the house had been sold to someone else. But when he returned from

California, he wasted no time, purchasing the house outright with money Dr. Curtis had paid him to do the 13th Power experiments.

Standing in the kitchen, he watched Tracy run her palms across the counter tops. She inspected the Jen-Aire grill and looked into the refrigerator, a monstrous thing, with double doors and special taps for ice, water, and beer. "This is incredible."

Janis chuckled, and folding his arms across his chest, he leaned against the counter. "I confess. I bought the place just for the refrigerator."

She flashed him a smile and peeked into the pantry. Janis thought she knew what she was looking for as she made her way around the kitchen. She seemed to be weighing the appeal of the place.

"Look over there." He pointed to the family room, which was set three steps down from the kitchen. A moss-rock fireplace stretched along the far wall, and in the corner, a triangular kiva had been built into the floor. Janis imagined spending a romantic evening in it with Tracy, drinking wine and listening to music.

"Let's go upstairs," she said, her eyes beaming.

"Oh, I don't know. You might not like it."

"Yeah, right." She headed up the staircase with a light bounce to her steps.

Janis blinked. Somehow the house seemed brighter and warmer now that she was here. He wondered if there was any way he could convince her to stay.

The master bedroom took her breath away. Mouth open, she stood in the doorway and scanned the vaulted ceiling and octagonal windows. Janis followed her across the room to a walk-in closet, and then she went through an archway into the bathroom. Above the twin-sink vanity, a lighted mirror stretched the length of the wall, and sunk in the floor, an oval bathtub glistened with white marble and gold fixtures.

"I love this place, Janis," she said and turned around. "Congratulations." She threw her arms around his neck and gave him a kiss, setting his heart on fire. He took in every sweet second of it, his mind reeling with thoughts of love and marriage, the kind of things that had eluded him all his life.

As she pressed her body against him, he was sure he was dreaming, or maybe he had gone to heaven. Perhaps the 13th Power had escaped from the MIGGS that day and sucked him into another world where wonderful things happened all the time. Whatever the case, since the 13th Power came into his life, everything had changed. He now had a fat bank account, a new car, a new home, and a new woman in his life.

She was beautiful and smart and a hard worker. For most of the day, as the movers unpacked the truck and carried stuff into the house, she was right there with him, helping tote and stow his things away. They worked side by side, just as they had done in Tech-Com Control when the fate of the world was in their hands.

"Janis, do you want the couch by the window or against the wall?"

"You chose."

"But it's your house."

"I trust you."

She winked.

He had to laugh as she made the movers lug things all over the place until she was satisfied that everything looked perfect. When the movers finally left, she'd organized the kitchen cupboards, put away the dishes, and stocked the pantry. And after making tuna sandwiches and iced tea for lunch, she helped Janis arrange the walk-in closet.

"Where do you want this?" she asked, holding up his favorite bathrobe.

He curled his finger to her. "Over here."

She walked toward him, the tip of her tongue touching

her upper lip and her eyes bright.

"Closer," he said softly.

She stood in front of him now, her eyes darting around his face. "Where?"

Janis slipped his right hand around her back and pulled her close. "Right here." Her body felt warm and inviting.

Tracy dropped the bathrobe, laced her arms around his waist, and kissed him. Her tongue pushed between his lips, and his ardor began to rise. His heart ached to tell her how he felt. There was no denying it; he was in love. But he worried that she wasn't in love with him. He didn't think he could take the rejection if she wasn't, but as it turned out, the passion in her kisses made him take the leap. "I love you, Tracy."

Her smile reached her eyes. "I'm homeless and out of work. I don't have anything to give you."

His heart skipped. "How about a little encouragement here?"

"Haven't you seen it in my eyes?"

"I don't often trust what I see."

"Then trust this." She kissed him, hard and long. When their lips parted, she buried her face in his chest. "I've so badly wanted you to love me, too."

"Too? As in *also*?"

"As in forever."

"Is this the way love was meant to be?"

"Yes," she whispered.

He switched off the closet light. Unpacking would have to wait.

***

On the back porch that evening, as the sprinkler system chattered across the sod, he sat next to Tracy in the swing and held her hand. They watched the sun go down over Flagstaff Mountain, its waning rays setting the clouds ablaze in pink.

Having poured Merlot into tall glasses, he offered a toast to the day. The wine tasted sweet and smooth, just like Tracy's kisses. Though he couldn't keep his hands off her the rest of the afternoon, they'd managed to make the house livable. He left a few boxes stacked in the living room, things he'd go through later, and he stashed away some odds and ends in the garage. They had done enough for one day.

The sky changed slowly from pink to orange and then bright yellow along the ridge of the foothills. As nightfall turned the sky into a wondrous dome of starlight, a chill began to set in.

Janis rubbed goose bumps on his arms. "Let's go inside." He poured more wine, and they nestled together in the kiva. Candlelight flickered on the walls, and a Travis Tritt CD played on the sound system, a waltz called *Drift off to Dream*.

Tracy snuggled up closer.

"I want you in my future," Janis said, looking into Tracy's eyes. His heart started pounding as her eyes searched his.

"I love you, Janis." She kissed him and hugged his neck. "I feel as though I've always loved you." Her breath was soft on his skin.

"I've been looking for you all my life. And now that I've found you, everything seems to be going so fast, so completely out of control."

"And so wonderful."

He blinked and wondered if he should ask her. After all, it was a wonderful world, and there was no reason to hold his feelings back. The 13th Power had brought them together. They were meant to be. But he feared she would think he was being foolish for rushing things. The wine made his body tingle all over, and his head was a merry-go-round from her kisses, her perfume, and the sound of her breathing in his ear. Though he was taking a big chance, he thought there would never be a better time to ask her. "Will you marry me?"

Tracy moaned and hugged his neck. Her lips brushed his ear. "Yes."

Janis's heart raced. This was indeed a wonderful new world, and today was the happiest day of his life.

Tracy held up her wine glass and smiled. "A toast to us."

He touched his glass to hers. "To love."

Bam! Bam! BAM! Wood cracked and splintered as the front door caved in. Janis jumped. The wine spilled.

"CIA," a loud voice announced.

Men in black fatigues and helmets poured into the house. They held big rifles, which emitted skinny beams of red light that darted about the candlelit rooms. There must have been a dozen or more men rushing down the hallway, sweeping through the kitchen, and piling down into the family room.

Janis cringed. They had nowhere to run, no time to escape. He held Tracy in his arms. She was trembling. He feared the CIA would kill her; maybe they'd kill them both. Something had gone horribly wrong with this wonderful world.

"Dr. Tracy McClarence?" one of the CIA men asked as he stood above the kiva, the red sighting beam of his rifle on her heart.

She pushed herself away from Janis and scooted into the corner of the kiva, her face pinched with anger. Two more agents stood above them now, their red lasers shining on Janis's chest.

"What do you people want?" he shouted. The wine and adrenaline was running rampant through his system. He needed his senses clear, but everything was a blur.

Two men stepped down into the kiva, grabbed Tracy

by her arms, and yanked her up.

"Get your hands off me, you bastards." Tracy started screaming and kicking.

Janis leaped to his feet but took the butt of a rifle in his stomach. The air came out of him, and he keeled over.

A man in a black suit walked up. "Hello, Tracy," he said in a voice that chilled the air.

"Stevens!" she yelled as the men dragged her out of the kiva. "What are you doing here?"

"*The Ark* has some unfinished business with you."

"Tell him to go to hell."

Stevens grabbed Tracy by the throat. "Listen real close," he snarled. "I've got orders to kill you if you don't cooperate. You know *The Ark* is dead serious, so don't make this hard on yourself."

"All right," Tracy rasped through a restricted windpipe.

Stevens let loose of her neck. "That's more like it."

Rubbing her throat, Tracy said, "Everybody just stay calm." She pulled in a breath. "I'll go, but leave Janis alone. He doesn't have anything to do with this."

Stevens shook his head. "On the contrary," he said. "I have a message for Janis from Dr. Curtis." Stevens stepped down into the kiva and lifted Janis's head by his hair. "You know Dr. Curtis, don't you?"

"Screw you!" Janis tried to pull away, but he couldn't. Clutching his stomach and gasping air, his insides ached as he thought about Dr. Curtis having a message for him, and worse, he wondered why the CIA was delivering it.

Stevens glared into Janis's eyes. "Dr. Curtis requests your presence at Solartech Labs to finish what you started. He paid you a million dollars for the 13th Power, and he wants his money's worth. Bring Lo Chin with you. If you refuse, Tracy will die. You have three days to comply." He let go of Janis's hair and turned away.

Janis coughed. "Don't you people get it?" he shouted

to Stevens. “The 13th Power will destroy the world.”

Stevens pointed an accusatory finger at him. “Not if you get the formula right this time.” He turned toward the door and signaled the others.

They dragged Tracy out of the house.

Janis sat up in the kiva and cradled his throbbing stomach. His heart sank. The house was suddenly darker and colder, and he shivered with dread. “Leave it to the fucking government to screw up my wonderful world.”

Chapter Seventeen

THE CIA'S FALCON JET, with Captain Wilfred Baines at the controls, touched down at Andrews Air Force Base just after four in the morning. Though Tracy was exhausted, she couldn't sleep during the flight. Her mind wouldn't let her rest as thoughts of Janis Mackey and *The Ark* spun around in her brain. The best and the worst men she'd ever known were doing battle, but it wasn't a fair fight. In every scenario, Janis was the loser and the world was destroyed. It all made her heart ache.

She looked at the CIA agents sitting around her: Craig Stevens, his rookie partner, Cisco, and some oaf they called Lester. Thoughts of escape entered her mind. Maybe she could make a break for it somewhere along the route, after all, CIA headquarters was a long way from the airfield and an opportunity might arise. She clenched her jaw and wondered if she dared to try making a break for it. Perhaps Stevens would shoot her in the back for *The Ark.*

The jet pulled up to the gate, and the cabin lights brightened. Stevens stood and offered his hand. She unfastened her seatbelt and allowed him to pull her to her feet.

It happened so fast she barely caught the motion. Stevens bumped her wrist with the cold steel of his handcuffs, which locked with a click that sent a chill through her body.

"Just in case you get any funny ideas." He snapped

the other cuff around his wrist.

Her stomach turned upside down. There was no escape. Now she'd have to face *The Ark*.

The agents hustled her through the terminal and into a black step van where unpadded bench seats stretched along the walls. Tracy squinted against the bright ceiling light as Stevens muscled her onto the seat. The walls loomed bare and shiny, and every noise sounded hollow. Cisco and Lester sat on the seat across from her, their faces void of compassion.

The back doors slammed shut then the engine rattled to life. As the van sped away from the terminal, she felt a chill, her bare legs turning to gooseflesh. She wished she had worn long pants instead of shorts. "I'm freezing."

Stevens got a wool blanket out from under the seat and covered her. "You're a bit underdressed to meet *The Ark*."

"You should have called ahead. What does he want me to do this time?"

"Directive Number 119," Stevens said, his voice warm. "You were supposed to get it for him, remember?"

Closing her eyes, the whole affair began to replay in her mind, and she wondered how she'd managed to get herself into this mess. It had all begun with the best of intentions: a call from John Nathan, a request from the President, a meeting.

The van bounced a little as she looked at Stevens. "It was supposed to be the greatest defense network in the world."

"And you blew it."

"Not me. General Brigham and the Department of Defense blew it. They raped the budget until Congress finally got fed up and cut the funding."

"But it's your tit that's in the wringer, Tracy."

The truck hit a bump and turned right.

"My God, don't you see? It was Star Wars, the

Strategic Defense Initiative...the boldest plan of all. Imagine," she pointed a finger in the air, "a network of orbiting laser resonators and sighting dish satellites patrolling the earth for ICBMs...an impenetrable defense grid. President Reagan issued the directive in 1983, a challenge to the scientific community to see if it was technologically possible to destroy a missile with a laser beam from space. I was hooked on the idea."

"Looks like you got more than you bargained for."

She thought about that, how far she had come since graduating from Cal Tech and working at Cavendish Labs in England where they specialized in laser research and development, a field that had consumed her every waking hour.

Brakes squealed and the van came to a stop, probably at a traffic light. She thought about how thrilled she was when Phillips Research came to Cavendish Labs, looking for help with their Department of Defense contract. They'd said they needed a special kind of laser beam, one that could accelerate nuclear particles with pinpoint accuracy, a particle beam that would disassemble the atomic structure of a target. Disintegration was what they wanted, but they didn't seem to care that it was a dangerous thing to fool around with, if it were even possible.

At first, when she saw the research agenda they'd put forward, she thought of Buck Rogers' ray guns, the Starship Enterprise, and all the science fiction gadgets that made space adventure sound exciting and dangerous. However, when she realized that a lot of that old sci-fi make-believe had already become reality, like Jules Verne's submarine and his rocket to the moon, it then became obvious: the particle beam would eventually become a reality, too, and she wanted to be there when it happened. As luck would have it though, Congress took the money away. It was all over, her dreams dashed.

In desperation, she'd submitted a request for more

funding through the Ballistic Missile Defense Organization's budget office, which landed on the President's desk, denied, of course. That was when *The Ark* contacted her and told her the President was fed up with the way the Department of Defense had mishandled the money. His only recourse was to reassign the directive to the CIA. General Brigham was fired from the project. He nearly lost his stars when Congress held him accountable.

The van accelerated loudly and made a left turn.

"Maybe you're right," she said to Stevens with a sigh, thinking how dangerous her liaison with *The Ark* had become. "Maybe I did get in over my head, but not any worse than the Russians. Boris Daglofska and his people didn't do so well, either."

Stevens nodded. "Yeah. Good old Boris. I remember when we cleared him through customs in Atlanta. He told us all about the experiments he'd done in Russia and how things kept disappearing into some kind of void. What a bunch of bullshit."

"You didn't believe him?"

"Did you?"

A shiver went up Tracy's spine. "Well...not really...I mean, the end of the world seemed a bit much at the time. Where's Boris now?"

Stevens shrugged. "I don't know and I don't care."

The van sped up as if merging onto an expressway. Tires began to whine. Tracy leaned her head back against the vibrating metal wall and closed her eyes, remembering that Boris had left Simi Valley. After all, he was a survivor. While the rest of his colleagues were locked up in a Moscow prison for tampering with the 13th Power, he'd escaped and hid out in the jungles of Borneo where he met Melvin Anderson. She opened her eyes and looked at Stevens. "This whole thing is Boris's fault, you know. He's the one who filled Anderson's head with visions of riches."

"Boris screwed up," Stevens said. "He bragged to the

wrong man, and when he realized his mistake, he turned himself in to the CIA, looking for political asylum. He kept babbling on about Melvin Anderson changing his name to Dr. Curtis, and how he was planning to do the same experiments the Russians had tried."

Grinding gears, the truck lurched. Stevens cast her a sullen glance. "So how did you get involved with *The Ark*?"

"My name was on the budget request to the BMDO. *The Ark* called me because the President wanted my help."

"You should have walked away."

"But I couldn't resist the challenge."

"Look what it's gotten you."

Tracy shuddered. Though her particle beam had worked, all her data was lost in the aftermath at Solartech Labs. If *The Ark* expected her to do it again, she would have to start over from scratch. She regarded Stevens sadly. "And look what it's done to us. We used to be friends."

Looking at her, he blinked. "I'm sorry I was rough with you back at the house. Just doing my job, you understand?"

"How far will you go for *The Ark*?"

He scowled. "Let's hope we don't have to find out."

"Christ, Stevens—"

Suddenly, the van slowed and rattled along as if it were negotiating the tight confines of an alley or maybe an underground garage. They were probably close to CIA headquarters by now. She shivered and ached to be in Janis's arms again. Yesterday was like heaven. He had asked her to marry him. They were going to share their futures together in Boulder. She had so much to look forward to.

The van squealed to a stop and doors slammed.

Now it looked as though *The Ark* was going to ruin everything.

Chapter Eighteen

DOWN IN THE BASEMENT OF CIA headquarters, Tracy was still handcuffed to Agent Stevens as they walked through a maze of hollow corridors devoid of any decorations. Bright ceiling lights hurt her eyes, and the whole place smelled like floor wax. Her sandals clacked on shiny tiles. Her knees trembled. They came to a door and stopped. Cisco keyed the handcuffs.

"Don't try anything stupid," Stevens said. "There's no way out of here."

She rubbed the red marks on her wrist. "Are you kidding? I wouldn't want to miss this party," she lied.

Inside the office, a woman dressed in a black pantsuit directed them into a conference room. The aroma of coffee filled the air, but that's where the pleasantries ended. Tracy's heart nearly stopped at the sight of the man standing at the coffee pot. It was Dr. Frank Curtis, AKA Melvin Anderson. His hair was combed back, his face shaved clean, and his tie was perfectly straight. The perfectionist, as always, he still wore a long black coat like he was perpetually ready for a funeral.

His gaze fell on her, cold and hard.

Seeing him there with John Nathan sent a chill up her spine. He too looked neat and perfect: freshly shaven, his salt and pepper hair parted just right, and his black suit immaculately pressed. He flashed deceivingly beautiful blue eyes, and a sense of evil filled her mind. This was an incredibly horrifying sight: Curtis and Nathan, the two of them together.

Then her eyes went to the man seated at the conference table. It was Jonathan Kyles, still looking like the butler who did it, also too pressed and polished for this early in the morning.

Nathan cleared his throat. “I trust you had a pleasant flight.” His smile was almost cordial, but Jonathan and Dr. Curtis just glared at her. She avoided their eyes, thinking they had every right to be angry with her. They once thought they could trust her, but now she was sure they never would again.

Walking around the table, she selected a chair and set her hand on the seatback. Her fingers tingled, but she had to be cool. She couldn’t let them know about the terror rifling through her body. “What does a girl have to do to get a drink in this place?” She sat down with a forced calm.

Cisco brought her a cup of coffee and a sweet roll.

Over the rim of her cup, she eyed Dr. Curtis as she took a sip of coffee. He looked the same as he always did: stern-faced. But something seemed different about him; something was missing. It wasn’t until he made his way to a chair at the table that she realized what it was: the golden staff he once carried with him everywhere, tapping it on the ground, pointing it with authority. Without it, he looked weaker and, dressed like a 16th century Count of Portugal, almost comical.

However, she knew that comedy was the last thing Dr. Curtis was about. He had to be the cruelest man in the world: the way he used his cellar of rats to exterminate his rivals, and the way he’d killed Alex Gibson with a golden dagger that ejected from the golden staff. Just thinking about it made her stomach sour. Worse, he seemed to enjoy the terror he had infused in the research team with his threats of death and torture and his *risk nothing, gain nothing* attitude. She thought he was certifiably insane.

Cisco sat down with a cup of coffee and a pile of donuts. Stevens sat next to him.

Lester stood at the door, his arms folded over his chest.

Nathan paced a few times before stopping at the head of the table. “Will Dr. Mackey go back to Simi Valley?” he asked Agent Stevens.

“That’s my bet. I told him we’d kill Tracy if he didn’t show.” He pointed at Curtis. “Dr. Frankenstein would enjoy that.”

Curtis sneered at Stevens. Jonathan shot to his feet with his fists balled.

As Nathan signaled him to sit down, Stevens stood with his hand hovering over his weapon. “This is turning into a freak show.”

“We’ll have none of that,” Nathan shouted. “Sit down...both of you.”

Jonathan showed his teeth.

Defiantly straightening his lapels, Stevens sat down slowly, still glaring at Jonathan, who followed suit with a groan.

Tracy blinked. It was an uneasy truce.

Nathan turned to her. “You’re in a difficult position, Tracy. Your chances for survival are bleak. Are we clear on that?”

She set her cup down, carefully masking the wave of terror now sweeping through her belly. “I have no idea what you’re talking about.”

“It’s really quite simple,” Nathan said evenly. “You know too much. I should kill you just for that.”

“You wouldn’t—”

He held up his hand. “I assure you I would.”

Tracy glanced at Curtis who grinned. Stevens didn’t look impressed. Then Nathan leaned on the table with both hands. “But there is a way to save yourself.”

She was speechless.

"Agree to help me fulfill Directive Number 119, and I'll let you live."

Her head buzzed with two big questions. Would he really kill her, or was he just talking tough? She tightened her lips and gave him a defiant glare. "You can't mean the 13th Power experiments."

"Precisely."

"And risk destroying the world? Are you crazy? You know what happened in Simi Valley. We barely got out alive."

Nathan huffed. "Do you call yourself a scientist?"

"It's too dangerous. Boris warned us about that from the beginning."

Curtis snickered. "Risk nothing, gain nothing."

"And if I don't?"

Nathan stood tall. "I'll not only kill you, I'll kill your boyfriend, Janis Mackey." He leaned forward. "Don't think for one minute that you people aren't expendable. There are other scientists and mathematicians in this country. You're alive only because it's convenient. You already know how to conduct the 13th Power experiments. Make it inconvenient and you'll be out of the picture, posthaste. Are we perfectly clear on this now?"

Curtis bobbed his head, grinning manically.

Tracy gulped. It was obvious to her that *The Ark* and Dr. Curtis had come to terms with each other. They'd made some kind of alliance, an alliance of evil. She couldn't imagine herself being involved with them again. Her mind started working through other scenarios, looking for another way out, a way that wouldn't get Janis killed.

Then she remembered seeing him curled up in the kiva, gasping for air. He looked pale and helpless. But she was sure he would go back to Solartech Labs. He'd never think of turning his back on her no matter how dangerous the 13th Power was to the world. After all, he was her hero.

The solution became suddenly clear, as if a fog had

lifted and sunlight shown through in her mind. She would do it for Janis. Together they could solve the problems and make the experiment safe. *The Ark* would have his particle beam, and Curtis would have his precious Higgs boson. It seemed like the only way they'd ever let her and Janis go back to Boulder to live in peace. Then she felt a jolt of fear. She couldn't trust them to keep their word. *The Ark* could kill them both when this was over.

"I want some assurances here." She poked her finger on the table. "When it's over, it's over for good. We go home. You leave us alone, forever."

Nathan nodded, his lips drawn tight. "With one condition."

"What's that?"

"You ever breathe a word about this to anyone: to the press, your next door neighbor, or even whisper it in your sleep, all bets are off. You die, Janis Mackey dies, and your kids die, if you have any."

Tracy stiffened. She wanted to know why Nathan was so damn paranoid about this. Something must've happened that she didn't know about. "For Christ sake, John. We did an experiment. It failed. So what's the big deal?"

His eyes narrowed. "Let's just say I won't tolerate any hint that I might be connected to this project in any way."

"What did you do, kill somebody?"

Nathan frowned. "You're a smart woman, Tracy. Don't say anything stupid."

She settled back in her chair and watched Nathan's eyes for any hint of compassion or human kindness. She saw nothing but cold blue emptiness. He must have killed someone, or at the very least, he was responsible for someone's death. If so, he'd never let her live, no matter what he agreed to here today. He couldn't be trusted, and she had no leverage against him, nothing to make him keep his word. She saw only one way to survive this: bluff. Make him think they had a deal. She pulled in a breath.

"Like you said, John. Not a word to anyone, ever."

He smiled. "That's what I like to hear."

"But what about Dr. Frankenstein?" She pointed to the imposter, Melvin Anderson. "How does he figure into this?"

Nathan set a hand on Curtis's shoulder. "If I get the particle beam, all charges will be dropped. Mr. Anderson will get a Permanent Resident Visa in the United States, as Dr. Frank Curtis. He can have the 13th Power to do with as he pleases. The Malaysian Federation will forever think he's dead. But if he screws up, we deport him to Sumatra. He'll probably end up with his head in a basket. I'd say I've got him by the balls."

Curtis grimaced.

The door flew open. Lester stepped aside as a team of agents rushed into the room, dragging an old man. He had bushy gray hair and wore dirty ragged clothes. They tossed him to the floor.

"You mothers. I damn you, mothers." The old man struggled to his feet, and with a discernable limp, shuffled up to Nathan and poked a rigid finger into his chest. "You I damn, also."

Tracy gasped. It was Boris Dagloskoff.

Chapter Nineteen

IN WASHINGTON D.C., THE FBI WAS investigating the crash of their Hawker jet which had suddenly spiraled into the ground only minutes after take off from Andrews Air Force Base. Onboard, the task force assigned to the 13th Power case had been en route to Simi Valley, California, to shut down Solartech Labs. They'd all perished. Inspector Anita Pollard had been working with the NTSB. They were trying to determine the cause of the crash, an especially difficult task because the Hawker's black box had mysteriously disappeared.

Spears of morning light beamed in through her bedroom window. Blinking sleep from her eyes, she knew this day was going to be as frustrating as all the others.

Lying beside her, Max let out a snort.

She gave him a nudge. "Time to get up."

He uttered a moan. The scent of Stetson cologne lingered in the air.

"Max?" Rolling out of bed, she stumbled over his cowboy boots and blue jeans and pulled the covers off him. Sunshine, knifing through the split in the curtains, fell across his tan, muscular back and the white curve of his buttocks. For a moment, she thought about last night, the late phone call and how she'd unlocked the door for him and jumped in the shower. She remembered her heart beating wildly as she got ready, and when he was finally standing in front of her, how her mouth went suddenly dry.

He was a long drink of water in the desert.

Max was her drifter, her once-a-week lover. He was good to her last night, made her glad she was a woman, and he took away the ache that lingered there so often. But now it was almost seven o'clock. He was going to make her late for work.

She sat on the edge of the bed and ran her fingers through his salt and pepper hair and down his back. When he didn't stir, she slapped his butt.

"Whip me, beat me, baby," he said softly.

"I will if you don't get out of here."

He rolled over, his morning hardness drawing her eyes like magnets to steel. Though her heartbeat skipped, she resisted the urge to touch him and start the whole thing over again.

"Come on," he said, those baby blue eyes beaming. "One more time?"

She showed him a playful frown. "I gotta get ready, Max."

He smiled, and putting his fingertips on her knee, walked them up her thigh like some kind of small animal scampering toward its nest of pubic hairs.

Grabbing his wrist, she stopped the little critter just short of home. "Don't make me call for backup."

"The bureau to the rescue? God, Anita, sometimes I think you're married to the FBI."

"I am." She stood and pulled on his arm, forcing him to sit up. "I'm happy there."

"Yeah. I forgot. Happy." Max got to his feet and struggled into his jeans and boots. No underwear. No socks. He had said the extra laundry only slowed him down. "How's the crash investigation coming along...anything solid?"

"Nothing." She didn't want to talk shop right now. She'd rather watch him pull his t-shirt over his head and carefully roll up the sleeves to show off his rounded biceps.

As he clasped the silver buckle of his belt, she stood there naked, thankful he'd come over and thankful he was leaving. She was happy, just as she'd promised herself when she cried over the ashes of her husband and son. Kevin had made her see the true value of happiness. They'd been married fifteen years. She was happy then too...until his anger ruined everything.

Max stood in front of her now, stroking her long brown hair with both hands. His eyes searched her body up and down. She liked showing him her sleek curves and round breasts. "Not bad for forty," he would tell her even though he knew she was forty-nine, the silver-tongued devil that he was. But his blue eyes told her he was sincere. She liked the way he looked at her, and she liked the feeling of being naked in front of him like this.

He took her in his arms and pulled her close, the cotton and denim now giving her goose bumps. His fingers caressed the small of her back. "I'll call you," he whispered into her ear.

"Soon, I hope."

After Max left, Anita sighed. "Soon" would be a week from now, give or take a day or two. It had been like this ever since the Hawker crashed. She hoped it would grow into a lifelong love affair.

Putting a pot of coffee on, she could still smell Max on her skin, so she inhaled a big breath of him. Max wasn't like all the other men she'd met, men that wasted her time in relationships that only ended succumbing to the pressures of her job. Chief Inspector of the Washington, D.C. division of the FBI took a heavy toll on her time, and now more than ever, she was glad she had Max in her life. He was genuinely interested in her problems, and he wasn't the least bit intimidated by her position: mostly sympathetic, supportive, and often inquisitive. It helped her to confide in him a little; after all, with the crash of the FBI's Hawker jet and the deaths of her top agent, Lou

Marston and his task force, her job had become suddenly heartbreaking. She only wanted to be happy...happy like her son Tommy had been. Not a day went by she didn't think of him. He'd taught her so much in such a short time.

The coffeemaker hacked and hissed. She poured a cup and shuffled into the bathroom. Sitting on the edge of the tub, she turned on the faucet and sprinkled strawberry bath crystals into the churning water. In an hour and a half she'd be battling traffic jams and bad tempers, but for now she'd be happy, like Tommy.

She always thought that Tommy had found happiness every day of his life, twelve years in all. If he wasn't playing ball with Kevin, they were off fishing and hiking, flying kites or collecting rocks. He did well in school and ate like a horse. Though he was a small-framed boy with skinny arms and big feet, he had the boundless energy of youth. His goodnight hugs were strong and warm, and his giggle would light up the night. Her son had the whole world as his playground...before he got sick.

That was six years ago. The doctors had said he'd come down with bronchitis, something they could fix with little white pills. How could they have been so wrong?

She slipped into the bubbles, hoping the hot water would wash away the memories...the grief of that horrible week her son lay in a coma, his life bleeding from his body like so much water down a drain. As he languished in pneumonia's grip of death, the doctors told her they were powerless to do anything to save him.

It seemed to her then that people handled the death of a loved one in different ways. Some thanked God for the time they were allowed to share with the one they lost, while others blamed God. Often, grief and fear took hold as they contemplated their own mortality. But poor Kevin, the man she'd loved with all her heart, chose anger. It consumed every part of him and set him to drinking. One night he went to the hospital with a shotgun, cursing the doctors that killed his son. The police were not sympathetic. When it was over, Anita was alone in the world.

She shivered, the water no longer hot enough to leach the chill from her bones. Be happy like Tommy, she told herself over and over. Happiness was life; anger was death. She'd strived to be happy like Tommy rather than angry like Kevin. Through the following years, she had taken great strength from that way of thinking and put all her energy into the FBI, the only family she had left. Now, with Max in her life, she saw love in her future, something she thought she'd never have again.

The phone rattled.

Puffing her cheeks, Anita blew out a big breath and took a sip of coffee, her son's memory still lingering in her mind. The answering machine in the hallway picked up the call. "Inspector Pollard. We need you right away. The scrappers found something in the wreckage of the Hawker."

Chapter Twenty

AN HOUR LATER, INSPECTOR POLLARD pushed through the door to her office, which stood like a glass sentry over a maze of cubicles in the Internal Investigations Division of the FBI. The place buzzed with the sounds of keyboards clicking and laser printers whirring. A copy machine churned out paper as if the stuff were cheap.

"What do you have?" Anita asked Agent Remsen. He was a squatty man with puffy jowls that gave his face the same hound-like look as Alfred Hitchcock, only black.

"NTSB found something that belongs to us."

"If it's not the missing black box, I'm not interested."

Remsen's jowls jiggled as he shook his head. "No, it's not the black box."

She set her purse on the desk. "Then we may never find out why our jet fell out of the sky."

Remsen shrugged.

At the window, she folded her arms across her chest. Morning sunlight beamed off the Capitol's dome. She could still remember the black plume of smoke rising into the sky that day, blocking out the sun and overshadowing the most powerful city in the world. Shuddering from the memory, she said, "I suppose the NTSB still claims they gave the black box to the CIA."

"And the CIA still denies it."

Anita shook her head. "What do you make of that?"

"Somebody's lying." Remsen stood next to her now. He may have been a little shorter than Anita, but what he lacked in stature he made up for in savvy. "Colonel Fallon told us he'd spoken with Agent Marston on the phone just prior to the flight. Marston had told him that a copy of the task force's report on the Atomtech disaster was safe on the plane."

Anita frowned. "But there's nothing left of anything that was on that plane."

"And there's nothing left on the hard drive in Agent Marston's computer, either. It was wiped clean."

She watched the traffic below. "So what do we have left?"

"We know that Agent Marston and the Las Vegas task force were headed for Simi Valley, California, to serve a Federal Marshal's warrant on a place called Solartech Labs. The judge who issued that warrant was found murdered in his chambers, and shortly afterwards, the Hawker went down killing all onboard. My guess is the whole affair has something to do with this lab in Simi Valley."

A few minutes following Remsen's account lingered in silence. Inattentively gazing out the window, Anita worked through the details in her mind, first accepting the simplicity of it all, then, as her analytical process took over, she rejected the notion that a research facility had that much political clout in Washington D.C., at least not enough to assassinate a federal judge and down an FBI executive jet. Two of the *five Ws* were missing.

Who, what, where, when, and *why?* In every investigation, she had to find the answers to all five. She knew *what* happened and *where*: the Atomtech disaster in Nevada, the assassination of Judge Freeman, and the crash of the Hawker in Washington. And she knew *when*: all within one week of each other. If these events were connected, she needed to know *who* was responsible, and *why*.

She turned to Agent Remsen. "We need to figure out who's lying."

Remsen bit his lower lip. His eyebrows furrowed in

thought.

"Is it the NTSB or the CIA?" she prodded him. "Let's think about motivation. Who would benefit from lying about the black box?"

"The NTSB would have no reason to lie about anything," Remsen said. "Besides, if they didn't want the information in the black box to become known, they would only have to say it was destroyed in the crash: end of issue."

Still looking out the window, Anita accepted that theory. "On the other hand, the CIA has been known to conduct covert operations, and then turn around and deny everything afterwards. Isn't that true?"

"I think people generally believe the spy business operates that way."

"Then do they have enough resources to orchestrate events from California to Washington?"

"They're capable of worldwide espionage."

"But this was a domestic case. Why would the CIA have their noses in it?"

"So you think they're lying about—"

A knock on the door interrupted him. An agent poked his head in. "It's downstairs," he said and left.

Anita turned from the window. "What's he talking about?"

"The air safe," Remsen said. "Colonel Fallon told me the task force's report was on the Hawker. Agent Marston had used the words, 'it was safe on the plane.' When an air safe turned up in the wreckage, I wondered if Marston meant the report was 'in' the safe on the plane."

"But it has to be ruined."

"The dial is busted off, and it's scorched pretty bad, but anything inside might have survived the crash."

That was enough to spark Anita's curiosity. "Maybe we won't need the black box after all. Let's go."

Chapter Twenty-One

AS THE ELEVATOR DROPPED toward the basement in FBI headquarters, Anita grabbed a quick breath. "Who found the air safe?" she asked Agent Remsen.

"The scrappers, the guys that cleanup after a crash."

"Sounds like a morbid job."

"They're a pretty tough bunch."

The Elevator clunked to a stop, and the doors slid open with a chime. Anita stepped out into a dimly lit hallway and caught a chill from the cold, damp air. She never liked coming down here. The smell of musty cement, the clanking and ticking of plumbing, and the constant groan of the air conditioning system made her feel ill.

Remsen followed her down the hall. On the left, they came upon the maintenance garage. In passing, she looked in through the door. Men dressed in gray coveralls were busy keeping the FBI's fleet of squad cars in running order. Air wrenches whirred and hammered, and sparks cascaded down from under a hoisted Ford where a mechanic wearing dark goggles worked a torch on a muffler.

Now there's a tough bunch of men.

At the end of the hallway, she came to a brightly lit loading dock where a pickup truck had parked with its tailgate backed up to the platform. A man in blue coveralls leaned against the front fender, chewing on the stub of a cigar. He held out a clipboard to them. "You gonna sign for this junk or not?"

"Sure thing." Remsen inspected the document as a forklift whined up to the dock and squealed to a stop.

Anita examined the blackened air safe that was chained to a wooden pallet in the back of the pickup. The air safe looked heavy, about two-foot square and two foot deep. A swath of soot had been rubbed off the door, revealing an FBI seal. This remnant of the plane crash sent a moment of terror rushing through her body. She imagined the horror on the task force agents' faces as the Hawker spiraled toward the ground. What was going through their minds in the final seconds? Now, she hoped that Agent Marston had left a clue to their demise inside the air safe.

Signing the voucher, Remsen asked, "What took you boys so long to get this back to us?"

The NTSB man grumped. "You're lucky we didn't scrap the damn thing."

The forklift stabbed the pallet and backed away from the pickup, which quickly roared off and disappeared out the garage door.

"Where do you want it?" the forklift operator asked Anita.

"I don't know yet." She walked around the air safe. It had thick hinges on the door and fat metal bands around the box, all secured with rivets. The dial had been broken off, and the handle too. Otherwise, it looked to be in pretty good shape. She knew the air safe was bombproof, fireproof, and impact resistant, so if there was anything inside, it was definitely well protected. She put a finger to her lower lip. "Do you know any good safecrackers?" she asked Agent Remsen.

He shook his head. "It'll take a torch to get into this thing."

Her mind flashed back to the maintenance garage and the mechanic working on the Ford. "I've got an idea."

A few minutes later, in the garage, a couple of mechanics cleared a metal bench of busted parts, making room for the forklift to set down the air safe. Remsen began talking with the shop foreman. Their eyes shifted from the air safe to the torch and back and forth.

Shortly, several mechanics gathered around. Some removed the chains with bolt cutters, while others inspected the challenge put before them. All in all, their long faces didn't look optimistic.

Anita stepped out of the way to let them do their work. Agent Remsen walked up beside her. "They said if Pete can't get it open, no one can."

"Pete?"

"The guy with the welding glasses. I told him to be careful. We don't want the inside set on fire."

The torch popped to life. Pete adjusted the knobs, turning the flame bright blue. He worked the oxygen trigger. The blue tongue of fire turned white and hissed. As he put it to the thick hinges, sparks hurled through the air. Anita wanted to watch, but she had to turn her eyes away from the intense glow.

Several minutes passed. The mechanics went to work with hammers and crowbars. They banged and pried and hammered some more, cursing the thing that defied them. The torch spit fire, and the safe spewed steel. Smoke swirled all around the men as a pungent odor of oxidized metal stunk up the air. Undeterred, they kept at it, assaulting the safe with brutal precision, until the door finally fell away with a clank.

Pete shut off the torch, and the men stepped back. Anita thought that was her cue. She moved forward and carefully leaned over to look inside the safe. Hot steel glowed red around the smoke-filled opening, but all she could see inside was blackness. Her shoulders sagged. There was nothing: no file folder full of papers, no report sleeve, not even a notebook. Only a shelf and black fireproof padding. It looked as empty as her heart suddenly felt.

Agent Remsen stepped up and fanned the smoke away with his hand.

Suddenly, a glint of silver caught her eye, way down at the bottom. She would have missed it if she'd turned away a second sooner. Carefully, she reached in and lifted out a black Sony flash drive with a silver USB connector.

"Will you look at that?" Remsen said with raised eyebrows.

The mechanics grumbled and walked away scuffing their feet. One said, "Big deal."

Anita thanked them and apologized for the feeble contents of the safe, that no treasure of gold or diamonds was found locked up inside. The mechanics had no way of knowing this little flash drive could be more valuable than all the world's riches.

Chapter Twenty-Two

THROUGH ANITA'S COMPUTER MONITOR, Agent Marston spoke to her now, and the Las Vegas task force was there with him, too. From their graves, they told her a story so incredibly fantastic that it made her skin crawl. Pages of notes from their laptop computers were merged with Marston's report and now scrolled down the screen in front of her, their words rolling around in her mind as she tried to comprehend the meaning of it all. Her temples throbbed as she read a horrifying tale of deception and mass murder.

"My God," Remsen said, looking over her shoulder. "Melvin Anderson was responsible for all this?"

Anita cleared her throat. "It says here, Agent Marston found out that Melvin Anderson was blacklisted by the World Society of Archeologists. His source for that information was a Dr. Church who had told him that Anderson was killed when his helicopter crashed into a croc-infested swamp in Borneo. 'A fitting end to the scoundrel' were his exact words." Anita looked up. "No love lost there, I'd say."

"You know..." Remsen winced. "Some time back, I'd read about an archeologist who'd turned to grave robbing. Come to think of it, his name was Anderson, and he supposedly started a war in Malaysia."

"A war?"

"He'd stolen several billion dollars worth of

antiquities and sold them on the black market. Hundreds of people died trying to get their stuff back. The Malaysian Federation listed him as their most wanted fugitive."

"But according to Marston's report, Anderson died in Borneo."

"Then how did he end up in the United States?"

"Obviously he's alive and well," Anita said. "And somebody had to pull some strings to get him here."

"The CIA, you think?"

"I wouldn't put it past them. It also says here that Walter Devin from the Atomtech facility in Desert Rock, Nevada, discovered Dr. Frank Curtis was an imposter. His real name was Melvin Anderson. He'd orchestrated the hostile takeover of Solartech Labs in California."

"That's where the task force was headed: Simi Valley."

"There are several pages of his testimony here..." She skimmed the material. "Something about a dangerous nuclear experiment, the 13th Power, and the end of the world." Anita's throat went dry. "What were these guys messing with?"

"Jesus."

She scrolled down to the next page where the task force talked about the Atomtech disaster. The terror of that day came to mind. The whole country had awakened to the news of an explosion at the atomic research and development company in Nevada. The horrors of Chernobyl on American soil became terrifyingly real. "Look here." She pointed to a paragraph in the task force report where it said that Colonel Fallon's investigation "came to the real and troubling conclusion that the explosion at Atomtech was not a nuclear accident, but rather the result of a direct military assault on the company, directed by Dr. Curtis and carried out by unknowns."

She read on aloud, "C4 explosives heavily damaged the facility, but no radiation leaks were detected. Employee casualties were high: thirty-seven dead, ninety-two injured, all wounds consistent with a battlefield scenario, trauma and death caused by firearms and grenades: *MILITARY.*"

Agent Remsen gasped. "Could that mean...?"

"Melvin Anderson had a military connection."

"But how?"

"More like, why?" Anita rubbed her throbbing temples. "Why would the government kill its own citizens for Melvin Anderson?"

Remsen shook his fatty chin. "Right here in the land of the free and the home of the brave? How could that have happened?"

"Maybe Melvin Anderson had something the government wanted, like that 13th Power thing Colonel Fallon was talking about."

"But what the hell is that?"

Anita scrolled down to the last page. Suddenly, the answer was right there in front of her. Agent Marston had found it, the only way Melvin Anderson could have acquired the military clout to conduct the attack on Atomtech. He had a powerful ally: *The Ark*. The connection was solid. "My God. This thing stinks all the way up to the White House."

"That's it," Remsen said. "*The Ark* knew Marston was onto him, so he sabotaged the Hawker and killed our men to shut them up."

"The son-of-a-bitch."

Chapter Twenty-Three

JANIS STOOD AT THE KITCHEN counter, still shaken from Tracy's abduction, the phone clutched in his hand. It was ringing on the other end. He hoped Lo Chin would answer it. Tracy needed his help, and if he was going to save her, he'd need the help of the only man he could trust.

A click came over the line. *"I'm sorry to be away so long to miss your call. Please be so kind to leave message at beep."*

"Lo Chin. It's Janis, Janis Mackey..." When he finished, he set the receiver down and hoped Lo Chin would get the message in time.

***

Los Angeles. An answering machine recorded an incoming message. In the room next to the small office, Lisa cinched the black belt around her gi a little tighter and stepped onto the mat. It felt cool on her bare feet. She felt good, all warmed up from the last hour of kata, the precise movements exercising form and control. When she attended school in Japan, the elders had taught her well.

Standing erect, arms at her side, she glanced around Lo Chin's workout room. Candles burned at the base of a little prayer station in the corner, and a stationary bike and treadmill stood at the other end of the room. Oriental paintings hung on the walls. The subtle scent of incense hung in the air. She bowed to Lo Chin who stood across from her on the mat.

He grinned back at her with confidence.

Saying nothing to him, she sidestepped left, her eyes on his eyes. He was a short and stocky man, sixty or so, with long gray hair that he wore in a braid. His flowing black pants hid his leg movements and made him appear to float across the mat as he countered her move to the right. With all the grace of a karate master, he settled into his stance, crouched, one arm up for defense, the other cocked at his side to strike. His hands opened slowly until his fingers were outstretched like claws.

She sighed and assumed the position, wondering when he was going to learn. “You sure you want to do this, Lo?”

Without warning, he attacked. He lunged forward in a flash, shuffling his feet, grabbing her arm, and tripping her legs.

The room spun, her shoulder blades hit the mat, and air huffed from her lungs. Lo was on top of her now, grinning, his fisted knuckles poised over her throat. “You like that move?”

“A little cocky, today, are you?” She shoved him up and over her head. He landed on his back with a thud. In an instant, she rolled to her feet, but he was already up and moving right. Balling her fists, she crouched, awaiting his next attack. Every nerve in her body tingled with anticipation.

He took three steps forward at lightning speed, his arms flailing. Lisa threw out a cross-block, stepped right, and put her left knee into his ribcage. He rocked back on his heels and gulped air.

“Give it up, Lo. You’ll be sleeping with the hot water bottle again tonight.”

Lo bared his teeth and came around with a spinning back kick. Lisa ducked, and with a leg sweep, knocked his pivot foot out from under him. He hit the mat with a thump.

In an instant, she leaped on him with her fists clenched. "Don't make me hurt you."

"All right, all right," Lo said, holding up his hands. "You win."

She helped him to his feet, faced him, and bowed.

"How did you get so good at karate, pretty Miss Lisa?" Lo tossed her a towel.

She draped it over her shoulder. "My father, well..." She hesitated. Those old feelings stirred in her gut again. Hate and anger had made her strong, and karate had given her a way to vent. She'd blamed all her problems on her father. It was only after she'd returned home that she found out how wrong she'd been about him. He'd only done what he had to do to protect her from her mother. Lisa looked at Lo who was damping his forehead with a towel. "It doesn't matter."

"It matters to me. When I get my butt kicked, I want to know why."

Lisa smiled. "No you don't."

Giving her one of those serious stares, Lo said, "Miss Lisa, I see there is still much hate in your eyes, not for your father now, but for your mother."

"I don't even know my mother."

"You know enough."

"I know she'd better never come back."

She pushed through the door to the outer office, thinking Lo was some kind of mind reader. He had an uncanny knack of knowing what she was feeling, and he really seemed to care. But she didn't want to tell him what her father had told her...about what had happened when she was six years old, how her mother had kidnapped her after losing a bitter custody battle, or how a year passed before her father found her in a trailer town outside North Las Vegas, wallowing in filth, underfed, and abused. She didn't have any memory of that time in her life. The shrinks had told her it was because the experience was so horrible that her mind had blocked it out.

"I don't want to talk about it, Lo." She leaned against the desk as he closed the door behind him.

"Very well, but remember this: just because the ostrich does not see the world with his head in a hole, it does not mean the world is not there." He shifted his eyes to the phone. "Ah, it looks like somebody called."

> *"Lo Chin. It's Janis, Janis Mackey. Pick me up at LAX. United flight 314 arriving at 7:40 tonight. I need your help. We have to go back to Simi Valley."*

Lisa gasped and looked at Lo. "He changed his mind...he's coming back, Lo." She threw her arms around his neck. "I get another chance."

Lo shook his head. "You're going to get your heart broken all over again, Miss Lisa..."

"Oh no, not this time," she said, her mind spinning with thoughts of the mathematician and a love rekindled. She pulled the towel off her shoulder and tossed it on the chair. "I'm going to the airport with you." She spun for the door.

"But...Miss Lisa..."

"I have to get ready." She grabbed the doorknob. "Janis is coming back."

Chapter Twenty-Four

JANIS BOARDED THE 737 AT Denver International Airport. Loosening his tie, he felt apprehensive about this flight, not because of a fear of flying, but because this was the same type aircraft that had fallen out of the sky over Colorado Springs and Pittsburgh for no apparent reason. There was something wrong with the 737. The NTSB and the FAA never figured out what had caused those aircraft to crash, though they suspected there was a problem with the rudder controls. Modifications were made, and fears were alleviated...well, not entirely. Though hundreds of 737s flew every hour of every day all over the world, he was still concerned, but this was the only flight out tonight. He had no choice, and neither did a hundred and fifty other people who were all jammed into the aisle at once.

In his seat by the window, he clasped the safety belt and fumbled with the aircraft evacuation card he found in the pocket in front of him. The nearest exit was four rows back.

An elderly lady wedged herself into the seat next to him and smiled. She seemed pleasant enough, but she smelled like a soap dish. He adjusted the air nozzle on the panel above his head and wondered if he could take two hours of her aroma. Again, he had no choice.

Twenty minutes later, DIA was just a concrete dot on the Colorado plains below. Now, the Rocky Mountains jutted up into a cloudless sky, and the setting August sun basked the peaks in a yellow glow. As the 737 climbed, Janis relaxed into his seatback and took in the soapy smell of flight 314.

Ray Crawford was on his mind.

In college, Ray had been engrossed in nuclear physics, the space-time continuum, Einstein's theories of relativity and the unified field. It was all he ever talked about: the atomic force, the speed of light, and his dreams of becoming a world famous physicist.

The jet leveled off at cruising altitude. A chime sounded. Janis swallowed and popped his ears as the *fasten seatbelt* light went out. A subtle drone from the engines filled the cabin. He looked out the window. The mountains were now just jagged bumps, some still marred with white slivers of glacial snow.

"Would you like something to drink, sir?" the flight attendant asked.

"No thanks." Janis closed his eyes and went back to his thoughts of Ray Crawford.

After one of their college projects failed, everything changed for Ray. Disillusioned with the university's tight purse strings and the narrow minded Board of Trustees, he dropped out without earning his degree. His travels to find employment in the field he loved had taken him to Atomtech in Desert Rock, Nevada.

While Janis was working on his doctorate in mathematics and eventually went on to teaching at the University of Colorado, Ray was struggling with his mediocre job and a boss that had no interest in experimenting with the 13th Power. Walter Devin had been adamant. The answer was always the same: No.

The jet hit a bump of turbulent air and made Janis's heart beat faster. Something else about Ray Crawford bothered him. As if his obsession with the 13th Power wasn't crazy enough, his choice of women went beyond that. He'd met Kate in Las Vegas, plying her trade on the

Strip during a convention he was attending. For some unknown reason, not unlike the demise of the 737s, Ray had thought he could rescue Kate from her life of drugs and prostitution. He was going to save her from herself. Oh, there was an attraction between them, no doubt about that, and Lisa was the result. But he'd had no more luck changing Kate's ways than he did changing Devin's mind about the 13th Power.

The jet made a gentle roll to the right. The engines quieted a little, and a subtle sinking feeling went through Janis's stomach. He opened his eyes and saw the soap lady flipping through pages of a magazine. Unnerved, he closed his eyes again and let the gentle motion of the 737 lull him to sleep. In uneasy dreams, he saw Lisa, Tracy, and Mother. They appeared and disappeared, here and there, as if playing a misty game of hide and seek. He called out to them, again and again. Lisa came to him naked. Tracy cried.

A chime echoed through the cabin. Janis suddenly became aware of the drone of the engines, and he jerked his eyes open, his heart beating wildly from the dream and the downward pitch of the 737's nose.

The *fasten seatbelt* light came on.

"Flight attendants... prepare for landing," came over the intercom. The soap lady tucked away her magazine and gave Janis a smile.

He held his breath as the jet rolled left, banked to the right, and shuddered when the landing gear deployed. A moment later, the wheels hit the runway, and the reverse thrusters roared.

Janis was back in California, and the gravity of his situation struck him like a blow below the belt.

Chapter Twenty-Five

HE'D JUST CLEARED THE GANGWAY from the plane when he heard his name called out. "Janis." The voice was unmistakable.

Lisa.

His eyes raced over the throng on the concourse, his heart beating as if he were a kid at a school dance. Old feelings were coming back to life, feelings he quickly suppressed as he scanned the crowd, looking for a tan-skinned blonde with shoulder length hair and long legs. In his wildest dreams, he'd never imagined seeing her again.

"Janis."

He looked to his right. There, by the bank of arrival monitors, Lisa stood next to Lo Chin, waving. Janis should have known Lo would bring her along.

Running toward him now, she brushed through the crowd, her blue eyes wide and her smile lighting up all of California. She wore cutoff blue jeans and a white sleeveless top tied in a knot just above her navel. Her eyes shined with tears.

"Oh, Janis." She threw her arms around his neck and hugged him. "My Colorado cowboy. You came back."

"Just like a bad dream," he assured her.

Lisa went to her tiptoes and kissed him quickly. "It's a good dream. I'm holding you again."

He set her back on her heels. "It's a nightmare, Lisa. Don't ever forget it."

She showed him a pouting face. “What? You’re not glad to see me?”

Janis bit his lower lip and glanced at Lo Chin. A loose green T-shirt hung on his stocky frame, and bone-white legs protruded from tan Bermuda shorts. He rocked on the balls of his feet, smiling as if he had all the time in the world.

Satisfied with Lo’s patience, Janis looked again at Lisa’s face, her cheeks now streaked with tears. The last thing he wanted was to turn those tears of joy into tears of sorrow, but the reasons he’d left her in California had not changed. Lisa was too young, he was too old, and where love was concerned, it mattered. He put a hand on her cheek and wiped away a teardrop with his thumb. “Of course I’m glad to see you, Lisa.”

Her smile widened. “Is there a chance you could ever love me again?”

“Not in the way you deserve.” He paused and took a breath. “Besides, I’m in love with Tracy. She’s the reason I’ve come back.”

Lisa’s smile faded to nothing. “You can’t be serious.”

“Dr. Curtis has kidnapped her. He wants the 13th Power in exchange for her life. I have to conduct the experiments again. I don’t have any choice.”

She just stared at him, her bleary eyes fixed on his. Even the noisy swarm of travelers jamming the concourse seemed muffled and distant. Janis couldn’t stand the tension any longer. “I’m sorry,” he said, though he wasn’t sure what for. He knew he wasn’t sorry for leaving her here with her father. This was her home; she belonged here. He definitely wasn’t sorry for loving Tracy, so he figured it must have been the look on Lisa’s face, that look of abandonment and loss that he had caused. She’d suffered enough of that from her mother.

“Come on. Let’s go.” He put his arm around her and coaxed her toward Lo Chin.

She took a couple steps, stopped, and spun out from under the crook of his arm. “No! It’s not fair, Janis. I found you first.” She took off down the concourse, her sandals slapping the floor, and disappeared into the crowd.

“Lisa, wait.” He started after her, but a strong hand grabbed his arm from behind, spinning him around.

“Let Miss Lisa go,” Lo Chin said with warm eyes.

Janis took a breath, looked again down the concourse then shook his head. “I don’t think I should.”

“She be all right. Give her time to get act together. Tell me now, why do we need to go back to Simi Valley?”

Janis explained about Tracy and Curtis.

Lo took a step back. “This isn’t going to end well.”

***

In the airport parking garage, Lisa climbed into the back of Lo Chin’s limo, a white stretched Lincoln with beige leather interior. Though she liked the scent of his new car, it didn’t help improve her mood. She wanted to scream but threw herself down on the seat instead. “How dare Janis come back for Tracy?” she whined. Her eyes stung with tears. Lo was right. Her heart was breaking again. In the back of her mind she had held on to the hope that someday Janis would come back, that they could fall in love again, this time completely. They were so good together. Janis was her Colorado Cowboy, and she was his California Girl. She wanted it all back again, the way it was before Tracy came along.

She clenched her fists. Tracy McClarence, that old bag? What was he thinking?

Just then, familiar voices echoed through the parking garage. Lisa pushed herself up from the seat to look out the back window. Janis and Lo were moving up the walkway from the terminal, Janis toting a big suitcase and Lo gabbing at him about something. They didn’t seem concerned about her problems.

She dropped back onto the seat, her heart beating hard. Now she felt foolish. Sure it was a childish thing to do, stomping out of the airport like that. She must have looked like a spoiled brat. But what did Janis expect her to do, say congratulations? No way. He wasn't getting off the hook that easily.

When the trunk lid popped open, Lisa sank lower in the seat. A suitcase clunked into the trunk, followed by the lid closing with a thud.

Lo opened the door and poked his head in. "You all right, Miss Lisa?"

She turned her head away.

Janis looked in, too, but he said nothing.

She folded her arms over her chest and put a pout on her face.

The door closed. She glared at the men now walking toward the front of the car. They got into the front seat as if nothing was wrong. Lo started the engine and drove away from the airport terminal.

She glared at the back of the men's heads and wondered why Janis hadn't turned around. Was he really so much in love with Tracy that he'd forgotten his feelings for her?

It wasn't fair.

Then a glimmer of hope came over her, a warm kind of feeling that swelled up inside. The solution was simple. Janis was here with her now, and Tracy wasn't. Lisa had the advantage. He was still fair game, and she was going to break all the rules.

Chapter Twenty-Six

THE SILVER TRANSPORTER GLEAMED under floodlights inside the new MIGGS. Ray stood on the interior catwalk and put his hands on his hips as he took in the sight. It was the most beautiful thing he'd ever seen. A mechanical arm with hydraulic cylinders and steel hinges suspended the transporter from the ceiling and made it appear as if it were floating in mid air. His heart pounded with excitement and trepidation as he wondered if the I.S.S.T. would take him into the 13th Power or be the death of him.

Men in gray jumpsuits and white hard hats scurried about inside the MIGGS, some toting gadgets and parts and tools, while others worked huge wrenches on black bolts. Another team was welding something to the thick collar that joined the MIGGS to the particle accelerator. Sparks flew and molten steel popped and hissed. The air tasted like tin. Hammering and clattering echoed all around, and the workers' voices were loud.

A crew on the scaffolding at the transporter's fuselage peeled off the backing of a decal, which revealed an insignia: a white lightning bolt piercing the nucleus of a blue atom on a gold shield background. Curtis had told him the gold shield represented the riches hidden inside the nucleus, while the lightning bolt was the power of the technology that would unlock the atom. Another decal read: *NASA USA*. After pulling their scaffold away, the men stood there looking up at their work. One guy took a picture with his cell phone. Ray thought they had done a fine job.

Stan Burton entered the MIGGS with a clipboard in hand. “Let’s go over the checklist.”

Ray followed him down the catwalk, ducked under a wing, and climbed the ladder into the transporter’s belly hatch. A tunnel went up about two feet. He found himself at the rear of the flight deck. Grabbing a handrail on the wall, he pulled himself inside.

The first thing he noticed was the subtle whirring sound of the APU, the auxiliary power unit. Lighting tracks on the ceiling and along the gray-carpeted floor lit the interior with a soft glow. The walls were smooth and beige and curved up to the ceiling from which hung panels of switches and glass-faced gauges that reflected the light like sparkling jewels. Foot-thick titanium ribs were spaced every two feet apart, reinforcing the flight deck, which smelled like the interior of a new car.

Stan entered the flight deck behind him.

Three high-back seats took up much of the floor space, two up front at the controls and one centered directly behind them. Made of a red material, they had the feel of fine leather. A titanium passageway on the right went toward the rear of the spacecraft. “What’s down there?” Ray asked, pointing aft.

Stan cocked his head. “Sleeping harnesses, galley, and a zero gravity water closet.”

“All the comforts of home.” Ray followed Stan to the front seats.

Stan sat on the left with the clipboard in his lap. Ray took the right seat, which felt plush as a captain’s chair in a luxury van. Looking out the thick windshield edged with chrome rivets, he saw the bustle of activity going on inside the MIGGS, but he couldn’t hear any of the noise.

Across the entire panel in front of him lay a maze of

instruments, rows of switches and dials and knobs of different shapes and sizes. There were keypads with LCDs, liquid crystal displays, and monitors showing graphics and charts. The mass of gadgetry spanned the forward flight deck and came down a console between the front seats. There were throttle levers, trim controls, and "Star" gauges that indicated thruster pressure and photon intensity, and there was a Space Probe screen with three settings: *ON, OFF,* and *RECORD*. A meter labeled *ION Shield* caught Ray's eye. "Is this the gravity deflector?"

Looking up from his clipboard, Stan said, "You'll feel some pressure." He tapped a gauge labeled *G-Force*. "This will tell you how many times the gravity is greater than earth's. You'll be all right."

"Will it feel like an elevator ride?"

"I don't know." Stan returned to his checklist.

Sitting upright, Ray thought about how he would fly this contraption and grabbed hold of the steering yoke with both hands. It was mounted to an aluminum control mast that came up out of the floor. He turned the yoke right and left, like any ordinary steering wheel in a car, and he discovered it also tilted forward and backward and leaned both left and right. He looked at Stan who was checking instruments on the ceiling panel. "How does this thing work?"

"Ever fly a plane?" He worked switches that clicked.

"I took lessons twenty years ago, if that's any help."

Stan chuckled. "Believe me, nothing's changed since then. Turning the yoke rolls the transporter right or left, keeps it level or even tilted if needed. Push the yoke: nose goes down. Pull the yoke: nose goes up, just like an airplane."

"Then what's with this?" Ray leaned the mast, first right then left.

"Yaw," Stan said. "Points the nose. In the vacuum of space there's no lifting force on the wings to make a turn, like a plane. In space, you have to lean the mast in the direction you want to go. The computer-controlled thrusters do the rest. Remember, this thing's been designed for precision docking maneuvers. It can rotate on a pencil point 360 degrees around all three axes."

"And I'm supposed to remember all this?"

"The computers do all the work. You'll be a pro before you know it."

"Easy for you to say." Ray buckled the six-way seatbelt harness. "You know this contraption better than anybody. I'm just a nuclear physicist, an atom smasher, not an engineer or an astronaut. Why don't you come along...keep me from crashing this thing?"

"You're the crazy one around here, not me." Stan motioned over his right shoulder. "There'll be two empty seats. Who's going with you?"

Ray shrugged and scanned the flight instruments, hoping the question would fade from his mind, but it didn't. He wondered if he had the right to ask anyone to go with him. Besides, he didn't know where he was going, how long he'd be gone, or how he was going to get back. Perhaps Stan was right: no one else was crazy enough to take this journey. Hell, for all he knew, the particle beam might disintegrate the transporter right at the get-go, especially if the Supers weren't programmed properly. It would be the end of everything in a flash of light.

He shook off the thought in favor of thinking that wasn't going to happen. Now that he knew the dangers of the 13th Power, the real risks he was taking, he could make the necessary adjustments to the programming schedule. Every angle would be covered, every scenario considered. This time he'd be prepared before the laser fired, and in the end, he'd have made a historic journey beyond the feats of Columbus, Lindbergh, and Neil Armstrong.

"Ray," Stan said. "Are you with me here?"

"Oh...I was just thinking."

Stan flipped through some papers on his clipboard. “Let’s start with the systems checklist first...then the operational. If there’s time, I want to go through the regenerator sequence.”

“Regenerator? What’s that?”

“Your round trip ticket, Ray.”

***

Four hours passed by the time they’d completed the operational checklist. Ray rubbed a crook in his neck. “Looks like most systems are functioning perfectly.”

Stan tossed the clipboard on the instrument cover. “I’ll get the technical team on the other stuff, maybe tomorrow. It’ll be perfect when it flies.”

“If we can call it *flying*.” Ray worked the control mast.

“When the transporter is degenerated into the 13th Power, it won’t be like any flying anyone has ever done.”

“Is that the technical term for what this transporter will do, degenerate?” Ray looked around the flight deck. “I’ve heard you use that word before.”

“I like it better than *zap*.”

Ray bit his lip. *Zap* didn’t sound like a very good thing.

Stan got out of his seat. “Follow me.”

“Where’re we going?” Ray unbuckled his harness.

“To the regenerator.”

“Is that anything like an *unzapper?*”

Stan nodded. “I rest my case.”

At the back of the flight deck, he pushed open a hatch on the wall. Ray stepped over the threshold and ducked through the doorway, feeling as if he were suddenly degenerated into a submarine. He found himself in a dimly lit chamber cramped with instruments on the walls. A ventilating fan whirred, and there were levers and knobs and things that looked like keys and gauges and meters and flashing LEDs. The smell of warm electrical circuits filled the air.

Stan stopped at a computer terminal on a wall cluttered with instruments and switches. “Look at this.”

Ray stood next to him, his nerves tingling from the complexity of the machinery around him. As Stan worked the keyboard, the monitor blinked on and revealed a galaxy of stars slowly rotating in the black void of space.

“Recognize her?”

Ray shook his head. “They all look alike to me.”

“The Milky Way galaxy, a computerized version, that is. And here.” He clicked the mouse button. “Home sweet home.” An *X* popped up on the screen near the lower edge of the galaxy. “It’s the MIGGS, in our solar system, of course. And this...” he clicked the mouse again, “is the transporter.” A circle appeared over the *X*. Together, they made an odd looking reticle, like a rifle scope, only crooked.

“Obviously, the transporter is in the MIGGS so the *O* and the *X* are in the same place, but after degeneration into the 13th Power, the regenerator will keep track of the transporter and its correlation with the MIGGS at all times. When you want to come back, pull this handle down.” He pointed to a chrome lever on the wall next to the monitor. “The regenerator will activate and home-in on the MIGGS, where the transporter will regenerate, in the same place it degenerated from...theoretically, that is.”

Ray groaned. “Theoretically? How good am I supposed to feel about that?”

“Relax.” Stan turned a key-like knob on the wall. With a whoosh of compressed air, a panel opened, revealing a window about eighteen inches high and three feet long with rounded corners and glass a foot thick.

Amazed, Ray looked in the window. A green light blinked on and off in two-second intervals. When it was on, he saw a shiny titanium cylinder hanging from the ceiling of a black tunnel-like chamber. When it was off, he saw a red glow coming from somewhere beyond his angle of view. "My God," he said, finding it hard to keep his breath. "You built a MIGGS in here?"

Stan grinned.

Ray took a step away from the thick window. "How did you do that?"

"We revamped the cargo bay. It was perfect for an onboard MIGGS."

Rubbing the side of his neck, Ray's mind reeled with questions: the 13th Power, the void of the universe inside the atom, the Higgs boson at the gateway, the Higgs Field expressway. "How's this going to get the transporter back home?"

Stan closed the panel over the window. "When you put the key in the ignition of your car, you don't have to know what makes the engine crank and run and all the things that happen to make it move. You just drive the damn thing. It does the rest, like magic."

"Look, Stan..." Ray frowned. "This isn't a car, and I'm not going on a Sunday drive. You'd better have some damn good science to back up your claims."

"Reverse physics," Stan said with raised eyebrows. "If taking the Higgs boson out of the atom sends the I.S.S.T. into the 13th Power, then putting it back into the atom will bring the I.S.S.T. out of the 13th Power, in the same place it degenerated from."

Ray thought about that. Could Higgs regeneration be as simple as electromagnetism? Concerned, he looked at Stan. "For the regenerator to work, the Higgs boson has to be contained in the titanium cylinder along with all the other particles of the atom so it can be put back together. We haven't been able to do that yet."

Stan patted Ray's shoulder. "That's your problem. I've done my part. Now it's up to you. Get the physics right, Ray. This thing doesn't degenerate until you do."

"But..."

"Hello. Anybody in here?"

Ray's knees went weak at the sound of her voice. He'd given security strict orders: the transporter was off-limits to Lisa.

"Dad?"

Fighting panic, he leaped from the regenerator room and onto the flight deck, but it was too late. Lisa's head had already popped up through the hatch tunnel. Her eyes were narrow and her brows taut. He felt a chill. How was he ever going to explain this?

She pulled herself into the transporter and walked around the flight deck. Running her hands across the seatbacks, she made her way up front, peered out the windshield, then plopped in the right-hand seat and worked the controls like a kid playing in the family car. "This is *so* neat."

"I'm glad you like it," Ray said coolly, though his heart felt like it would burst. Did she think this was some kind of toy? Or was she just toying with him? Either way, her being here was too bizarre.

"Sorry, Ray," a soon-to-be-fired security guard said as he stuck his fat face up through the hatch. "I couldn't stop her."

"You had your orders."

"But she brought some heavy muscle with her."

"What?"

As the guard backed down the hatch ladder, Ray glanced at Lisa who was bouncing in the left-hand seat and wearing a communications headset. He knew her childlike antics were staged. She was up to something mischievous, he was sure of it. Looking back to the hatch, he thought he was going to have a heart attack when he saw Janis climb up the ladder. "What are you doing here?"

"We found him at the airport," Lisa said, sliding into

the rear seat sideways and dangling her legs over an armrest. The headset was now hanging around her neck. "Are you surprised?"

"What do you mean 'we'?"

"Lo Chin and I, of course."

Ray gasped. "Lo is here too?"

Janis climbed onto the flight deck. "He's right behind me." He stooped, lent Lo a hand, and pulled him aboard.

Lo looked around with wide eyes. "What have we here, Ray?"

"What's going on?" Janis asked with an edge to his words.

Lisa's eyes zeroed in on Ray. "Dad?"

His heart skipped. "Ah...well..." He found himself stumbling for words. He looked quickly to Stan who was standing in the doorway to the regenerator room, mute. There had to be a way out of this, or he'd end up having to 'fess up. He really didn't want to do that. What he wanted more than anything was an answer to a question grilling his brain. Why were these guys here, so totally unexpected? Something had to be wrong. He planted his feet apart and folded his arms across his chest. "What are you doing here, Lo...Janis?" He shifted his eyes between them, waiting for the first one to cough up an explanation.

"Don't be such a butthead, Dad." Lisa rolled her eyes. "Aren't you happy to see them?"

"Only one thing could have brought them back to Solartech Labs: trouble. And I'll bet Dr. Curtis has everything to do with it. Am I right, Janis?"

He nodded. "It's worse than that, but we asked you first. What's all this?"

Lisa smirked. "I bet it has nothing to do with the Gindrich Phenomenon." She twirled the headset cord.

Lo was busy looking over the instruments up front and didn't question Lisa's remark. But a puzzled look came over Janis's face. Ray blinked. He knew there was no bullshitting the mathematician like he had bullshitted Lisa. Or had he? It wouldn't have been the first time he'd underestimated her intelligence. If he couldn't make this craft seem legit, they'd shut him down for sure. His only hope now was to convince them the I.S.S.T. was just a prototype orbiter NASA brought in for testing. "Well..."

"Star gauge," Lo said, examining one of the instruments. "I read about this in a NASA engineering magazine. Pulse light engines." He stabbed some buttons on the panel. A green liquid crystal display responded, *FUNCTIONAL*. "This is the real thing, Janis."

Ray dropped his jaw. *So much for the prototype line.*

Lisa's eyes glittered with fury. He was going to have to tell her the truth, which wouldn't be easy. Last time, it had taken him nineteen years to tell her the truth about her mother. But Kate wasn't the problem any longer...he was. His obsession with the 13th Power was about to put another rift between him and his daughter. He looked at Janis and then at Lisa.

They both stared back at him furiously.

His tongue felt dry as shoe leather. "Well...it's like this..." he began.

Chapter Twenty-Seven

CHOKING DUST SWIRLED UP FROM under the rented Chevy's wheels as it sped down the dirt road toward Desert Rock, Nevada. Kate rolled up the window and clicked on the air conditioning. Though she wore a sleeveless yellow pullover and white short shorts, her skimpy garb gave her no relief from the heat. She lit another cigarette, inhaled, and let the nicotine calm her nerves.

Sarah Beth had told her she could never go back and reclaim the life she had tossed away so many years ago. Someone else had told her the same thing: Willy, the drug-dealing pimp who had ruined her life in the first place. Until meeting him, she had worked alone, walking the Strip, dodging the vice squad, and finding her own tricks. It was a tough existence. Willy promised to make things better, the lying bastard.

Then Ray came along, a handsome man who took it upon himself to be her savior...an impossible task. She latched on to him anyway, hoping for a better life. But Willy wouldn't leave her alone. He kept pulling her down into the pits with him. There were times when she was so strung out on cocaine and booze that she couldn't even remember Ray Crawford existed. She didn't even care. Willy had kept her high and flat on her back. She'd kept the money rolling in for him, and all in all, he'd made her life a living hell for all her efforts.

She always believed that Willy had told her she could never go back to her family just to keep her under his control. She had accused him of it once, and his eyes had turned to stone. "Tricks don't like whores with black eyes," he'd warned her, balling a fist. Kate shuddered at the recollection.

Tires thudded over a stretch of washboard on the road. She took a long drag on her cigarette as she thought about Willy. Control was a big thing with him. He'd used the drugs as leverage and held on to her money. He owed her thousands of dollars, she was sure, but she would never have the nerve to call in her marker. He was too dangerous, too close to that agony that beckoned her daily.

And there was something unspeakably horrible about Willy. Drugs and alcohol had blinded her to it for the longest time. He liked little girls. "Child pornography is a big cash business," he'd said. By the time she found out what he was doing, it was too late; the damage was done. And Lisa was only six years old.

Kate's stomach turned sour. How could she have been so stupid? Willy had made it all sound so easy. "Take your daughter back," he had told her. Because she still had a key to the apartment, he put together a plan, and in the middle of the night, they snatched Lisa from her bed. Ray must have been deathly ill when he found her gone the next morning, but at the time, Kate didn't care; after all, Willy was right. Ray didn't deserve Lisa. With her daughter back, Kate hoped everything was going to be fine, but more cocaine went up her nose, and nothing got any better.

A coyote skittered across the road and disappeared into the sagebrush. Up ahead, the tumbleweed-infested chain-link fence around the Atomtech compound came into view. Her heartbeat quickened. It was time to put her plan into action. She'd drive right up to the main gate and show her old ID card to the guard. If he balked at that, she would insist on seeing Walter Devin. Certainly he would tell the guard to let her come through the gate. Then she would find Ray, and with any luck, he'd still have a soft spot for her and take her back. If only it could be that easy.

As she approached the main gate, she immediately noticed that something was wrong. Green jeeps and soldiers with rifles blocked the entrance, and Air Force helicopters sat motionless inside the compound behind them. A chill went through her when she saw the windows had been blown out of the buildings, and the antennas and satellite dishes on the roof had toppled over into twisted heaps. A bulldozer rattled toward one of the buildings, which had been reduced to a pile of charred rubble. Something terrible had happened here, she realized, as she stopped at the main gate.

A group of sweaty soldiers gathered around the car.

When one of them approached the window, she rolled it down. "Hello, fellas."

The sergeant seemed especially cautious. "What are you doing out here in the middle of nowhere, ma'am?"

She handed him her ID card, and watched his eyes narrow. "Is something wrong?" she asked him in her softest voice.

The soldiers nodded. "That's an understatement," one of them said, frowning.

The sergeant said, "You're going to have to turn around and go back the way you came, ma'am. I'm sorry."

"Look, soldier boy." Kate put on her tough street voice. "I didn't eat a hundred miles of dust to hear you tell me to turn around. I demand to see Walter Devin."

The guard's eyes widened. "That's not possible, ah, Mrs. Crawford," he said slowly. "I'm sorry to tell you, Walter Devin is dead."

Kate gasped. Her next thought sent a wave of terror trembling through her body. "Ray Crawford...and Lisa? Are they...?" She couldn't speak the word.

He shook his head. "I don't know about them. You'll

need to check the casualty list at HQ."

"Where's that?"

"Creech Air Force Base, Indian Springs, ma'am."

She snatched her ID card from the sergeant. "Big help you are." Spinning the Chevy around, she peeled away from the main gate. The shambles of Atomtech quickly faded away in the rearview mirror.

Fumbling to light another cigarette, her mind buzzed with questions. Whatever happened at Atomtech must have been horrible. She thought the story might have been on the news, but she never watched television while she was locked up in prison. The outside world was only a mirage. A world that didn't exist wouldn't be missed or yearned for. It was her only defense against going totally insane in that place.

As she sped past the spot where she'd seen the coyote, a moment of regret crept through her. If Ray and Lisa were killed in the blast that devastated Atomtech, then her only chance for survival had died with them. Without her family, she knew it would be just a matter of time before that lust for cocaine took hold of her again. She needed them now more than ever, and if they were gone...oh no. She took a heavy drag on her cigarette and wondered what would become of her.

An hour later, a dust devil danced across the Air Force base at Indian Springs. Kate pulled up to the main gate. An airman, not much more than a kid, approached her car. He wore fatigues, a khaki ball cap, and a blue band around his arm with *SP* embroidered in white. "Ma'am, may I help you?"

"I've come to find out what happened to my family." She sobbed and plied a tissue to her eyes, hopefully in a show of sincerity. "My husband, Ray Crawford, and my daughter, Lisa, they were at Atomtech. There was some kind of accident or explosion. I don't know what to do." She added a sniffle for effect.

The young man's eyes showed immediate concern. "One moment." He reached for a telephone inside the guard shack, and after a minute, he looked back to her window. "Help is on the way, ma'am."

Shortly, a siren wailed in the distance. Through heat waves rising from the pavement beyond the black metal-bar gate, she saw the distorted shape of a jeep speeding toward them, its blue and white flashing overheads pulsing with an ominous rhythm. Instinct told her to run, to get away from this place as fast as she could. The sights and sounds now bombarding her mind were far too familiar. She'd had enough problems with cops and the trouble they brought with them. Her palms started to sweat on the steering wheel.

The airman must have notice her fingers trembling. "It's just Lieutenant Briggs, ma'am. He's always in a hurry. The siren makes him feel important. Don't worry. He's going to take you to see Colonel Fallon."

She took a deep breath, which didn't make her feel any better.

***

Colonel Fallon put the golden staff on his desk and picked up the ringing phone. "Security Police."

"Bruce, how are you?"

Leaning against his desk, Fallon replied, "How's the arm, Carlton?"

"It's been working all right."

"And NASA?"

"You know how you've been hounding me for a front row seat at a shuttle launch?"

"That's right," Fallon said, his heart rate rising.

"Guess what I've got in my hand."

"I can't imagine."

"One firing room badge, VIP visitor, the best seat in

the house."

"That's great. When?"

"December nineteenth, Atlantis. Can you make it?"

Fallon chuckled. "Are you kidding? I'll be there with bells on."

A knock on the door pulled him away from the phone call. "One moment," he said to Carlton and covered the mouthpiece with the palm of his hand. "Yes?"

The door came open. An airman poked his head in. "Sorry to interrupt, sir. There's a woman at the main gate looking for Ray Crawford."

"Who is she?"

"His wife."

"Really?"

A siren wailed from down the road. "The lieutenant went to get her."

Fallon frowned. "Did he have to use the damn siren?"

"I told him not to, sir."

"When she arrives, show her in."

The door closed. "Sorry, Carlton," Fallon said into the phone. "Something's come up here. I have to go."

"No problem. See you on the nineteenth."

"I'll be there."

The phone clicked, but Fallon hesitated to put the receiver down, his mind returning to the Vietnam War. In those days, he was a captain, a Mission Specialist with an eye for finding enemy targets. He'd flown many B-52 missions over Hanoi with Carlton Nash, one of the best bombardiers in the squadron. The bombing runs went day and night until the last one, the one Fallon would never forget...the night he'd found himself in the hands of God.

Swallowing, he hung up the phone. Right now, he had a new problem: Ray Crawford's wife. Problem was, Ray didn't have a wife. Fallon picked up the golden staff, ran his fingers over the finely carved eagle-head handle, and wondered how he could turn her unexpected visit to his advantage.

***

Ten minutes later, after an ear-shattering ride in the jeep, Kate sauntered into Colonel Fallon's office. He was sitting behind a massive desk. A few cushy chairs were set in a semicircle in front of it, and she noticed the wood-paneled walls were plastered with pictures of old planes, jets, and groups of men in gray flight suits gathered together, shoulder to shoulder. Behind the desk, an American flag and an Air Force Security Police seal adorned the wall. The air held a faint scent of cigar smoke.

Fallon stood and offered her a handshake. His grip was firm but gentle. In his left hand, he held a golden walking staff with an eagle-head handle. "Mrs. Crawford. Please have a seat."

Approaching a chair in front of his desk, she searched his eyes for any clue to what might be on his mind. She thought she was good at reading men's intentions by looking into their eyes. In her profession, that talent had been necessary for her survival. The Colonel made it easy for her to study his eyes now, as they were locked on her while she sat down. A humming air conditioner in the window was the only sound.

The Colonel was an imposing man, baldheaded and thick-chested. The light blue shirt of his uniform was neatly pressed and adorned with multi-colored ribbons. He wore thin-framed reading glasses low on the bridge of his nose. A big ring of keys was clipped to his belt. With the golden staff, he looked impressive and ritzy. His eyes glittered with curiosity. "What brings you all the way out here?" he asked and sat in his chair.

"I'm looking for my husband and daughter, Ray and Lisa Crawford. Ray lived and worked at Atomtech, and Lisa may have been there with him."

The Colonel picked up a black report folder from his desk and opened it. "A terrible thing... The bad news is in here: thirty seven dead, ninety two wounded." He thumbed the pages. "The good news is Ray Crawford was not among them...nor was Lisa."

Kate put her hand on her heart. "Oh, thank God."

Colonel Fallon tossed the folder down, stood, and walked to the window, the one with the air conditioning unit. The golden staff thudded on the floor with each step. He looked out to the desert. "You realize, of course, I didn't have to give you this information myself." He turned and pointed the golden staff at the black folder. "Briggs has a list just like that one."

"I don't understand," Kate said, keeping her voice calm.

His eyes hardened. "I've another reason for seeing you personally."

Stiffening, Kate took a quick breath. "What do you want?"

"You're looking for your husband in the wrong place," he said matter-of-factly. "That tells me you don't know Ray Crawford resigned from Atomtech nearly a year ago. It means you haven't been in contact with him for a long time."

Kate sighed, keeping her cool. "I've been out of the country on business."

He looked her up and down. "What kind of business?"

Thinking quickly, she replied, "Top secret stuff for the government. I'm not at liberty to say."

"So you like a little espionage, huh?"

Kate swallowed. He wasn't supposed to buy into this line of bullshit, but she nodded anyway.

He sat on the corner of his desk and propped the golden staff between his knees. His eyebrows arched. "My guess is you're not his wife...at least, not now. Am I right?"

"Well, I was his wife, a long time ago. But I really

need to find him."

"Why?"

"It's personal. Where is he?"

Fallon didn't say anything, but his glaring eyes told her he wasn't satisfied with that answer. After a moment, he stood. "Have a nice day, Mrs. Crawford."

"But you haven't told me were to find my husband."

He tapped the staff on the floor. "You're not being straight with me. What do you expect?"

"Okay," she said, thinking the Colonel had nothing to gain by helping her. "I want to get my family back, all right?"

"How did you lose them in the first place?"

Kate lowered her gaze. "It's a long story." She sniffled then showed him one of her meekest smiles. "Will you help me?"

With piercing eyes, he stared at her for a long moment. "If I tell you where you can find Ray and your daughter, will you do something for me?"

She perked up. "Of course, anything. Just tell me where they are."

He grinned. "It's all very simple."

"Really?"

"Your ex-husband has been playing around with atomic particles, doing experiments that go beyond ethical restraints."

"Don't tell me," Kate said, frowning. "The 13th Power?"

"How did you know?"

"That's all he ever talked about. Bor-ring."

"Maybe to you, but Walter Devin told me how dangerous it was, something about global disintegration. He'd tried to derail the experiments himself, and someone retaliated by attacking Atomtech."

"It was horrible out there." Kate shuddered.

"It'll take six months to clean up the mess, but if it's

the last thing I do, I'm going to find out who murdered those people." He was pointing at the black folder. "And I think Dr. Curtis knows who did it."

She leaned back and crossed her slender legs. "Why not bring the *doctor* in for questioning?"

"It's not that easy. The CIA has him in custody. They won't let me near him."

"And Ray?"

"He's on his own. I fear he'll try to conduct the experiments without Curtis. That's where I need you to come in."

She was completely lost on his meaning. "What can I do?"

"Keep an eye on him for me. If he even talks about the 13th Power, let me know."

Kate fidgeted in her chair. "Don't you have your own people for that kind of thing?"

He shook his head. "I had to pull out my security police and terminate our investigation."

"Why?"

"There were some jurisdictional concerns. I tried to get the Pentagon to fund a private eye, or at least some lousy phone taps, but they turned me down. There's no budget for it."

"So you want me to stick my nose into Ray's business? Hell, it's going to be hard enough just to get him to talk to me much less let me in on what he's doing."

"You've got to get him to open up to you. If he doesn't, we could all die."

Kate scowled. "Yeah, right."

"I know it seems farfetched, but Walter Devin was adamant: the 13th Power is dangerous. It could destroy the world. So what do you say, do we have a deal?"

Colonel Fallon had a look of desperation in his eyes, as if he really believed what Devin had told him. But how could she help him? Why would she even want to try? She had enough problems of her own.

A minute went by, maybe two. The air conditioner hummed, and Fallon stared at Kate as she pondered her answer. “What if I say no?”

He shrugged. “No problem. You walk out of here no worse off than you were when you came in, still wondering where Ray and your daughter are.” His eyes didn’t flinch.

That was unacceptable. She was so close to finding her family. To leave empty handed would be the end of her. She let out a deep breath. “I’ll do what I can.”

“I have your word on that?”

She nodded. “Where are they?”

“Solartech Labs in Simi Valley, California. Lisa has a place in Santa Barbara, but she spends most of her time with her father.” Fallon handed her his card. “Call me if he’s messing around with the 13th Power.”

She took the card and slipped it inside her bra, on old habit she’d picked up hustling businessmen in Vegas. “I’ll need some money.”

At that, he turned his back on her. “Perhaps you didn’t understand me. We’re on a tight budget around here. You’re on your own.”

“But...”

“Good luck, Mrs. Crawford.”

She left Colonel Fallon’s office in a daze. Lieutenant Briggs drove her back to her Chevy parked at the main gate. After starting the engine, she drove away from Indian Springs and turned the air conditioning up full blast. The bleak landscape made her long for the bright lights of Las Vegas, the dimly lit bars where men couldn’t wait to part with their money, and the stuffy motel rooms where deals were made and lives were ruined.

It all seemed so simple compared to her mission for Colonel Fallon, the weight of which fell heavy on her shoulders. The fate of the world was now hanging on the back of a cokehead, a woman who prostituted herself for a quick fix, a mother who had abandoned her daughter. She wanted to cast it off, but she couldn't. Nervously, she lit a cigarette, thinking how she had to convince Ray and Lisa to forgive her, how they had to take her back. Everything teetered on her success or failure.

Her throat was desert dry. As she rummaged through her purse for a mint, her wallet fell open on the seat. In the money pocket, there were only a few loose twenties and a couple of ones, all that was left of her *walking money* from prison. It wasn't enough to buy a plane ticket to California, much less rent another car, or purchase new clothes and meals and more cigarettes. Fallon and his tight budget wasn't any help. Then she realized there was only one solution to her problem, a very dangerous remedy.

It was in Las Vegas.

She would have to call in her marker...on Willy.

Chapter Twenty-Eight

SOMEWHERE OFF THE LAS VEGAS STRIP in a sleazy motel, the soft glow of daylight seeped through a chink in the blinds. Jasmine sat up on the bed and moved her bleary gaze around the disheveled room. She was alone, but the implications of that hadn't registered yet. The air tasted of stale cigarette smoke, and the crumpled sheets smelled of liquor and semen. Chills rippled through her naked body as she licked the inside of her parched mouth. A sickness churned in her stomach. "Oh, God, not again," she said in a scratchy voice.

When a chip of mirror on the nightstand came into focus, a wave of relief poured over her. There was one line left, one for the road. Trembling, she fumbled with a straw and drew the line of cocaine up her nose, then dropped the mirror and fell back onto the bed. Her small breasts rose and fell with each deliberate breath as she awaited the full kick of the drug. Slowly, she rolled her head to the side and saw the dresser and the clock through the fog in her mind. It was past noon.

Suddenly, a tingling sensation rushed through her brain, and she sat up with a jerk. "Oh, my God." It was past noon. Sniffing and rubbing her nose, she shifted her eyes around the room, but only dark shadows stared back from the corners. He was gone. Her trick had slipped out during the night, sometime after she'd passed out from all the whiskey and cocaine. He'd wanted to drink and screw all night, and now she was late. Willy was going to be pissed.

Stumbling through the room, she found her bra and panties wadded up on a chair. Her white high-heel shoes were there, too, and her slinky red dress was hanging on the bedpost. She lifted it and gasped when she saw that the thin gold strap of her purse was gone.

Fighting hysteria, she dropped to her knees and crawled on the floor, looking under the bed and behind the nightstand. But her purse wasn't there, either. Terror raced through her mind. The trick had taken her money. No wonder he wanted to party all night: she got loaded...he got laid and paid. She had no idea how she was going to explain it to Willy.

The door burst open with a bang. Bright sunlight poured into the room. Still on her knees, she raised her hand over her eyes and squinted toward the dark silhouette now standing in the doorway. He wore baggy black pants, a loose white shirt, and a felt hat on his head. Long shaggy hair hung down to his collar. She grabbed the smelly sheet off the bed and covered herself just as he kicked the door shut. "There you are, bitch."

"Willy...please, I'm sorry." Her head was spinning. "I lost track of time."

He stood over her now. She kept her head down and closed her eyes so hard she saw colored swirls.

"How many times have I warned you?"

"But I..."

He took a handful of her hair and yanked her head back, forcing her to look up at his olive-skinned face. His eyes were narrow slits of anger. "What took you so long?"

"I had a bad night, Willy. Please."

He slapped her across the face. "Where's my money, Jasmine?"

She gasped, her face stinging, horror swelling in her stomach. "I'm sorry. It...it was an accident. I must've passed out. My trick took my purse. Everything's gone."

"What?" He let loose of her hair and shoved her head down to the carpet.

She sobbed over his black, pointy-toed boots. Then she heard the clink of his belt buckle and the sound of leather slipping through the loops of his pants. Every muscle in her body tightened. "Oh God, no, Willy, please don't."

***

Kate turned the Chevy onto the Las Vegas Strip, which was snarled with traffic, as usual. Droves of tourists choked the sidewalks. They moved along like cattle, an unnatural procession of humanity.

She hit the brakes when the taxi in front of her stopped suddenly. The driver laid on his horn and cursed out the window at some guy in a green Ford who flipped him the bird. She took the last drag on her cigarette. Las Vegas hadn't changed a bit.

Crushing the butt in the ashtray, she exhaled and clicked the air conditioner up a notch. The afternoon desert sun beat down relentlessly. Heat waves radiated off the pavement. It must have been a hundred and ten degrees out there. Traffic moved a little, the taxi blew a red light, and Kate braked again.

Idling at the intersection, she looked over the crowd scurrying by in the crosswalk: young people, old people, singles and couples. They all seemed to be in a hurry. She also saw a few overdressed businessmen with wandering eyes. They were easy to spot, the ones who had left their wives at home. Some were looking for the hundred-dollar *slam bam, thank you ma'am* in a cheap motel. Others were willing to plop down five hundred bucks for a full evening of uninhibited bliss. And some, for two thousand dollars, could have an all-nighter: take her to dinner and a show, take her up to their hotel room, and take her any way they wanted.

She lit another cigarette and toyed with an idea. Maybe she should find her own tricks, make some fast bucks, and forget about collecting any money from Willy. She inhaled smoke and realized she had to stay away from that scene: selling her body, doing dope and getting bombed, even though her insides still ached for the stuff. Finding Willy was the only way. He owed her a lot, but the thought of facing him made her feel sick to her stomach.

But first she'd have to find him. There were a few places she thought of to check, like maybe he still hung out at the Red Lace Saloon, or perhaps Danny's Café. She could always ask the working girls on the Strip tonight. Someone there would probably know where she could find him.

The light turned green, and she was about to press the gas pedal when she caught the sudden motion of a woman running into the crosswalk with no regard for the red pedestrian light. Horns honked, and tires screeched, but the woman kept coming, staggering, dashing wildly through the intersection. She was wearing a red dress and clutched a pair of white high-heel shoes in one hand. Suddenly, she stumbled, and with a bang, she fell against the fender of a Lincoln in the next lane, and then spun around and slumped over the hood of Kate's rented Chevy. Her arms were outstretched, and the shoes were still in her trembling hand. Kate gasped at the sight of the woman's black and swollen eyes. Willy's threatening words came back: *"Tricks don't like whores with black eyes."*

"Help me," the woman said. "Please. Help me."

Horns blared.

Kate clutched the steering wheel, her heart suddenly pounding. The hooker sprawled on her hood looked like she'd had a really bad night: a trick gone mad or a barroom brawl, or worse, she'd pissed off her pimp. Kate scanned the intersection quickly and saw nothing unusual, a few gawkers and tourists keeping their distance. There was no pimp chasing this woman. No one even seemed to care about her plight.

"Help me."

"Just great!" Kate threw open the door. Desert heat hit her like a club.

"Hey. Get out of the way," the man in the car behind her shouted.

Ignoring him and all the horns, she ran to the woman and pulled her off the hood. Her face was streaked with tears. "What's your name, honey?"

"Jasmine." She coughed.

"You live around here?"

She nodded.

"Get in."

Ten minutes later, with Jasmine tucked under her arm, Kate opened an apartment door. The place was dingy, stuffy, and smelled like cat piss. Her stomach turned sour as she stepped inside. By the faint light coming through the curtains, she saw a shambled room cluttered with beer bottles, greasy Chinese food cartons, pizza boxes, and newspapers scattered all over the floor. Overflowing ashtrays adorned the coffee table. She could hear a faucet dripping in the kitchen, and from down the hall, a toilet in need of repair hissed.

"I know it's a mess," Jasmine said. "Maid's day off."

Kate helped her to the couch, a brown and tattered thing. She cleared away dirty laundry, and Jasmine slumped into the lumpy cushions.

"We need some air in here." Kate walked to the window, pulled back the curtains, and lifted a cracked pane. "Whew." It wasn't much, but it would have to do.

Shuffling through the mess, Kate scouted the kitchen and down the hall to a single bedroom, and then peered into the bathroom with the noisy toilet. The rest of the place was just as disheveled. But it all looked familiar, the way she'd lived before, when Willy had control of her life. Cocaine and booze had a way of changing her priorities. Things like cooking, laundry, dishes, and even basic housecleaning were of no importance. Neither were husbands and daughters. Only the next hit, the next fix, and the next trick mattered.

In the kitchen, she found a towel, soaked it in cold water, and took it to Jasmine. She was lying down now, her head resting on the ragged armrest of the couch. Kate sat next to her and placed the towel on her forehead. “There. How’s that?”

“It hurts.” Jasmine looked up. “What’s your name?”

“Kate,” she said, taking note of the glaze in Jasmine’s bloodshot eyes, her thin, colorless lips and pale cheeks. “How old are you, Jasmine?”

“Twenty-six, why?”

“You don’t look a day under fifty.”

Jasmine turned her head away. “Considering the way I feel, I’ll take that as a compliment.”

“Who did this to you?”

“My old man.”

Kate frowned. “Husband or boyfriend?”

Jasmine shook her head a little. “You wouldn’t understand.”

Kate patted her shoulder, being careful of the bruises. “Must’ve been your pimp then.”

Surprise came over Jasmine’s face. “Is it that obvious, I mean, do I look—”

“I knew right away. Been there, done that, as they say.”

“Really...you?”

“Better believe it, honey.”

Jasmine sat up, took the towel off her forehead, and wrapped her arms around Kate. “I should have known,” she said with tears. “We take care of our own kind. No one else would have done anything for me out there.”

Kate, surprised at Jasmine's embrace, held her gently.

"Men." She'd said it as if the word tasted bad in her mouth. "It's all their fault. They scoff at us in the daylight, when wives and girlfriends are around, or bosses and clients. Whores and sluts they call us then. But in the middle of the night when they're lonely and horny, they come around calling us baby, talk sweet and flash their money. And we call them tricks instead of the pricks they really are. Last one stole my purse."

"So your pimp beat you up for losing his money?"

"That's not the half of it."

"Then what?"

Jasmine got a sassy look on her face, reached into a drawer on the coffee table and pulled out a folded white envelope.

Kate's mouth went suddenly dry.

"He was pissed off about this, too. I get the stuff from my tricks, sort of a tip, you know." She cleared junk off a corner of the table and dumped white powder out of the envelope. "I'm supposed to turn it over to my pimp. That's his rule." She took a razor blade from the drawer and cut four lines in the cocaine. From the clutter on the table she picked up a straw and offered it to Kate. "I don't share with pimps. That's *my* rule."

Kate's heart hammered. She sucked on her lower lip, her wide eyes shifting back and forth between the straw and those magnificent lines of cocaine. It had been more than three and a half years, and now, the old thirst for the stuff flared up inside her again. It would be so easy to satisfy that craving. "Really...I can't."

"It's all right."

Slowly, she took the straw with trembling fingers. "I really shouldn't," she said without conviction.

Jasmine smiled. "Go ahead. Two for you, two for me, and none for Willy."

Kate gasped. The air in the room turned to mud, thick

and unyielding to the will of her lungs as she realized it was Willy who had beaten Jasmine. Somewhere along the line he had started making good on his old threats. He'd become more dangerous than ever. A knot twisted in her stomach, tight as a noose around her neck. She knew she'd have to deal with him, once and for all, and the terror of that confrontation raged in her mind. How could she find the courage to face him?

Head buzzing, she focused on the lines of cocaine, white as snow, clean and pure. What she wanted and needed ached in her soul. Then she thought about Ray and Lisa, Colonel Fallon, and the 13th Power. She weighed her priorities and, with a racing heartbeat, threw her shoulders back and held in a long breath. But it was no use. "Oh God."

Leaning over the coffee table, she put the straw to her nostril. Two lines of cocaine disappeared in an instant. Through narrow slits in her eyelids, she looked at Jasmine. "Tell Willy I've come to get my money."

Chapter Twenty-Nine

SOMETIME BEFORE DAWN, KATE awoke. Her head pounded, her ears rang. A sour taste lingered in her mouth, and her stomach felt sick. She opened her eyes, just a tiny crack, and saw bed sheets. She was lying face down. A wave of panic jolted her. This feeling was too familiar: waking up in a strange place, the fear, and the uncertainty.

She moved her head just enough to see that she was alonc in the bed. But someone had been there. She could feel it between her legs, an aching sensation. It had been there before, many times. Some tricks liked their sex rough.

A sudden anger flared up inside, and she cursed herself for letting this happen again. Searching through the fog in her mind, she tried to remember what had happened earlier. An image of Jasmine with a bottle of Jack Daniels took form. They'd started drinking and talking, and she recalled telling Jasmine about Lisa and Ray and her mission for Colonel Fallon to save the world. Jasmine laughed, and they did more cocaine. They laughed some more, mostly at themselves. It was just girl talk between two whores: one old, one young. They were both Willy's property: one past and one present. Right now, that didn't seem so funny.

"Party 'til you drop," Jasmine had said. They were so much alike. But sometime during the night the party went blank in her mind: too much booze and too much cocaine. Time had slipped into nothingness...another black out.

Sitting up in the bed, she hugged her naked body and scanned the dark room. Long shadows stood in the corners and fell across the floor. Beyond an open door, she saw the dim glean of a toilet. Her bladder responded with a sharp pain. She pulled herself out of bed, and on unstable legs, stumbled into the bathroom and turned on the light. The sudden brightness made her eyeballs ache.

Squinting, she took in the room. A razor rested on the edge of the sink, an old style straight razor that opened up like a jackknife. That, and the cologne bottles lining the shelf below the mirror, told her this was a man's bathroom. The place was clean and pleasant, not like the mess in Jasmine's apartment.

Kate sat on the toilet and peed and fought to recall what had happened last night. How did she get here? Jasmine must've set her up with a wealthy trick, but Kate couldn't remember, and it frustrated her. After flushing the toilet, she walked to the doorway, pausing to steady herself on the doorframe. Her shadow fell across the bed, distorting the curve of her hips and the length of her arms. As she took another step, the light from the bathroom suddenly invaded the far corner of the bedroom, revealing a naked man sitting in a wicker chair.

She gasped.

Shaggy hair hung to his shoulders, and big round eyes glowered at her. A chill skittered up her spine. Sitting there naked like that, his skinny frame looked like bronze in the light from the bathroom. His penis lay limp to one side, resting on his inner thigh. He didn't move, just sat there staring.

"Willy?"

"What is the matter, Kate?" he said with a harsh Spanish accent. "You could not live without your Willy?"

A surge of panic welled up inside as she realized he'd been sitting there watching her the whole time. She thought to run for the door, but she couldn't go anywhere without her clothes. She was trapped, but she had to be tough. She couldn't let him see her fear. Slowly, she walked to the bed and set her knees on it first, then let her body down to the sheets, propping her head up on one elbow. "How did you find me?"

Willy snorted.

"What does it matter? We are together again."

"What did you do to Jasmine?"

"The two of you were smashed. She said you came to see me."

"I didn't mean like this."

"Kate, you do not know any other way." He cackled. "But I am glad you are back."

She looked around the room. "Where am I?"

Willy rolled his big eyeballs. "Do you like my new place?"

"How did I get here?"

"Oh, Kate," Willy said, grinning. "You followed me like a lost puppy dog. All I had to do was promise you more of the stuff you love so much. You went flat on your back for it, just like old times. You are a whore, Kate. A loser. Always have been, always will be."

She glared at him, denying the truth in his words, but she knew he was right. She had showed him her weakness, and he had taken advantage of it. Now she didn't know what to do. As denial raced through her mind, she hardened herself against the truth, sat up straight, and pulled the sheet over her breasts. Her stomach churned with that sickness again. What she wanted most was another hit of cocaine to make her feel better. She knew Willy could get her what she craved. All she had to do was obey him, pull a few tricks, and be his old lady. He'd take care of her. She suddenly caught herself on that thought. Jasmine's apartment flashed through her mind and the way things were when Willy had control. The recollection made her want to vomit, but she swallowed the bile that rose to the back of her throat. “I didn’t come back to be with you, Willy.”

“You could have fooled me.”

“I just got out of prison, for Christ’s sake. Jasmine and I cut loose a little. That’s all.”

Willy jumped up and leaped onto the bed, landing on all fours, his penis dangling. Nose to nose, his rancid breath hit her like a sharp slap in the face. “I can see it in your eyes, Kate. You need me.”

“I need my money, Willy.” It came out without thinking.

His nostrils flared, and he rose up on his knees. “Bitch.” He hit her in the mouth with his fist.

Her head popped back. She fell face-first to the bed, her mind blinking in and out of consciousness, the room spinning.

Then he jumped on top of her and started slugging the back of her head. “You ungrateful bitch.” Each blow made her skull feel like it would explode. Then he took hold of her hair and pulled her head back. “It is going be just like old times, Kate,” he growled into her ear. “We are going to get your daughter back again, too. Oh yeah, I will make you a mother-daughter team. Tricks will pay double for that pleasure. Hell, even I would take a piece of that action.” His words slurred, and drool dripped from the corner of his mouth. “I bet Lisa is even better now than she was back then.” He let go of her hair, shoved her head down, and cackled like a hyena in the night.

A new terror raced through Kate’s mind. The thought of Willy violating her daughter tore into her heart as painfully as if he’d plunged a knife into her chest. She now feared he had done more to Lisa than take pictures and videos.

At that thought, Kate’s bloodstream took a shot of adrenaline. “Bastard,” she shouted, flailing her arms and kicking. Because Willy always got his way, she knew that he had to be stopped, here and now. "You're not going to touch my daughter." Fighting nausea, she pushed herself up on her knees, and with Willy clinging to her back, she rolled over on her side. He fell to the bed, and still hanging onto her, his arm locked around her neck. Pain shot up the back of her skull, and she couldn't get a breath of air.

In panic, she swung her fist around behind her and hit Willy on the inside of his thigh, her wrist just brushing his penis. In that split second, her mind went blank and reflex took over. She slammed her fist into his groin as hard as she could.

Willy let out a guttural scream, a scream that could have come from the depths of hell. He released the chokehold on her neck and grabbed his crotch.

Gulping air, she rolled over and sat up as Willy writhed on the bed, his hands shoved between his legs.

"Damn you!" he yelled, spraying spit.

Kate leaped from the bed and ran for the bathroom, but Willy was right behind her, cussing. As she tried to shut the door, he threw his body against it, sending her flying backwards. She slammed into the sink and landed on the toilet. In an instant, he was on her, swinging his fists. Pain and a wave of dizziness came over her. Blood gushed from her nose. Falling, she reached out instinctively for something to grab on to. She felt the edge of the porcelain sink. She grabbed. The straight razor was suddenly in her clenched fist. Her body slammed to the floor.

Willy bent over her, slugged her again, but driven by a subconscious will to survive, she instinctively lashed out with the razor. It found the side of Willy's neck.

He let out a yelp.

Once, twice, three more times she slashed at him, his chest, and his arm, which he had thrown up as a shield. He hollered in panic and slapped a hand on the gushing gash to his neck. Stumbling backward, he glared at her with wild eyes. "You bitch!"

Without thinking, her eyes went to the part of him she hated most. It hung there, the organ he'd used to violate her young daughter, and terrifying images of that despicable act exploded in Kate's brain. One more time, she lashed out, but this time the razor sharp steel sliced through his flesh, cut his penis like so much hanging meat. Blood came out of it in a crimson torrent.

Willy fell backward, staggered out of the bathroom door, and landed on his back on the bed, holding his crotch and his neck as blood spurted between his fingers and spewed all over the sheets. "You goddamn whore."

Gasping and shaking, she pulled herself up from the blood-soaked floor and stood in the doorway, the bloody razor in her hand, still dripping, and her eyes on Willy's torment. Her body was shaking. She dropped the razor as if it were a hot coal and pressed her back against the doorframe, now fighting panic and unsure of where to go or what to do next.

Willy snarled. "I will kill you for this." With one hand clutching his bleeding groin, he clawed his way off the bed and stumbled to the dresser, his face contorted with pain, his naked body streaked with blood. "You are dead." He pulled on a drawer, and it fell to the floor spilling out underwear, socks, several wads of money wrapped in rubber bands, and a black gun.

Heart pounding, she searched for the bedroom door, which was on the other side of the room. The only way out was over Willy, who was now reaching for the gun on the floor.

"No!" Kate lunged at him, knocking him down as he bent over and picked up the gun. He landed on his back. The gun was in his right hand, his crotch in his left hand, and blood was spewing everywhere. Fueled by panic and rage, she jumped on him and sat on his stomach, which pinned his left arm under her. At the same time she grabbed his right wrist with both hands and fought for control of the gun. But even with only one arm free, the skinny man was powerful. Enraged like a wild beast, he jerked and twisted underneath her, fighting as if the devil possessed him. Hot blood spit from his wounds and showered her in a crimson mist.

Willy growled as his bloody finger slipped into the trigger guard. "I will see you in hell."

"This is hell, Willy." She tried to wrench the gun away, but he was too strong. He showed his teeth, and in spite of her grip on his wrist, he managed to turn the gun barrel toward her head.

Bang!

A blast and flash of light sent a wave of terror rolling through her guts. Ceiling plaster rained down, and the smell of gunpowder stung the air. Gritting her teeth, she desperately tried to keep the gun pointed away from her.

Willy snarled like a mad dog and spit, and again the gun banged. Wind from the round blew past her ear. She stifled a scream. Blood was dripping from her nose and mingling with the blood oozing from Willy's wounds. But she didn't dare let go of her tenuous hold on his wrist. She hung on with every bit of strength she could find in her body.

The gun wavered in the air like a cobra reared up to strike. She thought there had to be a way to stop him from firing it again. Frantically, she grabbed Willy's finger and pried it off the trigger. In response, he exerted more pressure, and she knew that if she weakened or let go, his finger would hit the trigger with full force and the gun would discharge. And even with all of her weight on his arm, his elbow remained locked. The gun barrel pointed at her face. She grimaced and held on as he kicked and cursed and tried to wrench his left arm out from under her. The life and death struggle went on forever.

"You should not have come back," he muttered just as he started shaking, a little at first, then more and more. His face turned a ghostly white. Gasping, he fought with less fury now, probably weakened by the horrific loss of blood. She didn't think he could hold on much longer. Keeping pressure on his arm, she felt him slowly succumb to his injuries. His elbow finally buckled. Now she was able to bend his wrist all the way back until the gun barrel pointed under his chin.

His eyes popped wide open. "Screw you, bitch."

"You'll never touch my daughter again." She let go of his finger, the one he had over the trigger.

Bang!

***

A short while later, Kate was sitting on a velour couch, her legs tucked underneath her and a blanket pulled over her bare shoulders. Her skin felt gritty, encrusted with Willy's dried blood, as well as her own. The clothes she'd worn yesterday had been on the floor at the foot of the bed. They too were blood soaked and unsuitable to wear.

She lit a cigarette and looked around the cavernous living room. A huge fireplace with a wooden mantel skirted one wall, and oil paintings of meadows and mountains and a few nudes hung on the other walls. Crystal lamps sat on polished end tables, and plush chairs were set around the room, chairs that matched the couch, and the coffee table matched the end tables. Willy had done well for himself while she was away.

Men's voices came from the bedroom, just down the hall. Inhaling smoke, she saw camera flashes pulsing like strobe lights in the shadows. She'd overheard the police calling it a crime scene in there. Officers scurried in and out of the house, conducting their investigation. She was waiting for them to interrogate her further.

At first she thought it would have been much easier to grab the money and run, but she knew she wouldn't have gotten far. The cops would have figured it out eventually, with fingerprints and forensic evidence. They would have thought she'd murdered Willy, and they'd have hunted her down, branded her a killer, and sentenced her to death by lethal injection. So instead of taking the easy way, she'd called 911 and told them what had happened, after all, it was self-defense. She didn't do anything wrong. She had nothing to fear.

Two detectives emerged from the hall and walked toward her. She felt a chill as her eyes shifted between them. Earlier, one had said his name was Carter. He had compassionate eyes. The other man never said his name. His eyes were cold.

"Did Willy do that to you?" Carter asked.

Kate took a drag on her cigarette, exhaled and pointed to the split in her lip. "It took a while for my nose to stop bleeding." She indicated a handful of bloodstained tissues beside her, then lifted her chin and touched her throat. "It hurts when I swallow." The paramedics had told her she'd have some nasty bruises, and that the knots on the back of her head would go away in a few days. Clutching the blanket, she tightened it around her neck and started shaking. She was beaten and bloody, but at least she was alive.

Carter blew out a breath. "I'd say it's a case of self-defense."

The cold-eyed detective turned to Carter. "Come on Lieutenant, you're not falling for that cockamamie story. She's a hooker, an ex-con, for Chrissake, fresh out of the joint. She came back to kill the guy. I say we book her. Murder One."

At that, she lowered her head, knowing full well they'd never believe her. Case closed. Lock her up. The whore deserved nothing. She had been so stupid to let that craving take over again. It had gotten her into one hell of a mess. She'd let herself down and everyone else too: Ray,

Lisa, Colonel Fallen, and the whole damn world.

"Kate?"

A familiar voice. She looked to the door. "Oh, thank God."

Jasmine rushed in wearing blue jeans and a white t-shirt. Today she didn't look like a hooker. She looked like a college student, or even the girl next door, but with black eyes that made her face look raccoonish.

"Oh, Kate. Oh, my God. Look what he did to you." Jasmine dropped onto the couch and hugged her. "I came as soon as I heard."

"I killed him, Jasmine," Kate said with tears flooding her eyes.

"Murdered him is more like it," the cold detective said. "You damn near cut his pecker off and blew his brains out."

"It wasn't like that." Kate took a drag on her cigarette. "He tried to kill me. Don't you people get it?"

"Look, lady..."

"That's enough," Carter said, cutting his partner short. "Go find some fingerprints to dust."

The cold detective stalked away.

Jasmine patted Kate's back. "He just doesn't understand," she whispered and hugged her again.

Carter got a notepad out of his pocket. "What do you know about all this, Jasmine?" He wrote something.

She turned toward the detective. "Willy was brutal. Look what he did to me." She pointed to her black eyes. "And look what he did to Kate. The world is better off without that bastard."

Carter stepped forward, inspected Jasmine's wounds. "Why did he do that to you?"

"He mugged me," she said in a voice reeking of sarcasm. "He took all my money."

"Did you file a report?"

She took the stub of cigarette from Kate, helped

herself to the last drag and put it out. "I'll do it when I'm feeling better."

A uniformed policeman came into the room with both hands full of money, the bundles of cash that had fallen out of Willy's drawer. "Five grand," he said, dropped the blood-splotched bills on the coffee table then walked away.

Carter picked up one of the bundles. "This the money he stole from you?"

Jasmine nodded.

Kate stiffened and wondered what Jasmine was up to. That wasn't her money.

"How did you get it?" Carter asked, with raised eyebrows.

"Stashed it," Jasmine said. "A little at a time. How else?"

The detective put his notebook away. "You know, my grandmother used to keep all her cash under her mattress. Always said she didn't believe in banks. Funny thing about that. The house burned down one night. Oh, she got out all right, but the money, well, it was destroyed along with the rest of the place." He tossed the bundle on the coffee table with the others.

"What are you going to do with all my money?" Jasmine asked.

Carter folded his arms over his chest. "Come on, now, just who do you think you're kidding? I was born in the dark but not last night. We both know he didn't steal that money from you, but I'm sure he owed it to you, one way or another. I know what the two of you are...what you do for a living..."

"Did," Kate interjected.

"And I also know how guys like Willy operate, how they treat women, how they hold on to their money. And we've had our eyes on that sleazeball in there for quite some time." He pointed toward the bedroom. "Whether you know it or not, he's no small fish. He comes from a whole family of bad blood. But what I'd like to know is how the two of you got mixed-up with him in the first place."

"We made some bad choices," Kate said. "But don't you see, we could never get free of him. He kept all our money. He kept our heads all screwed up."

"We need that money," Jasmine said. "It's ours."

"And what would you do with it?" he asked. "Buy more dope to put up your nose? Blow it on booze?"

Jasmine was quick to answer. "I'd get the hell out of this town, that's for sure. I'd go back home to Virginia."

"And I'd find my daughter," Kate said. "In California."

Carter knelt down on one knee. "If it were up to me, I'd let you have it, but it's not." His eyes went to Jasmine. "Follow us down to the station. I'll give you a property claim form to fill out. Then we'll see what the captain has to say about it. Fair enough?"

"But what about me?" Kate asked. "It was self-defense...you said so yourself."

He looked at her with caring eyes. "That's what I'm going to tell the DA. I'm sure he'll go along with it."

"Do I have to go to jail?"

"Only until we sort everything out. Besides, I want the doc to look you over."

"Then I'll be free to go?"

As Carter acknowledged with a bob of his head, a team of men with *CORONER* on their jackets rolled a gurney out of the hallway. He stood, walked to them, and started talking.

Kate stared at the shiny black body bag on the gurney. "Willy's taking his last trip," she said to Jasmine.

"And you're going to get your money back," Jasmine whispered.

"How do you figure?"

She winked. "I know the captain. He's one of my regulars. You can have half the money. I hope you find your daughter all right."

"Jasmine..." Kate said with more tears. "Twenty-five hundred dollars?" It wasn't nearly what Willy had owed her, but it was a miracle just the same. "I can't thank you enough."

"You don't have to. We take care of our own kind, remember?"

As the gurney rolled out the front door, the coroner handed Carter a clipboard. "Sign right here. One dead body. Willy Herrera."

Chapter Thirty

AT THE HACIENDA IN CONCORDIA, Mexico, hidden deep in the jungles of the Sierra Madre, Miguel Herrera paced the hardwood floor. A ceiling fan whirred above his head, and he could hear the guards' footsteps patrolling the balcony outside his window. He scanned pictures on the wall, family portraits from the old country: his grandfather's family, and his father and mother, and photographs of his wife, Maria, and their seven boys, all smiling. A crucifix hung there too, Jesus giving his life to save the Herrera family gathered around him.

Miguel stiffened. The family was now broken, shattered like glass and scattered into the winds of heaven. His heart ached for the loss of his sons: Carlos, his oldest, Ricardo, Philip, and now Willy, his youngest.

"Oh, Maria," he moaned and fell to one knee, his eyes uplifted to her picture on the wall. "I have failed you." Tears fell without restraint. "Since that day you brought Willy into this world and passed onto the Lord, I promised to take care of our sons, make them great, feared among the people, and mighty next to God." Clutching the silver bear on his necklace, he raised it to the image of his wife. "This gift of yours I have kept near to my heart. It has given me strength and courage over the years. Now, it shall lead us into battle against those who have torn us apart. The power of the bear shall wreak vengeance on our enemies...smite them from the earth as the wind would sweep the chaff from the wheat. I shall not rest until they have all perished." He put the silver bear to his lips. "Mother of the saints, it is to be this way or I shall die."

***

That afternoon, a breeze swept through the dining room. The dinner table was set with fine china, silk cloth, and silverware that glistened. Miguel and his sons took their usual seats. The aroma of roasted chilies and refried beans wafted from the kitchen where Lila prepared the evening meal. She set a platter of tortillas in front of Miguel.

"Gracias." He selected a tortilla, still steaming hot from the griddle, and glanced at Juan and Pedro. Their young faces were etched with hard lines of anger. They hadn't smiled since Willy's funeral. Miguel sensed their hatred in the air.

Pedro was the ruthless one. He was quick with a knife, and his temper was just as sharp. He'd rather kill a man than argue with him. Juan was more the cold and calculating type. He had a way of curling his upper lip to instill fear in the people. The street vendors were easily intimidated by this. They paid up protection money to him without hesitation.

To his sons, Miguel indicated the stack of tortillas. "Eat. You will need your strength."

Pedro's eyes lit up. "Then you have decided. We will go to America?"

"Simi Valley?" Juan added, that notorious curl forming on his upper lip, showing his teeth.

"I have promised your mother." Miguel scooped a spoonful of beans from the pot Lila had set on the table. "Donardo is checking our connections now. We will find all the killers." He slapped beans on the tortilla. "They will pay for what they have done to this family."

Those who were foolish enough to cross the Herreras had to face Donardo, the bulkiest of the clan. Working the weights had made him into a brute of a man. He found great joy in breaking the ribs of those who owed the business money.

"Who will stay to run the business?" Juan asked. "We are now so few."

"I shall handle things here," Miguel replied. "The killing will be yours to savor."

Pedro reached for the salsa. "We are honored, Father, but are you sure? We are all you have left. Would it not be better to send the Vigil brothers? They are the best assassins for the money."

Miguel balled a fist and slammed it on the table. "No. Carlos would want his brothers to seek revenge...and Ricardo and Philip and Willy...and so would you. We keep this in the family where it belongs. Mother would agree."

Pedro's shoulders slouched. "Yes, Father, we will do Mother proud."

Just then, Donardo came in through the veranda doorway. The only hair on his olive-skinned head grew on his face, a thick black mustache that came down past the corners of his mouth and ended in sharp points below his chin. A blue sleeveless shirt stretched over his thick chest. Biceps bulging, his arms hung at his side as if he were carrying suitcases. Baggy green shorts revealed muscular legs; and he wore leather sandals. There was no grace in his gait. His massive frame caused the wooden floor planks to creak with each step. "You will not believe this, Father." He sat at the table and reached for the platter of tortillas.

"You have news?" Miguel asked.

"There are five killers in all. I've learned that CIA pigs named Craig Stevens and his partner Cisco Mendez killed Carlos in Atlanta." He slapped a spoonful of beans on a tortilla. "We already know of Jonathan Kyles and Melvin Anderson who killed Ricardo and Philip. They have fled to Simi Valley." Donardo shifted his eyes around the table. "Where's the jalapenos? Hey, Lila. We got any jalapenos?"

"Si, Señor Donardo." Lila scurried off to the kitchen.

Donardo rubbed his chin. "Willy's killer was much harder to find. Some of the boys in Las Vegas got a lead on a hooker named Jasmine. They had to beat it out of her, but they got the name before she died."

"Who?" Miguel scowled.

Donardo grabbed the bowl of diced jalapenos Lila had rushed from the kitchen. "Some whore named Kate Crawford."

Miguel's breath hitched. "A woman killed our Willy?"

Pedro pulled his knife. "I will gut her with this."

Juan leaned forward. "There is no honor in dying by a woman's hand, only disgrace. And there is no honor in killing the woman to avenge our little brother."

"This is not about honor," Miguel boomed. "It is about family. She dies like the rest of them." He clutched the silver bear on his necklace and raised it to his sons. "I swore to your mother that we would not fail."

"It will be easy," Donardo said.

"And why is this so?" Miguel asked with raised eyebrows.

Donardo folded his tortilla. "They will all be in Simi Valley: the gringos that killed Ricardo and Philip, the old whore, and the CIA pigs...all of them, Father, in one place. It will be like shooting ducks in a barrel."

Chapter Thirty-One

JANIS HAD HEARD THE WEATHER forecast earlier. A storm was coming in, but right now, sunshine beamed down from the misty California sky. The air over Simi Valley held that subtle nip of autumn, humid but warm enough for the blue t-shirt and tan shorts he'd chosen to wear. Stepping out the back door of Solartech Labs' cafeteria, tray in hand, he stood on the patio deck and looked out over the courtyard and swimming pool, scouting for a place to sit and eat his lunch. Big gold umbrellas shaded round white tables that were arranged on the lawn in a casual manner. Many employees had chosen to eat outside, and the buzz of their conversations electrified the air. Janis headed for a vacant table under a palm tree that swayed lazily in the cool breeze.

After unloading his tray, he started eating his spaghetti and meatballs when the diving board clattered. He looked toward the pool in time to see a tan body and yellow bikini cut the water with hardly a splash. The diver bobbed up to the surface and swam a leisurely breaststroke toward the ladder. He almost choked when he recognized her. Lisa.

He couldn't take his eyes off her as she came out of the pool, her wet body sparkling. She sauntered back to the diving board, dripping water on the pool deck. Each step had all the grace of a Miss America contestant. His pulse went up a notch as he watched her climb the ladder and sashay to the end of the board. Her curves were perfect, he observed, her shoulders square, arms and legs smooth. Inhaling, she looked right at him, smiled, and then dove into the water.

Janis gulped. She put on quite a show. Then he realized her antics were meant especially for him. He thought to shout at her, to tell her to stop flirting with him. It wouldn't do her any good. He'd come back to Simi Valley for Tracy, not her.

When Lisa surfaced, she smiled at him again, making it obvious that she wasn't concerned about Tracy. She paraded back to the diving board, her gleaming eyes on him while he sat in front of his unfinished meal, perplexed as to what to do about her. This time she did a dance on the end of the board, her hips gyrating, her hands clasped behind her head, earning an applause from some of the other diners. She dropped a shoulder strap for Janis and dove into the water. He decided to ignore her and went back to his meal.

Just as he finished the last of his iced tea, the wind started to rise. He popped a mint into his mouth and returned his attention to Lisa who sat quietly on the edge of the pool, her legs dangling in the water. She curled a finger to him.

He blinked and thought he should head back to the executive suites and take a nap. Until Tracy arrived from Washington, there was nothing for him to do around here. Ray was busy playing with his new toy, the transporter. "Flight training," he had said, though Janis thought insanity was more the case.

Or maybe Janis was the crazy one, looking at Lisa, allowing her to tempt him like that. A part of him didn't mind, but with Tracy in his life now, he was immune to Lisa's come-ons. Thinking no harm could come from talking to her, he moved to the edge of the pool and sat with her on the deck. After pulling off his tennis shoes and socks, he put his feet in the cool water next to hers. The sun's heat radiated off her body in sensual waves. He showed her a slight smile. "How have you been?"

"I've missed you, Janis." Her eyes sparkled. "Some days are worse than others." She put her hand on his arm and batted her eyelashes. "And you?"

The sun ducked behind a cloud, chilling the air. Janis rubbed his hands on his knees and arched his back a little. He couldn't let her think for one minute that she might be able to wriggle her way back into his life. Even so, flames of desire flared up in his heart, heating him to the core. He held his breath, hoping to smother the fire. "I didn't sleep much at first."

"Good," she said with a sly smile.

Janis let a minute of silence slip by. "My mother died."

"I'm sorry." She regarded him a moment. "Are you happy, Janis?"

"I'm working on it, but Dr. Curtis keeps interfering."

She scooted closer to him, and as her leg touched his thigh, electricity shot through his body. Warm sunshine reappeared. He felt an urgent need to get away from her.

"You're trembling," Lisa said.

"Guess I caught a sudden chill." He looked into her eyes.

"Hold me, Janis."

Confusion engulfed him, but he pulled her into the crook of his arm anyway. He knew he should've stood and walked away, but he couldn't find it in his heart to treat her that coldly. After all, he had hurt her enough already. He'd seen it in her eyes at the airport, the shock, hurt, and anger, none of which he saw in her eyes right now. He wondered if she had accepted the fact that he and she would never be a couple.

Her hand touched his thigh. She snuggled up close to him, her lips brushing his cheek. "I want you so bad," she whispered.

The electricity turned to lightning bolts. He released her, pushed himself back, and tumbled into the pool, the cool water easing his torment and filling his ears with the sound of bubbles. He heard a splash behind him and realized she'd followed him. She wasn't going to make it easy. He swam off toward the deep end, his eyes burning from the chlorinated water, but his lungs were full of air, and he felt strong.

Beneath him, Lisa glided along, stroking through the water with the grace of a mermaid. Her beauty could not be denied. His imagination started running wild with visions of her naked, visions that he instantly suppressed as he recalled the dream he had on the plane. At the deep end of the pool, he surfaced, took a breath, and grabbed the tiled ledge.

The sun went behind a cloud again, graying the rough surface of the pool. Palm trees whipped in the rising wind.

Lisa surfaced in front of him. Her arms went around his neck, and she pressed her body against his. "Gotcha," she said and kissed him. Her lips were cold, her mouth hot. He found himself wanting to kiss her back, to return the passion, but instead, the instant the thought came, he tore his lips away from hers.

"You still have it for me, Janis. Admit it."

He knew he had to stop this before it got out of hand. "Lisa...I can't."

"Why not?"

"Because of the way I feel about Tracy. You have to understand."

"But what about the way I feel about you?"

He had to make her understand how serious he was. "I asked Tracy to marry me."

Lisa gasped. "No." That look of hurt and anger reappeared in her eyes, like at the airport. "You didn't. You couldn't..."

"Please don't...don't do this to me."

She pushed herself away from him, treading water up to her chin. "Do this to you...?" A wind-driven wave splashed into her mouth. She spit. "Look what you've done to me. All I've ever asked is that you love me, Janis. Nothing else. I'd have given up everything for you. My home, my father, even this California lifestyle you think is so damn important to me. You could have me, Janis, all of me. Just love me, that's all I ever wanted."

"Lisa, listen..."

"But no. You can't. Not you. Not the brilliant mathematician. Somewhere in that calculating, analytical mind of yours you think all the bullshit matters, our ages, our lifestyles, even my father. It's all bullshit, Janis. Love is what matters. When are you going to see that?"

"Lisa..." He reached for her.

She shot him a blue-eyed glare and moved out of his reach.

"It would never work for us," he said softly. "You're too young to see that now."

"And you're too old to take the chance." She spit again, still treading rough water.

Janis blinked. "I know how I feel. I'm just being honest about it. I don't love you like that."

"Like what?"

"To marry you."

Her mouth fell open. "What's wrong with me?"

"Nothing's wrong with you, Lisa. You're a wonderful woman, beautiful and smart," he hesitated, "and well, a bit bull-headed at times."

"Who me?" Her eyes brightened a little.

"Yes, you."

"Any wonder." She swam closer, her wet hair clinging to her cheeks. "I've had to fight for every scrap of affection I ever got. My whole life has been all screwed up, my mother abandoned me, my father sent me away. I want to be loved, Janis. When's it going to be my turn?"

Janis searched her eyes now welling with tears. "It may seem hard to believe right now, but your turn will come. Be patient. Sometimes love comes your way, sometimes it doesn't. It's a bitter fact of life. But one day you'll find the right man, I'm sure, and you'll be happy then. Please try to understand. Tracy and I are the same age. We have a lot in common. Love has come our way. Be happy for us."

She frowned. "Easy for you to say."

"It's the truth. You deserve that much."

She stared at him for a moment, intently, as if she were studying him, or perhaps seeing him clearly for the first time. Finally, she said, "Maybe you think I should thank you for being so thoughtful, so honest, but you're breaking my heart again."

"I didn't mean to."

"That doesn't make it hurt any less."

He offered his hand. "We were never lovers, but we were always friends. Can it be like that again?"

She swam toward him. "It won't be easy."

"All I ask is that you try."

She put a pout on her face and took his hand.

"That's a start." He pulled her to the edge of the pool with him. Goose bumps appeared on her shoulders. Only then did he realize that he too had caught a chill. He looked around the courtyard and noticed the place had been vacated. Even the gold umbrellas were folded down and tied. All around them, Palm trees thrashed, and the sky churned with angry gray clouds. He could smell the ocean in the wind. "Let's get out of here. All hell is going to break loose."

Chapter Thirty-Two

THUNDER RUMBLED ACROSS A GRAY California morning sky. Fierce rain pelted the staff car's windshield as the engine idled on the tarmac at Solartech Field. The heater was going full blast. Janis, sitting behind the steering wheel, clicked the wiper switch to high. He wrung his hands to work the chill from his fingers. An uneasy fear churned in his stomach. Tracy was up there somewhere in that raging storm.

"She should be here any time," Ray said, wiping fog from the passenger door window with the palm of his hand.

"She is late," Lo said from the back seat.

"I just wish they'd picked a better day for this." Janis shivered. Raindrops rattled on the roof, and wind-driven sheets of rain whipped across the airfield. The torrents swirled and pooled on the rubber-scarred runway. In the distance, white balls of light pulsed from the approach towers.

Lo reached up and patted Janis's shoulder. "I'm worried about her, too." As always, Lo had an uncanny way of picking up on Janis's feelings. They'd been through a lot of tough times together, and it seemed as if Dr. Curtis had more of the same planned for them. Looking over at Ray, Janis restrained a sudden urge to choke him for getting them into this mess. And as if the experiments weren't dangerous enough, Ray was planning a journey into the 13th Power as well. His obsession would be the death of him.

Lisa seemed to think so, too. Janis recalled the hateful look that came over her face when Ray told her about his plans: that same pinched-lipped expression, wrinkled nose, and searing glare she used to give him before they'd made peace with each other. But this time there'd be no peace. She had stormed out of the MIGGS shouting, "You're crazy." And Janis had to agree with her. Ray was completely out of his mind.

"Lisa's right, you know," Janis said to Ray, rolling his thoughts into words. "You are crazy."

"Think what you like. I've got a second chance at this. We're going to make the most incredible scientific breakthrough in history. A new dimension in time and space is at our fingertips. The 13th Power is the gateway, the key, the answer."

"It's suicide."

"It's my life."

A chill went up the back of Janis's neck. "What makes you think Curtis will let you go anyway? He's never been interested in the 13th Power. All he cares about is the Higgs boson, and for what, turn lead into gold? He's nothing but a greedy bastard."

"He has his agenda," Ray said flatly. "And I have mine." He suddenly squinted through the rain soaked windshield. "I think I see them."

Janis swiveled his attention back to the sky. Twin landing lights encircled by immense halos appeared through the haze, then the white form of a corporate jet emerged from the clouds right above the approach light towers. It dropped lower and lower, pitching and yawing in the wind. The wing flaps deployed, and the landing gear reached down like the talons of a falcon about to snatch its prey. With a screech, the tires hit the concrete. A spray of water erupted from the runway, swirling madly in the wake of the speeding jet. The nose gear touched down followed by the roar of reverse thrusters. Only the tail and wingtips could be seen protruding from the wash as the jet screamed by. At the far end of the runway, it had slowed enough to turn around and taxi toward the tarmac.

As the whining jet approached, Janis's heartbeat began to race. Tracy was on that plane. It had been an agonizing week since the CIA yanked her out of the kiva and dragged her away. Finally they'd be together again. He couldn't wait to hold her in his arms.

Horns blaring, a long black executive car with Solartech flags flapping from the fenders suddenly sped through the airfield gate. Two black staff cars followed close behind it. The official procession splashed toward the tarmac.

After the jet coasted to a stop, the engines shut off. Lightning flashed across the sky and reflected off the jet's white fuselage slicked with rain. High up on the tail, the silver seal of the CIA glistened. A moment later, the executive car slid to a stop alongside the jet. Doors flew open. Attendants in yellow rain coats appeared and deployed umbrellas.

"Welcoming committee," Ray said with a sting to his words.

"Let's go." Janis grabbed his umbrella off the seat, pushed open the door, and stepped into the tempest. Cold wind knifed through his jacket as he made his way toward the jet, its cabin door now open, and the retractable steps dropped to the ground.

First, a shadowy figure appeared in the jet's doorway. He wore a long black coat, perfectly pressed slacks, and polished shoes. Janis felt a surge of anger as he recognized Dr. Curtis. His face was pale and thin, and the gray glare from his eyes penetrated the core of Janis's body. He shuddered at the sight of this man, knowing the chaos was going to start all over again: the impossible demands, the mind games, and the battle of wills. Janis had survived the last round, and the world was spared. Never in a million years would he have agreed to endure it again, except for Tracy.

Attendants with umbrellas rushed to the open cabin door. Curtis descended the steps to the tarmac. He grabbed an umbrella from the nearest man, and with a long gait, the wind whipping his black coat, he stormed up to Janis, smiling his sly smile. “Glad to see you could join me, Dr. Mackey,” he said with an air of satisfaction in his voice. Rivulets of rain cascaded from both of their umbrellas, a watery partition between them. “Looks like I’m going to get my money’s worth after all.”

Janis set his jaw. The pompous bastard was always so formal, so totally in control. “I wouldn’t have missed it for the world,” Janis replied, dismissing the lie in his words. He craned his neck, the rain rapping on his umbrella, and tried to see beyond Curtis and the throng of attendants with umbrellas. He hoped to see Tracy, but it was Jonathan Kyles who stooped through the cabin doorway next. Disappointed, Janis’s impatience became stretched to the limit. “Where’s Tracy?”

Curtis sneered. “Ah, yes, the spying little bitch. You might say she’s all tied up right now.”

“You better not hurt her.”

“She’s CIA property.” Curtis regarded Janis with a crooked smile. “My, my, things have certainly changed around here.” He let out a throaty laugh.

“I want to see her.”

“Tech-Com Control, tomorrow, 10am sharp, Dr. Mackey. I’ll spell it out for you then.” Curtis dipped his chin. “Have a good day.”

Janis showed his teeth as Curtis strutted to the executive car and ducked into the back seat. Jonathan climbed in after him. Attendants closed the doors, and the car roared off.

Cursing mad, Janis returned his attention to the plane

just as a man wearing a dark suit stepped through the doorway, and then Tracy appeared with another agent behind her. Handcuffs on her wrists unleashed Janis's anger. "Tracy!" He took off running toward her.

Ray shouted, "Janis, wait."

One of the agents grabbed Tracy's elbow. The other held his left hand up like a traffic cop. "CIA. Hold it right there," he warned while reaching under his jacket lapel with his right hand.

Janis stopped, remembering his last painful confrontation with these CIA agents. "Tracy!"

She looked at him with mournful eyes. "I'm sorry, Janis."

"You can't help her," the agent said, and ducking against the fury of the storm, they hustled her into an idling staff car. The doors slammed shut, and the car sped away in the rain.

When it was out of sight, Janis dropped his gaze to the sopping tarmac. His heart felt heavy, like a boulder in his chest, and he wondered when he would see her again.

"Dr. Janis? Is it you?"

Startled by the familiar voice, Janis looked up and saw an old man descending the jet's steps. He had bushy gray hair and perfect teeth. The sight made Janis's stomach cramp. "Boris?" He couldn't believe it. Curtis had reassembled the entire team. And the CIA had helped him do it. But why?

The Russian limped toward Janis, rain dripping off his sideburns and thick mustache. "This weather is not so good." He ducked under Janis's umbrella and gave him an exuberant handshake. "But it is good that I see you."

Confusion swam in Janis's mind. "What's this all about, Boris?"

Ray and Lo had gathered around them, both wrestling their umbrellas against the biting wind. Ray asked, "What are you doing here, Boris?" His voice barely peaked the splatter of rain.

Lo bowed to the Russian, as if preferring silence to questions.

Boris furrowed his bushy eyebrows, his eyes darting between Janis and Ray and Lo. “You I will tell,” he said as they huddled together in the storm. “Curtis is a phony. Melvin Anderson is his real name. Him I meet in Borneo, and too late I discover he was a wanted criminal, a killer, and all-round general psycho. But now he has made a deal with a big shot in Washington.”

“Who? The President?” Ray asked.

“CIA top dog,” Boris shivered. “*The Ark*. They talked about Star Wars. You know what that is?”

Ray nodded. “The Strategic Defense Initiative. What’s it got to do with us?”

“The sneaky bastards want particle beam...shoot from space. Phony Curtis agreed to develop it in exchange for freedom in this country. We must help him or die. *The Ark* has told us that.”

“The Ark?” Janis felt a lump in his throat. The rain felt colder, the wind more intense. “So that’s it? The CIA puts the squeeze on us to arm the country with a particle beam...a weapon of unimaginable power.”

Ray bobbed his head. “For defense, of course, right?”

“You can’t believe that,” Janis spat. “In the wrong hands,” he looked around, “like the bastards who are orchestrating this affair, this weapon could be put to a much more cynical use.”

Lo grabbed Janis’s arm. “Hold cities hostage from space, maybe whole countries. Not a good thing for CIA to have this power.”

“Or the Department of Defense,” Ray put in. “They could assassinate leaders of nations, generals on the battlefield, anyone...just zap them from orbit.”

“And Tracy can give it to them...but only with our help.” The horrors of a world under siege from space rushed through Janis's mind: lasers buzzing out of the sky, targets destroyed with surgical precision, smoke and ash covering the land. "Nothing good can come of this, Ray. Once we have a space-bound particle beam, other countries will develop them. No one will be safe, anywhere."

Ray's face turned a ghostly shade of white. "How are we going to stop them?"

Chapter Thirty-Three

THE NEXT MORNING, HEAVY GRAY clouds hung over Simi Valley. Janis turtled his neck against a cold wind whipping in from the ocean and ducked into a staff car idling under the carport. It was almost ten o'clock, time for the showdown with Curtis in Tech-Com Control.

"They're ready for you, sir," the driver said.

"When's this storm going to be over? The wind howled all night." Janis shut the door.

"I've seen worse." The driver put the transmission into drive.

"So much for sunny Southern California."

The staff car sped away from the executive suites. Leaning his head on the seatback, Janis sighed. His eyelids felt like boat anchors from lack of sleep. Though his room had all the comforts of home, it had been a restless night with the clock ticking away the hours of insomnia, the wind blowing, and his troubled mind only allowing him to doze off from time to time. Even then he'd found no rest. In uneasy dreams, Dr. Curtis's glaring eyes tormented him, Tracy's terrified face haunted him, and the 13th Power eluded him. Numbers and formulas scrolled through his brain, but nothing computed; his calculations were always wrong. Curtis's maniacal laughter echoed through his mind. Tracy screamed. He'd jumped straight up out of bed, sweating, wishing it would all go away, the nightmares and the howling wind.

Dawn had brought him no relief.

As the staff car careened up the ramp between the twin steel and glass buildings, he looked up at the new arch spanning the entryway. *Welcome to Solartech Labs,* it read. *Gateway to the Atomic Universe.* The whole concept filled him with dread.

The staff car sped under the arch, and once inside the vehicle reception lobby, came to a screeching stop in front of the glass doors at the entrance to the labs. Inside the atrium, chrome and black escalators moved up and down. Video cameras swept back and forth in ever-silent vigil.

Janis got out of the car and shut the door. As he turned toward the entrance, the staff car sped away, engine roaring. Damp air sent a shiver down his neck. Taking in a deep breath, he pulled on a door handle and stepped inside.

"Janis." His name echoed all around him. He looked up to the top of the escalators where Lo Chin stood, waving. "Hurry. Dr. Curtis gets impatient."

"What else is new?" Janis stepped on the escalator. He was entering a world of technology, a place concerned only with the hard facts of nature. Inside these walls dwelled men of science, and everything in here was designed for discovery. Questions about right and wrong were not asked here, and no one talked of God or creation. The *Big Bang* had started everything. God didn't exist inside Solartech Labs.

"Did you sleep well?" Lo asked.

"Barely a wink." Janis stepped from the escalator.

"Me too."

Janis gave him a half-hearted bow and headed toward the semicircular counter on the other side of the main lobby. His heels ticked on a black marble floor inlaid with gold atomic icons. Tilting his head back, he looked up to the ceiling, a dizzying five stories high and supported by six pillars of gold. At least to Janis, they looked like they were made of real gold.

At the reception counter, a security officer dressed in a white shirt and tie greeted him. “Welcome back, Dr. Mackey. I didn’t think I’d ever see you again.”

Janis didn’t smile as he scanned the rows of video monitors on the wall behind the counter, each revealing various locations within the building. Labs, hallways, offices, and even the restrooms were under constant surveillance. Some screens showed workers in white coveralls plastering and painting walls and repairmen in gray jumpsuits fiddling with electrical fixtures. But most monitors revealed no activity at all, just empty labs and vacant halls. “There’s not much going on around here,” he said to the guard.

“That’ll change once you guys get the 13th Power experiments back on track.” He pulled a file folder out of a drawer. “I’ll say one thing. The maintenance boys have done a great job fixing things up around here.”

“So I see.” Janis remembered the blackened halls littered with dust and debris following the concussion that rocked Tech-Com Control.

An old woman, her silver hair wound into a bun on top of her head, approached carrying two folded white lab coats. She squinted behind thin spectacles. “Let’s see...” She eyed Janis up and down. “This one should fit you.” She helped him put it on, wrestled with a stubborn button, and then stepped back to inspect the fit. “Very nice.” She turned to Lo. “Such a handsome man.”

Lo gave her a funny look as she helped him put on his lab coat.

The security officer presented them with two ID tags, one of which he clipped to Janis’s coat lapel, the other to Lo’s. It wasn’t any different from the one he’d worn before. There was no picture or name on it, just a black-on-white barcode under a Solartech Labs insignia: the atom, the lightning bolt, and the gold shield. He noticed the security officer didn’t have an ID tag clipped on his coat. “Where’s yours?"

With a sly smile, the officer pulled up his left sleeve and showed him a twenty-four-pin microchip complete with a green LED, surgically implanted in the skin of his arm. Its black-on-white barcode was sealed in clear plastic. "Never leave home without it." He pulled his sleeve down. "Laser beams scan these buildings in random sequences and report the whereabouts of everyone to the main computers. This one on my arm is digitally encoded. Yours have to be out in plain sight. So don't be sticking them in your pockets or under your lab coats. We don't like false alarms. Got that?"

Janis double-checked to be sure his tag was in plain view.

"Mr. Chin," the officer said as he inspected the ID tag's position on Lo's lab coat pocket. "I was wondering, weren't you on the Polaris programming team a couple years back?"

Lo nodded.

"I read in Computer World magazine that you debugged the transcription program single-handedly. Pretty impressive feat, considering the number of brainards who tried and failed."

"Thank you, but please, all in day's work." Lo looked at Janis. "Magazine make big deal of nothing."

"To you, maybe." Janis was good at math and computers, but Lo was the undisputed expert.

The security officer took a step back and looked over his charges. "They're waiting for you in Tech-Com Control."

After a long walk through a maze of corridors, Janis stopped just inside the doorway to the main control room. The whole place was sparkling clean. The smell of fresh paint reminded him of his new house in Boulder, which made him feel suddenly glum. He scanned the gleaming white console that stretched across the room, its glowing monitors and the gray swivel chairs at each station. Gauges and meters and dials glistened, and rows of lights pulsed with a steady rhythm: reds, greens, blues, and yellows. Technicians wearing white lab coats attended to the machinery like ever-vigilant mothers caring for their young.

Taking a deep breath, Janis walked in and went directly to the windows overlooking the supercomputers. They were housed in an environmentally controlled room set below the main floor. A master control panel monitored the Supers. Pulsing green lights indicated that they were ready and awaiting commands from the terminals in Tech-Com Control. Cooling fans hummed.

Satisfied, Janis's gaze moved to the long window on the other side of the room, the foot-thick glass of the MIGGS. He walked over and looked inside, startled to see a new titanium-ribbed chamber, bigger than a railroad car. Green lights blinked on and off in two second intervals. When the lights came on, he saw the I.S.S.T. suspended from the ceiling by a mechanical arm. The nose faced to the left, the cockpit windows shining black as mica. The rear of the transporter faced the accelerator collar on the right. When the lights went out, a crimson glow came from somewhere inside the accelerator tunnel deep under Simi Valley.

Nerves tingled down the back of his neck.

"Dr. Mackey." Curtis's booming voice echoed through Tech-Com Control.

Janis looked up the metal staircase to an observation platform where Curtis stood overlooking the control room. Light from office windows behind him silhouetted his frame, the black suit coat and a black hat, of all things. Several men stood with him: Ray and Boris, Janis recognized, and technicians Roger, Johnson and Roberts, and Stan Burton, Solartech Labs' best mechanical engineer. Tracy was nowhere in sight. Janis gritted his teeth. "Where is she?"

"I'm glad you could join me," Curtis said as he made his way down the stairway, his boots clunking heavily on the metal steps. The group followed him down and gathered at the bottom of the stairs. Dressed in black, he looked out of place among the other men who were wearing white lab coats.

"I know what you're up to," Janis growled. "And I don't like it." He wanted to hit the bastard. "I want to see Tracy, right now."

Curtis grinned. "Relax, doctor, she'll be along shortly. While we wait, what do you say we get down to business?"

"You're nuts if you think we're going to do this experiment again. It's too dangerous."

"What's the matter, Dr. Mackey? Can't cut it? The math too tough for you? Maybe you're right. This thing is way over your head." Curtis put his nose in the air.

"I've already told you not to tamper with the 13th Power."

"What do you know?" Curtis replied. "You can't even get the formula right. You screwed up. You failed. You don't know anything about it."

"Mankind is not meant to know—"

"I'm giving you a chance to redeem yourselves...both of you." He indicated Ray, too. "I suggest you take it. If not, *The Ark* will have you killed. Personally, I'd like to watch that."

Janis frowned. "Just who does *The Ark* think he is, anyway?"

"Somebody we don't want to cross," Curtis said. "You think I'm a mean son-of-a-bitch. *The Ark* makes me look like your best friend."

"He wants the particle beam," Ray said. "Let's just give it to him, get him off our backs so we can get on with more important work."

"Smart man." Curtis tipped his hat to Ray. "Particle

beam first, the Higgs boson second, and then I'll let you guys play with the 13th Power all you want. Deal?"

Janis glanced at the men standing around them. Their faces showed no hint of emotion, like condemned men walking to the gallows. "You guys are going along with this?"

Some of them nodded, and Lo shrugged. Stan stepped forward. "We have no choice, Dr. Mackey."

"Of course you do. You can say no. Just walk away."

"No," Roger said, his face pale. "We can't."

"Why not?"

"I've got a wife and t-two kids in St. L-Louis..." He choked on his words. "If we don't cooperate...well...it's not just me I'm worried about." He paused to glance around at everyone, as if to be sure they were listening. "*The Ark* will have them killed, as well."

Curtis bobbed his head. "That's what he said. And the same goes for the rest of you." He pointed to the other members of the team. "Do it or die, but know this. Everyone you love will die too."

Janis now realized that not only was Tracy's life in peril, but also the entire team and their families' lives hinged on his willingness to cooperate with Curtis and *The Ark*. If he refused, they would all die. If he agreed, they would all die anyway. Their only hope to survive would be to conduct a perfect experiment. Every one of his formulas would have to be flawless in order to avert a global disaster. He glared at Curtis. "You know the 13th Power can destroy the world."

"Risk nothing, gain nothing," Curtis replied.

"With that attitude, you're going to end up killing everybody."

Curtis lifted his eyebrows. "That *is* entirely possible. I suggest you brainards put your heads together and get it right this time. We'll all be better off."

"You can't believe that," Janis said, his cheeks hot

with anger. “You give *The Ark* the particle beam...it’ll be like putting a loaded gun in the hands of a child.”

Curtis shrugged. “What’s wrong with that?”

“The Department of Defense will wreak havoc with it around the globe.”

“Look into my eyes,” Curtis said, going nose to nose with Janis. “Do you see any hint that I might even give a shit?”

A sinking feeling came over him. He could only shake his head in dismay. Nothing in Curtis’s cold gray eyes even faintly resembled sympathy for a world in peril.

“You people don’t have any choice,” Curtis said. “So what do you say, doctor? Are we going to get down to business now?”

“Not before I talk to Tracy.”

“I’m right here, Janis.”

He spun around. Like a ray of sunshine, she was standing in the doorway, her white lab coat glowing. His heart took a jump to light speed. Every red hair on her head was perfect, her face bright, though her smile looked strained. Her wrists were free of the handcuffs, but two CIA agents in black suits stood behind her, their hard eyes boring into him.

“Tracy!” He ran to her and gathered her into his arms. She felt warm and soft and wonderful. The agents put their hands on their guns, but he didn’t care. He just held her.

Chapter Thirty-Four

BENNIE'S COFFEE SHOP SAT ON the corner of First and Los Angeles Avenue in the city of Simi Valley. Kate had heard it was a favorite haunt of the locals, many of whom worked at Solartech Labs down the road. They'd gather here after the night shift and indulge in high-powered coffee and rich chocolate fudge, for which Bennie's was famous.

As Kate walked in, she inhaled the aroma of freshly ground coffee. An espresso machine hissed and hacked. A young man wearing a stained white apron busied himself with filling a row of mugs on the counter. She moved directly to a corner booth and peeled off her jacket, revealing a low-cut black evening dress and a diamond necklace. The diamonds were fake, the cleavage wasn't.

Rowdy voices erupted from across the room, drawing her attention to a table where men wearing gray jumpsuits joked and laughed. They looked young and wild in the eyes. Emblems adorned their work clothes: bolts of lightning, atoms, and gold shields.

The waitress approached. She looked to be about thirty, amply-breasted and blue-eyed, and her smile beamed as she approached. "My name's Suzie. What can I get you tonight?"

"Tell me, honey," Kate said, heavy on the barroom accent. "Those boys work around here?" She pointed a sleek red fingernail at the men making all the noise.

Suzie nodded. “The regular bunch from the research lab. Ruffians mostly. The big one’s a mechanic. The others are welders and electricians.”

“Tough guys, huh,” Kate said, eyeing the waitress up and down. “Any of them take a liking to you?”

“They’re animals, like all men.”

Kate smiled. “I’ll have a small mocha, extra whipped cream, and one of those fudge-swirly things. It’s going to be a long night.”

“You be careful now.” Suzie sauntered off.

A few minutes later, as the men drank their coffee and told their jokes, Kate sipped her mocha and pondered her situation. The thought of what she was about to do ached in her heart, but her body was the only asset she could use to get what she wanted. It had never failed her before. Like Suzie had said, men were animals. They possessed predictable instincts, the most powerful being the urge to breed. It made the majority of men careless. She figured that one of those men at the table had to be lonely tonight, possibly the guy with the sharp chin and deep brown eyes that landed on her from time to time.

She’d catch him looking at her. He’d blink and look away, and she’d smile when she caught him looking back. It was a game: a dance of the eyes, a sort of ESP between potential sex partners. Kate knew all the tricks. She was a pro. Brown Eyes didn’t stand a chance.

An hour later, she was sitting in the back seat of a four door Ford as it roared toward Solartech Labs. Her dress was hiked up past the top of her nylons, and cool night air chilled the inside of her thighs, as well as Brown Eyes’ cold hand.

“Impatient are we?” she whispered and let her knees come apart.

“We’re never gonna get away with this,” Billy said. He was the driver, and sitting next to him, a skinny guy named Leonard said, “It’ll be a piece of cake. She can duck on the floor when we get to the main gate."

"Come on, you guys," the guy riding shotgun muttered. Earlier, she'd heard somebody call him Ralph. He looked like a mamma's boy. "We're going to get killed if we're caught with her."

Billy shook his head. "I think we should find a motel room and do the bitch there."

"Let's just do her right here in the car," Brown Eyes said in an airy voice.

Kate huffed. "Now come on, boys, you were the ones bragging about your rooms at Solartech Labs, big-shot employees with the fancy digs, and how you've snuck women in there before. Don't back down now or nobody's going to *do the bitch*."

Brown Eyes put his tongue in her ear. A hand slipped down the front of her dress. Calloused fingers found a tender nipple. It was the mechanic's hand: Tom. Up until now, he'd been sitting quietly on her right, his elbow propped on the seatback. Tom was the bruiser of the bunch, a big boy with tattoos of snakes and naked women on his arms. He'd said he wasn't afraid of anything, not even the security guards at the main gate.

"Then it's settled," Tom said, pinching her nipple. "Our place. I get seconds...after Lloyd."

"Why does Lloyd get to go first?" Leonard demanded.

"'Cause I saw her first," brown-eyed Lloyd said and slipped his fingers under the leg seam of her panties.

She stiffened but let him have his way, her stomach clutching as it had done so many times before. But Brown Eyes was a beginner. He was fumbling around, his trembling fingers probing all the wrong places. As if on cue, Tom took her breast by the handful. Billy's two buddies up front turned around, their eyes ringed in white, almost glowing in the dark interior of the car.

Leonard said, "I don't care if I have to go last. My God. I got a boner already."

Kate forced a smile. Men, they were so predictable. If this were a paying job, she wouldn't have to work for a week.

***

The next morning, sunlight knifed through the window. "We gotta get you out of here," Billy said, pulling on his skivvies.

Kate rolled over. She was under the sheets and squinting as she glanced around the bedroom. Big Tom was slumped in a corner chair, still wearing his white t-shirt and naked down to his socks. Leonard had sprawled out on the floor, belly up with nothing on. Brown Eyes Lloyd was lying on his back next to her, snoring. He'd cupped his hands over his limp penis, which had been his problem all night long. The only man missing was Ralph. He'd taken off running as soon as the car came to a stop in front of the employees' quarters.

"Get up," Billy persisted.

She saw her dress hanging on the bedpost. Her nylons were balled up on the nightstand, and her shoes were setting on the rug by the door. Her cheap necklace got busted during the night's activity. A hundred glass diamonds sparkled in the sunbeams striking the floor. But she was in. She was at Solartech Labs. She'd gotten past security, now nearer to her goal: Ray and Lisa. All she had to do was find them.

"Come on," Billy said as he pulled on his socks.

Kate propped her head up on an elbow. "I'm not going anywhere."

"What the hell are you talkin' about, bitch? You can't stay here. Hey guys. Let's move it."

Tom let out a moan and licked his lips before his eyes came open. "Huh?"

Leonard rolled over and got up on his knees. "What

time is it?" His eyes looked like bowling balls.

"Six-thirty," Billy said.

Brown Eyes didn't budge.

Kate sat up and let the sheet fall from her breasts. "Breakfast in bed would be nice."

Billy didn't give her a second look. "We're going."

"Give her a break," Tom said, his gaze fixed on her nipples. "She's got to be starved."

"You guys don't get it," Billy said, his voice rising. "We'll be killed if we get caught with this bitch." He threw on a shirt. "We breached Solartech Labs' security. You all know the penalty for that."

Leonard got up and climbed into his gray jumpsuit. "Billy's right. If we get busted, we'll end up in the rat cellar."

Tom frowned. "There ain't no such place."

"Don't listen to him," Leonard said. His eyes were on Kate as he tied his boots. "Sorry, but you gotta go."

She looked at each of the big-shot employees of Solartech Labs. They sure talked tough last night, but now they suddenly got a case of nerves. All this talk about getting killed and rat cellars was just a ploy to scare her, to make this place sound dangerous in order to get rid of her. It wasn't going to work. This wasn't the way she had it figured. "How about if I just hide out here?" she suggested. "Then we can have some more fun tonight."

"We had enough fun." Billy threw her dress in her lap. "Let's go."

In the staff car, she sat in the back seat next to Tom as they headed for the main gate. He smelled like he needed a shower. Billy drove and Leonard rode shotgun. She had to think of something fast or she'd be right back where she started: Bennie's coffee shop.

"We'll do it just like last night," Tom said. "Get on the floor. I'll put my coat over you."

Up ahead, the stone archway of the main gate came

into view. The steel drawbar, painted in black and yellow stripes, was down across the road. Security cars, white Fords that looked like police cruisers, were parked off to the side. Men in blue uniforms and helmets checked cars coming in for the workday. Surveillance cameras swept back and forth.

"Get down," Billy said.

Kate ducked behind the seat. A coat went over her head and dowsed her in darkness. She held her breath, thinking how she could cause a ruckus. She had to make enough trouble to warrant the attention of management and maybe even Ray Crawford. She was too close to her family to let it all slip away now.

The car came to a stop, and Billy rolled down the window. "Supply run to town," he said to the guard.

It was now or never. Kate let out a scream and started kicking. "Help." She screamed again.

"What the hell?" the guard demanded.

The next thing she knew, she was thrown against the seat as the staff car engine roared and tires squealed. Billy had slammed the car into reverse, spun around, and was now racing away from the main gate.

Leonard gasped. "Billy. What'd you do that for?"

"They'll kill us, I tell yah. We need to get some help."

Sirens pierced the California morning air.

Kate sat up. "You guys are in big trouble, now."

"Look what you've done," Billy shouted as he wrestled the steering wheel and careened the car down a dirt road. "Why'd you do that?"

"I told you I wanted breakfast."

"They probably think we kidnapped you," Tom said, looking out the rear window.

Kate turned around. The pulsing blue and white overheads of three security cars slewed side to side through the staff car's tail of dust. Sirens wailed. Kate smiled with inner satisfaction. She'd wanted a ruckus. By golly she got one.

"What are we gonna do?" Leonard squeaked as the car rattled down the dirt road. Loose gravel pummeled the undercarriage.

"Oh man, oh man," Billy said over the roaring engine. "I'm thinkin' as fast as I can drive." A bump sent the car fishtailing.

"You guys really screwed up," Kate said. "But you were right about one thing."

"What's that?" Tom growled.

"I *am* a bitch. You shouldn't have reminded me."

Billy shook his finger at Leonard and bared his teeth. "I told you she was trouble."

Kate grinned. "You ain't seen nothin' yet, boys."

The dirt road wound down the hillside and broke out across a stretch of valley bottom strewn with boulder fields and scrub oak. Vultures soared on thermals overhead, and black crows perched like sentinels on barbed wire fence posts along the road. Up ahead on the right, the sun-rotted remains of an old ghost town came into view. A lopsided sign read, *Morrison Ridge: KEEP OUT*.

Kate cringed at the skull and crossbones painted in red under the sign. "I hope we're just passing through." She gulped.

Billy sped down the main street lined with splintered and collapsing wood-framed buildings. A general store, livery stable, and even a windowless saloon were still recognizable. Roofs had caved in, doors lay askew, and tumbleweeds choked the sun-rotted boardwalks. On the left, set apart from the rest of the place, stood a two-story structure with a large porch, glassless windows, and a pitched roof full of holes. Some intricate woodworking had survived the ravages of time: on the railings, window frames, and eves. Kate thought it must have been a fine hotel in its day.

The staff car skidded to a dusty stop in front of the

porch.

"You gotta be kiddin', Billy," Leonard shouted.

"It'll buy us some time."

"But what about the rats?"

"Screw the rats," Tom said, and the doors flew open, letting in dust.

Kate's stomach seized. "What rats?"

Tom grabbed her right arm and pulled her from the car. The security cars slid to a stop behind them, bullhorn blaring: "Don't anybody move. Stay where you are."

Billy took hold of Kate's left arm, and as she tried to break free, the men shoved and pushed her toward the entrance of the old hotel.

"I'm not going in there." Fighting panic, she struggled harder, but they forced her up the porch steps, which were broken down as if a heavy vehicle had driven up them. She could make out the wheel ruts that marred the porch, and the entrance's double door framework had been ripped from the wall, leaving a jagged hole.

"Stop!" crackled over the bullhorn.

They pushed her inside anyway and rushed her into the main lobby. Here the ceiling hung down, buckled at the center, and the far wall had another big hole busted through it. Splintered wallboards littered the floor. Hurrying, their footsteps kicked dust into the air.

"That way," Billy said, pointing.

Warily, Leonard led them through the jagged hole in the wall and into the adjoining room. Kate did a double take at what she saw there. The back bumper of an All-Terrain Vehicle with fat knobby tires was sticking up from a large opening in the floor. She recalled the tore up porch, the missing doorframe, and the big hole in the wall. Someone had driven into the hotel and tore the place up.

As Billy and Tom rushed her past the crashed ATV, she glanced down into the cellar-like opening where the wreck rested nose first on the shadow-darkened floor. She saw the remnants of rotted stairs, and a fecal stench wafted up from the depths.

"Keep moving," Billy said, pushing her toward a debris-strewn staircase with a broken railing. Kate struggled to keep her footing on the rickety steps as the men forced her up to the second floor. Boards creaked as they made their way to a window at the front of the old hotel. Leonard kicked aside a busted bed frame, and Tom helped him prop a smelly mattress against the front wall, as if it could stop a hail of bullets.

Billy grabbed Kate by the shoulders and placed her in front of the window. "Don't shoot," he shouted down. "We want to make a deal."

Below, the security officers were crouched behind their cars, guns drawn, frightened eyes cast up to the window. One big fellow leaned on the roof of his car, holding a bullhorn. Her rescuers seemed well trained. She counted eight men with plenty of firepower, but their eyes were filled with dread. She bit her lower lip and wondered why.

"Come out," bellowed from the bullhorn.

"What's with you guys?" Kate shouted down to the men hiding behind their cars. "These guys are unarmed. Come in and get me."

The men shook their heads, and one of them said, "We ain't goin' in there, lady."

Lifting the bullhorn to his lips, the big man hollered out, "Why don't you all just come down real peaceful like?"

Billy got to his knees and poked his head out the window. "We wanna talk to Ray Crawford first," he yelled down. "This bitch got us in trouble."

The bullhorn crackled. "You all right, lady?"

"Peachy," she said with a smile, thinking how things had suddenly turned in her favor. "Like the man said, we want to talk to Ray Crawford, so hurry up. We don't have all day."

Billy gave her a funny look.

"Yes, ma'am," the big man said and took the radio mike in his hand. "But wouldn't it be safer to wait for him out here?"

She frowned. Safer? Looking at Billy, then Tom and Leonard, she felt a hitch in her throat. "What's he talking about?"

"The rats," Leonard said with wide eyes.

Kate swallowed dryly. "What rats?"

"Vicious Kangaroo rats," Billy said.

"Kangaroo rats aren't vicious," Tom argued.

"These are," Billy replied.

Her curiosity piqued, Kate asked, "How's that possible?"

"The story goes like this," Billy began. "A hundred fifty years ago, a bunch of kangaroo rats got into the hotel's wine cellar down there. It was a cool place to get away from the heat, and anyway, they gnawed their way into the barrels and did a little wine tasting of their own. After thousands of generations of drinking and screwing, they got mentally deranged, you know, like it messed up their DNA."

"You're full of shit," Tom said.

"Now, they hunt the valley in packs," Leonard put in. "Mostly in the morning and evening hours, but when the day heats up, they come back to the cool cellar to nap and breed some more. A real happy family."

Kate made a sour face. "Why not just get rid of the damn things, like with rat poison or something?"

"Dr. Curtis found a use for them," Leonard put in. "The rats don't leave any remains, no bones, no hair, no nothin'."

Aghast, Kate put her hand on her heart. "Are you telling me Curtis tossed people into that cellar so the rats could eat them?"

Billy looked at Tom. “She catches on real quick.”

“It’s hogwash,” Tom spat.

“No, it’s true,” Leonard put in. “I’ve heard stories.”

“Then what the hell are we doing in here?” Kate said. “For Christ’s sake, rats can climb. They could swarm the hotel. No wonder those security guys won’t come in here. My God!”

“Relax,” Billy said. “The rats ain’t even here. They’re out in the valley, feeding on a cow that some poor alien is going to get blamed for mutilating.”

Kate frowned. “Ray Crawford had better hurry.”

Leonard pushed the mattress over. It went flat on the floor with a thud and hurled a cloud of dust into the air. Kate coughed and took a seat next to Tom who’d already claimed a corner of the nasty thing. She found a run in her nylons, and her stomach made a gurgling sound. “Well, boys, here we are.”

Billy sat on the floor with his back against the water-stained wall. “We’ll be lucky to get out of this mess with our lives.” He glared at Kate. “No thanks to you.”

She grinned. “You’ll be thanking me before this is over.”

Tom raised his eyebrows. “I get a funny feeling you’re not just some slick bitch looking for a good time.”

“Think not?”

An hour passed, and then two. Midday sunshine heated the old hotel, and soon, the fecal odor in the rat cellar wafted up from below and filled the room. Kate stood and moved to the window again, like she had done every few minutes or so, to take in a lungful of fresh air.

Leaning on the sill and looking out, she imagined a time when this ghost town thrived: women in long dresses strolling, men in denim and leather riding, horses trotting and buggies squeaking. But today, only security men sweltered in the sun below, standing by their cars, waiting, their eyes constantly moving, probably watching for the rats. In the distance, a plume of dust rose into the air, kicked up by a car speeding toward Morrison Ridge.

As she turned to tell Billy about the car, an eerie sound began to fill the air: a chittering sound.

"Listen." Billy leaped to his feet. "The rats."

"They're coming back to the cellar," Leonard said.

Faint at first, the chitter started getting louder and louder with each passing moment. The clamor soon filled the hotel with its sheer volume. A hard knot of terror formed in Kate's stomach.

Leonard rushed to the door and stuck his head out into the hallway. "I wonder if they'll come up the stairs."

"If they get a whiff of us," Billy said, his sweaty face pallid.

"Then let's get out of here right now," Kate said. "A car's coming anyway. It's probably Ray Crawford." She pushed Tom and Leonard into the hall. Billy followed close behind.

At the top of the dilapidated staircase, she froze at the sight on the floor below. A seething mob of rats had gathered, their furry bodies hopping about in total chaos. Skinny tails, each tipped with a fluff of fur, protruded straight up from the horde like the masts of a million ships bobbing on an angry sea. Her mind filled with terror. The sound of them all chittering tore at her sense of reality.

"We're trapped," Billy said.

Leonard put a finger to his lips. "Shhh."

"What's with you guys?" Tom said. "Just stomp the little bastards. We can kill a hundred of them between here and the front door."

Billy reached for Tom's arm. "No."

But it was too late. Tom went banging down the stairs and stomped into the mass of rats, kicking and cursing the little critters. He made it halfway across the room before the rats swarmed his ankles and then climbed up his pant legs, swelling in numbers, gnawing and clawing their way up to his thighs. Tom's cursing turned to screams of terror. He started running in circles, dragging rats, kicking rats, and screaming in pain. Just then, another wave of rats scampered up the wrecked ATV in the cellar and joined the melee, their chitter deafening as the gnawing horde brought Tom down to his knees. More rats piled on. The floor was alive with chittering death. Wide-eyed, he fell backwards into the sea of crazed rats. Muffled screams turned to gagging as the rats infested him. The swarm covered his body and hid the hideous feast.

Kate screamed.

Suddenly, the rats jerked their noses toward the stairs, their ears perked. They began scampering up the steps like a rolling wave of fur, hopping over each other, jumping, pouncing, their chisel-sharp teeth gnashing.

Billy pulled on her arm. "Come on."

She turned and followed him back into the front room and to the window. Leonard was already there. He jumped out. With a thud, he hit the dirt, rolled, and got to his feet running just as a staff car skidded to a stop and doors flew open.

Kate clutched the window frame, paralyzed with fear. "I can't."

"Go!" Billy gave her a shove.

The fall wasn't too bad, and the landing didn't hurt much either, but her feet came out from under her, and she ended up doing a belly flop in the dirt.

She spit dust.

Suddenly, the chitter was right above her head, loud and grating. Every muscle in her body constricted. She turned slowly and looked up. Her stomach knotted.

There must've been a thousand rats lined up along the steps, the length of the rotted porch, and on the railings. They teetered on their hind legs, their jaws snapping and their beady black eyes probing for weakness.

A scream lodged in her throat. She didn't dare move,

knowing any moment they could spill from the porch and cover her.

Then Billy jumped to the ground. Footfalls scuffed the dirt around her, but she didn't move. She couldn't take her eyes off the angry mob of rats looming above her. Then someone grabbed her arms and pulled her to her feet. Her legs had no strength, no stability, and she stumbled. More hands grabbed her. A few strides and she fell behind a security car. She looked back to the porch with its horde of rats hopping about. Still terrified, her eyes went to the window from which she had jumped. The rats were there too, chittering from the sill. But they didn't attack. They didn't leave the sanctuary of the old hotel, which Tom had so violently invaded. And now, with the intruders gone, the rats retreated. Not a one was left anywhere to be seen. Only their chitter remained, echoing from inside the rotted wooden walls.

Kate slumped to the ground, face in her hands, shaking.

"Are you all right?"

Her heart skipped. How well she remembered that voice after all these years. She looked up. "Ray!"

He dropped to one knee. "Kate?" His eyes filled with disbelief. "What are you doing here?"

Billy coughed, his mouth falling open. "What? You...you know her?"

"She's my ex-wife," Ray spat.

"Shit." Billy slapped his forehead. "This thing gets worse every time I turn around."

Kate shook her head. "Sorry, Billy."

"What's that supposed to mean?" Ray asked.

"She set us up," Leonard said, pointing an accusatory finger at Kate. He told Ray what they'd done, less the sleazy details, and how she'd blown her cover at the main gate. "Now Tom is dead, and Billy and I are about to be served up to the rats. I tell you, it's all her fault."

Ray glared at Kate. “Why?”

“I had to see you, Ray.”

“Wrong answer.” He stood. “You wrecked our lives, Kate. I’m not forgiving you for what you did to Lisa...and to me. We don’t want anything to do with you. Ever.” He turned to Leonard and Billy. “You boys breached security.” Ray signaled the big man holding the bullhorn. “Take them to D-block.”

“Yes, sir.”

Billy and Leonard hung their heads as the security officers took them away. They ducked into one of the cars with flashing overheads, and the doors slammed. The car sped off in a cloud of dust, but even the roaring engine couldn’t overpower the chitter coming from inside the old hotel.

Kate shuddered. “You better not hurt them.”

Ray’s hate-filled eyes bored into her. “I’m not going to let you ruin their lives, too, Kate. I need those men. They’ll be all right. But you...I have no use for you at all.” He took a step back and turned to the security guards. “Take her to the main gate. She can walk back to town.”

Two men yanked her to her feet and took her to a car. “Give me a chance, Ray,” she said. She had to convince him to let her stay, to help her get her life back, and Lisa, and for Colonel Fallen and the world. “That’s all I’m asking, Ray, a chance.”

“Get her out of here.”

From the cloud of dust on main street came the long black form of a limousine with Solartech flags flapping from the fenders and tires crunching dirt. The security men who had hold of her arms stood silent. Ray stiffened and held his breath. She watched the car skid to a stop, her heart beating faster.

The back door flew open. A tall man stepped out. He wore a black suit, wide-brimmed hat, and a sinister smile.

Kate felt a wave of panic roll through her stomach.

She felt suddenly vulnerable and confused.

The man in black treaded toward Ray. "What's the meaning of this?" he growled in a voice that chilled the air.

Ray rushed up to him, looking small and frail in his shadow. "Security breach, sir."

"Who the hell is she?"

"My ex-wife, but don't worry, Dr. Curtis. We're getting rid of her right away."

Dr. Curtis, the man who fed people to rats, cocked his head and looked her up and down. An icy shiver crept down her back. His gaze made her feel naked, violated. Her heartbeat raced.

After Ray explained how she'd duped the employees into getting her past security, the mysterious Dr. Curtis approached her, and for the first time she saw his gray eyes. But instead of anger, she saw admiration, which surprised her. She smiled shyly, suddenly noticing the dirt on her dress, the run in her nylons, and the tacky sheen of her skin. In spite of these things, he took her hand anyway. "Mrs. Crawford, I'm delighted," he said softly. "You've had yourself quite an adventure...a truly remarkable feat, I must say, breaching security like this."

"I really didn't mean to intrude," she said, her heart now pounding.

"Yes you did," Curtis accused her...then grinned. "However, you showed cunning resourcefulness and courage. May I ask why you went to all this bother?"

"I just want to see my daughter." Surely he'd understand.

"Ray? You hear that? She wants to see her daughter."

"No way," Ray said. "She's leaving."

Curtis furrowed his brows. "Seems he wants to be rid of you. I'd say he doesn't know you very well, your real worth, your wonderful talents. May I be so bold to say I fully recognize all of those things?"

Kate nodded. "But of course."

"Then you agree...Ray is obviously wrong about you."

"She's a liar," Ray said.

"I think it highly unwise to be so hasty in this matter," Curtis said to Ray and gave Kate a wink. "She sounds like my kind of woman."

"Then I can stay and see my daughter?" Kate asked, her hopes rising.

"Only if you allow me to be your gracious host."

"Absolutely."

Curtis smiled. "Very well then, it's settled. Ray, inform Lisa that her mother is here."

Chapter Thirty-Five

IN THE TOWER OVERLOOKING THE border crossing at Nogales, Mexico, an INS supervisor peered through his binoculars at an old Chevy Suburban idling at the drawbar. Blue smoke pumped from its exhaust pipe, rust had infested its fenders, and sunshine glinted off a crack in the windshield. A California license plate hung from the front bumper, crooked, and he could make out the forms of three men inside. The driver, a big Mexican talking with the border guard, passed some papers through the window. The two passengers were skinny men, brothers perhaps, who seemed disinterested in the conversation as they glanced around casually, like tourists.

On cue, two uniformed inspectors and a German Shepherd approached the Suburban. The men looked in the windows as the dog went around sniffing at door seams and underneath.

The supervisor picked up his radio mike. "Post to seventeen, what's their business?"

Looking up to the tower, the guard radioed back. "Aunt died in Los Angeles. Their visas are in order."

"And the vehicle?"

"It's registered to a cousin there."

The inspectors backed away from the rusty Suburban. One wrote something on a clipboard while the dog sat next to him, tongue flopping from his mouth.

"Let them through."

The drawbar came up, and the old Chevy coughed and wheezed its way into the United States.

***

In the executive suites at Solartech Labs, Ray broke the bad news to Lisa. Holding her hand, they sat on the sofa in her room, facing each other. "You're mother is here."

"No," Lisa cried out and slumped onto the sofa. "I don't want to see her."

Ray's heart felt heavy. For nineteen years, he'd feared this day would come. And Curtis wasn't any help in the matter. He was adamant about Kate staying. Incredibly, he'd taken a liking to her. He'd convinced her he wanted to help her patch things up with Lisa. Ray knew Curtis had never done anything nice for anyone in his life. He had an ulterior motive. Perhaps he'd fallen for Kate's phony pleas, or else he just wanted to endear himself to her, the sleazy bastard, in order to use her as leverage against Ray.

Obviously, Kate had him right where she wanted him, curled around her little finger. She had a way of ruining everyone's lives. It was no wonder Curtis thought highly of her. They were so much alike. Ray put his hand on Lisa's shoulder. "We'll figure a way to get out of this."

She tucked her knees up to her chest and wrapped her arms around her legs. Her eyes were fixed orbs of blue rage. "You can't make me see her."

"I won't make you do anything."

"Why don't I remember her?" She rocked back and forth. "There's something so wrong about that."

Again, Ray took her hand. "I've always thought it best that you'd forgotten your mother. Seeing her might bring back memories better left buried."

"You mean, about the time in the trailer?"

"The doctor believes you've repressed those memories for a reason, a self-protective thing."

"Shrinks. They're no help."

"The doctor said it would be risky if you were to see her again."

Glancing down, she whimpered, "But my mother must've loved me."

"In her own way, I suppose."

She looked up. "Why else would she have kidnapped me?"

"She didn't want me to have you."

"Because the judge gave you custody?"

"I thought it was the end of our problems."

Lisa glared at him. "You know what happened to me in that trailer, don't you."

Ray turned his head away.

"Why won't you tell me?"

Taking a deep breath, he lowered his eyes. He didn't want to tell her what the private investigator had found: the glossy black and white photos, the videos, or what the doctor's examination had revealed. When the police went in to make the arrests, the trailer was empty. The suspects were gone without a trace. Kate had disappeared too. Ray looked up. "You don't really want to know."

"Something horrible?"

"Consider yourself lucky to have forgotten."

"A piece of my life is missing, damn it."

"It's better that way."

"Still protecting me, dad?"

He nodded. "From Kate, always."

She put her chin between her knees. "Was she all that bad?"

"Just remember what the doctors said. You shouldn't see her."

"Then I'd better get out of here."

"Where will you go?" he asked, not wanting her to leave, yet knowing it was the best course of action.

"Back to Santa Barbara."

There came a knock at the door. Ray cringed and looked at his watch. Kate wasn't due for another half hour. "I wonder who that could be." He got off the sofa, strode to the door, and looked through the peephole. It was Curtis. Leaving the security chain in place, Ray pulled the door open a crack. "She's not ready yet."

"Come now," Curtis said. "What's to get ready?"

"I want to see her now," Kate said, stepping out from behind Curtis.

"Go away," Lisa shouted.

"You see? She doesn't want to see you." Ray shut the door.

"Not so fast," Curtis bellowed. He knocked on the door, harder this time.

"Go away," Lisa cried out.

Ray rushed to her side and hugged her.

"Please make them leave," she said, now sobbing on his chest.

Curtis kept pounding on the door.

"Lisa, please," Kate said.

Looking into Lisa's teary eyes, Ray felt trapped. The entire situation had gotten out of hand. "She's never going to go away, you know."

Lisa hugged him tightly. "I'm afraid."

"I know." He patted her back, restraining his own tears. He wondered if there was any way to end their fear of Kate, or whether any attempt at reconciliation would just be the beginning of another nightmare.

Curtis banged on the door. "Ray. Open up."

#

Lisa shot up from the sofa and rushed to the window, but three stories down, an asphalt parking lot swayed her from jumping. There was no escape. Wringing her hands, she paced back and forth as Curtis pounded on the door with nerve-wracking relentlessness. She looked at her father sitting stone-faced on the sofa. He wasn't to blame. He'd tried to protect her. He'd spent his whole life protecting her from Kate: the drug addict, the kidnapper, the mother that never was. She had no right to be here. She'd done enough damage.

Anger boiled up in Lisa's stomach. Her shoulders went tight, and a vein in her neck throbbed. Uncertainty clouded her thinking as she wondered what horrors resided in the recesses of her mind, hidden from her consciousness because of the woman outside that door. Why couldn't she remember what had happened to her when she was six, when she was living in that trailer somewhere in the desert north of Las Vegas?

Curtis pounded on the door as if possessed. The whole room echoed with the sounds of his insistence.

Maybe her father was right. Though the risks were high, maybe it was time to put an end to this madness. Hardening her heart, she turned to Ray. "Mother wants to see me." She gritted her teeth. "Let her in."

Ray's face drained. "You sure?"

"I'm not sure of anything."

"What if...?"

"Open the door before I change my mind."

"Christ!" He went to the door, slowly released the chain, and pulled on the knob. A rush of wind came in.

Dr. Curtis stood there, dressed in his new Halloween costume and taking up most of the doorway, sweat glistening on his radish-red cheeks. He took a step forward, somewhat breathless from ranting. "I'm glad to see you've all come to your senses in this matter." He bowed slightly. "Lisa, may I present your mother?" Stepping aside, he revealed a shapely woman standing behind him. She had short black hair highlighted with streaks of silver. Her black eyelashes were heavy on the mascara. She wore a short red dress that matched her lipstick, and black high heels that accentuated the shape of her legs. Enjoli perfume overwhelmed the room.

Lisa's mouth went dry. She expected something inside her head to explode with horrifying images of the past...but nothing happened.

"Hello, Lisa," Kate said, smiling. "My how you've grown."

Lisa stood by the window, speechless, seeing her mother for the first time in memory. Her voice sounded soft, sincere, and it chipped at the chill in Lisa's heart. Lower lip trembling, chin quivering, she felt an urge to run to this woman, hug her, and weep, but she couldn't bring herself to do it. Instead, she lashed out, like she always did when things weren't going her way. "You waltz in here with a lot of nerve, Kate. What the hell are you thinking?"

Curtis cleared his throat. "This is where I leave you all to sort things out." He touched a finger to his hat brim. "Good day." The door closed as he left.

Kate took a step forward.

Lisa put her hand up. "Don't come near me."

"I know this is awkward for you...it is for me, too." Kate's voice sounded soft and caring, like a mother's.

Ignoring the feelings that tugged on her heart, Lisa stood firm. "What do you want?"

"I've come to apologize for what happened. Please believe me. I am so sorry."

"I believe you're one sorry excuse for a mother." Lisa folded her arms across her chest and glared at Kate.

Kate's red lips formed a pout and her eyes drooped. She looked sad and lost.

Lisa fought the urge to break down, to run to her mother and tell her everything was going to be all right. Through tear-blurry eyes, she glanced at her father. He shoved his hands in his pockets. His gaze shifted between the two of them: mother and daughter standing in the same room. They were all together again, a family, a crazy mixed up family. The thought warmed her heart, but the reality of the past quickly iced it over. This fucked up family didn't stand a chance. "So you've seen me. Now what?"

"It's been a long time," Kate said with a slight smile. "I'd like to know more about you, how well you've gotten along, the places you've seen and the loves of your life. You know, mother-daughter things. Could it be like that for us?"

"You expect too much."

"She's right, Kate," Ray said, touching his mustache.

"Stay out of this, Ray," Kate barked.

Lisa felt a sudden surge of contempt. "He comes with me. We're a package deal."

Ray took a step back. "Now wait one minute...I...I don't want anything to do with her."

"Both of you had better get the picture here," Lisa said. "I'm not doing this alone. I haven't had a real mother my whole life, and I don't need one now."

Kate said, "I didn't mean to—"

"You never mean to do anything, Mother. You just did things that hurt us."

"I know, but your father—"

"Stop." Lisa put her hand up. "Don't go there...don't even try. My father didn't do anything to deserve what you did to us."

"I did the best I could."

"Not good enough."

"She's right," Ray put in.

"You're both right." Looking defeated, Kate took a seat on the edge of the sofa. She put the hem of her dress over her knees, daintily, as if she were royalty. "I can only blame myself for my problems. But I've changed. I spent three and a half years in prison for what I did. I'm not the same person anymore. You'll see."

Ray huffed. "You'll never change, Kate."

"Yes I will...I mean I have. All I'm asking for is a

chance to prove it."

Lisa looked at her father. His iron gaze was on Kate, glaring at her as if he'd never be foolish enough to trust her again. He'd never give her another chance. Why should he? And furthermore, why should she? But strangely, welling up from somewhere deep inside her, Lisa wanted to try. She just couldn't figure out why she felt that way. It had to have something to do with what happened in the trailer.

"Please try to understand," Kate said.

"There's only one way I'd consider letting you back into my life, Mother."

"Anything, dear. What can I do?"

"Tell me about that trailer...when I was six."

Kate stiffened as if someone had knifed her in the back. Her eyes went wide. She stared across the room, mute.

"When I was six, Mother."

Ray said, "Don't tell her, Kate."

"Stop protecting me, Dad."

"But the doctor said..."

"Mother, I need to know."

Kate's eyes rotated to Ray. "You haven't told her anything?"

"Nothing."

"Dear God." She looked down and fussed with the hem of her dress. "It wasn't my fault."

"Are you going to lie to her now?" Ray asked.

Lisa wanted to scream. "Will you two stop treating me like a child? I have every right to know what happened."

Leaning forward, Kate put her elbows on her knees and clasped her hands in front of her. Her eyes locked on Lisa. "I'm not sure what happened." Sweat beaded her forehead. "But I can imagine..." She hesitated, took a breath. "You see, I was gone a lot, on assignments with clients in the city, mostly. When I was home, well, this guy kept me pretty much bombed on my ass. He took care of you."

"Who?" Lisa said, her heart clutching.

Kate flinched, rubbed her knuckles, and looked down again.

"Mother!"

"I'm not proud of him." She looked up. "Or what he did."

"What did he do?"

"You've got to understand, Willy was very protective of you."

"Willy?" Lisa put her hand over her wide-open mouth. All the breath came out of her. Her mind blinked in and out of consciousness, like a faulty light bulb in a cellar. She saw a man's face above her now. His hair hung shaggy and long and went all about. He had dark skin and the red nose of a clown, but his face wasn't happy. His teeth were showing like a growling dog, and spit dripped from his mouth. He was sweaty and heavy on top of her. Then there was pain, horrible pain. He was pushing and pushing. It hurt. It hurt. His eyes were like a dragon's. He made grunting noises deep down in his throat. And the pain, so much pain. *"Mommy! Oh Mommy!"* She screamed. She screamed. She screamed.

Lisa's knees buckled, the floor rushed up to meet her, and the memory flew mercifully away.

Chapter Thirty-Six

RAY WAS IN THE WAITING ROOM of Solartech Medical when Janis pushed his way in through the double doors. “I’d hoped for an excuse to get away from the MIGGS spreadsheet,” he said. “But I didn’t have this in mind. What happened to Lisa?”

Ray jumped up from his chair. “It all came back to her. What a shock. She keeled over, and when she came to, she was babbling incoherently.”

“What came back?”

“She’s has problems, Janis, things about her past. The doctor is running some tests.”

“Is she hurt?” Janis looked at the clock, and then he noticed Kate sitting in a chair by the reception counter. A look of shock creased his face. “What’s she doing here?”

“She found us,” Ray said, shoving his hands into his pockets. “I tried to get rid of her, but Curtis insists that she stay.”

“Why would he do that?”

“He likes her.”

“Figures,” Janis said with disdain in his voice. “When can we see Lisa?”

“It’ll be a while.”

“What happened?”

“It’s all Kate’s fault.” Ray glared at his ex-wife. He was angry, but at the same time confused. It had been a long time since he’d seen her, and he thought he’d never care if he ever saw her again, but now that she was here, he was glad to know she hadn't ended up dead somewhere. And even with red eyes and black mascara streaking her cheeks, she still looked beautiful to him. He knew she was genuinely upset about all this, but it still didn't excuse her for what she'd done.

"What does she want?" Janis asked.

"She wants us to forgive her, take her back. Imagine that."

"How did she know you were here?"

Ray pinched his mustache, thinking that was a good question. He'd been so involved with Lisa's problem that he hadn't had time to worry about how Kate had found him. Sitting next to her, he asked, "Who told you we were here?"

"What difference does it make?" Kate said, sniffling.

"For Christ's sake, Kate. Look what you've done to your daughter. You should have stayed away."

"I had to come."

"Haven't you done enough harm?"

She stuck out her chin. "It wasn't my fault. It was the drugs and booze. It was Willy and his arrogance. I wasn't thinking straight. I'm over that now. It's behind me."

"But it's not behind us, Kate."

"Lisa will get over it," she said, slipping a cigarette from her purse. "I'll help her."

"You can't fix this." He grabbed the cigarette, broke it in two, and dropped the remains on the floor. "It's no wonder her moods have been so flighty, her temper tantrums, her bouts of childish behavior, Christ, she's had a monster living in her skull."

"That's Willy's fault."

"What's she talking about?" Janis asked, frowning.

"It's none of your business," Kate said.

Ray didn't want her to start a war with Janis, so he decided to go back to the original question. "How did you find us, Kate?"

She dropped her gaze. "Forget about it. I need a cigarette."

A hot flush of anger shot through Ray's stomach. "Then you can forget about seeing Lisa."

"You..." Kate sat up straight. "You wouldn't."

"I'll call security right now and have you removed from this medical department."

Janis picked up the phone on the reception counter and offered it to Ray.

Kate shouted, "Dr. Curtis said I could see my daughter."

"Wrong! He said you could stay. I can't make you leave Solartech Labs, but I can keep you from seeing Lisa."

"You'd better tell him," Janis said, still holding the phone.

Her eyes darted back and forth between Janis and the phone in his hand. Finally, Ray had enough of her stalling and reached for it.

"All right," Kate said. Her shoulders sagged. "Colonel Fallon told me you were here."

"There." Janis hung up the phone. "That wasn't so hard. It was only Colonel Fallon."

But Ray's brain went on overload. The Colonel hadn't forgotten about the 13th Power experiments. Though he was legally obligated to withdraw his Apaches from Solartech Labs, he was still vigilant. The last thing Ray needed was another incursion by the military. Colonel Fallon could ruin all his plans. That would be totally unacceptable. He glared at Kate again. "What are you, his little spy?"

"I don't care what you're doing. I came because of you, and Lisa." Kate clasped her hands. "Without you, I'll end up back in prison again. I need your help. I can't kick my bad habits alone."

"So Colonel Fallon told you we were here just so you could get us to help you?"

"Yes."

"I don't believe it. He must've asked you to do something for him in return."

"Nothing...really."

Ray could tell she was lying by the look on her face. He'd seen that look so many times before. "Come on, Kate." A few moments passed in silence, and finally, he got tired of waiting for an answer. "Janis, hand me the phone."

"No, wait. He wants to know if you guys are doing any of those 13th Power experiments again. That's all."

Ray could hardly breathe. She was a spy, after all, and that changed everything. "We're not doing those kinds of experiments anymore," he lied. "You've got to tell him that."

"Then I can see Lisa?"

"Kate, you don't understand. If Curtis finds out you're a spy for Colonel Fallon, you'll be rat fodder."

Gasping, Kate put a hand on her chest. "Oh my God. You wouldn't let him do that to me, would you?"

The fear in her eyes startled him. He wanted to tell her that he'd never let Curtis feed her to the rats. After all, he wouldn't want that on his conscience. He didn't hate her that much. And then he felt that old "rescue" mode kick in, the way he'd felt when he met her, when he took her in, when he tried to save her from herself. She was beautiful. She needed help. He didn't have anyone special. He was lonely...it was more emotion than he could handle. The solution seemed simple. "Do us all a favor, Kate. Just leave. We'll all be safer that way."

"I can't."

"Sure you can," Ray said. "Just walk away. You're good at it."

"I'm this close to my daughter," she replied with tears.

"But you're risking your life by staying here."

"Please don't make me go."

There was that look in her eyes again, that look she'd used on him so many times before. How many times had he fallen for her apologies? *It'll never happen again. I'm sorry. I love you.* Rubbing his temples, he tried to resist the emotions tugging at his heart. It surprised him that he still felt that way about her, but deep down, he feared he could lose a lot by giving in to her. She wasn't worth the risk. "How do I know you won't bring it all back, the drugs, the all-nighters, or Willy?"

She lowered her gaze to her fingernails, absently scraped at a chip of polish.

"What if Willy comes back?" Ray prodded.

"He won't," she said, not looking up.

"I want guarantees here, Kate."

"He's dead."

Ray sprang upright in his chair. "You sure?"

"Is that enough guarantee for you?"

Glancing at Janis, Ray didn't know what to think. He needed more than just Kate's word. "How do you know he's dead?"

"I killed him." She looked up from her fingernails. "It was self defense. He's not a threat to us anymore."

"You killed him?" Ray tried to understand how that could have happened. And what about the police? Was she wanted by the law? "How...?"

"It's all right," Kate said, her voice calm. "I'm not in any trouble over it."

"What happened?"

Nervously, she glanced at Janis. "This isn't the time or place to discuss it." She set a gentle hand on Ray's knee. "What's important is...I want my family."

Ray jerked his knee out from under her hand. "You had us once and threw us away."

"Please, take a minute to understand."

"It would take me the rest of my life."

"I know I was wrong, but I couldn't help it." She

buried her face in her hands. "Damn Willy..." Tearfully, she looked up and found Ray's eyes. "He's gone. It won't happen again."

"You bet it won't. You've got to get out of here, Kate. Curtis has a way of finding out about things. The CIA is backing him, and you're in grave danger."

"I'm not leaving my daughter."

Ray frowned. He had to convince her to go. "Lisa and I don't want you here, Kate."

"Doesn't she have a say in this?"

"She doesn't want you. Can you get that through your head?"

Kate threw her shoulders back. "Let her tell me that for herself."

"Let me get this straight," Ray said. "You'd risk your life for Lisa?"

"I already have."

Ray thought about that and knew Kate was right. Just coming to Solartech Labs as a spy for Colonel Fallon could have gotten her killed. She'd risked everything. The least he could do was give her and Lisa a chance.

He sighed. "We'll see what Lisa has to say about it."

***

The doctor didn't allow visitors for two days. Kate left the waiting room only to eat, and she slept in a chair every night. Her back felt like a chunk of wrought iron. Ray and Janis had checked in once in a while. Dr. Curtis's project left them little time for hanging around Solartech Medical. Ray had assured her they weren't working on the 13th Power project. He wanted her to call Colonel Fallon to tell him so...which she didn't. But most importantly, Ray had agreed to let her see Lisa again.

When footsteps echoed from down the hallway, Kate looked up. A doctor in a long white smock approached.

"She wants to see you, now."

"But Ray said he had to be present..."

"I'm the doctor. I say you can see her. It'll do you both some good."

Shock rippled through Kate's stomach. She was going to see Lisa, alone, one-on-one with her daughter. There was something scary about that, especially after how Lisa had reacted to Willy's name.

The doctor showed Kate into a small room, brightly lit, with white walls. Lisa was lying on the bed with her head on a pillow and her blond hair tied back. She wore a white gown. Her skin looked sickly pale.

Approaching the bed, Kate's heart beat faster. Lisa's blue eyes shined with tears. She didn't make eye contact, just stared at the ceiling. Though Lisa was a twenty-six-year-old woman, Kate only saw a young girl lying there, her child. All the years they'd been apart came to mind, and the enormity of that loss began to weigh on her. She had no idea what to say to make things right. "Lisa?"

There was no response.

"The doctor said you wanted to see me."

Mute, Lisa's gaze was fixed. A single tear trickled from her eye.

"My God. What have I done?" Kate stood there, her heart filled with sorrow and regret. She'd been so selfish, caring more about her own sanity than her daughter's. The chasm between them turned out to be much wider than she'd realized. She'd rather have put a gun to her head than to have caused her daughter to suffer this way. Kate's tears flowed without restraint. "I'm so sorry I did this to you." She turned toward the door.

"Wait." Lisa's voice sounded frail.

Kate's heart leaped. She rushed back to the bedside but hesitated to touch her daughter. "Lisa?"

"I want to see my mother," she whispered.

"I'm right here, dear."

"No, my mother, my real mother."

Kate didn't know what to say.

"My mother made me cookies, read me stories, taught me to sew pretty dresses."

"We can still do those things."

"My mother and I had tea parties. She always wore the finest hats with long feathers."

"I like tea..."

"Did you bring your hat?"

"I didn't know..."

"My mother liked to laugh." Lisa turned her head and looked at Kate now. "She was always happy. Not like you."

Kate longed to hug her daughter but didn't dare. "I want to be happy."

"And I want my mother."

"I am your mother, Lisa."

Lisa's bleary blue eyes glared. "You're not the mother I remember."

Kate blinked. *The poor child...* "You made her up...in your imagination."

"My mother would never leave me."

"I..." Kate felt a chill, the truth stinging.

Lisa blinked away tears. "My mother wanted me, but my father sent her away, and then he sent me away, too. He kept us apart, don't you see?"

"Is that what you thought?"

"It's true. My mother cried for me, like I cried for her. Every night we went to sleep with our tears. We cried for each other."

"I cried..."

"You left," Lisa shouted. "You're not my mother. Where is she? What have you done with her?"

"I ruined her life," Kate said softly, the guilt of her past breaking through. "Just like I ruined yours...and Ray's."

"I want her back," Lisa shouted. "Give her back to

me."

Kate felt sick. She now realized this was all her fault...not Willy's. She's the one who made the wrong choices along the way. She should've gotten professional help for her problems, instead of destroying everything she held dear in an effort to erase the nightmares of her father. "I'm sorry." She hung her head. "I'll leave."

"Just like before?"

"What are you saying?"

"You're going to leave me again?"

"I don't understand."

Lisa sat up on her elbows. "You were right about my mother. I made her up. She was all I had." Lisa looked away. "Is she all I'm ever going to have?"

"But look at the mess I've made."

"Mistakes." Lisa looked at her again. "You made mistakes. It was Willy who took advantage of those mistakes."

Kate felt a pang in her heart. "What do you remember?"

Lisa's eyes went big around. She sat up and covered her mouth as if she might vomit.

"Can you tell me about it?"

"I'm afraid," Lisa rasped.

Suddenly, Kate had second thoughts about pushing the issue. It could send Lisa over the edge again. "It's okay. You don't have to tell me anything..."

"I remember..." Lisa trembled; her eyes stared into infinity.

"No, dear. It's all right."

"I remember...Willy. I saw him, blurry images of him, as if shadows in my mind suddenly took form. Children were giggling and crying. Cameras clicked and flash bulbs popped. Willy was taking pictures of us."

"Oh my God. There were others?" Kate reached out for her.

Lisa flinched and pulled back. “Willy was teaching us a game.” She started taking deep breaths, her face drained of color.

“You need to rest,” Kate said, not wanting to hear anymore.

“We played body games...that’s what Willy called them...body games. Some games tickled, some hurt...down there.”

“God no.”

“Then he got on top of me, and I remembered calling out for you. ‘Mommy. Mommy!’” Lisa clasped her hands, knuckles white. “I cried, and I screamed, but you never came.” Her eyes zeroed in on Kate’s. “Where were you, Mother? Where were you?”

“I...”

Tears streaked Lisa’s cheeks. “Why didn’t you stop him?”

“He...”

“Stop him, Mommy. Stop him, Mommy. Stop him...”

Kate cupped her hands over her ears, wishing she could end Lisa’s torment. “He’s dead,” she blurted out. “I stopped him.”

Lisa blinked. “You...you did?”

“He can’t hurt you anymore.”

“Mother?” Lisa threw her arms around Kate’s neck. “You stopped him?”

“I promise.”

Lisa hugged her. “Please don’t leave me.”

Kate held her daughter, tears stinging her eyes. She wanted to take all the hurt away and make everything better, but she knew she couldn’t do that. It was beyond the power of any mother. Instead, she hoped it would be enough to hold her, to let her know she was loved, and above all, protected.

“Why do men play body games?” Lisa asked, sobbing on Kate’s shoulder.

"No, dear," Kate said softly. "It's not just men. Women play the game too. You should know that...unless...have you ever?"

"Never." Lisa shook her head, still clutching Kate.

Kate hugged her daughter, thankful they were talking to each other. It was a start. The healing process had only just begun. Lisa's regression to childish behavior would pass, and in time, the cruel effects of the Abandoned Child Syndrome would diminish as well. Meanwhile, Kate could only hope to measure up to Lisa's imaginary mother.

The door swung open, and Dr. Curtis walked in. "How is she?"

"She's strong," Kate said.

Lisa looked up. "My mother stopped Willy. She's not leaving me...ever again, right, Mom?"

Kate melted. She was 'mom' again. Deep inside her rose a wisp of hope. "Maybe, in time, your father might give me another chance, too. We could be a family again. What do you think of that?"

"I've always wanted a family."

"Very well," Curtis said. "We shall celebrate this evening. I have special plans for us."

Kate cringed as she looked into Curtis's gray eyes and saw a mischievous sparkle there, like the eyes of those Las Vegas businessmen who'd left their wives at home. That look meant only one thing: body games.

Chapter Thirty-Seven

LOS ANGELES AVENUE IN SIMI VALLEY was jammed with rush hour traffic. Inside Bennie's coffee shop, Suzie put a rag to a tabletop. Her feet ached and her back complained with needle-like pains. A fresh batch of ground coffee made the whole place smell of French Mocha.

A customer pulled his rounded body out of a chair. Tip change clinked on the counter. "Thanks, Suzie."

"Have a nice day, sir."

The front door chimed, and he was gone.

Just then, Bennie waddled out of the kitchen with a fresh tray of fudge. He sprinkled it with crushed walnuts and added streaks of vanilla frosting. "Suzie, cut this up," he said and disappeared into the kitchen.

"My favorite."

"Keep your fingers out of it," Bennie's voice boomed.

Suzie chuckled. There were so many good things around here to eat. Maybe that's how Bennie got so big around the middle.

Outside, an engine backfired. Suzie looked out the window just in time to see a dilapidated green Suburban pull into the parking lot: rattling, coughing, and wheezing. It looked like a piece of junk.

Moments later, the front door chimed, and three Mexicans lumbered in. One was a brute of a man. The other two were skinny brown twigs in comparison. Though they wore the soiled clothes of migrant workers, their faces didn't show the harsh effects of sun and wind. The odd trio took seats at the counter, and Suzie handed them menus, noticing their hands were smooth and nails well manicured. They didn't smile.

"Can I help you, gentlemen?"

***

At Solartech Labs, Lisa aimed her red Z28 Camaro toward the main gate. As the sun warmed her face, she thought how convertibles were made for mornings like this. The throaty rumble of high performance exhaust made her pulse race. It was a good diversion from the ache in her heart, the one her mother had put there.

Sitting in the passenger seat, Kate braced herself against the dash. "Where are we going in such a hurry?"

"Santa Barbara." Lisa shifted gears as the wind whipped through her long blond hair. She wanted to forget the past and move on with her life. Taking her mother to see her home seemed like a good way to start the healing process. They could get away from the bustle of Solartech Labs and spend some quality time together. "I have a really nice place, lots of plants and oil paintings. Do you like pillow furniture?"

"I could get used to it." Kate buckled her seatbelt as Lisa slammed fifth gear. "How long have you lived there?"

"Two years, since I came back from Japan."

"Your father moved you around a lot, I hear."

Mute, Lisa braked for a stop sign.

"I'm sorry about that," Kate said, her voice soft. "But you saw Europe, Canada, and the Orient, and didn't you get a good education along the way?"

"Sure." Lisa turned the car right and throttled up. "I see that now, but you've got to know it was hell for me back then. I was too young to appreciate the world. I was hurt and angry." She shifted gears harder than necessary.

"My world was very frustrating."

"It was no cakewalk for me either, honey."

Lisa glanced at her mother sitting there preoccupied with herself again. "Nor dad," Lisa reminded her.

Returning her attention to the road, her eyes swept past the rearview mirror and saw a black executive car lurch onto the road behind them. Jonathan was driving. In the passenger seat, Curtis's dark form was harder to make out. Their sudden appearance caused her breath to hitch. "What do they want?"

Kate twisted in her seat and looked out the rear window. "I told him we'd be back tonight."

"Christ. They'll follow us all day."

The color drained from Kate's face. "Doesn't he trust us?"

"He doesn't trust anybody."

Settling back in her seat, Kate suggested, "Maybe he's just concerned about me."

"Curtis only cares about one thing." Lisa groaned. "Himself."

At the main gate, the guard waved them through. She divided her attention between the road and the rearview mirror. In the mirror, she saw the executive car stop at the gate. The guard approached the driver's window, saluting. Curtis leaned over as if to say something to the guard. She looked forward and saw a Suburban parked on the shoulder. Blue smoke puffed from its exhaust pipe. As she sped past the junker, she noticed three men sitting in the front seat, watching her go by. The bulky driver pointed at her and shouted something in Spanish.

"Creeps." Her eyes returned to the rearview mirror. She couldn't believe what she saw. The Suburban was throwing gravel as it pulled onto the road. She wondered if they were following her, then decided she was being paranoid. However, thinking it best to error on the side of caution, she let the Z28 run wide open.

Roaring down the road out of Simi Valley, the sports car quickly left her pursuers far behind. She let go of the tension in her shoulders, and steering with one hand, took in the scenery around her.

An hour later and north of Ventura, the highway dogged the coastline, passing through small towns and along sandy beaches where palm trees shaded seaside resorts and seabirds hung on lofty winds. The air tasted of salt from the ocean, which stretched like a slate-gray slab toward the horizon. Cool, moist air moving in off the water gave Lisa goose bumps. Her yellow sundress was no longer warm enough for this drive, but determined to leave the convertible top down, she switched on the heater full blast.

Reaching into the back seat, Kate retrieved her sweater. “It’s beautiful here.”

“Ever been to California?”

“I’ve never been anywhere,” Kate said, the wind ruffling her short locks. “Well, except New York when I was three.”

“Hardly counts.”

“My dad said there was too much crime in the Bronx.” Kate donned her sweater. “We moved to Las Vegas were he got a job dealing cards. Turns out Mom got into some dealing of her own, too. They didn’t like each other much.”

“So that’s how it was: like mother, like daughter?”

“Perhaps.”

“I’m not like you, Mom.”

“You have your father to thank for that.”

Lisa steered the Camaro into a left-hand curve. She knew she had a lot to be thankful for when it came to her father. In solitude, they’d both suffered a lot. She owed him more than she could ever repay. There wasn’t anything she wouldn’t do for him.

“What’s that?” Kate pointed at a beachfront coming into view.

"Stearns Wharf."

The pier stretched out over the breaking surf. It looked like a shantytown on stilts, its massive platform cluttered with pitched-roof shops and restaurants.

Lisa found a parking spot, shut off the engine, and pressed the switch that put up the roof.

Kate looked around. "You live here?"

"I want to show you this place first, before it gets too late. Besides, I'm hungry, and they've got the greatest seafood here."

A stiff breeze off the ocean tugged on Lisa's sundress as she led her mother past a dolphin fountain at the waterfront's entrance. On the wharf, people lined the wooden railings with fishing poles in hand and plastic buckets of caught fish at their feet. Colorfully dressed tourists and shoppers milled about the bird-dropping-splattered boardwalk. Some were eating ice cream cones and corn dogs while others watched children feed baitfish to Pelicans that danced and cawed for their meal. All around, couples strolled hand-in-hand and gazed out at the ocean swells.

Overhead, gulls hovered about, shrieking, while their counterparts hunkered down on the gables of white shit-streaked roofs, complaining to the wind...a fishy, salty smelling wind.

"Come on," Lisa said. "Let's hit the Shellfish Company. I'm starved."

While snapping crab legs and peeling shrimp over a bottle of wine, Kate talked about the heartbreak of losing her daughter, not one time, but twice: after the divorce and after the private eye had tracked her down.

"When you were gone..." Kate crushed out a cigarette in a shell-shaped ashtray. "I couldn't sleep, I couldn't eat." She held her glass of wine tightly. "There wasn't anything I could do about it, so I hit the drugs and booze harder. Willy worked me day and night. The sickness in my stomach got worse."

"Was it like that for your mother?"

"She was a hard case."

"Where's my grandma now?"

Kate took two gulps of wine. "Dead." Her eyes shined with tears. "And your grandfather. They both died the same night."

"Oh no." Lisa felt suddenly sad. "How did they die?"

"Trust me, dear, you don't want to know."

"Don't treat me like a child, Mom. What happened?"

Another swallow of wine went down before Kate put her hand on Lisa's arm. "There was a time when I blamed your grandfather for all my problems. He blamed your grandmother."

"They argued?"

"I was only thirteen, for God's sake."

"What happened?"

"I was torn between the two of them." Kate swished the wine around in her glass. "Who was right, who was wrong, it didn't matter to me. I just wished they'd stop fighting."

"Mom, how did they die?"

Kate drained her glass. "I was in my room that night." Her hands began to tremble, but she clung to the empty glass. "I could hear them shouting downstairs...even with my head buried under my pillow." She swallowed, her eyes staring into space. "Dishes shattered on the kitchen floor...and...and then I heard a pop."

Lisa felt a chill.

"There was silence," Kate whispered. "It went on and on, and I was more terrified than when they were fighting. I couldn't take it, anymore. I ran downstairs and..." She quit in mid-sentence, took up the bottle, and shakily poured wine in her unsteady glass.

"Mom?"

"I can't..." Kate raised the glass to her mouth, began

gulping down wine.

Lisa grabbed her arm. “Mother, don’t drink so fast.”

“I’ve never told anyone before.” She tried to pull away, stiff-armed, spilling some wine.

“Drinking doesn’t help. Haven’t you learned that much?”

Slowly, Kate relaxed her arm. “I’ve spent my whole life trying to forget.”

“It hasn’t worked,” Lisa said, releasing her mother’s arm. “Try something different.”

Kate looked at her daughter, a long silent look, and then set down the wine glass. “All right.” She sat up in the chair, shoulders back. “My mother was lying on the kitchen floor.” She lowered her head, wringing her hands. “There was so much blood.”

“My God.” Lisa felt a pang in her chest. “He shot her?”

“He was standing over her with a gun,” Kate went on. “I don’t know what I was thinking. I just ran to her, fell on my knees...I huddled over her, bawling, pleading with her to look at me. I don’t remember what all I said, but I remember her eyes. They were empty.”

Kate reached for the wine glass.

“My father just stood over us, his eyes filled with rage. There was no hint of concern or remorse or compassion anywhere on his face.”

“You must’ve been terrified of him.”

“Until he pointed the gun at me...I was, but I shouldn’t have said what I said.” Kate swallowed wine. “It was all my fault...what he did next.”

“What did you say, Mother?”

“You can’t imagine what was going through my mind as I stared into that gun barrel. It was the last thing my mother saw, the last thing I would see. I wasn’t afraid anymore...it made me so angry...I just shouted out: ‘I hope you rot in hell, you bastard.’”

Lisa leaned toward her. “And he shot you?”

Kate finished the wine. “Sometimes I wish he had, but instead, he put the gun in his mouth and pulled the trigger. I watched the back of his head hit the kitchen wall.”

Lisa groaned. “What a horrible thing to see. What did you do?”

“I stayed with my mother, my knees in her blood, my nightgown soaked. Three days passed before anybody found us.”

“It must’ve been awful.”

She shivered. “I’ll never forget the smell.”

Lisa pushed away her half-eaten meal, trying not to visualize that horrific scene, but failing. Now she understood her mother’s torment and how that ordeal had affected her. “Dad thought something was bothering you, something you wouldn’t talk about.”

“Sober, I couldn’t rid my mind of my dead mother, my father’s crazed face, all the blood, the smell, and the days of silence that followed. And the nightmares...my mother lying there staring at nothing, my father’s head exploding. I couldn’t sleep.” She shivered. “I’d wake up screaming in the middle of the night. I couldn’t handle it. His memory was tormenting me, so I set out to fix him. I got drunk and stoned out of my mind. It was the only way I could put an end to him. I killed him...in my own way, for what he did to my mother.”

“What did you do...I mean...without your parents?”

“For a while, Social Services tried to help. They put me in a couple of foster homes, but I always ran away...I just couldn’t get far enough away from myself.”

“You blamed yourself?”

Kate blinked. “I wondered what would have happened if I hadn’t cursed my father. He might still be alive.”

“That’s nonsense.” Lisa couldn’t grasp the guilt her mother had put on herself. “He could have shot you instead.”

"I didn't realize that. I just ran, living on the streets, at first, hustling for food, panhandling. I fell in with a rough crowd, runaways mostly. They got me into cocaine. It helped me forget my father, but it was expensive. Handouts didn't begin to cover the cost. So I sold blood 'til they wouldn't take me anymore. Then I started doing favors for my dealer in exchange for the stuff."

"Willy?"

She nodded. "I was sixteen when he took me in. It was all right at first, but the favors I did for him soon turned to favors for his clients. I went from a liability to an asset within a month. From then on, he made my life hell."

"And Dad?"

"The dear man." Kate sighed. "Your father came along a couple years later. He tried to save me from myself...God bless him. He didn't have a prayer. It was prison that finally turned everything around for me, Lisa. Now I want to start fresh. I want to do things right this time. I don't ever want to go back."

Lisa looked at her mother's tears. How similar her story sounded: fathers blaming mothers, and daughters left to deal with the anguish caused by all the chaos. Then a stark reality came over her. Kate and Ray were her only family. She had to hold on to them. She had to be strong for them, and they had to be strong for each other.

"We should go." Kate stood. "I want to see your place before it gets too late."

Leading the way outside, Lisa took in the salty air as she walked along the wharf and held her mother's arm. The fishermen, shoppers, tourists, and noisy birds seemed only a blur to her now. Finally, she was with her mother, a mother that was as much a victim as herself. Their bond was their suffering. They had a lot in common after all.

At the Camaro, Lisa keyed the door lock. Suddenly, a god-awful rumbling came from behind her, the annoying sound of a bad muffler. Curiosity made her turn and look.

What she saw almost stopped her heart. It was the junker Suburban. "Get in, Mom, quick."

As she fastened her seatbelt, a big Mexican got out of the Suburban and bolted toward her. Hot panic rose in her chest. She fired up the engine and roared backwards out of the parking space. The Mexican ran after her, now brandishing a gun.

"Get down, Mom."

A bullet zinged off the hood.

Lisa floored it, spun the car around. In first gear and under full throttle, the tires squealed and spewed blue smoke. Wrestling the steering wheel, she fishtailed the Z28 through the parking lot, scattering pedestrians and birds. The car banged over a curb and onto Garden Street. She hit second gear and lit up the tires again. By the time she jammed third gear, she flew over a double set of railroad tracks. The Camaro hugged the S curves. In fourth gear now, she blew a yellow light, hung a hard right, and careened onto Highway 101. She barely had time to catch her breath when the Suburban cut a diagonal path toward the highway as it barreled down an on ramp.

"Oh, dear," Kate said.

The Suburban skidded onto the highway into the lane in front of her, fishtailing wildly.

"Do you know those guys?" Kate shouted.

"I thought they were your friends." Lisa floored the gas and tried to go around the Suburban, but it swerved and cut her off.

Kate shook her head. "I don't recall—"

Suddenly, the Suburban's brake lights lit up. Smoke swirled from its tires.

Lisa yanked the steering wheel left. The Camaro went into a skid. She counter-steered and punched the throttle, causing the Z28 to dart up alongside the braking Suburban. Immediately, gunfire erupted from the open windows.

The Camaro's passenger window exploded.

Kate screamed.

Bullets pelted the door, fender and trunk, and ripped through the convertible top. The windshield spider-cracked. Like a shotgun blast, the right front tire blew.

The steering wheel shuddered in Lisa's hands. She hit the brakes. The car skidded off the highway. In a wild ride, the car banged up a rugged embankment, soared across a railroad track, and crashed into a thicket of scrub oak with a bone-jarring bang.

The hood folded up and the airbags exploded. The engine stalled.

Dazed, Lisa looked at Kate. "Are you okay?"

"You wrecked your car." She pushed back a deflating airbag. "What are we going to do now?"

Hissing radiator steam swirled in the wind. "We'd better get out of here."

Kate tugged on the door handle. "It's jammed. I can't get out."

Lisa put her shoulder to the driver's door. It popped open with a creak. "This way." She helped her mother crawl over the console and out of the car.

"Hola, Senoritas!"

Fear stabbed Lisa's chest. Three Mexicans stood on the railroad tracks, the Suburban parked beside them, one big man and two little men, all with guns drawn. Their loose-fitting clothes rippled in the wind.

"What do you want?" Lisa shouted up at them.

"Come here real easy like, *por favor*," the big Mexican said. "We don't want to shoot you where you are. Be like a dog to die down there."

"Run." Kate said.

"No." Lisa grabbed Kate's arm. "We wouldn't get far. They'll just shoot us in the back."

"What do they w-want with us?" Kate's voice was raspy with fear.

"Let's ask them," Lisa replied.

"You can't be serious."

"Got a better idea?"

"No."

"Stay behind me." Lisa plodded up the embankment. Loose gravel lodged inside her sandals. The relentless wind tugged at her sundress. During the steep climb, she paid close attention to her breathing, kept her panic in check and her mind focused on the menace above: three men and three guns. The guns would be the hard part.

Reaching the tracks, she joggled rocks from her sandals. The sound of traffic whizzed by on the highway. She knew that no one would see them on the tracks, pretty much hidden by the scrub oak on each side. They were alone. She had to be cool. Eye contact. Show no weakness. "What do you guys want?"

"Kate Crawford?" the big one asked, his black eyes on her mother.

Kate took a step back. "Y-yes?"

"Our father sends his regards."

"Your father?"

"Miguel Herrera."

Kate put her hand on her heart. "Willy's father?"

The big Mexican grinned. "*Si*. And now you must die." He brought up the gun and pointed it at Kate's heart.

"No." Lisa's shout caused the big man to flinch. In that stalled moment, she kicked the gun from his hand, which sent it tumbling down the embankment and into the scrub oak.

Before the smaller men could react, she planted a spinning back kick to the stomach of the nearest armed man. Air huffed from his lungs. He fell backwards and slammed to the ground. She kicked the gun free of his hand, then pivoted with one smooth motion and struck the last armed man's wrist with a karate blow. Bones cracked. He dropped the gun. Buckling to his knees, he wailed in agony, his hand dangling from the stub of his arm.

Without a wasted movement, Lisa spun around and set her feet apart, crouching, her hands rigid, and her eyes fixed on the last brother standing, the big one coming at her, teeth bared and eyes but narrow slits of fury. She sidestepped his bullish charge and tripped his feet. He fell forward, hit the Suburban's fender face-first, and slumped to the ground, moaning.

She picked up the dropped gun and, while pointing it at the Mexicans, looked at her mother. "It appears Willy's father wants you dead."

Kate stared at the men writhing on the ground. "How did you do that?"

"Mother, Miguel Herrera is out for revenge."

"I don't...I...I don't even know the man..." She took a step back. "My God, he sent his sons to kill me. He's got to be crazy. He'll stop at nothing—"

The sound of a roaring engine interrupted her. Skidding and throwing gravel, the black executive car careened around a bend in the tracks and raced toward them, tires thudding on the washboard railroad ties.

"Oh, shit," Lisa said. "It's Curtis."

"Thank God."

"God's got nothing to do with him."

"He'll know what to do."

"He's going to make things worse."

The car stuttered to a stop, dust swirling in the air. Doors flew open. Curtis got out first, ducking against the wind. "What's going on here?"

Jonathan sprinted to his side.

Kate ran to Curtis and hung on his arm. "They tried to kill me."

"Is that so?" Curtis pushed her away and kept walking toward Lisa.

Kate tried to stop him. "Where the hell did you come from?"

"We had trouble finding you." Jonathan pointed to the

executive car. "It's not a four wheel drive truck, you know."

With his black coat thrashing in the wind, Curtis stepped up to the men sprawled on the tracks. He took the gun from Lisa and tossed it to Jonathan. "Who are they?"

"The Herrera brothers," Kate said, her voice faltering.

Curtis turned to Jonathan. "Do you suppose they're related to the Herrera boys we killed back in Juchitan?"

"Could be," Jonathan replied, holding the gun on the Mexicans. "Sure looks like them, except the big one there."

"Check the truck." Curtis motioned to the Suburban and turned to the sniveling Mexican with the broken arm. "What are you boys doing here?"

"*No hablo Ingles*," he replied and cowered away from Curtis.

"Hey, boss," Jonathan called out. "Looks like we were next." He held a folder he found in the Suburban. "Our names are in here, and our pictures, and look, here's one of Kate." He held up a glossy black and white that showed more flesh than Lisa cared to see. "Says here she killed Willy, Miguel's youngest son." He flipped some pages, the wind working against him. "And guess who else they're after...our CIA buddies, Stevens and Cisco. Seems they killed his oldest son in an Atlanta shootout. Hell, you know what this is, boss? We've got us an assassination squad here."

Curtis curled his upper lip. "Is that right?" He kicked the big Mexican in the ribcage.

Lisa had seen that look in Curtis's eyes before: anger and hate, edged with a little glee, as if he enjoyed the thoughts that entered his mind. She felt a chill, took her mother's hand, and they backed away from Curtis.

"Leave them alone," Kate shouted. "Let the police handle this."

"*Si*," the brother with the broken arm said. "We go to jail and not come back."

"No English, hey?" Curtis snarled. "You lying scum. Guess all you Herrera boys are stupid." From under his long coat, Curtis pulled out a gun and slid back the breach, chambering a round.

"Don't," Lisa shouted, clinging to her mother.

Gunshots banged: three, six, nine of them echoed away on the wind.

Curtis stepped back. "That'll teach the bastards."

"You...you killed them," Kate yelled. "In cold blood."

Curtis turned to her. "Shut up or you'll be next."

Lisa gave him a shove. "Leave her alone."

"What's with you and that pathetic father of yours?" Curtis pointed at Kate. "Don't you know you can't turn a whore into a housewife?"

Kate turned away and sobbed in her hands.

Lisa resisted an urge to kick the grin off Curtis's face. "My mother is not a whore, but you...you're a murderer."

"Serves Miguel right," Curtis replied coldly. "Now all his sons are dead." He turned to Jonathan. "Throw the bodies in the Suburban and drive it back to Solartech. You know what to do with them."

"The rat cellar, boss?"

Curtis nodded. "Make it quick. While you clean up this mess, we'll go into Santa Barbara, file an accident report, and get a wrecker out here for the car. Nobody will be the wiser."

"What about this pile of junk?" Jonathan kicked a tire on the Suburban.

"Have Materials Handling cut it into scrap metal and ship it to Utah with the next batch nuclear waste."

"You got it, boss."

Curtis glared at Lisa and Kate. "Get in the car."

Chapter Thirty-Eight

IN TECH-COM CONTROL, TECHNICIANS sat at their terminals as Janis studied the supercomputer printouts. All the rows of figures, equations, and formulas were making him dizzy. And fatigued. He'd been working twelve-hour shifts, seven days a week, and the grueling schedule had worn him down. The entire team exhibited the strain, as well. After two month's work, Tracy's earlier success with the particle beam had not been duplicated. Tomorrow was Thanksgiving. "No particle beam, no turkey," Curtis had threatened.

Janis pushed his glasses up and pinched the bridge of his nose. "I don't see anything wrong with this program."

"Take 47D out," Lo said. "Grid sequencer keeps stacking."

Janis flipped through the printout, found the sequencer stack, but didn't see a problem with it. He looked up and saw Boris and Ray talking it over. "What do you guys think?"

Nodding, Ray said, "Give it a try, Lo."

Lo went to work on his keyboard.

At the laser terminal, Tracy was crosschecking the firing voltages again. Her monitor flashed ERROR, and Janis saw frustration grow on her face. Undaunted, she typed some more.

"Check this out," Ray said, now watching a replay on the MIGGS monitor, his face etched with concern.

"What is it?"

"The escape velocity is wrong." He typed something. The monitor displayed a swirling funnel made up of distorted squares, a transparent graph rolled into the shape of a cone. It spun faster and faster and began to turn colors.

Janis had seen this all before. Rows of yellows and greens turned to blues, and then to a radiant orange that became more vivid as the funnel narrowed at its base.

"Right here." Ray pointed to a band of red squares appearing at the top of the vortex. "The Laser fired at 0-33, down here. That's not right. It needs to be 0-47, in the red band, up here, the event horizon: escape velocity 186,000 miles per second."

Janis looked at Lo still bent over his keyboard, typing like mad. Something wasn't making any sense. If 47D kept stacking, he wondered how taking it out of the sequencer would fix the grid problem at 0-33. "Tracy? Is anything wrong with 0-33?"

"I'm working on it."

"You'd better hurry," Robert said from his chair in front of the accelerator terminal. "She's topping out at 15TEV." Fifteen Trillion Electron Volts: the highest energy level the accelerator could produce and still hold the particles on course for the laser.

Boris, now perched in his chair at the main control console, cleared his throat. "Keep it online, Robert."

"I'm trying."

Frustration rising, Janis rushed back to his terminal and punched in the formula reprogramming schedule. They were running out of time, again. The accelerator was about to max out. They'd have to shut it down and wait until tomorrow. He slammed his hand down on the counter. It was always tomorrow.

He glanced up to the office above the control room. As usual, Dr. Curtis stood at his window, his arms folded across his chest, watching like a vulture from a high branch. The CIA agents stood with him, Stevens and Cisco. Janis didn't like either one of them. They were nothing more than jailers, bringing Tracy to work in the morning and taking her away at night. They always looked angry, their eyes cold and jaws set as they enforced *The Ark's* will.

Returning his attention to the glow of his monitor, Janis started reworking the formulas for 0-33, but everything he tried failed. If 0-33 was the key, then why didn't it fit the lock? Or perhaps he had the wrong lock. "Tracy, can you fire the laser at 0-47?"

"That's too high," she said, shaking her head.

"Try it anyway."

She shrugged and typed. Columns of figures scrolled down her screen. Then she got an error message. "No. It's got to be 0-33."

Janis's hopes sank. He needed more from 0-33. There had to be a way to amplify it. On a hunch, he turned to Roger at the power distribution console. "Can you send more power to the MIGGS?"

"How much do you need?" he asked, swiveling in his chair.

"All you've got."

"Tech-Com Control can only take a fifteen percent overload before the breakers start popping."

"It's too dangerous," Boris shouted out.

But Tracy's eyes lit up. "Now I remember. The grid wasn't buffered before, when the particle beam worked."

Janis knew the buffers were supposed to prevent a repeat of the last disaster. Now they were interfering with the success of the entire project.

"Take out the buffers," Ray said.

Janis looked at Lo. He was still working on 47D. "It'll take a month to reformulate the programmer."

"Then let me try it with more power," Tracy said and reset the values plus fifteen percent and ran the simulator again. The vortex on the MIGGS monitor started spinning wildly and changing colors. Moments later, her screen flashed *O-33=0-47*. "That's it." She turned to Janis. "I can fire the laser at O-47...but what about the MIGGS?"

Janis's temples throbbed as he watched the MIGGS monitor. The last time they changed a formula, the MIGGS failed, a mistake that nearly cost them their lives. But this time, the MIGGS monitor displayed a bright red rotating vortex: escape velocity 186,000 miles per second. "Yes." He jabbed a fist in the air. "The simulation works. What do you think, Ray?"

"I say it's a go for the experiment."

Pumped with renewed excitement, Janis turned to Boris. "Should we give it a try?" The ex-Russian scientist had final say.

Fear creased his face. "It's too dangerous."

Tracy huffed. "Come on, Boris. Do you want us to spend the rest of our lives in this dungeon?"

Boris's face drooped. "All right, but you I have warned."

Finally, Lo looked up from his keyboard. "I finished take out 47D."

"Put it back in," Janis said. "And hurry."

Lo frowned. "Make up mind, will you?" He went back to typing and deleted his changes.

"Johnson, bring the MIGGS online," Boris said.

Johnson worked the controls. The MIGGS began to hum as electromagnets and ion fields energized.

At his power station, Roger started turning knobs and checking dials. Sweat beaded his forehead. "Come on, baby." Power levels rose fifteen percent. The lights in Tech-Com Control brightened.

Janis rushed to the MIGGS' window and looked inside. A red hue from deep within the accelerator reflected off a rocket fuselage on the floor and the mirror-like refractors of the space transporter's pulse light engines. The cockpit windows stared back at him, cold and charcoal black. He shivered, knowing that once the particle beam was perfected, the transporter could then be degenerated into the 13th Power. Ray was going to get himself killed. But that was another day's problem. Today, the transporter wasn't going anywhere.

"Engage the sighting system," Boris said to Tracy.

A thin red beam of light shot into the MIGGS and hit a shiny titanium dish positioned in front of the transporter's engines. The sighting dish angled the red beam down thirty degrees to the MIGGS' grated floor.

Working a knob on her terminal, Tracy moved the sighting dish. The red beam shifted toward the target, a ten-foot section of missile fuselage anchored to the floor with steel bands. When the beam shined directly on the center of the target, Tracy announced, "Laser locked."

Ray joined Janis at the MIGGS window. "Let's do it."

At that, Johnson pushed the MIGGS acceleration lever forward. "Here we go. Better hang on."

A hum got louder and louder as the MIGGS' power came up, its gravity field boosted by the extra voltage Roger had sent to the machine. An ion shield appeared, glowing bright blue around the transporter, protecting it from the crushing gravity produced.

Janis shifted his eyes to Johnson's monitor where a faint yellow vortex began rotating on the screen. *RECORD* flashed in the lower left corner.

"She's coming up nicely," Johnson said. "Forty percent. Fifty!"

"The temperature is climbing into the red," Robert announced from his chair at the accelerator terminal. "Two minutes."

"She'll make it," Johnson said, patting the side of his MIGGS monitor. Then he whispered, "You can do it, baby." On the screen in front of him, the vortex swirled with a mix of colors, yellows and greens. A blue band appeared. "Seventy!"

Janis watched through the thick window. A black mist began to boil up inside the MIGGS, an ungodly swirling fog. The MIGGS started howling under the strain of the gravity field, and then roared like an oncoming freight train, vibrating the glass, the walls, and the floor.

"Eighty percent," Johnson said. "Orange."

"Sixty seconds," Robert shouted.

"0-33," Tracy reported.

In awe, Janis watched the black mist churn inside the MIGGS. It whipped around the transporter, expanding faster and faster, roiling like an angry storm, pitching and curling, growing bigger and thicker with each passing second.

"Soul of tiger," Lo said.

A shiver rippled down Janis's spine.

"0-40," Tracy said, her voice pitched an octave higher.

The transporter, sighting dish, and fuselage became shadows, nearly swallowed up by the mist swirling wildly inside the MIGGS.

"0-43."

Sound pounded Janis's chest and hurt his ears. "Come on..."

"Ninety percent."

"Thirty seconds," Robert shouted.

Tracy said, "0-44."

"We've got red," Johnson reported. "One hundred percent, Tracy. Whenever you're ready."

"Not yet," she shrieked. "0-45."

The transporter disappeared, completely engulfed in the swirling black mist.

"0-46..."

Everything was black inside the MIGGS: the red hue, the sighting beam, and the blue ion haze were all gone. Not even light could escape the gravity field now. Janis's formulas proved out. The MIGGS was working flawlessly.

"0-47."

"Fire," Boris ordered.

Tracy pushed the button.

From out of the synchrotron came the buzzing particle beam, a laser saturated with protons and accelerated to the speed of light. It cracked like thunder and shook Tech-Com Control. The power of the sun fused and focused on a single point, all of which was hidden from Janis's view within the thick black mist. But he knew a head-on impact with the atoms of the target meant its complete disintegration. If it weren't for the gravity field that trapped the particle beam inside the MIGGS, there'd be nothing to stop it from disintegrating Tech-Com Control, Solartech Labs, or perhaps all of Simi Valley, California.

"Tracy, status report." Janis had to shout over all the noise.

"I'm checking."

Johnson pulled back on the MIGGS deceleration lever. The roar subsided to a rumble. Vent fans whirled on, and the air began to smell like burnt metal. Electromagnets wound down to a hum. Inside the MIGGS, the swirling mist broke into small vortexes and twisted down floor grates as the gravity equalized.

Now Janis could see the transporter glistening under the green ceiling lights. The black mist settled into an eerie sort of rolling ground fog.

"Janis," Tracy shouted, excitement shrieking from her voice.

He looked toward her station just as she twisted around in her chair, her smile beaming.

TARGET TERMINATED flashed on the monitor behind her.

"You were right," she said. "0-47 did the trick."

"Brilliant." Ray slapped Janis on the back.

Janis wasn't as quick to celebrate. He swallowed and looked into the MIGGS window again. The black fog wisped away, revealing the jagged remains of the steel bands that once secured the missile fuselage to the floor. Nothing was left. The target had been disintegrated. The particle beam had shattered the missile's atoms and scattered them like specks of dust in the universe. With that realization, he felt a mix of pride and relief. Perhaps he deserved the reputation of a top-notched mathematician after all.

Unexpected applause suddenly echoed through Tech-Com Control. It came from the office landing upstairs: from Dr. Curtis, his sidekick Jonathan, and the CIA jailers, Stevens and Cisco.

"Bravo. Well done." Curtis cheered as he moved down the steps.

Tracy's printer clattered and rolled out paper. She tore it off and examined it with wide eyes. "It's all here." She rushed to Janis's side. "The particle beam formulas."

"I'll take that." Curtis snatched it from her hand. "*The Ark* will be most pleased. Now maybe we can get on with my agenda: the Higgs boson."

"And don't forget about the 13th Power," Ray said.

"Certainly," Curtis replied under his breath.

Janis shook his head, thinking they'd never be satisfied.

Stan Burton rushed in, followed by his team of engineers. With his hand outstretched, he went directly to Ray. "You did it. Congratulations."

"Now we can all go home," Janis said.

"Correction," Curtis replied sternly. "You boys aren't finished yet. The Supers may have printed out this technology, the results of your hard work of which, I must say, I am quite proud, but there is still the issue of delivery. We must have the hardware."

"Leave that to us," Stan said. "My team has built seven sighting dishes with pulse light thrusters. We've fitted them to Lockheed's AUX satellites. With the data you have in your hand there," he pointed to the printout, "we'll have two Proton Laser Resonators operational within three months. *The Ark* will have his damn hardware, and he'll have no more reason to use our families as pawns in his Star Wars scheme."

"Very well." Curtis handed Stan the printout. "Three months." He turned toward the steps. "Come on, Jonathan. I say it's time to celebrate." They tromped up the stairs.

Boris shuffled up to Janis, his gray hair tousled. "We have made a powerful weapon for powerful men."

Lo shook his head. "Not a good thing, Janis."

"I know." He turned to Stan. "What have you guys been doing, working nights?"

"Twenty-four-seven."

"What's the rush?" Ray said. "Now they'll have Star Wars in orbit three months from now."

Janis frowned at Stan. "You should have stalled. Now you've laid this weapon right in their hands."

"We all want to go home," Stan replied. "We just gave them what they wanted."

"And damn the rest of the world?"

Glancing at his team, Stan said, "We're engineers, Janis. You guys invented the particle beam."

"But you're helping them put it in orbit."

"Don't worry. We've built in our own safeguards."

"There's no such thing."

"I know what I'm doing, Janis. We haven't given them anything we can't take back."

"What do you mean?"

"Call it an insurance policy."

"An insurance policy?"

Ray jumped in. "For Christ's sake, Janis. He's on our side. Give him a break."

"This whole thing stinks like a shit house." Janis swallowed his frustration and looked over his team who had gathered around: Robert, Roger, Johnson, and some of the others. Tracy was standing with the CIA men, talking. Janis realized that no one in the room had any choice in the matter. "You all did a really good job. Thanks." Handshakes and uneasy smiles went all around.

"Janis?"

He turned to the sound of Tracy's voice, thinking it almost gleeful for a change.

The CIA men walked out the door...without her.

As she came toward him with a slight saunter to her step, he noticed a different look in her eyes, full of sparkle from bridled tears. "Tracy?"

"They let me go."

Janis felt a surge in his bloodstream. "Oh my God."

"Finally." She threw her arms around his neck and kissed him like she did before, when they were together in the kiva that evening before this nightmare began. He took in the sweetness of her tongue, the heat of her breath in his mouth. "I love you," he said and hugged her.

Then Curtis's voice boomed down from his office above Tech-Com Control. "One more thing, people."

Janis looked up. "Now what?"

Curtis grinned. "Turkey for everyone."

Chapter Thirty-Nine

JOHN NATHAN HELD THE REPORT in his hand and fell back into the chair behind his desk. He needed to catch his breath. They'd done it. Star Wars was his. Directive Number 119 could go into the history books. The greatest day of his life was here, finally. He couldn't believe it.

Without a knock, the door burst open. Chief Lawrence came in, nearly at a full run. His bald head gleamed with sweat, and a fat cigar smoldered between his fingers. "Congratulations, John. Have a cigar." He lifted a stogie from his breast pocket.

"You know I don't smoke those nasty things."

"Suit yourself. Does the President know yet?"

Nathan combed his fingers through his hair. "I'll tell him right after I check the launch schedules at NASA."

"You don't have any clout with those boys," Lawrence said.

"Kennedy Space Center will cooperate with the CIA."

"But you can't tell them what to launch."

"True." Nathan sat forward, propping his forearms on the desk. "However, the President can."

"Perhaps," Lawrence said. "I'm just glad our involvement in this affair is over." Then his expression hardened. "Now we can tie up those loose ends."

Nathan knew what Lawrence was referring to, the elimination of witnesses. "What's the rush?"

"I'm telling you, John, we've got to do it right away."

Lawrence pointed a stiff finger. “You’re pressing your luck.”

At that, Nathan stood. “I made a deal with Melvin Anderson. He needs Boris and Tracy to get his Higgs boson.”

“I say damn the deal.”

“After they’re done, you can have them both.” He paused. “Hell, kill Melvin Anderson while you’re at it.”

“They know too much, John. You’re on the brink of making history, for Christ’s sake. Don’t take any more chances.”

Nathan sat in his chair, which creaked eerily in the silence that suddenly permeated his office. He wondered if Lawrence was right. Would killing Tracy and Boris ensure his place in history? If they talked, it would be federal prison instead of fame, or maybe a needle in his arm. It was too risky. He took in a breath. “I’ll get Stevens to do it.”

“Do you want me to tell him?”

“I will.” Nathan pushed the intercom button. “Get Agent Stevens on the ComLink. And scramble it.”

“Yes, sir.”

***

“Isn’t this great?” Cisco said, piling his plate with turkey, mashed potatoes, and gravy...lots of gravy. The cooks at Solartech Labs’ cafeteria had set out a feast for the employees. Dr. Curtis had declared Thanksgiving a holiday. What a guy.

The cafeteria buzzed with the clatter of utensils and conversation. Many of the technicians who’d gathered for this meal had a look of relief on their faces; after all, a big load had been lifted from their shoulders. Some held cell phones to their ears, calling family and loved ones, but Cisco had already spoken with his parents. Besides, home was where the food was, and this was home sweet home.

"Come on," Stevens said and gave Cisco a shove down the serving line. "Save some for the rest of us."

Cisco took in the wonderful array of aromas wafting from the kitchen: sweet potatoes, pumpkin pie, chocolate cake, and cranberry sauce. "Look at the size of them rolls. Yum."

Sitting at the nearest table, he dug in. "I sure am glad we don't have to baby-sit Tracy anymore," he said through a mouthful of mashed potatoes. "The rabbit food she eats would kill a grown man."

"There's no kind of food that would kill you, Cisco." Stevens unfolded his napkin. "Tracy takes good care of herself."

"No doubt. Working out two hours every night in the gym. Hell, I got tired just watchin' her." Cisco downed a sweet potato.

"But isn't she a beauty?" Stevens fiddled with his fork.

Cisco looked up from his plate and thought he saw a starry-eyed Stevens. "What's with you, man? She was an assignment. The assignment is over. So eat."

Stevens mulled that over in his head. "You're right," he said finally and forked a chunk of turkey. "I'd be better off thinking about those big fish in Canada."

"Yeah, sure...like we're ever going to catch any of them." Cisco ripped his roll in half and reached for the butter.

Just then, the ComLink buzzed from Stevens' belt. He put his fork down and answered the call. There was a long moment of silence that got Cisco's attention. Looking up from his dinner, he saw Stevens' eyes go wide and stare at the wall. "Sir?" Stevens said with a sharp gasp.

Every muscle in Cisco's body went tight. "Who is it?"

Stevens shook his head, listening, his eyes glazing over.

Squinting, Cisco wondered if it was another

assignment. His curiosity was unrestrainable. "What's going on?"

"Yes, sir," Stevens said with dismay in his voice, as if he'd suddenly resigned himself to some horrible fate. "Right away." He closed the ComLink.

"Jesus, Craig, you look like you've just seen a ghost. What was that all about?"

Stevens leaned forward, shifted his eyes back and forth and whispered, "It was *The Ark*."

"He called you personally?"

Stevens nodded, a look of shock etched on his face.

Cisco's appetite left him, as a soul would abandon a dead body. "What did he say?" A moment of silence held the answer in limbo, which wore on his already-frazzled nerves. "Agent Stevens...what the fuck?"

"He's ordered us to kill Tracy and Boris."

Cisco's throat clutched, then he realized it had to be some kind of sick joke. "Yeah, right."

But Stevens sat stone-faced, his dinner steaming in front of him.

Cisco swallowed. "You're not kidding?"

"Nope," he said, hard-lipped.

"We're finished with this assignment. It's over, done, we're out of here. Killing them wasn't part of the deal."

Stevens picked up his fork and looked down at his dinner. "Tracy and Boris did their jobs. They gave *The Ark* what he wanted. *The Ark* assured them they'd be free to go when it was over."

"Now *The Ark* wants to alter the deal." Cisco felt a stranglehold of contempt for his boss. "Well, I've got news for him. I'm not going to have any part of it."

"I knew you wouldn't," Stevens said flatly.

Cisco leaned forward, unsure what that meant. "Are you going to do it?"

Examining his fork, Stevens explained, "I followed my father's footsteps into the CIA to help weed the bad guys out of this world." He shook his head in disgust. "Funny thing about that. Only now have I come to realize I've been working in the shadow of the worst villain of them all...and in the name of national security, no less."

"Maybe we should kill *The Ark*."

"There's been enough killing. Let's go fishing instead. Canada awaits."

Cisco held up his fork. "I'm with you, partner. Let's eat."

***

A bitter December wind swirled across the White House drive as a black limousine screeched to a stop under the portico. The car door flew open, and Nathan pulled himself out. Secret Service agents greeted him with stiff-armed salutes.

"Gentlemen."

With the wind cutting through his black trench coat, Nathan climbed the steps to the front doors, two at a time. He clutched a briefcase in his right hand. In it were the particle beam data sheets, test results with scientific verification from nuclear physicist Ray Crawford, and the launch schedules for the next six months from Kennedy Space Center.

"Morning, sir," the guard said, holding open the door against the wind.

Inside, the President's aide took Nathan's coat. "He will see you now, sir." As usual, she recorded his visit in the appointment log. Curtains in the Oval Office were drawn, and a rich coffee aroma lingered in the air.

The President seemed anxious, his brown eyes intense, his fingers laced together as he sat at his massive desk. Behind him, two flags were crossed: one with the Presidential seal and the other, the Stars and Stripes. "What's so important?" he asked, his eyes fixed on his top snoop.

Nathan set his briefcase on the desk and popped the clasps. “May I?”

“Of course.”

He took out the papers and set them in front of the President.

“What do we have here?”

“History,” Nathan said.

An aide brought in a cup of coffee and a plate of pastries. As the President thumbed through the documents, Nathan sat in a cushy chair, sipped his coffee, and chose to pass on the sweets. His nerves tingled with the turn of each page.

Shortly, the President looked up. “Is this what I think it is?”

“Star Wars, sir. Directive Number 119 has been fulfilled.” He set down his cup. “I expect history will reflect my accomplishment.”

“Indeed, John.” The President stood and offered a handshake. “Indeed it will.”

Bursting with pride, Nathan stood and accepted the President’s congratulations.

“Job well done,” he said with conviction. “What’s next on the agenda?”

“In three months, *Pledge* will be ready for launch.”

“*Pledge*?” The President returned to his seat.

Nathan chose to stand in front of his desk. “P-L-E-D-G, sir. The Proton Laser Energy Defense Grid. Look over that launch schedule from Kennedy Space Center. I suggest knocking off the communications satellite...the one marked Inter-Con Wireless. We have enough cell phones. Tell NASA to put ours up instead.”

“Fine. I’ll brief the Department of Defense right away. Our country will no longer be vulnerable to ballistic missiles.”

“It’s your greatest hour, sir.”

Suddenly, the President arched his eyebrows. "Does anybody else know about this?"

"I'm leaving that to you. Call a press conference. Tell the world of our achievement."

At that, the President's smile faded. "Oh...but no...we can't do that. Don't you realize the stir it would cause?" He sat upright, shoulders back, brows furrowed. "Russia, the Middle East, China, hell, even Pakistan would be up in arms."

Confusion clouded Nathan's thinking. "Sir?"

"How would you like it if someone was holding a big club over your head? You'd be outraged."

"A club? How do you figure? *Pledge* is defensive."

The President frowned. "Is that what you think?"

Nathan was beginning to get his drift. "You mean it's an offensive weapon?"

"It's whatever I say it is." The President wagged a finger. "So you see, John, *Pledge* must be kept top secret."

"But what about my place in history? You told me this assignment was my chance to be a hero."

Rubbing his chin thoughtfully, the President conceded. "I did, didn't I? Well, then...how about a time vault? Sure. We'll lock your credit for Directive Number 119 in a time vault. A hundred years, tops."

"A hundred years? Christ!"

"Sounds about right."

Restraining his temper, Nathan said, "That wasn't the deal."

"Our business here is finished," the President concluded. "I've got work to do."

"But..."

"You're dismissed."

"I didn't bust my butt on this project just to be..."

"Go!" the President demanded. "Or I'll have you forcefully removed."

Appalled, Nathan stepped back from the desk. "That's

no way to talk to *The Ark*."

"I gave you *The Ark*," the President hissed. "I can take it away. Now get the hell out of my office."

***

Back at CIA headquarters, Nathan stormed in. "I don't want to be disturbed," he ordered his secretary and slammed the door. Plopping into his chair, he pounded a fist on the desk. This time the President had gone too far. Seething mad, he retrieved a .38 revolver from his desk drawer and spun the cylinder, checking that it was full of bullets. The bastard was in for a big surprise.

Just then, the intercom beeped.

"What is it?"

"Sorry, sir. There's someone downstairs to see you."

"I told you I didn't want to be disturbed."

"It's the FBI, sir."

Nathan took a hit of adrenaline. The President must've sent them. "Get Lawrence in here."

***

Inspector Anita Pollard stood at the security desk in CIA headquarters while a guard hung on the phone. She had showed him her FBI identification and explained she and her partner, Agent Remsen, needed to see John Nathan, the CIA's top operative. "No—we don't have an appointment," she had told the guard. "It's an investigation, that's why." Her insides ached with foreboding.

Putting down the receiver, the guard said, "Have a seat," and pointed to a row of chairs next to the magazine rack. "He'll see you shortly."

Reluctantly, Anita took a seat, her palms sweating.

Agent Remsen paced. "I still think we should have pressed for a grand jury indictment," he said. "At least we'd have some authority here."

"But what if we're wrong?" Anita crossed her legs. "If Nathan isn't *The Ark*, the real one could get away while we're wasting time with a grand jury."

Jowls flopping, Remsen shook his head. "We don't even have a picture of the guy."

"He's clandestine. The CIA erased his past: no military records, no high school or college transcripts, not as much as a driver's license."

"According to the appointment log, he's the only operative with White House connections. We know the President gave someone that code name and the assignment in Simi Valley. It has to be Nathan." Remsen shoved his hands deep into his pockets and, straight-armed, paced some more.

"I didn't know such a thing even existed in this country," Anita grumped.

"When the President wants something done and doesn't want to be involved or connected to it in any way, he gives one operative complete authority over the assignment. *The Ark* doesn't answer to anyone, not the President, the Cabinet, or even to Congress."

"What do they say, *Absolute power corrupts absolutely*?"

In front of her chair, Remsen stopped pacing. "And we're about to go up against that power alone."

"Just play this thing like we planned." Anita patted the holstered pistol beneath her black blazer.

"He's never gonna buy the mechanic bit."

"Just sound convincing. It's taken us two months to finger Nathan. Don't get skittish on me now."

"I just wish we'd brought a task force with us." He rubbed his chin.

"We can't waltz into CIA headquarters with a posse, for Christ's sake. Will you relax? They'll show us to his office. It's the only way to find out who he is."

"I don't like it," Remsen replied. "Bombarding him

with questions will just get us kicked out of here."

"We have to throw him off balance. He has to slip up, admit he's *The Ark*, or we don't have a case."

"There's no way. He didn't get to be the CIA's top dog by being stupid. We'll end up dead, I tell you, just like Marston and the task force."

Anita shivered. This wasn't like her partner. He was usually cool under pressure, but this time his concerns were well justified. The FBI verses the CIA, a dangerous confrontation if ever there was one.

The elevator chimed as the doors slid open. A young woman emerged wearing a sharp olive pantsuit, her blazer adorned with a gold butterfly brooch. She nodded to the guard who pointed to the FBI agents.

Anita tensed.

"Good afternoon," the woman said with a pleasant smile. "I'm John Nathan's secretary."

"Chief Inspector Pollard and my partner, Agent Remsen," Anita said, shaking her hand.

Remsen nodded without smiling.

"You'll need these." She clipped two guest ID tags to their pockets. "Follow me."

They rode the elevator up in silence.

At Nathan's office door, the secretary said, "They're here."

"Send them in," a man's voice returned.

Anita looked into the office and saw him leaning on the desk inside. He was a brute of a man, bald, and smoking a cigar. "John Nathan?"

"Who do I have to thank for this surprise visit?"

Anita stepped inside, followed by Agent Remsen, and slowly sidestepped right, putting a gap between her and Remsen who was now standing next to her. She assured herself enough elbow room for a clean sweep. Drop left, drop right, clear front and rear. Nerves tingling, her senses were on full alert. "Chief Inspector Pollard." She cocked her head to her left. "Agent Remsen."

"What can I do for you today?"

"We have some questions."

"Please, have a seat." He indicated the chairs in front of his desk.

"This is fine," Anita said, not wanting to give up her strategic position. "We believe you might have some information that will help us on a case we're working?"

"Concerning?"

"The crash of our Hawker jet for starters."

The big man took a drag on his cigar and studied the swirling smoke. "Horrible accident," he said finally. "Sorry about the loss of your men."

Anita kept her demeanor hard. "We have evidence your Chief of Internal Affairs, Bret Lawrence, had a beef with our agent, Lou Marston. Care to tell us about that?"

"Why don't you ask him yourself?"

"We plan to," Remsen said. "Right after we're done with the mechanic who sabotaged the Hawker."

"The mechanic? What mechanic?"

"They tell me he's singing like a canary at HQ."

The big man huffed. "May I suggest...?"

"We just want some answers," Anita said. "Not suggestions. Tell us about the Atomtech disaster."

"Have you read the papers?"

Anita bit her lower lip. He was cool, but she was sure something had to rattle him. "What about the 13th Power Project in Simi Valley?"

"Thirteen what?"

"You know: Melvin Anderson, Dr. Curtis, Star Wars?"

The big man stood and walked to the window. "I don't know what you're talking about."

While his back was turned, Anita edged her hand closer to the pistol under her blazer. It was time to make him sweat. "Isn't it true that you are *The Ark*?"

A long moment of silence electrified the air with tension.

Without turning from the window, the bald man replied, "You read too many horror novels, Miss Pollard. Don't you know there is no boogeyman?"

"I'm looking at *The Ark*, John Nathan."

Suddenly, he whipped around, a .44 magnum drawn, its black silencer pointed at Anita's heart. "You think you're so smart."

Anita froze. Something was wrong with this picture. The man standing there with the gun couldn't possibly be the nation's top espionage agent. He was too quick tempered, too out of control. How had she figured it wrong? She cast a quick glance to Remsen. With narrow eyes, his hand hovered over his weapon. "Easy," she said and returned her focus to the man she believed an imposter. "Who are you?"

"*The Ark*," he snapped as if he enjoyed saying the words.

"I don't think so." Anita took another step right, her hand close to her holstered gun. "*The Ark* wouldn't have blown his cover so quickly. He's a spy, a covert operative, a professional at deception. He wouldn't have caved. You're a phony."

"Call it what you like." The big man aimed his gun at Remsen.

Remsen drew.

Gunfire erupted.

Dropping right, she reached for her gun as bullets flew. She saw Remsen buckle over, and though she wasn't set, she fired at the big man who was already ducking behind the desk.

Remsen hit the floor with a thump and wheezed.

At the same time, she came down on her right knee and concentrated on the desk across the room. Her gun in both hands now, elbows locked, she swept back and forth, searching for any sign of her target. Heart pounding, she forced a breath of air. Tunnel vision set in as she tried to guess where the imposter would appear next.

Then a click came from behind her head.

She held her breath, the cold steel of a gun now pressing on the back of her neck.

“Drop it,” a booming voice ordered.

The air in the room turned to ice. It was the voice, a voice that sounded disturbingly familiar.

“I said drop it, Inspector Pollard.”

A shot of pain blasted up the back of her head, the pressure of the gun now grating against the base of her skull. She suddenly lost track of time, her mind creating fiction from fact. Remsen wasn’t down. He was back at the office working on a new case. And she was soaking in her tub at home, hot and bubbly and happy. Only a few minutes ago, she’d kissed Max good-bye, her lips still burning, and Tommy just ran through the house. “Mom, where’s my baseball mitt?”

“Drop it now.”

She let the gun fall. It clunked on the floor, the sound of total defeat. Craning her eyes right, she strained to get a glimpse of the man behind her, hoping beyond hope that she was mistaken about his voice. An open door by the bookcase caught her attention. It may have been a closet or an anteroom, but it was definitely a trap. How could she have been so careless? She should have cleared the room first. Turning more, she finally saw him, her eyes meeting his, beautiful blue and cold as ice. His neatly combed hair was touched with gray, his jaw handsome and lips soft, lips that she knew so well. “Max?”

“Get up,” he ordered.

She found wobbly legs and stood, her perception of reality strangling the breath from her lungs. “Max? How could you?”

“Don’t take it personal, sweetheart.” He looked

toward the desk. "Lawrence, you're a fool."

Lawrence showed himself, gun in hand. "They know everything, John."

"I told you to keep your mouth shut. They had no idea who *The Ark* was. They had nothing to pin on me."

"What makes you so sure?" Lawrence asked, standing behind the desk.

"She told me." He traced her chin with the cold barrel of his gun. "In bed the other night, as a matter of fact."

His smile made her feel sick inside. She glared at the man she'd once thought was the love of her life, her future. Now, she had all she could do to keep from scratching out his eyes. But as much as she wanted to take this personally, she held firm to her professionalism. "So you are *The Ark*, Max."

"Gives you a chill, doesn't it?"

Lawrence said, "Let me kill her right now."

"There's no rush, Lawrence." Max grinned.

She suddenly felt cheap and used. Her professional demeanor slipped. "You lied to me, Max."

"I'm a spy. I was doing my job."

"You make me want to puke."

"That's not what you said the other night."

"Will you lovebirds knock it off?" Lawrence spat. "We've got a serious problem here."

"Relax," Nathan chirped. "I'll handle this my way, after all, she's my sweetheart."

Anger tore through her insides. She wanted to lash out at the bastard but remembered how anger had gotten her husband killed. Happiness was life; anger was death. It was her motto for survival. Subduing her rage in hopes of saving her life, she gave *The Ark* a scornful look. "You had me fooled, Max. I guess that proves you're a damn good spy."

"Cut the *Max* crap." He looked down at his gun and back to her face. "I'm curious though...you never told me how you found out *The Ark* was responsible for the crash."

Anita didn't answer him. It was one thing to talk about a case after the throes of passion, but entirely another to divulge any specific details. Glancing down at her partner on the floor, her heart ached. Remsen was lying on his side in a pool of blood, a hand spazzing, and a foot twitching. It was a horrible way to die, and she knew she was next. Her only hope now was to stall *The Ark*, to answer his questions and keep him off balance. Perhaps someone had heard the gunfire. They might rush in to investigate and discover his treachery. Pointing to the pocket of her blazer, she said, "I've got something to show you."

Eyeing her suspiciously, he nodded.

She retrieved a flash drive and held it up for his inspection. "You may have murdered Judge Freemen, destroyed his files, sabotaged our Hawker, and killed our task force, but you didn't know about this one little device Agent Marston had stashed in the jet's air safe. It's all here, John Nathan, enough to put you on the gurney with a needle in your arm. Personally, I'd like to be there for that show."

Snatching the drive from her hand, he dropped it on the floor and crunched it under his heel.

She shook her head. "It's no use, *sweetheart*. That was a copy. There are more just like it, lots more. One's even on its way to Congress as we speak. I made a paper trail you can't erase this time. Oh yes, you're going down, John Nathan: forty-four counts, murder one: thirty-seven at Atomtech, seven FBI task force agents and their flight crew, and one Federal judge. We aren't going to talk about attempted murder, conspiracy, and illegally importing a Malaysian criminal into the country, or have you forgotten about Melvin Anderson? He was your Achilles' heel, you know. Marston found his connection with *The Ark*. All I had to do was figure out who *The Ark* was. Trouble is, I didn't expect to find out I was sleeping with the son-of-a-bitch all along."

He grinned as if he thought himself cunning.

Disgusted, she turned to the bald man. "I couldn't have done it without you, Lawrence. You gave it all away, but you should've cut a deal with Marston, like he offered. Now you're going down with Nathan."

Lawrence scowled. "You're in no position to make threats."

"Promises," she replied. "Justice will be served, one way or another."

Nathan lifted his gun to Anita's forehead. "Too bad you won't be around to see it."

A gunshot suddenly banged. Nathan huffed and staggered backward. Anita whirled around and saw her partner sitting up with his gun pointed at Nathan. It banged again. Just as quickly, Lawrence pumped two rounds into Remsen. His gun went flying as his body slammed back to the floor.

The next second went by in a flash. Anita's instincts and years of special training dropped her to the floor. She spun around, snatched her gun up in both hands, and rolled right just as a bullet zinged past her head. Tumbling and without conscious thought, she came up on one knee and squeezed off three rounds into Lawrence.

He hit the floor like a wet towel.

Jaw clenched, she immediately spun around and fixed her aim on *The Ark*, who was now standing with his back against the wall, blood turning his suit coat red. He clutched his stomach with one hand, and in the other, the gun wavered. His eyes stared out blankly, those beautiful blue irises ringed in white.

"Drop it," Anita ordered, hard as any man.

"I only wanted to do something great for my country," he said, his voice raspy. "Now everything is ruined."

"Explain it to a judge. You're under arrest."

He put the gun barrel under his chin. “I won’t give you the satisfaction.” Clumsily, he pulled the gun’s hammer back.

“Drop it.”

“Screw you.” He pulled the trigger. The contents of his skull hit the wall behind him.

Anita slumped to the floor. There was no way to be happy about this.

Chapter Forty

IN THE FIRING ROOM AT KENNEDY'S Launch Control Center, amidst the faint smell of warm electrical circuitry, clicking keyboards, and a variety of voices, Carlton stood next to Colonel Fallon in front of the observation windows. They were looking out at launch pad 39-B, where Atlantis sat poised for flight. It was a moonless December night, and from three miles away, the orbiter glowed ivory white in the beams of intense floodlights.

"An impressive sight." Fallon leaned on a golden staff. A VIP firing room badge dangled from his left pocket.

"It gets better." Carlton scratched the jagged scar on his left arm, a constant, itchy reminder of that terrifying day over North Vietnam.

"Does it still bother you?" Fallon asked.

Uninvited, the memory of that last bombing run came to mind. He'd just centered a railhead in his bombsite when a horrendous explosion tore the B-52 apart. The air became fire and ink. The next thing he knew, flares lit up the night sky, and chopper blades thumped overhead. He felt rough canvas against his bare back, and a face appeared above him. It was Captain Fallon, the B-52's mission specialist. *"Hang on, Carlton."*

"What happened?"

"We were hit by a goddamn SAM."

A dagger-like pain throbbed in his left arm, and when he looked, he saw it had been wrapped with bandages. Everything went ink black again. The next time he opened his eyes, he was in a hospital room where Captain Fallon explained how Carlton's main parachute had deployed prematurely and tangled the lines. As he fell at near terminal velocity, his left arm was flailing above him like a scarf in the wind. During the plunge, Fallon managed to grab Carlton's harness, cut him free, and pull the reserve chute. He owed his life to the Colonel, a debt he could never repay. Rubbing the scar, he looked at Fallon. "It reminds me of you."

"You've come a long way since then."

"I was Chief Flight Engineer for Apollo, you know."

Fallon stood upright, golden staff in hand, his chin held high. "How do you like being Launch Director for Kennedy Space Center?"

"With the help of my team of directors, I make all the final decisions around here: what flies, who flies, and sometimes why they fly."

"What's that they say about *boys and their toys*? Thanks for inviting me."

"You can't get any closer than this, unless of course, you were going up."

"I'd like to do that," Fallon said.

"I bet you would."

"I've always wanted to fly higher than a B-52."

"Atlantis's not like getting on a bomber, Bruce."

"No doubt. What took you so long to get me cleared to watch this launch?"

"Security's especially tight for this flight. I had to do some finagling."

"I thought they were going up to repair the Hubble," Fallon said, his eyes fixed on Atlantis. "What's the big deal?"

"This place is crawling with Department of Defense

big shots," Carlton whispered to Fallon. "Something to do with the payload. They told me it was Hubble upgrades, but when I conducted my final inspection of the orbiter, I thought the hardware in Atlantis's cargo bay looked more like something out of a science fiction movie."

Fallon looked thoughtful. "You think they're up to something?"

"Scuttlebutt is Star Wars."

"It's got to be a rumor. Congress hasn't approved anything like that."

"Regardless, it's my job to see that STS-103 gets off the ground without a hitch."

Scanning the room, Fallon noted, "It takes a small army to do it," nodding toward all the launch technicians seated at the consoles.

"The NASA Test Directors and other flight operations managers, like OTC and MMT, the Mission Management Team, help me make critical decisions concerning the flight. Teams of test conductors and engineers keep tabs on the hardware aboard the orbiter. They report any problems to the NTD boys, who keep me informed. I can call this thing off at any time." His finger made a wide sweep. "There are 249 people in this room, all hard working professionals dedicated to one thing: a safe launch. No one wants a repeat of the Challenger accident."

"I see," Fallon said.

"T minus 12 minutes," the flight controller's voice came over the loudspeaker.

"Enjoy the show." Carlton donned a headset. "I've got work to do." He glanced at the Shuttle Project Engineer who gave him the thumbs up.

"Launch teams report," Carlton said into the mike on his headset. Placing his fingertips on the right earpiece, he awaited a reply.

"Ice Team, all clear," a foreman reported. His final inspection of the pad had been completed.

"OTC, crew module closeout," the Orbiter Test Conductor said. Atlantis's astronauts were ready.

Carlton paced as NTD gave him the *GO* for liftoff. Seventy-one hours and forty-five minutes ago, this countdown had begun. Now the safety tests were completed, and the computer checks were done. All 25,000 plus measurements and parameters had passed their tests. Everything was ready.

"T minus nine minutes."

"NTD, Launch Commit Criteria has been met," Carlton announced.

"Ground Launch Sequencer on," came the reply. From here, the GLS computers took automatic control of the countdown. In less than nine minutes, when the solid rocket boosters ignited, Carlton's responsibility to STS-103 would end, and Johnson Space Center in Houston would assume command of the flight. To Carlton, these seemed like the longest minutes of the countdown. If the computers detected any glitch on the orbiter or ground equipment, they'd automatically scrub the launch.

No matter how many times he'd been through this, the tension made Carlton's arm ache. As he watched the seconds tick away, he scanned the firing room, looking for any sign of trouble.

"T minus five minutes." The intercom crackled. *"We're* go *for auto sequence start. Atlantis's onboard computers have primary control of all the vehicle's critical functions."*

Time dragged by as MMT and NTD directors huddled in whispered conversation. Their meeting ended with thumbs-up to Carlton.

Looking at Colonel Fallon, he felt a moment of thankful pride and wondered if there was any way he could ever fulfill Fallon's wish to fly in space.

"T minus one minute."

Carlton moved behind the NTD consoles and checked

the monitors for any red flags. Numbers and formulas scrolled down the screens at breathtaking speed, and green lights pulsed on the panels. The GLS had complete control.

At T minus sixteen seconds, the sound suppression system was activated. Three hundred thousand gallons of water began flooding the launch platform and spilled down the flame chute.

"Ten seconds," the flight controller said. *"Nine...eight... We have a go for main engine start*."

Carlton's scar itched.

"Six."

Flares spewed sparks across the launch pad to clear away any residual hydrogen gas, then Atlantis's three main engines ignited, sending flame and smoke down their respective deflector chutes. A sound greater than thunder rumbled up from the launch pad.

"Three...two...one..."

The SRBs roared to life, glowing white-hot and hurling a tower of steam into the air. At the same time, four exploding bolts freed the orbiter from the pad.

"We have liftoff of the space shuttle Atlantis."

Like a rising sun, Atlantis rose from the pad. The engines' thunderous roar rattled the observation windows.

Squinting against the fireball now rocketing into the night sky, Carlton approached Colonel Fallon. "What do you think of that?" he yelled over all the noise.

"Incredible!"

"Houston, Atlantis, r-roll program," the shuttle commander announced over the radio. His voice sounded choppy from the rough ride.

"Roger roll, Atlantis," Houston returned.

The shuttle, illuminated by its yellow tail of fire, rolled on its back and streaked toward the heavens, black and studded with twinkling stars.

Carlton folded his arms across his chest. "In eight and a half minutes, she'll be in orbit, 315 nautical miles up and somewhere over Africa."

"Seven hundred miles per hour. Three miles altitude. Atlantis is a little more than a mile downrange from Kennedy Space Center."

Colonel Fallon tapped the golden staff. "Must be one hell of a ride."

"An understatement," Carlton said.

"Atlantis, Houston. Go with throttle up."

The radio crackled. "*Atlantis c-copy. G-go with throttle up.*"

A brilliant tail of fire and smoke arched across the dark sky and shined off the ocean like a full moon.

"One minute into the flight, Atlantis is already ten miles in altitude and downrange seven miles from the launch site, traveling one thousand five hundred miles per hour. All systems looking good."

"That's it, boys," Carlton said. "Wrap it up. Scrub teams dismissed."

"The windows haven't even stopped rattling," Fallon said.

"She's not our bird anymore. Next shuttle up is Odyssey, in four months. You want to come back for that launch?"

Fallon tapped the golden staff on the floor. "I'd rather go up in it."

"Odyssey would be my choice," Carlton said. "She's more user-friendly than Atlantis."

"How's that?"

"Technicians and mission specialists have to spend months preparing to ride an orbiter. It costs us a fortune to train them, and most fly only once. However, with Odyssey's environmental upgrades, in two hours we can brief passengers on everything they need to know."

"Everything?"

"Considering most of them will just be ferried up to the space station, they don't need to know much." Carlton smiled. "Odyssey is the flagship of *NASA Aerospace*, our orbital airline of the future."

"Airline?" Fallon's brows lifted.

Carlton chuckled. He could see in Fallon's eyes that unmistakable desire to fly like he'd never flown before.

Atlantis roared, rumbling like distant thunder. Its main engines were now only three dots of white light dwarfed by the flaming SRBs.

"Approaching one minute, forty seconds into the flight. Awaiting burnout and separation of the SRBs."

With a flash, the solid rocket boosters fell away from the orbiter, leaving its three dots of light alone in the night sky. Only a subtle drone came from Atlantis now, fading away as if on a breeze.

Fallon pointed the golden staff toward the last glint of light from the orbiter. "Incredible, Carlton. You and your boys did a fine job."

"Now we've got to get ready for our next Delta II project."

"What's that?"

"DOD system going up, seven satellites, staggered deployment with global positioning. High-tech hardware."

"What for?"

Carlton leaned to Fallon's ear. "Between you and me, more Star Wars stuff."

"Do you think those satellites have anything to do with Atlantis's payload?"

"Could."

"Who's the contractor?"

"Solartech Labs in California."

Fallon's cheeks went pale as if he'd come to some horrifying realization. "DOD is strangely busy these days. Who's in command?"

"General Brigham, an arrogant son-of-a-bitch, I must say."

Fallon nodded. "I know him well."

"Then you should know he carries a lot of clout. He's monitoring all launch operations. The President's right hand man, I've been told."

"That surprises me."

"Why?"

"A while back, the President took Star Wars away from the Department of Defense."

"I remember," Carlton said. "About two years ago, wasn't it?"

"The General and his cronies were accused of pilfering funds from SDI's budget. In retaliation, Brigham testified to a Senate committee, claimed there was a conspiracy between the White House and the CIA over Directive Number 119. The President was furious. Brigham almost lost his stars over it."

"Perhaps Brigham and the President have come to terms."

Fallon leaned on his staff. "Scary proposition, if you ask me. Brigham will never trust the President again. He told me so himself. And he abhors the CIA, for good reason, but just the same, there's no telling what he'll do in a crisis."

"What's your best guess?" Carlton asked.

"Get revenge."

Chapter Forty-One

FLICKING A LOCK OF RED HAIR from her cheek, Tracy snuggled into the crook of Janis's arm. Nestled on the couch with the man she loved, she felt cozy all the way down to her toes. In the fireplace, blue and white gas flames danced silently. Christmas in California. It was eighty-six degrees outside.

A Bing Crosby CD spun out her favorite yuletide song. *"I'm dreaming of a White Christmas. Just like the ones I used to know."*

From the kitchen, the teakettle whistled. A fake tree in the corner gleamed with twinkling red and green lights, which reflected off sparkling silver ornaments. Earlier, Janis had placed two presents under the tree, one sporting an exceptionally large red and white bow. The other, smaller and not as fancy, sat on top of the bigger one, begging to be opened first.

"Where the tree tops glisten, and children listen, for sleigh bells in the snow."

Janis hummed along as if singing the words aloud would somehow ruin her impression of him.

The teakettle shrieked in urgency. Tracy got up and kissed Janis's cheek. "Honey in yours?"

"That'll be fine."

"Anything else?" She winked and pulled the strap of her top down off her shoulder.

"How about some snow?"

"You brat." She sauntered off to the kitchen.

"Next year," Janis said over Bing's singing. "You'll love Boulder during the holidays, the snow, the lights, and the Pearl Street Mall."

"If we ever get out of here." She poured two cups, the aroma of Irish tea permeating the air. "This suite is nice and all, but I really miss our kiva."

"I miss it all, including the university, if you'll believe that."

"I do." She spooned honey into the cups. "Those kids have been your whole life." She headed back to the couch, teacups in hand, and the strap of her top still hanging at her elbow. She hoped he'd get the hint.

Bing began another song: *Silver Bells*.

Snuggling into Janis again, her heart danced to the music as she felt his soft breathing and thought of the wonderful rhythm he'd brought into her life. The tea tasted sweet and smooth. She glanced at him as he took a quiet sip from his cup, seemingly content that they were together on Christmas Eve in spite of Curtis and his stiff-armed tactics. The man didn't know the meaning of peace on earth or goodwill toward men. Shivering, she knew that someday they'd leave Simi Valley. The 13th Power project was nearing an end. Janis had recalculated the math, and Lo had reprogrammed the Supers. They'd solved most of the problems that had plagued the experiment, and each accomplishment brought them closer to going home.

"We've got the day off tomorrow," she said softly. "What should we do?"

Janis's eyes went to her dangling strap. He smiled and held up his cup. "We got anything stronger than this?"

***

Later that night, the phone rang. "Who could be calling at this hour?" Janis rolled over and grabbed the receiver. "What?"

"Dr. Mackey...we need your help." Stan sounded breathless, and in the background, Janis heard the control room's emergency horns blaring.

"What the hell are you guys doing? It's Christmas Eve."

"Curtis has been working us all night," Stan said. "The idiot tried to get the DM on line himself."

"The de-materializer?"

"The welds haven't even cooled. My men are beat and now this. Lo is on his way. A staff car should be there for you in five minutes. And bring Tracy."

Janis rubbed his eyes. "Christ! The laser!"

"Curtis really screwed up. The Supers turned it on. They think it's the real thing. Countdown's at forty-four minutes already. Changes locked out."

"Freeze the rescrambler and set the program mode to optimal."

"Done."

"I'll be there." Janis hung up, his nervous system on sudden overload. That damn CIA spy program, *The Worm*, kept locking out changes in the scheduler. Lo had tried everything to delete the damn thing. At least he'd found a way to work around it. By writing new script to block each troublesome command, they'd been able to assure a reasonable measure of safety. Problem was, the DM segment of the scheduling program wasn't ready yet. The Supers didn't know that because the script hadn't been written. "Tracy, get up."

"What is it?" she asked from under the covers.

Janis flipped on the lights. "Curtis jumped the gun on the DM. He tried to start the sequencer."

She sat up. "But the DM isn't finished."

"Yes it is, and Curtis wants gold for Christmas."

"But Lo's not done with the programming." Tracy scrambled to her feet.

Janis threw on a shirt. “The MIGGS isn’t interlaced. If the laser fires, it’ll burn a hole through the transporter, and I don’t have to tell you what’ll happen if it hits the hydrogen storage tanks.”

“Oh, dear.” Tracy slipped into a pair of shorts. “Can we stop it?”

Janis grabbed his shoes and socks. “I don’t know.”

***

Blaring emergency horns resonated through Tech-Com Control as Janis pushed through the doors with Tracy right behind him. She went directly to the laser terminal at her station. Janis found Lo tapping his keyboard. Lines of code scrolled down the screen in front of him, a mathematical nightmare.

“Any luck?”

“Ho, Ho, Ho,” he said, not looking up.

“Where’s Stan?”

“At the ionizer, venting hydrogen. If the laser fires, we’re dead.”

“What about the backdoor?” Janis asked him.

“It’s not responding.”

“Then delete the whole damn scheduler.”

“Like this?” Lo typed and looked up.

ACCESS DENIED flashed in a window labeled *WORM SECURITY.*

“Or this?” He typed again.

OVERRIDE FAILED.

“It’s no use, Janis. Curtis made a mess of the whole thing. We need to change the script.”

“But where?”

Lo shrugged. “With a million plus lines of code, it’s anybody’s guess.”

“Can you shut off the damn alarm?”

“We must solve the problem first.”

Still buttoning his lab coat, Ray ran into the control room. "What's wrong now?"

"The Supers won't allow us access to the laser," Tracy said. "We can't shut it down."

"Can we get the MIGGS online?"

Janis shook his head. "Not without Johnson."

"Where is he?"

"It's Christmas, who knows?"

"I can't find Kate, either," Ray said, flipping through switches on his console.

Janis frowned. "Why were you looking for Kate?"

"We were going to spend Christmas together."

"Reconciliation?"

"We've been talking."

"Really...?"

"Let's get to work on the code," Tracy shouted.

"All of it?" Lo asked.

"We don't have enough time," Janis said. "The sequencer runs too fast. How about the laser-scheduling program? Maybe we can change a command line."

"It's a long shot," Ray said. "Send us the figures, Tracy."

She pushed a button on her keyboard. "They're all yours."

On Lo's monitor, columns of mathematical formulas appeared, equations recalculating as the Supers worked through the sequence of firing commands.

"Scroll the program ahead," Janis told Lo.

New formulas appeared, frozen on the screen as if they were soldiers waiting their turn to fire in a mathematical battle. Line 42372 caught Janis's eye, a single command: *YES*. The line before it read *Resonator Charge: YES or NO* followed by a formula referring to transformer voltages applied to the field. Maybe, if no field voltage existed, there would be no laser output.

"Change that *Yes* to a *NO*."

Lo typed.

ACCESS DENIED.

Janis winced.

"What next?" Lo asked.

What else could he do? *The Worm* was obviously programmed to block command line changes, but now Janis wondered about re-scripted equations?

"Think fast," Lo said nervously. "The scheduler is catching up."

"Can we change a formula?"

"Which one?"

"Change the field voltage to *zero*."

Lo typed.

Nothing happened: no access denied, no errors.

"Ha!" Lo grinned. "*The Worm* did not recognize the change. Good work, Janis."

"Brilliant," Tracy said.

Satisfied, Janis stood over Lo's shoulder and watched the scheduler scroll down the screen. Seconds later, the altered formula calculated, and the laser firing sequence stalled. The emergency horns shut off automatically.

ERROR flashed on the monitor. *NO LASER FIELD VOLTAGE.*

Janis, his ears ringing, swallowed dryly. "That did it."

"All right," Ray said, his cheeks flushed.

Tracy gave Janis a thumbs-up and smiled.

Lo stood and bowed. "Merry Christmas to all and to all good night."

"Not so fast!" Curtis was standing in the doorway, feet spread and hands on his hips.

Janis gathered Tracy under his arm. "The emergency is over, Curtis, no thanks to you. We're going back to bed. Santa Claus is coming, or have you forgotten?"

"Screw Santa *and* his reindeer. I want the scheduling program finished and the DM on line before breakfast. I've called in the rest of the team. You boys are making gold tomorrow whether you like it or not."

"The gold can wait," Janis said.

"You dare to argue with me?"

"Haven't you caused enough trouble for one night?" Ray blurted out.

Curtis lifted his eyebrows. "Oh...you ain't seen nothin' yet. I was afraid you lightweights might need a little motivation." He grinned like a maniac. "Jonathan?"

"Come on, Tracy." Janis started walking toward the door. Just then, video monitors flickered on all around Tech-Com Control. A woman's scream pierced the air, and an awful chittering sound filled the control room.

Ray stepped toward a monitor, his mouth hanging open.

Janis couldn't breathe. As much as he wanted, he couldn't take his eyes off the screen. The image coming into focus sent a sudden spike of terror through his chest. Kate, wearing only a black bra and panties, was hanging upside down by a rope around her ankles. She appeared to be in a room with a fallen staircase, rotted wallboards, and a buckled balcony. The air was clouded with dust, illuminated only by a glowing lantern. But worse, the floor was moving, churning, teeming with...with rats. They were chittering, jumping, and clawing for Kate's hair, which dangled just inches out of their reach. Her screams ripped through Tech-Com Control.

Horror staggered Janis's sense of reality. "My God."

"Kate!" Ray shouted. He grabbed hold of a counter as if he were going to fall over.

Jonathan stepped into the picture. He was standing on the balcony, holding the end of the rope. "You heard Dr. Curtis," he shouted. "Get back to work or I'll give her to the rats." He let the rope slip through his hands a little, dropping Kate closer to gnashing jaws and flailing claws.

She screamed.

The chitter became deafening.

Tracy shrieked.

Ray fell to his knees, his eyes on Curtis. “All right. We’ll do it.” He turned to Janis and Lo. “Tell him we’ll do it.”

Curtis laughed.

Stepping back, Janis finally tore his eyes away from the monitor. “What’s the rush?” he shouted at Curtis.

“I don’t like waiting.”

“But tomorrow’s Christmas.”

“In case you’ve forgotten,” Curtis said. “I’m king shit around here, and if you don’t like it, that’s tough shit. If I say you work, you work.”

Janis stared at Curtis. He seemed pleased with the terror he’d brought into the room. There was no limit to the man’s cruelty. But Janis knew they had no choice in the matter. To stop the madness, they’d have to give Curtis what he wanted. They’d have to give it to him for Christmas.

The rope slipped some more.

Kate wailed.

The rats jumped.

“Please, Janis,” Ray said, trembling. “Lo? Tracy? For Christ’s sake. He’ll kill her.”

“A few inches lower,” Curtis said. “She’ll be rat fodder.”

Janis felt the wind go out of him. “Okay. We’ll do it.”

Lo fell back into his chair.

“Then it’s settled,” Curtis said, grinning. “You’d better get to work. It’s going to be a long night.” He turned and left the control room, disappearing down the hall like a black shadow merging into darkness.

Tech-Com Control was silent, except for the chittering of the rats and Kate’s screams.

Chapter Forty-Two

CHRISTMAS DAY DAWNED. A thick fog rolled in from a languid sea. The sun was merely a dull orb in the sky, its rays barely able to filter through the haze. Rubbing stubble on his chin, Janis leaned against the railing outside Tech-Com Control and wondered whatever happened to Christmas: the love, the joy, and the peace on earth.

Yawning, he rubbed his burning eyes. He had to take a break from the monitors, the rows of formulas and figures, and the mathematical ordeal that Christmas had become. Now, everything but the programming was finished, and Lo was working on that.

Seagulls yammered from somewhere unseen.

Last time he saw Tracy, she was slumped over her keyboard, sleeping on her forearms. She hadn't complained, working with Lo on the sequencer programming codes while Janis compiled formulas for the DM, the dematerializer, a marvel of modern engineering, as Stan had called it. The nuclear imploder was able to change the atomic structure of lead and turn it into gold.

Ray appeared at the door. "Program's ready, Janis."

Swallowing hard, he took a last look at Christmas in California. Boulder seemed like it was on another planet. "Is everybody here?" he asked Ray.

"And nobody's happy about it."

Inside the control room, the humming of electromagnets filled the air.

"10TEV and climbing," Robert reported from his accelerator terminal.

Janis moved to the MIGGS window and looked inside. The transporter had been covered with a plastic sheet. Two of Stan's men were lowering a gray brick of lead into the DM, which was set on the floor in the same place the rocket fuselage had been strapped earlier. Not much bigger than a suitcase, the DM's titanium liner sparkled under the green ceiling lights. After Stan closed the lid, his men set the locks and backed away. Stan aligned the DM's optical lens with the sighting dish mounted on a tripod behind the transporter. Finished, he led his team out a hatch-like door that closed with a thud. The locking mechanism creaked as it engaged. At the same time, the green ceiling lights started blinking in two-second intervals.

The MIGGS was ready.

"Bring up the power," Boris ordered from his control console.

Roger worked his dials intensifying the hum in the room.

"12TEV and rising," Robert said as the synchrotron picked up speed.

Boris pointed to Tracy. "Sighting beam."

A skinny red beam of light came out of the synchrotron, reflected off the sighting dish, and shined into the DM's optic lens, dead center.

"Laser locked," Tracy confirmed and leaned back in her chair.

Lo turned to Janis. "The sequencer is up and running," he said. "The Supers have complete control."

Taking a deep breath, Janis wondered if his formulas would hold up this time. Did he have the math right or would the DM disintegrate like the rocket fuselage? He looked up to the office window where Jonathan was standing next to Curtis, their eerie forms silhouetted against the glass.

"14TEV."

Janis glanced at the video monitor that had once revealed Kate hanging above the rats. Now it showed an empty, disheveled room and a dangling rope. He wondered what Curtis had done with her. Then he thought about Ray who hadn't said anything about her for hours. Janis couldn't help but wonder what was going on between Ray and his ex-wife. As impossible as it seemed, he was sure that Lisa had something to do with them getting back together.

"Bring the MIGGS online," Boris ordered.

"CEI engaged," Ray reported, obviously keeping busy with details the Supers were already handling.

The roaring MIGGS began to vibrate the control room.

"Fifty percent," Johnson announced.

Janis watched the black mist form and swirl inside the MIGGS, getting thicker.

"Seventy..."

The mist spun and expanded, filling the gravity chamber, consuming the red glow from the synchrotron, the sighting beam, and finally the transporter and its blue ion shield.

"Ninety percent..."

"15TEV," Robert yelled and patted his synchrotron monitor. "She's ready."

Janis winced against the pounding sound waves.

"One hundred..."

"Fire!" Boris commanded.

Tracy pushed the button.

A pulsing white light buzzed through the synchrotron, propelling protons into the MIGGS at the speed of light. The particle beam crackled for a second, and then it was gone.

Johnson pulled back on the MIGGS decelerator; the roar subsided, first to a rumble and then a hum.

The black mist inside the MIGGS broke apart into small vortexes and twisted down floor grates as the gravity equalized. Green ceiling lights came on, revealing the one-eyed DM, still intact.

Janis's stomach fluttered as he contemplated the possibility that lead had actually been turned into gold. A small part of him wanted the experiment to succeed. He and Tracy could go home, but a bigger part of him wanted to see it fail, so he could see the look on Curtis's face and the rage in his eyes.

The MIGGS hatch opened. Stan and two of his men entered warily, their boots hidden in the dissipating black mist. Bending over the DM, they released its locks.

Ray stood next to Janis now. Lo, Johnson, Tracy, and Boris gathered at the MIGGS window, too. They didn't say a word. Janis caught himself holding his breath as the DM lid was opened. Stan's men stooped, reached inside, and all smiles, lifted out a brick of glimmering gold.

"That's it." Ray cheered. "We did it." He patted Janis's shoulder. "We did it. We did it."

Janis clenched his jaw, refusing to get caught up in Ray's excitement. The DM had shaved off three electrons and three protons from the atoms of lead, reducing its atomic weight from 207.19 to 196.967: Gold. It seemed an ungodly thing they had done.

Curtis bounded down the stairs, ran across the control room, and pressed his face against the MIGGS window. He didn't say anything, but merely stood in awe of his new God of gold.

Janis watched his admiring gaze and felt wary of the financial power they'd created for Curtis and the damage he could do to the world markets.

Joining in the elation, Jonathan slapped Curtis on the back. "Congratulations, boss."

Without warning, Ray turned around and slugged Jonathan in the jaw, which sent him staggering backwards.

He lost his feet and fell flat on his back. Ray jumped on him and hit him again. “You son-of-a-bitch. Where is she? I’m gonna kill you.”

Jonathan covered his face with his arms but took two more punches before Janis got to Ray and pulled him off. “What’s the matter with you?”

“What have you done with my wife?” Ray demanded.

Janis shook him. “Get hold of yourself.”

“She’s your ex-wife,” Jonathan said and spit blood.

Ray kicked him in the leg. “She’s the mother of my child.”

“She’s just a whore.”

Curtis grinned as if he were enjoying the show.

“I should kill both you bastards,” Ray shouted.

Holding Ray back from another lunge at Jonathan, Janis said, “They’re not worth it.”

Jonathan wiped blood from his lip and got to his feet, fists balled. “It’s all right, Janis. Let him go. I wanna see what he can do without throwing a sucker punch first. Let him come on.”

“Forget it.” Curtis grabbed Jonathan’s arm and turned to Ray. “You fool. You’re in love with a whore.” Curtis grabbed his crotch. “And I’m going to dip into some of her real soon.”

“You bastard.” Ray lunged at Curtis.

Janis held him back. “Knock it off. This isn’t the way to settle anything. Just remember, every dog has his day. Curtis will have his.”

“Don’t count on it,” Curtis said in a gravelly voice. “And don’t count on going anywhere in the transporter either. You’ve got gold to make, and lots of it. I hardly think there will be any time to play.”

Ray squared his shoulders. “You gave me your word.”

“I gave you nothing.” He looked at Jonathan. “Come on. I need a drink.”

“Where’s Kate?” Ray shouted.

Jonathan flipped him a key. “D-block. Unlock the whore yourself.”

Curtis pointed at Ray. “The gold production schedule will be posted tomorrow morning. Any deviation and she’ll be checking into the rat hotel permanently. You got that?”

Ray bared his teeth.

Chapter Forty-Three

IN MEXICO, RAIN CAME DOWN in straight lines, bending the jungle and ticking on the hacienda roof. Miguel stood on the balcony, caressing the silver bear of his necklace. His heart ached for the loss of his sons, all seven of them now gone. Donardo, Juan, and Pedro had not returned from the states. No one had seen nor heard a word from them. They had disappeared, gone without a trace. Some horrible fate must have found them at Solartech Labs. They had failed, and he, in turn, had failed Maria. The chill of the rain seeped into his soul, and he shivered.

A rattletrap taxi squeaked to a stop below the balcony, rain tapping hollow notes on the roof and hood. Its muffler made the rumbling sound of a truck.

Then sandaled footsteps clapped on the hardwood floor behind him. Turning, Miguel saw Lila approach, waddling, her eyes red and cheeks streaked with tears. She wore a blue dress with yellow flowers, and he noticed how different she looked today, not wearing her apron. In her right hand, she carried a leather-strapped suitcase, water-stained with age. "Señor, I must go now."

"*Si*, Lila." Miguel tipped his head. "My heart is heavy. I am truly sorry for the way things have ended. You have been a faithful nana."

She brushed aside a lock of black hair. "I will miss this place, the sound of the children, the smell of the *cocina*."

"*La casa* will never be the same. Where will you go?"

Lila held her chin up. "Ecuador. My sister's home. She has a spare room."

"I wish you would stay."

"The boys are gone. It was for them I was here and because of a promise I made to Maria, to help them grow to be men. Now I am not needed."

"Only you think—"

"What I think is of no concern to you."

Miguel clutched the silver bear, his housemaid's quick tongue striking a nerve. "You've something on your mind? Speak it at will."

Lila bit her lip and remained silent. Rain patted the roof.

"Do not let words fail you now, Lila."

She took a slow breath. "Your sons were dear to me, Miguel. But they were bullies, like their father."

"They were good boys."

Shaking her head, she replied, "Perhaps at one time, when they were small and Maria was alive. Somehow you changed them. Now they are dead, and the business, the dirty business that it is, that will die too."

Miguel knew that Lila was right. Without his sons, there was no business. He could not handle every part of it. "I do not care anymore."

"Did you ever, Señor? Really? I watched you use your sons to gain wealth and power. Now you are left with nothing. You have reaped what you have sowed, Miguel. God may forgive you." Her eyes narrowed. "I cannot."

Miguel raised his hand. "You have spoken enough."

She sighed. "Only I have spoken too late."

Brushing past him, she took the stairs down to the taxi. She didn't look up before disappearing inside the car. The door closed with a thump, and the driver drove away.

Miguel listened to the sound of noisy exhaust fade into the rain-soaked jungle. His guts clutched. He was alone. The place in his heart once filled with the joy of his family had become an empty pit burrowing deep into the very core of his soul. The weight of it made him cling to the railing, his knees weak with anguish. He wondered if Lila was right. Was all of what happened his fault?

"Maria," he cried, his eyes raised to a slate gray sky. "What do I do now?"

Thunder rumbled in the distance.

"Jesus, Son of God! Why do you punish me so? You take my wife, my sons, my reason for life." Miguel fell to his knees and slumped over the railing, anger at his God tearing his faith apart. The savior on the cross had failed him too, and his sons as well. He wanted to cry out like a child, wash away the pain with tears, but he could not. Instead, hate and anger boiled up inside and hardened his heart. It gave him energy and a renewed determination.

He would have to do the killing himself.

Chapter Forty-Four

AT INDIAN SPRINGS, COLONEL Fallon stood at the window overlooking the flight line and leaned on the golden staff. Behind him, Flight Operations buzzed with activity. Com-Center airmen were handling radio communications between aircrews and ground controllers. Weather officers passed information to flight planners who studied them like college exams.

"Falcon Six-Seven-Whiskey," came over the speaker. *"We have the field in sight. Close our flight plan from Washington D.C."*

"Roger, Six-Seven-Whiskey," an airman replied.

"Welcome to Indian Springs," the tower radioed the Falcon jet on final approach. *"Winds light and variable. Clear to land runway two-six."*

From the window, Fallon scanned the rows of Apache helicopters sitting motionless on the tarmac, some being attended by mechanics, others radiating heat waves under the desert sun, which glistened off Security Police insignias emblazoned on camouflaged fuselages. In the distance, he watched the sleek Falcon touch down.

She's here.

He headed for the stairs. Donning sunglasses, he rushed outside with Lieutenant Briggs on his heels. "Are you sure this is a good idea, sir?"

"She's got agent Marston's report and information on Melvin Anderson. I'm going to catch that bastard if it's the last thing I do."

"From what I've heard, sir...it just might be."

Fallon shuddered.

The jet taxied to a stop. A silver and blue CIA seal glistened from the tail. The engines wound down, and the cabin door came open. Shortly, a woman in a black blazer and skirt stepped off the plane. Shifting a satchel to her left hand, she offered the Colonel a firm handshake. "Bruce Fallon?"

"At your service, ma'am."

"Chief Inspector Anita Pollard, FBI. Thanks for seeing me."

"I should be the one thanking you...but I'm wondering, how did you get the CIA to fly you out here?" He directed Anita toward the front doors to Flight Operations.

"The CIA has been very cooperative since I nailed their top dog John Nathan and his puppet of a chief. The scandal gave them a black eye. Headquarters' brass wants this mess cleaned up as soon as possible."

"Must have been one hell of an embarrassment," Briggs said, walking beside her. "Thanks to your agent Marston."

"He opened the proverbial can of worms," she replied. "Cost him his life."

"A good man," Fallon added.

"But he didn't leave us empty handed." Anita walked briskly alongside the men, her high heels clicking on the concrete. "I've been sorting through things for months now, and I finally figured it all out."

Briggs pulled open the doors.

"What do you need from me?" Fallon allowed Anita to go inside ahead of him.

"I understand you executed an MPA on Solartech Labs," she said as they walked down the hallway.

"The last time they conducted the 13th Power

experiments, I intervened with a Military Police Action, yes."

"You're going to have to do it again."

Fallon frowned. *Another MPA? How many of my men will die?* Solartech Labs' security force was top rate and heavily armed. He followed Briggs into the conference room. The air conditioning made the desert's heat seem far away.

Anita set her satchel on the table.

"Get us some coffee," Fallon told the lieutenant.

"Yes, sir." Briggs left them alone.

Anita sat, pulled a newspaper clipping from her satchel, and laid it out for Fallon's inspection. The headline read, *Secret Satellites Launched.*

He leaned the golden staff against a chair, picked up the article, and read it out loud:

"Kennedy Space Center and Cape Canaveral, Florida. Multiple Delta II rockets blasted into orbit late last night, rousting many Floridians from their sleep. The Department of Defense is tight-lipped about the array of satellites aboard, citing Top Secret national defense issues. Launch Director Carlton Nash was unavailable for comment."

Looking at Anita, he said, "This was a month ago. What's it got to do with Melvin Anderson?"

Anita fished a brown folder from her satchel and set it in front of him. "In here, I have the transcripts from Marston's report. John Nathan was in cahoots with Melvin Anderson on a project to develop a particle beam. He sent his top agent, Alex Gibson, into Solartech Labs with strict orders to protect the project...at all costs. Your friend, Walter Devin, set out to derail them, and Atomtech suffered a catastrophic disaster in the aftermath. According to your investigation, included here with Marston's report, you found evidence of a military assault."

"Exactly," Fallon said. "I believe Melvin Anderson

ordered the raid, but I'm at a loss as to who carried it out for him."

Anita looked at Fallon with confidence. "*The Ark* authorized the raid, and the CIA carried it out."

Fallon stepped back. "That's a serious accusation."

"But you're wrong about Melvin Anderson. He knew nothing about it."

"A covert operation?"

"All the way. So I looked into Gibson's past." She drew a bound report from her satchel. "It's all in here." She tossed it in front of the Colonel. "His buddy, James 'Red' Colburn, a right wing militant who still thinks he's at war, keeps a paramilitary army of mercenaries encamped in the mountains east of L.A. Phone records indicate he and Alex talked the day before the raid."

"Could be a coincidence," Fallon said, thumbing the pages.

"They had a special bond."

"Vietnam?"

"Virginia. She was Alex's lover until Red came on the scene, wooed her away from him, and married her shortly thereafter. Who better to send into battle than the bastard who stole your girl?"

Fallon tried to swallow. "That's the only connection?"

Anita shook her head. "One more." She handed him a copy of a flight log posting twelve hours in a C-130-M transport, dated the night of the Atomtech disaster. The pilot had logged the time as *domestic*. "Since when do C-130-Ms fly domestic?"

"Who logged this?"

"CIA Captain Wilfred Baines," Anita replied, grinning.

Fallon didn't understand the grin. "We need to find this guy."

"I brought him with me," Anita said conspiratorially.

"Huh?"

"He's the pilot of the jet that brought me here."

"Does he know you're onto him?" Fallon asked.

"Clueless. I believe he's having coffee in your mess hall right now."

"I'll be damned."

"And another thing," she added. "I assume you know Melvin Anderson is back."

"He's in CIA custody, I heard."

"That's not entirely true. *The Ark* made a deal with him. He's at Solartech Labs, and I'm betting he gave Star Wars to the Department of Defense." She pointed to the newspaper clipping.

"They wouldn't deploy an unauthorized weapons system."

"They did, thanks to Melvin Anderson. I'm not sure what was in it for him, but I am sure that whatever it was, it's not in anybody's best interest but his own. You need to go in to Solartech Labs and extract him."

"With an MPA?"

Nodding, she added, "And while you're at it..." She pulled an aerial photo from her satchel and handed it to Fallon. "I suggest you send a strike force into Red's mercenary encampment. 'X' marks the spot. These are the guys who murdered thirty-seven employees at Atomtech. Americans, like you and I."

"They're only suspects until proven guilty."

"Call it what you like, but you can bet they won't give up peacefully just to get their day in court."

"Then I'll need a warrant for all of this."

"Federal Marshal's Warrant okay?" She flipped the document on the table.

Fallon's mouth fell open. "Why all this? I mean, why didn't you execute this yourself, take the collar?"

"No thanks." She shook her head. "You've got the firepower to take these *suspects* down. Besides..." she closed the satchel. "I lost enough of my people over this. In the end, I got *The Ark*. That was enough."

The Colonel set his jaw. "And I'm going to get Melvin Anderson."

Briggs came in with the coffee. "I hope you like—"

"Lieutenant." Fallon turned to Briggs. "Get Captain Stanton and his team together. We're going to the mess hall. And put Major Ellington and his squadron on full alert. Schedule a full briefing for O-eight hundred hours."

"What's up, sir?"

The Colonel snatched the golden staff from the chair. "The Apaches are going back to Simi Valley."

Chapter Forty-Five

RAY CLIMBED THE LADDER TO THE transporter's belly hatch and pulled himself onto the flight deck, which was only illuminated by the MIGGS' green ceiling lights that filtered in through the thick windshield. In shadowy silence, he went directly to the Auxiliary Power Unit controller and switched it on. Interior lights flickered and glowed as the APU came up to full power, humming softly.

Sitting in the Captain's chair, he flipped through a series of switches, checked gauge readings, and booted the main flight computers. There were seven of them: four control and three backups. Stan had showed him how to do all this. "The I.S.S.T. can fly itself," Stan had told him. All he had to do was point it in the direction he wanted to go. The computers would do the rest.

For a moment, he stared beyond his reflection in the windshield and tried to imagine what sights he would see when the transporter degenerated into the 13th Power. He tried to picture what worlds he would find there: what supernovas, what star systems, what other wonders might reside on the other side of the galaxy. Curtis may have reneged on his agreement, but Ray wasn't going to let that stop him from achieving his goal.

"Ray, you up there?" a security guard called up the hatch.

"Yes."

"I brought them like you told me."

Feeling a sudden jolt of trepidation, Ray cleared his throat. “Send them up.”

As footsteps ticked on the ladder, his heartbeat took a jump to light speed. He’d chosen his crew for this journey. Now all he had to do was convince them to go with him. After all, the 13th Power was the new frontier. This expedition would reach farther into the unknown than Columbus, Lewis and Clark, or Neil Armstrong had ventured. Also, this journey would be fraught with unknown dangers, but the rewards would be boundless. In the end, they’d all be famous. He didn’t understand how anyone could say no to that?

Getting out of the Captain’s chair, he straightened the lapels of his lab coat and prepared to greet them. The mathematician and the laser physicist were absolutely invaluable to this expedition, as well as the engineers and the computer techs. Without them, degenerating into the 13th Power wouldn’t be possible. They were brilliant professionals, the best in their fields.

Ray swallowed. As for Janis, Tracy, Stan and Lo, he needed their expertise, but not aboard the transporter. Rather, he needed them at their stations in Tech-Com Control. If this project had taught them only one thing, it was how to solve problems. They were good at it, good enough for him to stake his life on, and the lives of his crew, a crew that didn’t need any special skills, only the desire to be together.

Lisa came up through the hatch first. She wore cutoff blue jeans, a yellow t-shirt, and brown leather sandals. Then Kate appeared, wearing a short black skirt, red lacy blouse, and white high heels. They stood next to each other on the flight deck, holding hands and glaring at him, their faces etched with questions.

“Why did you call for us?” Lisa asked.

Kate wet her lips. “What’s this all about, Ray?”

“Sit down...please.” He motioned to the high-back

chairs. "Let me show you something." As they seated themselves, Ray worked switches on the console. A monitor dropped from the ceiling, its screen a blank gray.

"We're going to watch TV?" Lisa asked.

"Not like any TV you've ever seen," Ray said. "This is the viewfinder for a high-resolution space probe mounted in the nosecone of this transporter. Stan built it himself."

"What's it for?" Kate asked.

"On this gadget, we'll be able to observe star systems in astonishing detail."

"Turn it on," Lisa said. "I want to see."

Shaking his head, Ray explained, "It only works in the vacuum of space." He quickly glanced at Kate.

Her mouth dropped open as if she'd suddenly gotten the gist of this conversation. "Ray?"

"Dad...you're scaring me."

Kate put her hand on her chest. "You want us to go up in space in this...this...thing?" Her eyes darted around the flight deck, "...with you...to watch that probe gadget?"

"That's right, both of you. A family adventure...kind of like Robinson Crusoe."

"No way." Lisa shot up from her chair. "I'm outta here."

Ray stepped in front of her. "Didn't you say you wanted a family again, the mother and father you didn't have all your life?"

"Because of you...and her." She thumbed in Kate's direction. "I grew up without a family."

"I'm sorry about that. And your mother is sorry too. Now it's time to put it behind us."

"But this..." Kate said, aghast. "This is too much to ask."

"Anymore than you asking us to forgive you for what you did, to take you back into our lives, forget about the past, start over? A bit much to ask, don't you think? But because your daughter is willing to try, I'm willing to try.

What are you willing to do?"

"But you said..."

Ray put his hand up. "I know what I said. The sooner we finish this project the sooner we get out of here. After the way Curtis and Jonathan treated you, I'm surprised you're still hanging around here."

"My daughter and I are just getting to know each other. I'm not about to let those bozos interfere with that."

"By staying, you've convinced me of one thing. You're sincere about wanting this family back together. Because of that resolve, and yours, Lisa, I've decided to ask you to go with me. I believe in you. Now the question is...do you believe in me?"

Lisa sat in the chair again. "I do, Dad, besides...you wouldn't ask us to do this if it wasn't safe."

"I didn't say it was safe. I don't even know how dangerous it is. But does it matter? We wouldn't be the first people to venture into the unknown...risk it all, life and limb, not knowing what we'll find out there. The point is we'll be doing it together."

Kate pointed to Ray with a red-nailed finger. "How can you ask us to risk our lives like this...in the name of our family? What if your daughter gets killed? Don't you care?"

"I don't believe we're going to die. If I did, I wouldn't go. I'm not being reckless here. The math and physics are solid. The Supers have proven it time and again. I'm sure it's going to work. You've got to trust me."

"Blind trust is a lot to ask of us," Lisa said.

"What else have I ever asked of you?"

Lisa looked at her fingernails. "Nothing," she said softly.

"You know how to fly this thing?" Kate asked.

"Stan taught me everything I need to know."

"Is it going to be like a shuttle launch? God, I don't think I can do it."

"No launch, no fire, no noise," Ray said. "We'll slip into the 13th Power like a hand into a glove."

Kate gasped. "The 13th Power?" Her face turned ashen.

"Don't worry."

She looked as if she were going into shock. "Isn't it dangerous?"

"Who told you that?"

"Colonel Fallon...but I wasn't sure..."

"Don't get any ideas about telling him what I'm doing."

She looked appalled. "I would never..."

"Good. We're leaving in twenty-four hours, so he won't have time to stop us anyway. Now...are you with me on this?"

They didn't say anything, just glared at him.

He wasn't about to give up. "You've been bugging me for a month, all this talk about reuniting this family. Now it's time to step up."

Lisa and Kate looked at each other, then at Ray and back and forth a few times. They put their heads together and whispered. Ray held his breath. A moment passed like an hour. Finally, they looked at him, and Kate broke the silence. "Are you sure we'll come back safe?"

"Stan says it'll work. That's good enough for me."

Lisa asked, "What does Janis have to say about this?"

"I haven't told him yet."

"He'll never agree," Lisa said.

"You leave that up to me."

Kate looked at Lisa and then at Ray. "If Janis says it's okay, we'll go."

"As a family," Lisa added without smiling.

"But if he says no," Kate put in. "Nobody goes."

Ray was sure he could talk Janis into it. "Agreed. The briefing is in one hour."

They embraced.

A shiver ran up Ray's back. His family was going on an adventure, the Crawfords, a crazy mix of souls: a scientist, an ex-hooker, and their daughter. Over the years, they'd done nothing but tear each other apart, as lust and fear and hate all worked against them. He could only hope that the 13th Power would be strong enough to unite them.

***

After leaving Ray in the transporter, Kate stepped out the MIGGS hatch. A cold sweat formed the back of her neck. This incredible turn of events had caught her off guard.

Lisa came out behind her. "I hope you're not doing this because of me."

"We both want our family together." Kate hustled toward the exit in Tech-Com Control.

"But what if Dad's wrong?"

"And what if he's not?"

"Mother, aren't you afraid?"

"I'm petrified."

"Then why...?"

"I'm not feeling very well," Kate said, which wasn't entirely a lie. Her stomach felt like it had twisted in knots when Ray mentioned the 13th Power. Colonel Fallon's concerns shot through her mind: oblivion and the end of the world.

"What about the briefing?" Lisa asked.

"You go ahead."

"You look kind of pale, Mom."

"Tell Ray I had to lie down."

Lisa turned, hesitated a moment. "Are you going to be all right?"

"I'll catch up with you later."

Shrugging, Lisa headed toward the conference room.

Kate watched until Lisa disappeared around the

corner. Ray had said he planned on leaving on his *great adventure* in twenty-four hours. There wasn't much time.

Hurrying down the escalator in the atrium, she pushed through the doors to the vehicle lobby. A staff car pulled up to the curb, and she climbed in. "Executive suites."

The car roared out of the parking garage.

She needed to make a phone call. Colonel Fallon had put the fate of the world on her shoulders, after all, if not for the deal she'd made with him, she'd have already left this horrible place. She'd have gotten as far away from Curtis and Jonathan and the rats as possible, but she'd lived with abuse before. Willy, his drugs, and the prostitution had just been a different kind of abuse. And risking her life was nothing new. Any of those smelly men in those cheap motel rooms could've easily killed her. She figured this journey with Ray was the price she'd have to pay to put it all behind her, to start a new life with her family. Nothing was going to stop her now, not even the 13th Power.

The staff car glided to a stop under the carport. She got out and shut the door. As the car sped away, she looked back at the twin stainless steel buildings of the lab complex nestled against the rocky hillside, the steel arch clearly visible above the roofline. She was on a mission, and she had to stick it out. Her throat aching, she fished Colonel Fallon's card from her purse and pushed her way inside. Once in her room, she kicked off her high heels, sat on the edge of her bed, and dialed the house phone.

"Lieutenant Briggs."

"Colonel Fallon, please."

"He's in a meeting. Can I take a message?"

"It's Kate...Kate Crawford."

There was a moment of silence, as if Briggs had put his hand over the phone. Then he said, "I'll patch you through, Mrs. Crawford." The line clicked.

"Kate. What's wrong?" The tension in Fallon's voice gave her a chill.

"The 13th Power."

"My God! When?"

"In twenty-four hours."

"We'll be there at noon. Get out as soon as you can."

Kate's stomach clutched. "I'm staying, Colonel."

"Don't be a fool. Get out of there."

She gripped the receiver a little tighter. "How far can I run if the world is going to be destroyed?"

"You don't understand. All hell is going to break loose. You'd better hurry."

"My place is with my family, no matter what. Thanks for everything and goodbye." She set the phone in its cradle, ending the protests on the other end of the line.

Chapter Forty-Six

RAY LEANED ON JANIS'S CONSOLE in Tech-Com Control. "You've got to do it for me."

Janis glared at the maniac, the madman he called his friend. He was completely out of his mind. "There's no way we can get away with it. Curtis will notice the changes in procedure. The countdown is different, liquid hydrogen has to be brought in from LA, and the ionizer has to be charged. Hell, the electron target makes more noise than the MIGGS. For Christ's sake, forget it."

Ray pinched his mustache. "We'll tell him it's a new procedure that'll increase our gold production. You know he's not happy with only five DM shots a day. The greedy bastard will go for it if he thinks it'll double his take. What do you say?"

"When do you want to go?"

"Tomorrow."

Janis pushed his glasses up the bridge of his nose. "Why are you in such a goddamned hurry to kill yourself?"

"Nobody's going to get killed, Janis. I'm so sure of it I'm taking Lisa and Kate with me."

Janis almost choked. "You've got to be—"

"My family is going with me."

"Like hell they are."

"They've already agreed to go."

"Why in God's name would they do that?"

"It's a family matter. The math is correct, and the

Higgs boson is contained. We can do this thing, Janis. Now's the time."

Janis glanced at the MIGGS window. "What about the transporter?"

"Stan signed it off yesterday. All systems *go*."

"You're nuts." Janis sat in front of his terminal. He knew he should've gone out for coffee with the rest of the team. Then he wouldn't be having this ludicrous conversation with Ray. This morning, Curtis had shipped in another pallet of lead bars, creating more work. Janis had stayed behind, electing to work them into the DM scheduler now, rather than tonight, when he'd rather be with Tracy.

Ray folded his arms across his chest. "You miss Colorado, don't you?"

Janis ignored him.

"You have a cushy job waiting for you back at the university," Ray went on. "Bet you miss that, too."

"Where's this leading?"

"I don't have anything to go back to, Janis. When this job is done, I've got nothing. I can't go back to Atomtech. It's a junkyard. This is the end of the line for me. My career is over, finished, kaput."

Janis swiveled in his chair and faced Ray. "Is that any reason to suck your family into the void of the universe?"

"Recognition for the discovery is my one shot. I'll be set for life: the Nobel Prize, a book or two, and lecture tours. I've dedicated my whole life to this project, its theories, its speculations, and its controversies. I have a vision. Let me see it through to the end, Janis. I've earned it."

"And if you don't come back?" Janis set his jaw.

"Then nobody will ever know what we found out there."

"Exactly what do you expect to find, Ray?"

"The answer to a question mankind has been asking for centuries, ever since our ancestors looked up into the night sky. We all want to know one thing: are we alone? Were we created or evolved, the deliberate act of a higher power or an accident of nature?"

"You can't be serious."

Ray put his hands on his hips and his glare on Janis. "The answer is beyond our reach from earth. The distances are too great for rockets or space stations, or even radio signals. But because the rules of math and physics don't apply at the 13th Power, the transporter will travel 100,000 light years in an instant, proving the smallest equals the largest and negative equals positive. It'll take us across the galaxy where other worlds, other forms of life may exist. I want to see what's out there."

"A lot of empty space," Janis said. "Just like the atom."

"But we might get close to something."

Janis rocked back in his chair. "What if you don't find anything?"

"At least I'll have tried."

"Worse yet, what if you find something you wish you hadn't...you know...like hostile aliens, creatures more horrifying than anything in the movies?"

Ray frowned. "I'll take my chances."

"But Lisa and Kate don't have to take those chances. Why not just go alone?"

"You've never had a family," Ray said. "You wouldn't understand."

"That's not fair."

"We'll be back in two days."

"I can't believe Lisa and Kate agreed to this. What's the catch?"

Ray swallowed. "You have to approve."

"That's just great. Lay it all on me. I say no."

Ray gritted his teeth. "Give me one good reason."

"The transporter can't reenter the atmosphere, for one. How will you get back?"

"We'll be regenerated back inside the MIGGS."

"And you know that for a fact?"

Ray nodded. "Stan said so."

"If not, how will I know you even survived degeneration?"

"Look." Using the mouse on Janis's terminal, Ray clicked on the regenerating program icon and double-clicked an animated swirling galaxy. The monitor switched to a rotating mass of stars. "Stan showed me how this works." Ray pointed. "As long as you see this *O* and this *X*, we're okay. The regenerator is locked-on to us. If there's no *O*, we didn't make it." He said the words without blinking.

Janis stared at the monitor, his mind trying to comprehend the distances involved, the amount of time it would take to traverse the expanse of the galaxy. Incomprehensible. If something went wrong, they'd be lost forever. How could he agree to such a thing?

Just then, Stan came in, his shoes squeaking on the tile floor. "Here's the latest tally." He handed Janis a printout. "When the pallet's full, we're going to move it from the MIGGS to a vault in the assembly room, probably in two days."

"What's the hurry?"

"Curtis is always in a hurry," Stan replied and walked out.

Janis looked over the inventory of new gold, somewhat relieved his mind had something else to work on besides Ray's insistence. "Get a load of this." Janis showed Ray the list. "One hundred forty nine ingots, twelve-point-one million dollars. And this is just the beginning. It's a crime, I tell you. If he dumps this stuff on the open market, the price of gold is going to plummet. Our economy, banking system, and global exchange rates are going to end up on the shit pile."

Ray peered at the printout. "Curtis is going to

exchange the gold overseas. Someone else's country is going to suffer...at first anyway. By the time the damage is done, he'll have made off with billions."

"But his money won't be any good if gold is worthless."

"He's going to buy up the world's diamond reserves. When he's finished, there'll be no more gold standard, Janis."

"It's insanity."

"Then let's do something about it."

"What do you suggest...shoot the bastard?"

"Better men have tried...and died." Ray smiled. "But we can hit him where it really hurts...in his back pocket."

Janis raised his eyebrows. "What do you have in mind?"

"You heard Stan. He's going to move the gold out of the MIGGS in two days. If we degenerate the space transporter, everything in the MIGGS disappears into the 13th Power with it, including the DM and the gold. Poof. It's all gone. The old *kill two birds* routine. I get the 13th Power. Curtis gets the shaft."

Janis huffed. "He'll just make us start over. I want to go home." He moved to the MIGGS window.

Ray followed. "Everybody wants out of here, Janis. But we haven't finished what we started. The 13th Power is still up for grabs. The true science of this thing is waiting for us, begging us to take the leap. Let's do it, and then we can go home, when we're done."

"And what about Curtis?"

"Weren't you the one who told me every dog has his day?"

Janis's breath fogged the MIGGS window, his reflection staring back at him like a ghost in the glass. The thought of screwing Curtis out of his gold made his pulse race, but the repercussions made his stomach cramp. Would the satisfaction of seeing Curtis ruined be worth risking

Ray's life, and Lisa's and Kate's? What would the real price of satisfaction be in the end?

A few technicians wandered in from their break, coffee cups in hand, the hubbub of their voices rising. Tracy and Lo were with them. Boris took his place at the main control console. They were getting ready to do another DM shot.

Ray whispered, "Come on, Janis. What do you say?"

Curtis stomped onto the deck outside his office and shouted down to the control room. "Get back to work."

Janis's neck hairs tingled. "Asshole," he said under his breath and then looked Ray in the eyes. The nuclear physicist just stared back at him.

"Let's do it," Ray said and offered his hand. "Don't let him get away with this."

Curtis bellowed, "You too, Janis. Or do you want a lunch date with the rats?"

Taking a deep breath, Janis shook Ray's hand. "You're on...tomorrow at noon. I'll call the team in at seven o'clock. Be ready to board the transporter then, before Curtis gets here."

"You won't regret this, Janis."

"That remains to be seen."

Chapter Forty-Seven

THE NEXT MORNING, A TWINGE OF dread pinched Janis's stomach as he looked into the MIGGS window and saw Ray standing at the transporter's belly hatch. Kate and Lisa were with him. They were dressed as a team, all wearing white tennis shoes, gray jumpsuits, and red baseball caps. Standing with them, Stan handed Ray an inventory sheet, the same one Janis had signed off an hour ago. It listed the supplies Stan's men had loaded during the night. A moment later, they shook hands.

Boris approached Janis with the coffee pot.

"No thanks."

As the Crawfords climbed on board, the transporter teetered on the mechanical arm that suspended it from the ceiling. Stan secured the belly hatch, took a step back, and looked up to the MIGGS window. Janis nodded to him. After a quick salute, Stan headed toward the exit hatch, stopping for a moment at the pallet of gold bars that once were lead. He shook his head in disgust and ducked out.

Janis turned his attention to Tech-Com Control. The countdown clock showed four hours and twenty-one minutes. Green lights twinkled on the Supers' main control panel. Lo's monitor lit up with lines of information as he typed on his keyboard, his eyes fixed on the language he knew so well, constantly checking and rechecking formulas and codes.

The MIGGS monitor read *STANDBY* in the operations

window. Johnson fidgeted in his chair, and Roger worked switches and dials on the power distribution console, while Robert started the warm up sequence for the accelerator. At the laser terminal, the monitor scrolled a message: *STANDBY MODE*. Tracy leaned on the instrument panel at Boris's station, coffee cup in hand, locked in conversation with the Russian. The only other sound, a soft hum, came from cooling fans in the electronic consoles. Curtis's upstairs office window was dark.

Janis put on a communications headset. "Ray, you on?"

A moment passed. *"With you, Janis. Just getting settled in."*

"So far, so good," Janis said, his eyes on the transporter's black windshield. "The liquid hydrogen is due in from LA at 10:30, another hour prep and we'll be ready to go by noon. Lo's checking the Supers one last time."

Ray's face appeared in the windshield. *"Stan told me his men tested the electron target field magnets last night. They had to be realigned with the transporter's onboard MIGGS port. Other than that, everything went without a glitch."*

"Stan's checking the ionizer right now. It hasn't been sequenced since the last time we did the 13th Power experiment." Janis shuddered. "What a disaster that could have been."

"But it wasn't," Ray said. *"The particle beam and the DM were child's play compared to the 13th Power experiment. We'll make it this time."*

"Sure," Janis replied under his breath.

***

Meanwhile, Indian Springs basked under a balmy Nevada sun, and snow clung to mountain peaks far off to the west. The air hung still and dry over the Air Force base as Colonel Fallon climbed into the jump seat of his UH-60L Blackhawk helicopter, clamped the golden staff between his knees, and slipped on a headset.

The pilot started flipping switches. Rotors began to spin, slowly at first, then faster and faster as the whine of turbine engines rose to a fever pitch. As the blades collided with the air, they made a thumping sound Fallon could feel in his chest. He positioned the mike in front of his lips. "Start 'em up, men."

On the tarmac stretched out in front of him, four rows of sixteen Apaches came to life. Engines threw smoke and rotor blades started to whip around. The desert dust rose and swirled with a mix of power and fury.

A spotter gave the signal, a rotating motion with his hand over his head, and the Blackhawk lifted off the pad with the smoothness of an elevator. As the flight line fell away, Fallon watched his squadron rise into the air as if summoned up by an invisible conductor. The Apaches were on the move, rotor blades flashing in the sunshine, the formation now speeding over the desert, rising higher and higher. From his left, a dozen brown Hueys, each carrying a squad of heavily armed security police, converged with the formation. Fallon nodded. The whole affair made his pulse race.

"Red Leader One to Command," squawked over the radio.

"Command," Fallon replied.

"Green Leader Two reports choppers away from Nellis. ETA to target, ninety minutes."

The Blackhawk copilot came on the intercom, his voice bitter. *"The lucky bastards. While we're rounding up a bunch of civilians at Solartech Labs, they'll be blasting James 'Red' Colburn and his mercenaries."*

"At ease, Captain," the Colonel said, looking up to the flight deck. "Red and his soldiers will be shooting back. Green Leader Two will have his hands full. Some of his men are going to die today. Be glad you got the gravy this time."

"I'm sorry, sir."

Fallon returned his attention to the Apaches flying in formation below the Blackhawk and grabbed the golden staff. The last time he executed an MPA on Solartech Labs, the security force didn't resist. If they put up a fight this time, some of *his* men were going to die today, too.

***

Sixty minutes to laser firing, the electronic voice from the Supers announced. Stan rushed into Tech-Com Control with two engineers in tow. "The ionizer's ready, Janis. Bring it online."

Janis turned to Lo. "How's she look?"

Lo typed. The Supers put the ionizer-sequencing program up on the monitor. He nodded. "Good to go."

"Okay, Boris..." Janis turned to the main control console. "Initiate the experiment."

Boris reset a series of switches on the panel.

As the ionizer buzzed and came online, *ACTIVATED* appeared on Lo's monitor.

Suddenly, Curtis stomped in. "What the hell is going on in here?"

Janis flinched. "Sir?"

"Why is the ionizer online?"

Stan answered without hesitating. "Good news, sir. We've figured a way to double the DM's gold output by using the transporter's pulse light engines."

"You don't say." Curtis strode to the MIGGS window and peered inside. "How's that?"

Janis approached Curtis. "The pulse light engines can magnify the ionized particle beam twofold." He looked into the MIGGS. "Now we can put two lead bars in the DM at a time. Twice the gold."

Curtis shifted his eyes back and forth. “Where’s the sighting dish?”

Stan cleared his throat. “We moved it inside the transporter’s number three pulse light engine chamber... more refraction that way.”

“Refraction? Of course.” Curtis frowned as if he wasn’t buying any of this scientific mumbo jumbo. He looked at the clock ticking off seconds then back to the MIGGS window and the transporter.

Janis folded his arms, his gaze on the transporter and his heart racing as he worried over Curtis’s next question. But as luck would have it, Lisa’s face appeared in the windshield.

“What’s she doing in there?” Curtis bellowed.

A hand pulled Lisa away, and another face appeared. Ray’s.

Curtis grabbed Janis by his lab coat lapels and slammed him against the wall. “Get them out of there. Now.”

Janis grimaced. “I can’t.”

“You better.”

“They’re going, Curtis. And your gold is going with them. You’re finished.”

“Like hell.” His eyes shifted to the countdown clock above the windows, then to the MIGGS, then to Tracy’s monitor. *LASER CHARGED* flashed on her screen. “Twice the gold, why you lying bastards. Boris, shut down Tech-Com Control.”

The Russian flipped through a row of switches. *ACCESS DENIED* flashed on the monitors. “The Supers...get in I cannot.”

Curtis shifted his attention to the power station. “Roger...turn it off.”

Roger worked dials and knobs. “No response, sir. The Supers have complete control.”

Rage turned Curtis’s face to stone. From under his

black coat, he pulled out a gun and shoved it under Janis's chin. "Lo, shut down the Supers, or I swear I'll kill Janis right where he stands."

As Lo typed, Janis fought a hot rush of panic.

CHANGES LOCKED OUT appeared in a window titled *Worm Security*. "Sorry, Janis," Lo said.

Curtis let out a yell and shoved Janis into the center of the room. "You have been a pain in my ass ever since the very beginning. I am *SO* going to enjoy this."

"No." Tracy leaped from her chair and dove in front of Janis. The gun went off, and Tracy hit the floor.

Shocked, Janis fell to his knees, his hand going to the wound in her chest that was gushing blood. "Tracy!"

As Curtis took aim again, Jonathan ran into the control room. "Boss. We got big trouble. Choppers are comin' in. There must be a hundred of them."

Curtis glared at Jonathan. "Son-of-a-bitch."

"We gotta get out of here." He grabbed Curtis's coat sleeve.

"Like hell." Curtis pulled his arm free, the gun wavering. "I'm not going anywhere without my gold."

Forty-five minutes to laser firing, announced the electronic voice.

"They'll be here any minute," Jonathan said. "There's no time."

"Call security. Condition Red."

Jonathan took a step back. "A full scale attack...against those choppers? Our men will be slaughtered."

"Risk nothing, gain nothing," Curtis said. "It'll buy us some time. Get the gold loader and meet me in the MIGGS."

As their running footsteps echoed away down the hall, Janis clutched Tracy's limp body in his arms. "Oh, God. No."

***

The squadron of Apaches approached Solartech Labs from the north, flying low and fast. Below, Fallon spotted men dressed in combat fatigues, lining the perimeter barriers, firing 50-caliber machineguns and M-16s. Rounds plinked off the Blackhawk's fuselage. A Stinger missile streaked skyward and blew an Apache out of the sky.

"Evade!" Fallon ordered.

The pilot veered right, then left as four Apaches flew in underneath them, mini-guns rattling off two thousand rounds per minute, shredding open a hole in the defensive perimeter. Men fell, broken and bloody. A Hellfire missile took out the main gate with a blast that sent a yellow fireball churning into the air. More Apaches joined the battle: hovering, firing, slewing sideways, and firing again. Two at a time, a dozen Folding Fin Rockets spit fire and smoke from the underbelly of an Apache and slammed into a building where defenders held positions on the roof. Black smoke pumped into a hazy California sky.

Pressing on, the Blackhawk flew toward the twin stainless-steel buildings and its landmark arch. As bullets ricocheted off the Blackhawk, Fallon saw columns of armed men rushing for cover below, jumping over walls, crawling under cars, and ducking around corners. He figured Melvin Anderson had given orders to defend the main lab complex, no matter how many men would die.

Fallon keyed his mike. "Send in the Hueys."

The Blackhawk stayed aloft as the Hueys came in, touching down on well-manicured lawns, cement parking lots, and blacktopped roadways. Security Police leaped into battle, guns blazing. Wreaking havoc, four Apaches strafed the defenders' positions, blowing out windows and felling trees. Small arms fire popped and banged.

Men screamed. Security Police fell.

A Hellfire twisted a tail of smoke into the top level of

the parking garage. It exploded, sending men airborne, tumbling to their deaths. Another barrage of Folding Fin Rockets blasted the steel arch, which twisted, teetered, and crashed to the ground.

It might have been another fifteen minutes, though it seemed longer to Fallon, before makeshift white flags started popping up all over the place. The SPs surrounded the last resisters and soon gave the all clear. "Take us in," he told the pilot.

The Blackhawk settled to the roadway. Apaches landed on either side of it. Others set down on the roofs and lawns, their engines whining and rotor blades thumping. They were everywhere, like a swarm of hornets descending on a nest.

Fallon clutched the golden staff and ran across the lawn, a squad of men at his heels. The main doors were locked. He stepped back. His men fired at the locks and kicked open the doors.

Inside, remembering his last incursion here, he led the way down a hall, through the main lobby, and down a corridor to a catwalk, which crossed over to Tech-Com Control. The first thing he saw was a man huddled over a woman lying on the floor in a pool of blood.

"Get the medics in here," Fallon ordered.

"She's dying," the man said and looked up. "Help us!"

Fallon thought his heart stopped. "Janis?" His eyes went to the woman's pallid face. "Tracy? What are you doing here?"

"T-that bastard, Curtis," Janis said, his voice faltering. "He shot her!"

"Where is he?"

"In the MIGGS," Janis said, nodding to the thick glass window in the wall.

Twenty minutes to laser firing.

Fallon flinched. "What's that mean?"

"The 13th Power experiment," Janis said. "The Supers are running the programs automatically."

"Can you stop it?"

"No, damn it...Tracy...please, God!" He rocked her.

Colonel Fallon rushed to the MIGGS window. Inside, he saw the silver transporter and a man wearing a black suit stacking gold bars on a pallet.

Clenching the golden staff in his fist, Fallon snarled. "Finally...Melvin Anderson." He turned to Janis. "How do I get down there?"

"The stairs...down that hall."

Medics rushed in. "Take care of her," Fallon ordered and ran for the stairs, the jingling key ring on his belt echoing off the walls. He soon found himself in a cold cement room with yellow and black warning stripes painted around the ceiling and floor. A hatch-like door hung open at the far end.

Fifteen minutes to laser firing.

A sudden humming sound came from beyond the door, getting louder and louder.

Jaw set, Fallon leaped into the MIGGS.

Melvin Anderson turned around, dropped a gold bar, surprise etched on his ashen face, then sheer delight as his gaze landed on the golden staff in Fallon's hand. "I see you brought it back to me," the impostor said with a crooked smile.

"Melvin Anderson, you're under arrest," Fallon ordered. "Federal Marshal's Warrant."

"It's Dr. Frank Curtis to you, Colonel. Now, hand over my Pharaoh's staff and be on your way."

The humming increased, filling the air with a tingling vibration.

"Don't try to bullshit me, Anderson, or Curtis, or whoever the hell you think you are. I know the whole scam. *The Ark* is dead. Your charade is over."

"My ass." In a flash, Curtis pulled a gun, but the grin

on his face faded swiftly. His lips tightened, and he glared wide-eyed at the gun in his hand, which began quivering, then vibrating and now shaking wildly, the barrel jerking up and down, back and forth. As Curtis fought for control of the gun, his face contorted like an arm wrestler straining against a fierce opponent.

Humming louder now, the MIGGS walls started vibrating, rumbling. Fallon's key ring flew from his belt and stuck to the wall.

Curtis clenched his teeth and groaned. "Ahhh!" The gun ripped from his hand and stuck to the ceiling with a clang.

Fallon couldn't take his eyes away from this oddity, the roaring noise and the gun's strange behavior distorting his sense of reality. Some kind of powerful force field made his skin feel as if it were crawling off his body.

The green ceiling lights went out, leaving the MIGGS awash in a crimson glow coming from a tunnel at the other end. Momentarily blinded, chills rippled down Fallon's spine. Curtis lunged at him and grabbed the golden staff. With every muscle on full alert, Fallon held on to the staff with both hands and grappled with his cursing nemesis. Like gladiators in a red arena, they jockeyed for position, each seeking the best advantage over the other. Fallon gritted his teeth. "I've waited a long time for this."

"Hope you're not disappointed," Curtis growled.

Shuffling left, Fallon rotated the golden staff upward. "Walter Devin was my best friend."

"He was a pain in my ass." Curtis forced the golden staff around the other way. "Like you." He pushed the Colonel backward, slamming him into the wall.

Pain rifled up his backbone, but he mustered all his strength and shoved Curtis back. "You haven't seen anything yet." Years of military training kicked in. He dropped onto his back, pulling Curtis over the top of him and sending the impostor tumbling across the MIGGS. He landed under the transporter on his face.

"Boss, I got the loader."

Spinning around, Fallon spotted Jonathan ducking in through the hatch. In that split second, Fallon sprang to his feet and swung the golden staff, connecting the eagle-head handle squarely on Jonathan's temple and sending him to the floor with a thud.

At the same time, Curtis charged across the MIGGS, teeth bared, and black coat flailing in his wake. Fallon stood firm and pointed the golden staff at him. "You want this so damn bad, you can have it." He pressed the eagle's emerald eye.

With a zing, a golden dagger shot out from the tip of the staff and straight into Curtis's chest, buried to the hilt. He staggered backward, his eyes wide, and his hands clutching the dagger's gold handle.

Fallon threw the staff to the floor. "That's for Walter Devin."

Curtis stumbled in a semicircle, slumped over his pallet, and embraced his bars of gold.

Ten minutes to laser firing.

The Colonel ducked out of the MIGGS and slammed shut the hatch. Locks squeaked into place. Brushing his hands together, he now had to stop the experiment before everyone got killed.

Upstairs in the control room, only a pool of blood remained on the floor where Tracy had fallen. Medics had lifted her to a gurney and were wheeling her toward the door. Running alongside, Janis huddled over her.

"Hold it!" Fallon grabbed Janis's arm. "Where do you think you're going?"

"To the hospital with Tracy."

"No you're not."

"The medics are going to fly her out of here."

"And they'll take good care of her," Fallon assured him.

"I'm not..."

"I need you here."

"But..."

Fallon fixed his eyes on the mathematician. "Trust me, Janis. These guys are the best combat medics in the business. Bullet wounds are their specialty."

Janis looked into a medic's eyes. "Don't let her die," he said and stepped back.

The medics hurried out and down the hall, the gurney wheels rattling with speed.

Fallon patted Janis's shoulder. "We have to stop this thing."

"We can't."

"You've got to try."

#

Janis thought this had to be worse than any nightmare he could have ever conjured up. Tracy was mortally wounded, and she was wheeled away, perhaps out of his life forever. Though he might never see her again, he knew the Colonel was right. There was nothing to gain from going with her and everything to lose. He realized that Tracy chose to stop that bullet for a reason. She knew that Ray, Lisa, and Kate needed him. His place was here at the controls. He had to see this experiment through to the end. "Lo," Janis said, not giving the Colonel a second look. "Status report."

Rumbling electromagnets resonated in the air.

"Scheduling program initiated, Janis."

"Try blocking lines of code."

Lo typed on the keyboard. *ACCESS DENIED.*

"What about changing the laser firing voltage?" Janis asked, stepping to the MIGGS window and donning a headset.

"I'm locked out," Lo replied. "*The Worm* won't let us

stop the 13th Power experiment. Thank CIA for that fucking problem."

"Damn!" Janis keyed the mike. "Ray! The military guys are back. We can't abort this thing. Come out before it's too late."

There was no response.

"Ray?" Janis looked into the transporter's windshield. Ray's face appeared. He was shaking his head no. "Come on, Ray. Get out of there."

Colonel Fallon put his face to the glass. "There's somebody in that thing?"

"Ray Crawford."

"Let me talk to him."

"Good luck." Janis handed the Colonel a microphone and switched to the intercom speakers.

"Ray. This is Colonel Bruce Fallon. Remember me?" The Colonel's voice echoed through Tech-Com Control.

Nothing.

"You know I can't let you do this."

More silence.

"Don't make me bring in my demolition team. I'll blow this contraption to smithereens."

There was still no reply.

"Where's Kate? Where's your daughter? Maybe they can talk some sense into you."

"Hello, Colonel." Kate's voice came over the speakers.

He thought he was going to faint. "Jesus. Get out of there, Kate."

"We're not coming out, so you may as well forget it."

"What in God's name are you doing?"

"I've got my family back."

Eight minutes to laser firing.

"The ionizer is loading," Lo reported.

Janis looked at the Colonel. "It's the way they want it. Now we have to get them off safely."

"What?"

"They're going into the 13th Power, Colonel."

Fallon thrust his shoulders back. "And risk the whole world?"

"Relax." Janis checked the programming schedule scrolling down his monitor. "Those problems have been solved."

"Walter Devin told me we'd all be disintegrated."

Janis glared at him. "Last time my formulas were wrong. I screwed up. But this time I've got them right."

"You can't be serious."

"The MIGGS will work. We're safe. The Crawfords on the other hand, I don't know about them."

"What's the worse case scenario?" Fallon asked, frowning.

"The transporter gets vaporized."

"Then get them out of there."

"It's too late." Janis turned to the control panel. "Robert? How's the synchrotron?"

"13TEV and rising steadily."

"Johnson?"

"MIGGS coming up, Janis. Twenty percent."

He turned to the power distribution station. "Roger?"

"Maximum online. Boost to one hundred fifteen percent in six minutes. The Supers have complete control."

The rumble became a roar, and the walls began vibrating.

"Electron target in five seconds," Lo said. "Three, two, one..."

The Supers energized the huge magnetic fields of the electron target, which now sounded like a freight train running through a tunnel at full speed.

Five minutes to laser firing.

"Buckle up, Ray."

"We're ready, Janis," crackled from the speakers.

"Good luck." He waved goodbye through the MIGGS

window. Ray's hand appeared in the transporter windshield, waving as the black mist began to form in the MIGGS, swirling like a devil's wind.

Suddenly, a contorted face appeared in the MIGGS window. Janis jumped back. Colonel Fallon gasped. It was Jonathan. He was pounding on the glass with the palms of his hands. His face looked awful: cheeks thin and sunken, lips puckered. An invisible force was pulling down on the skin of his forehead and jowls. His eyeballs were big around and popped halfway out of their sockets.

"Thirty percent," Johnson reported.

"My God," Janis said. "The gravity field."

Behind Jonathan, the black mist thickened and swirled, gaining momentum and form, whipping around the transporter, expanding and engulfing the blue ion shield. As if anchoring himself against a hurricane wind, Jonathan clung to the window frame, his fingers bleeding, his face etched with pain, mouth open wide, screaming in anguish, a scream that could not be heard in Tech-Com Control. Suddenly, blood spurted from his nostrils, and his eyeballs burst. The black mist reached out to him, touched him, yanked him away from the window and spun him around in midair, head over heels. His legs and arms were spread wide, and his clothes were ripped from his body and whipped away in the tempest.

"Fifty percent..."

Jonathan imploded, crumpling like a wad of paper under the crushing weight of the MIGGS building gravity field until he became just a spec, and then nothing as the gravity crushed every last atom in his body.

Three minutes to laser firing.

Janis turned away from the window, gasping, not realizing how long he'd been holding his breath.

"Ionizer charged," Lo said. "Ready for synchrotron."

"Seventy percent," Johnson said.

"CEI engaged," Lo reported and looked at Janis.

Shaking his head to clear his mind of the horror of Jonathan's demise, Janis checked the scheduling program. To his relief, there were no errors. The sequencer was right on time, each element of the experiment coming online with perfection. Every formula computed. Every equation checked. His mathematics calculated with staggering precision.

"Ninety percent," Johnson said. "We've got a red event horizon, Janis. One hundred. It's perfect."

One minute to laser firing.

The ceiling lights brightened as the Supers increased power to Tech-Com Control by fifteen percent. Roaring, the MIGGS rattled windows, consoles, and monitors.

"Synchrotron charged," Lo yelled.

"15TEV and holding," Robert confirmed.

"Electron target loaded." Lo spun around in his chair. "Laser resonator on maximum."

Janis looked at the clock, its red digits now at thirty seconds...twenty-nine... His eyes shifted to Tracy's station, the monitor flashing *ARMED*, the chair empty. Through it all, she had been here with him, up until now, when all their efforts would come to fruition in the next twenty seconds...nineteen...eighteen...

He glanced at Lo. Eyes closed, the computer wiz sat with his hands clasped in his lap. Johnson and Robert had their attention on the monitors in front of them as if intently watching the screens would have some positive affect on the outcome. Ten seconds...nine...eight...seven...

Janis rushed to the MIGGS window again. Boris was already there with Colonel Fallon, looking inside the black chamber where the swirling mist now completely cloaked the transporter and all those neatly stacked gold bars. Three...two...one...

ZERO.

The laser fired with intensity, buzzing through the synchrotron with the force of the sun, beaming into the

MIGGS with a thunderous clap. Hidden from view by the black mist, the particle beam collided with the electron target suspended in the onboard MIGGS. Protons smashed together at the speed of light and atomic particles were hurled into the transporter's titanium cylinder, releasing their Higgs bosons.

Tech-Com Control shook.

Slowly, the black mist opened up like the iris of an eye, revealing a cluster of lights that began to glow, spin, and undulate in waves, growing larger and larger as it raced forward, rotating now like a galaxy of a billion trillion stars.

Janis couldn't take his eyes away from this beautiful sight. It looked as if the universe had appeared within the MIGGS in all its splendor, tempting him to reach out for it, to grasp it in his hands. The brilliant swirling mass of stars expanded into a shower of sparkling lights and quickly blinked out, returning the MIGGS to darkness.

A clunk came from Roger's station as the Supers reset the power to normal. The roaring electromagnets wound down to a rumble, then a hum. Walls and windows stopped vibrating. Janis forced himself to breathe as he watched the black mist thin, break apart, and swirl down the floor grates. Green ceiling lights flickered on, and Tech-Com Control fell silent. Janis's heart beat wildly as the mechanical arm became visible, swaying back and forth from its anchor on the ceiling, broken. With wide eyes, he searched for the transporter in the dissipating mist.

"It's gone," Colonel Fallon said. "Where'd it go?"

Janis gulped. "Into the 13th Power."

Chapter Forty-Eight

THE TRANSPORTER STARTED SHAKING. Ray could see only blackness out the windshield. Titanium joints creaked under the heavy strain of the MIGGS' gravity field. He felt pressure on his chest and eyeballs, checked the *G-Force* gauge, and watched it climb past *2Gs*. Though he expected to hear the roaring of the MIGGS, everything was surprisingly quiet inside. He took one last look at Lisa sitting stiffly behind him as was Kate sitting in the chair on his right. Their eyes were fixed on the windshield as they wrung their hands in their laps.

The G-Force gauge read *3+*, and the ION Shield meter was in the green safety band.

"Dad. I can't breathe."

"Any moment now."

Holding his breath, he grabbed the steering yoke, his heart hammering as his eyes searched the swirling black mist beyond the windshield. Seconds passed like hours.

Suddenly, a pulsing light appeared in the darkness, faint at first, approaching from perhaps a million miles away, or maybe just a few feet. The nearer it came, the more brilliant it shined. Beams of light arced from its core, reaching out, twisting and bending like tentacles and racing forward at incredible speed.

"The Higgs boson," Ray said.

Lisa gasped. "Wow."

"It's scaring the hell out of me," Kate shrieked and

clutched the armrests of her chair.

Shaking, the transporter groaned as Ray scanned the hull pressure gauges. Their needles were bouncing in the red. "Come on, baby, hold together."

The G-Force gauge read four times the force of gravity, and the intense glow of the Higgs boson lit up the flight deck like a rising sun. Squinting, he didn't want to shut his eyes. He didn't want to miss a thing. Then something popped, and he flinched, the pressure on his body suddenly gone.

In an instant, the radiant Higgs boson broke into a billion sparkles that started spinning around the transporter, slowly at first, then faster and faster, producing lines of light that streaked the darkness and formed a brilliantly lit tunnel, bending and twisting and swirling down and up and around. Ray gripped the yoke is if it were the hand bar on a rollercoaster, but he soon realized the sensation of speed was just an illusion. There were no centrifugal forces pressing against his body. He was sitting still while everything around him was going by at breakneck speed.

"Look at that," Lisa said, pointing.

Glistening gold bars passed in front of the transporter, tumbling down the tunnel ahead of them now. "Curtis's gold. It's gone forever," Ray said. "And there, look, it's his golden staff." It was twirling like a baton, end over end, following the gold bars into the void as the transporter streaked through the luminous tunnel, which spun faster and faster, changing colors like a wondrous kaleidoscope.

Ray felt suddenly off balance, his sense of direction and orientation dizzily perplexed. Vertigo-induced nausea upset his stomach. Everything was spinning out of control.

Abruptly, the tunnel ended in what seemed like a freefall into a funnel, its shape outlined with billions of sparkling lights that seemed to be millions of miles away.

Lisa screeched.

"Oh my God," Kate shouted.

He swallowed hard as the transporter plunged down into an empty well of black space. A hollow feeling took hold of his stomach, a kind of floating sensation that made his whole body tingle. The G-Force gauge read zero, and he instinctively tightened his abdominal muscles as if that would help to hold his insides together. Nearby, a communications headset floated in the air. The transporter seemed to be upside down, and his sinuses began to drain. He remembered Stan saying that spatial attitude didn't exist in outer space. In weightlessness, there was no up or down. "Don't try to fly the transporter," he'd said. "Just hang on."

Down in the narrowest part of the funnel, lines of luminous dust emanated from the center of black space and curved outward toward a rim of stars, much like a giant pinwheel. Ray blinked. He thought his eyes were deceiving him because he couldn't see any hint of light beyond the pinwheel, as if it were not transparent, like a solid cosmic wall, or perhaps they were approaching the bottom of some kind of space well or black hole. His heartbeat took a leap of dread.

"What's that?" Lisa shrieked.

"We're going to crash!" Kate shouted. "Do something."

"I'm thinking," Ray said, trying to quell his own rising panic. Whatever that pinwheel was, they were headed straight toward it at horrendous speed.

Kate pounded on her armrests. "Stop this thing!"

"I'm scared, Dad."

"Go back!" Kate cried. "For God's sake, we're going to be killed."

Ray scanned the instruments and found nothing that could help him decide what to do now. But something looked vaguely familiar about this scene looming before him, as if he'd seen it all somewhere before, though he couldn't imagine how, or where. He wondered if he should trust his instincts and ride it out...or abort.

"Turn around, Dad!"

"Your daughter is going to die," Kate screamed.

The fear in Lisa's voice and the terror in Kate's made the decision for him. Abort. But he didn't know how. He didn't dare leave his seat and go back to the regenerator control room to pull the chrome handle. He had to think of another way. A list of things to check raced through his mind. Pulse light engine switches: *ON*. Refractors: *EXTEND*. Light speed indicator: *0 Point 9*. Full reverse: *INITIATE*. He shoved the throttles forward. A shrill whine came from the engines, but the transporter continued its plunge toward the ominous black wall in the middle of space. Shuddering and shaking, the light speed indicator still read *0 point 9*.

Kate gasped. "We're not slowing down."

"Dad!"

Ray flipped the COM switch. "Janis, are you there?"

Static.

It was no use. The wall was now looming before the transporter like a giant black barrier suspended in a luminescent web, an end to everything, straight ahead.

Light speed: *0 Point 9*.

Ray rechecked the throttles. They were all the way to full. The reverse thrusters were at maximum. He tried to pull back on the yoke, but it wouldn't budge. There was nothing else he could do. The space-bound aberration seemed intent on pulling the transporter down. Everything he'd worked for all his life was about to end in a fiery crash. It was over. With despair gripping his heart, he turned around and looked solemnly at his daughter and then over at Kate. "I'm sorry."

"Sorry, hell!" she shouted. "You promised we'd be all right. You told us to trust you, so don't let us die, Ray."

"Please, Dad, do something."

"I was so sure we'd be okay."

"You were wrong," Kate cried, and then surprisingly

her mouth fell open in awe.

And Lisa's expression suddenly changed from sheer terror to instant glee, her eyes glittering. "Dad! Look."

Ray whipped around, and what he saw outside the windshield took his breath away. The center of the pinwheel was moving. It was opening up like the iris of an eye, revealing an incredible inter-galactic gateway.

It was the 13th Power.

Ray didn't blink. "Of course." He recalled seeing this before, on the monitor in Tech-Com Control, when the CEI replayed the 13th Power experiment, but he never thought he'd see it for real. And beyond the ballooning hole in the darkness, a galaxy appeared, rotating in the star-studded blackness of space, its bulbous middle glowing with white and yellow clusters of supernovas, and its stellar plain swirling trails of sparkling stars in its wake.

"Oh my God," Ray said, suddenly feeling like a tiny, insignificant spec of matter. "Will you look at that?" The rules of physics and math had been nullified beyond the Higgs boson. Negative and positive were now one in the same at the 13th Power. He had been right all along. The universe resided in every atom.

The transporter streaked through the expanding iris and across the galaxy plain. "We made it!" Ray shut down the reverse thrusters.

Kate gulped air. "You damn near gave me a heart attack."

Lisa laughed out loud. "But Mom, this is *so* cool."

"We're dead," Kate said.

"Then we must be in heaven," Lisa responded. "Look at all those stars. They're so close, I could reach out and touch them."

Leaning forward, Kate gazed at the view out the windshield. "I don't believe this."

"Dad was right."

Not taking her eyes from the window, Kate replied,

"I'll never doubt him again."

Smiling, Ray looked at the flight clock on the overhead instrument panel. It was running. Next, he inspected the Higgs gauge, which vibrated in the green band, meaning the regenerator had been charged with Higgs bosons. The onboard MIGGS had trapped the particles needed for the return trip home. "All systems go," he reported to his family of deep space voyagers. He felt incredibly proud of them for their courage and their will to be together. Throttling up the pulse light engines, Ray let them run full open. The light speed indicator now read: *10 point 0.*

For all the wonders that lay before him, he asked himself that question again: *Are we alone?* Was there another world like earth and other intelligent beings seeking the same answers as mankind? With so many possibilities among so many stars and so many more millions of galaxies beyond this one, there had to be life somewhere within this immense expanse of incalculable distances.

Kate sighed. "It's so beautiful, Ray."

"No one has ever seen this before."

"Where are we?"

"On the other side of the Milky Way galaxy." Ray switched power to the regenerator monitor. It blinked on and showed a galaxy, similar to the one stretched out beyond the windshield. An *X* rested just inside the galaxy's bottom rim. "Like Stan said, look, here's earth." He pointed to the *X*. "And this is us." He pointed to the *O* on the other side of the galaxy. "Magnificent."

"It's so big," Lisa said, looking out the windshield, her eyes gleaming.

"Makes all our problems seem small," Kate said.

"It's better than any trip you've ever taken, huh, Mom?"

Kate winked. "Now I can't say that I've never been

anywhere. I just don't understand how we got here."

Ray switched on the space probe monitor as the transporter zoomed through a star-studded sea. "Mathematics," he said. "The Higgs boson is the 13th Power negative, a trillionth the diameter of the atom, deep inside the nucleus, a place so small that the space around it is as vast as the universe we see in the night sky.

"The 13th Power positive is a hundred thousand light years, a distance equal to the diameter of the Milky Way. So here we are, transported across the galaxy via the Higgs Field, just as I had calculated."

"But, h-how will we get back?" Kate asked, her voice cracking.

"Stan's got it all figured out." Ray scanned the instruments. "We'll regenerate back inside the MIGGS, in the exact place we left."

"Has Stan ever been wrong?"

"Not that I know of."

"Look at that," Lisa said, pointing like a kid at Disneyland as the transporter streaked past a star system floating within an interstellar cloud, glowing like a thousand radiant suns. Ray watched it go by in awe as the flight control computers kept him clear of its gravitational pull. On the monitor, the space probe showed a planet rotating around a star on the outermost edge of the cluster. *NO LIFE FORMS DETECTED* scrolled across the screen.

"How does this contraption know that?" Kate asked.

Ray pressed *STANDBY* on the space probe's record function. "Stan says it analyzes the planet's atmosphere with infrared and x-rays, like the Venus probes and Voyager I and II. If elements are present which are conducive to life, it mathematically predicts the possibilities based on the data it receives. That planet there is shrouded in hot, poisonous gases."

"That's a bummer," Lisa said. "But couldn't organisms evolve and thrive in that environment?"

"Maybe."

Kate made a face. "Like aliens?"

Ray nodded. "I think somewhere, it's possible."

"Are they dangerous?"

"If you mean more dangerous than humans, I seriously doubt it."

***

In Tech-Com Control, Lo reported the transporter's flight status to Janis. "Clock is running."

Sitting upright at his terminal, Janis switched to the regenerator program and held his breath as the monitor came on, fluttering and focusing.

"Where are they?" Fallon asked.

"There." Janis pointed at the *O*, which was clearly visible now. A wave of relief rushed through his body. "They're on the other side of the galaxy, Colonel. They made it."

Fallon stared at the rotating mass of stars on the screen, his jaw muscles flexing. "Jesus. How are they going to get back?"

"They'll regenerate inside the MIGGS."

The Colonel rubbed his chin. "Really?"

Janis shrugged. "That's what Stan says."

"When?"

"Day after tomorrow."

"Can't you bring them back right now?"

"Only Ray can initiate the regenerator. It's onboard the transporter."

Fallon looked around the control room. "You mean there's nothing we can do?"

"Nothing but wait."

The ComLink buzzed. "Colonel Fallon," Lieutenant Briggs said.

"Yes?"

"Green leader reports mission accomplished. After a bloody battle, they have Red in custody, sir."

"He'll be on death row in Leavenworth when I'm through with him."

"Good work, sir."

Janis cocked his head. "What was that all about?"

Fallon smiled. "The Atomtech investigation is complete. The murderers are in custody." He pulled out a fat cigar. "It's time to celebrate."

"Congratulations. Now it's time for me to see Tracy."

"She's in good hands."

"You don't need me anymore."

Fallon examined his cigar. "You're not leaving, Janis, not until this is over."

Janis stood. "But that's two more days."

"You heard me."

"If she dies—"

"The medics will call me."

"But—"

"No news is good news."

"Then call them right now." Janis pointed to the ComLink.

Fallon held his breath a moment, glaring, then as if he knew Janis wouldn't back down, spoke into the radio. "Bravo Leader Gray, give me a medical report on Tracy McClarence."

Noisy chopper blades hammered over the radio crackle. *"We're trying to get the bleeding under control. She's critical."*

Chapter Forty-Nine

LATER THAT AFTERNOON, COLONEL Fallon strolled into Tech-Com Control. Janis bolted from his chair at the regenerator monitor. "Where have you been?"

"I've got a squadron to run, you know."

"Is she all right?"

"Relax." Fallon approached the MIGGS window and peered inside. "The medical team called. She was lucky. Another two centimeters, the bullet would have exploded her aorta. Doc says she'll be on her feet soon."

Janis felt faint with relief.

Just then, Lieutenant Briggs rushed in. "Call for you on the ComLink, Sir. We patched it into the intercom."

Fallon frowned. "Who is it?"

"Carlton Nash."

Janis handed Fallon a mike. "When can I see Tracy?"

"When this is over." He keyed the mike. "What is it, Carlton?"

"Hello, Bruce," came over the speakers. "*Odyssey is going up in eighteen hours. Do you want a VIP pass for the launch?"*

Glancing around Tech-Com Control, Fallon shook his head. "You don't know how bad it hurts me to say this...but not this time. I'm in the middle of a big mess."

"Maybe next time," Carlton replied. *"Keep in touch."*

The connection went dead. Fallon sat in the chair at Ray's terminal and set the mike on the console. "Good man, that Carlton."

"Have you known him long?" Janis asked.

"Since Vietnam. Last time I saw him was back in December. He got me a pass for the Atlantis launch."

"It's good to have friends in the right places."

"You never know when you'll need a friend." Fallon leaned forward and looked at Janis's monitor. "How are they doing out there?"

"I wish I knew."

The monitor showed the *O* inside the galaxy's rim where billions of star clusters sparkled like glitter. Janis glanced at the useless headset hanging on the communications console. He knew it would take a hundred thousand years for a radio signal to reach Ray.

***

General Brigham hated Texas, especially this time of year. An ice storm had delayed his flight twice, but now that he'd finally arrived in Houston's Orbital Operations Center, he could get down to the mission at hand, one that the President had given him, personally.

The target was Federico Duran, the self-proclaimed leader of a rebel faction in Honduras where he bludgeoned his way into power over the bodies of slaughtered missionary nuns. His ties to the drug cartels in Columbia, where all his capital came from, and his animosity to the United States, won him no favors in the White House. Granted, the people generally liked him. He built a couple schools and a hospital. However, those who opposed him were languishing in Federico's prisons under the most inhumane of conditions. The President wanted him and his dictatorial regime dispatched immediately.

A controller looked up from his terminal. "System checks completed, sir."

Cigar smoke swirled around Brigham's head as he studied the big screen on the wall, which charted the position of the PLEDG defense system in orbit. He had seven SDSs, Sighting Dish Satellites, and two PLRs, Proton Laser Resonators, orbiting the earth. Star Wars was fully operational. PLR-ONE had been given a new course that would take it over Honduras.

"SDS-3 will be in range within two minutes."

"Very well." Brigham checked his watch, knowing SDS-3 would forever change the way war was waged. "Where's my spy satellite?"

"The SSS is in position, sir. We have twenty minutes to azimuth."

"What's the weather like?"

"Partly cloudy."

"Let's have a look, shall we?"

The big screen flickered, and now San Pedro Sula appeared, an aerial view from 300 miles up, only a few areas obscured by clouds.

"Zoom in on Casa del Sol, the palace," Brigham said.

The scene changed, tiling squares of detail as it magnified city streets, open-air markets, donkey trains and pedestrians, cars and jeeps, buses and bicycle riders. They had no idea what was about to happen.

Seconds later, a palace came into focus, a fortress of reinforced concrete and sandbags surrounding a spacious green lawn cut from the jungle, a pool, a fountain, and a limo parked in the semicircular drive. The images came in sharp and clear, thanks to the technological advancements the scientists at Atomtech had developed for the Sky Spy Satellite before the disaster that destroyed the place.

"SDS-3 is over the target," the controller reported.

"Sighting screen," Brigham ordered.

The PLEDG window opened, and crosshairs traversed the palace, the grounds, the drive, and finally zeroed in on the limo. Moments later, an entourage appeared on the sidewalk between the limo and the palace front doors. It was a group of men wearing business suits, all except one, who wore a military cap and quickly ducked into the limo, followed by the others.

"Sighting beam," Brigham ordered.

LASER LOCKED flashed on the screen.

"Gotcha!"

"PLR-ONE is charging, sir. Sixty seconds to laser firing."

As the limo sped away from the palace, the sighting crosshairs locked on its roof and followed every turn as the car negotiated narrow streets choked with pedestrians, and then raced along a blacktopped boulevard lined with trees. A minute later, the limo careened around a bend and headed toward the city center.

READY flashed on the monitor and a chill worked its way up Brigham's neck. "Fire!"

***

Lieutenant Briggs rushed into Tech-Com Control. "Message on the ComLink, sir. The President is going to address the nation. All the networks are carrying it live."

Janis's stomach turned over. Had someone gotten wind of what they had done?

"Patch it into the control room," Fallon said.

"Already done." The television monitors flickered on just as the buzz of conversation in the White House pressroom subsided. Reporters took their seats.

"Ladies and Gentlemen, the President of the United States."

Fallon's jaw muscles twitched.

The President, dressed in a gray suit, grasped the edge of the podium, straight-armed. "I'll make this as brief as possible," he said, his voice booming. "Federico Duran is dead. Witnesses in San Pedro Sula claimed to have seen lightning come out of the sky, a bolt so powerful it disintegrated the delegation's limousine, killing all on board, including under secretary Roberto Cordova,

Commandant Delarosa, and their aides. It's an unimaginable tragedy. I'm here to tell you that we, the citizens of the United States, send our condolences to the people of Honduras in their time of grief. Some religious zealots are saying that Federico's death was an act of God. Scientists, on the other hand, have blamed it on a tragic freak of nature, as yet unexplained. Whatever the case, America mourns with all of Honduras."

The President turned from the podium. Reporters leaped to their feet, hands waving. "Mr. President. Mr. President." He didn't respond to anyone and quickly disappeared through the doorway. The monitors blinked off.

Janis couldn't believe it. "Act of God...a freak of nature, like hell! We all know better than that. The bastard lied to the whole world, and with a straight face, no less. How's he going to get away with it?"

Fallon's eyes narrowed. "The Department of Defense is behind him, that's how. And I'll bet General Brigham is running the show. He's crazier than all of them, but political assassinations are illegal."

"I wonder who put him up to it."

"The President, that's who."

Janis squinted. "A conspiracy?"

"Worse," Fallon said, steel-eyed. "Brigham has a vendetta against the President. I've a bad feeling this is going to backfire on him."

"A double cross over Star Wars?"

"I wouldn't doubt it."

"Can we stop him?"

Fallon slumped in a chair. "I don't know."

"What's this world coming to?" Janis turned his attention to the regenerator monitor, its sparkling galaxy slowly rotating. He hoped the Crawfords were doing all right out there.

Chapter Fifty

AS THE TRANSPORTER STREAKED through interstellar space, Ray settled back into his Captain's chair and took in the intoxicating view out the windshield.

Floating across the flight deck, Lisa tumbled and twirled, playing with weightlessness as if it were a new toy. "I'm thirsty."

"See what you can find in the galley," Ray said.

"I'll go with you." Kate unlatched her seatbelt and rose like magic. "Oh my." Together, they disappeared down the aft hallway, the soles of their tennis shoes the last thing Ray saw of them. He returned his attention to the instruments.

The light speed indicator read: *10 Point 0,* the flight clock: *Six hours, twenty-seven minutes.* The Higgs Field gauge was in the green band. Satisfied, he set the space probe to swivel in a 180-degree arc. It reached out with its electronic feelers, searching the vast plain of star-studded space. Amazed, he then checked the video and record switches, insuring they were in the 'on' positions.

Soon, another star system loomed ahead. The transporter was fast approaching an array of glowing stars clumped together in a strange gravitational dance set against the black background of deep space. Some stars shined yellow, like earth's sun, while others emitted reds and blues. The smaller ones shone bright white, and they were all getting closer and bigger. As the flight computers deviated the course away from this system, Ray checked the trajectory readout, which showed a curving flight path toward two yellow suns glowing in the distance.

Suddenly, the space probe began beeping wildly. Ray shifted his eyes to the monitor where oscillating lines appeared, jumping up and down on the screen, blinking on and off, and erratically changing intensity. His breath hitched, and he flipped through a series of tuning switches to see if it was detecting a signal. Or perhaps a glitch in the main computer had set off the alarm. Amazingly, the LCD showed no errors online.

Lisa and Kate floated in. "Cherry or apple juice?" Lisa showed him two plastic packets with polyethylene straws.

"Cherry," Ray replied. Lisa let the packet float toward him, and he caught it with one hand. His eyes went back to the monitor, its weird lines rising and falling and flashing.

Kate settled into her seat and buckled her harness, her drink packet hanging in midair in front of her. "What's all that?" She pointed at the monitor.

"I think it's some kind of computer foul-up." Confused, he switched off the beeping alarm.

"It looks like a radio wave pattern to me," Lisa said. "A broadband of some kind, too wide for microwave and weak...or old, as if it were transmitted a long time ago."

"You think?"

"I've seen similar patterns in college lab."

Ray thought she might be right.

"Can we listen to it?" Kate asked.

"Let's see." Ray flipped the *AUDIO* switch. A speaker crackled and hissed. "Static," he said. "I wonder where it's coming from." He typed on the keypad, and a locator beacon came up on the screen. The arrow pointed toward the two yellow suns up ahead. "Couldn't be gamma rays."

The static turned to high-pitched squealing, oscillating in volume, and then a clear bass tone came over the speaker followed by another tone an octave higher. It faded into static again.

Ray's heart beat faster. "Did you hear that?" He turned to his family.

"Music?" Lisa said. "Is it coming from that star system, the one with two suns?"

"Or somewhere around here..."

"Maybe it's from earth." Kate sucked on her straw.

"We didn't have radios a hundred thousand years ago," Ray said. "It would have taken that long for a signal to reach this far across the galaxy, assuming it was strong enough. This signal is coming from somewhere close by." He worked a series of switches that would allow the computer to fine tune the space probe.

Suddenly, a vocal sound came over the speaker, fading in and out, barely discernable from the background noise. Ray flinched. It sounded like a voice, a cadence of sounds making up syllables or words completely without meaning. Baritone jabber. A different sound came after that, higher in pitch and clearer, to which the baritone again resounded, as if in response to the other.

"They're talking," Lisa said, her voice rising. "Dad?"

Ray felt light-headed. He could hardly move. The speakers hissed, and a sudden burst of spontaneous sound came next. It was a familiar sound that made Ray's stomach turn over.

"My God," Kate said, her hand on her heart. "They're laughing."

Trembling with excitement, Ray checked the recorder to be sure it was running. Satisfied, he turned to his family. "We're not alone," he said in awe. "We've just made mankind's greatest discovery."

"Just wait until everyone back on earth hears about this," Lisa said.

"You'll be famous, Ray."

He didn't even want to think about that right now, wondering instead where the voices originated. Then the space probe started beeping like crazy.

From around the backside of the two yellow suns, a planet appeared like a green marble floating in the darkness, one side gleaming with sunlight, the other side darkened by night. It was bigger than earth, and a color-streaked ring encircled it like Saturn. The space probe wailed, and a message scrolled across the screen.

MULTIPLE LIFE FORMS DETECTED.

"We found them." Ray laughed out loud. He couldn't help himself. "We did it." Questions started tumbling through his mind. What great civilizations prospered on the surface of the Green Planet? How advanced was their technology? What did they look like?

He wished he could fly the transporter down to this new world, to land and see it all for himself, but he knew he couldn't do that. The transporter would burn up entering the atmosphere. He had no choice but to stay out here and wonder, although he thought it couldn't hurt to get a little closer.

Tapping the keyboard on the flight computer, he set the controls to manual. The transporter suddenly rolled right, and Ray turned the yoke, countering the roll but overcorrecting to the left.

"Dad! What are you doing?"

The transporter started to tumble, and Ray fought the controls. "It's about time I got some practice flying this thing." He rolled the transporter over and, tilting the controls right, he brought the nose around and pitched it up until the Green Planet wobbled in the middle of his windshield. Finally getting the feel of it, he steadied the transporter and his nerves.

"You're not going down there," Kate said.

Setting the navigation computer, Ray busied himself with chores Stan had taught him.

"Ray!"

"Dad?"

"Will you stop worrying?" Ray pulled the throttles back, and with pulse light engines running at half power, the transporter streaked into orbit around the two yellow suns. The trajectory readout displayed a course that intersected with the Green Planet's orbit. A subdued whine came from the engines, and the light-speed indicator slowed to *2 Point 0*.

"Easy, baby." The transporter was approaching the planet at breathtaking speed. Ray eased back on the throttles again, slowing to sub-light speed. He prompted the flight control computers to initiate a low altitude orbit, just inside the wide, rainbow-like ring of the planet.

"I hope you know what you're doing, Dad."

Ray shrugged. He didn't, but the excitement of this close encounter had set his heart to racing. Sweat beaded his forehead as he flew over the planet's ring-plane and the engine power subsided automatically.

The view out the windshield took his breath away. On the planet below, white bands of clouds drifted in the atmosphere, and red islands with mountains and river basins dotted vast sparkling-green seas. Surface scanners on the space probe indicated an abundance of fresh-water algae, oxygen, hydrogen, nitrogen along with small quantities of carbon dioxide and hydrocarbon, but oddly, the total absence of sodium.

"There's breathable air, but no salt down there."

"Is that bad?" Kate asked.

"Life on earth depends on salt, in one degree or another."

"I like salt," Lisa said. "On popcorn especially."

Ray agreed with her. As the trajectory readout indicated a sustained orbit, the transporter passed into darkness. Lights appeared on the surface below, some in huge clusters, each with a network of luminous arms radiating outward and connecting with other bright clusters.

"My God. Will you look at that?" Ray thought the

scene below looked like nighttime satellite photos he'd seen of earth, and he quickly came to the conclusion that there were huge cities on the Green Planet, clearly visible from space at night.

Several minutes later, the transporter emerged into daylight again, the twin suns now revealing the most horrifying sight Ray had ever seen. His heart almost stopped. Wedge-shaped spacecraft, gray and white, with massive towers of girder-like steel, had gathered above the planet's ring-plane. A fleet of these ships, a dozen or more, came together, pitching and rolling as if tossed about on the swells of an invisible sea. Ray's mouth went dry. "We're in trouble!"

A brilliant ball of light came at the transporter. "Hold on." Ray pushed the nose down. The flight deck shuddered. There was a boom, and alarms went off.

"Dad."

He pushed the throttles full forward. Another boom, and then a vibration wracked the transporter.

"Hold together, baby."

Kate gasped.

On the horizon, another armada of ships appeared. They came from out of nowhere, suddenly materializing in front of them and now hovering above and below, to the left and the right, the front and the rear. "My God, They're everywhere." Ray tilted the control mast left, putting the transporter into a tight circle.

"Dad?"

"Get us out of here," Kate said with pleading eyes.

Ray clenched his jaw. They were trapped. If he tried to break out between the space ships, he feared they'd destroy the transporter. Besides, the fleet was quickly closing up the gaps and encasing them in an ever-tightening sphere.

Kate clutched her armrest. "They're going to kill us."

"They could have done that by now," Ray said with

conviction. "If they wanted."

"Then what do they want, Dad?" Lisa said, trembling. "Oh my God. Do you think they're going to capture us...experiment on us...dissect us like frogs?"

"I hope not," Ray said.

"I bet they can do anything they want with us."

Ray knew she was right. "We've got one other option."

"W-what's that?" Kate stuttered.

"End this trip right now."

"But we just got started."

"Don't give up now, Dad. At least try to escape."

Ray saw the fear on Lisa's face, and his fingers went numb. He knew he couldn't risk making a run for it. He had to activate the regenerator. There was no other way of ensuring their safety. He shut down the throttles. "We've got one chance to get out of here, and I'm taking it, for us. There's no time to lose."

"I love you, Dad."

Kate touched his arm. "Me too."

Ray held onto those words as he rose from his seat and floated toward the hatch in the back wall. Climbing into the regenerator control room he went straight for the chrome lever, and holding his breath, he pulled it down.

Something clicked.

Regeneration in three minutes came a computerized female voice. A hum began to fill the transporter, getting louder and louder.

Satisfied, he made his way back to his seat and buckled in. As much as he wanted to stay, to learn more about this planet and the people or creatures that lived here, he had to think of his family. He knew that going into the 13th Power had its risks, but they were calculated risks based on known constants and predictable variables. However, this impending capture by aliens had no scientific basis on which to predict an outcome. He didn't know if they'd be treated like special guests of the Green Planet, or examined like lab rats, condemned to horrific experimentation, dissection and death; after all, that's what humans had supposedly done to the aliens at Roswell, if one were to believe the stories, which he didn't. So there was no way he was going to take the chance...not with Lisa, and not with Kate. His dream-come-true adventure would soon come to an end. Heart pounding, he was sure he'd made the right decision as he watched the forces gather around him.

Regeneration in two minutes. The humming intensified to a rumble, and the transporter shuddered under the strain.

Suddenly, a huge gray ship, the biggest one of them all, maneuvered into position in front of the transporter. Ray watched in horror as a giant door started to open on the bow of the spacecraft, like the jaws of a beast gaping wide, awaiting to partake of a meal.

"Do something, Ray!"

With fear pumping through his veins, he scanned the instruments. The Higgs Field meter was bouncing in the red zone, and the rumble from the onboard MIGGS became a roar and started shaking the transporter violently.

Regeneration in one minute.

The giant alien door loomed closer now, and inside the spaceship's brightly lit chamber, figures moved about in columns, running upright, identically dressed in loose fitting uniforms. Black-gloved hands with extremely long fingers held weapons of some kind, and yellow helmets with silver shields covered the alien's faces. The reception committee quickly took up positions around the chamber.

"They look human enough," Lisa said.

Ray swallowed. "Maybe. But either they're impervious to the vacuum of space or there's some sort of barrier at the door that holds in atmosphere and blocks out space. If that's the case, it will also block out the regenerator. We don't dare get caught inside that thing."

"We gotta get out of here," Kate said.

"Put it in reverse, Dad."

Ray balked. "They might blast us again."

"Do it, Ray, before it's too late."

Near panic, Ray switched on the pulse light engines and extended the reverse thrusters. He eased on the throttle, but they still kept moving closer to the ominous maw.

"More power, Dad."

He gave it full throttle. The engines whined, but nothing happened. "It must be pulling us in."

Regeneration in ten seconds...nine...eight...

At the chamber's threshold, the space outside the window seemed to turn to clear liquid, blurring and distorting the scene inside the alien ship. The creatures held their weapons extended, and the barrier bulged as if resisting the transporter's mass.

Six...five...four...

"We're not going to make it," Kate cried.

"Get ready," Ray said and held his breath.

"Dad!"

Two...one...

The roaring onboard MIGGS shook the transporter.

Zero.

In a flash of light, the alien ship vanished. The Green Planet disappeared into a well of black as the transporter plummeted down a funnel and spun into a spinning tunnel of starlight. It was another wild ride until, suddenly, the transporter was floating motionless in the silent black sea of space.

Ray took a deliberate breath to be sure he was still alive. "Everybody all right?"

"What a rush, Dad."

"I'm okay," Kate said.

Ray looked out the windshield. Something wasn't right. There was no blue glow, meaning the ION Shield had not been activated. And where was the MIGGS' swirling black mist? On top of that, he expected the pressure of G-forces on his chest. None of this had happened.

"Where are we?" Kate asked.

"It looks like we're still out in space, Dad."

Ray checked the regenerator monitor. The *X* and the *O* were now perfectly aligned, one on top of the other. "We should be inside the MIGGS."

"It doesn't look like the MIGGS to me," Lisa said.

Hot panic rose in Ray's chest. "Something went wrong."

Kate crossed her arms. "Is that a scientific observation?"

He looked to the left of the transporter and saw one yellow star shining brightly. All the other stars were far away. He switched on the engines and pivoted the transporter right. What he saw then made his heart skip. A blue and white planet hung in the black void, half lit by the sun, the other half darkened by shadow, and a small moon, reflecting a similar-shaped glow, floated there too, eternally tied to the other as they traveled through the dark void. The space probe started beeping wildly.

MULTIPLE LIFE FORMS DETECTED.

Ray shut off the engines. "How did we end up out here?" He grabbed the headset and reached for the COM switch. "Janis. What's going on down there?"

Chapter Fifty-One

A BUZZER SOUNDED THROUGH Tech-Com Control, ripping Janis out of an uneasy nap at his terminal. "What's that?" Then the MIGGS electromagnets started humming, and Stan rushed in with three engineers. "The regenerator's been activated." He shut off the alarm.

Janis examined the flight clock. "It's only been ten hours and twelve minutes for Christ's sake. What's Ray's hurry to get back?"

Stan shrugged. "Lo, status report."

"Two minutes to regeneration," Lo replied.

"Somebody get the Colonel in here," Janis ordered.

"He's on his way," Stan said. "Two of my men were with him at C-Wing, assessing the damage to the cafeteria. We should have it up and running by breakfast."

"I hope so," Janis returned. "I can't take anymore of his army chow."

"Air Force chow," Colonel Fallon said as he entered the control room. "It grows on you after a while."

"I hope not." Janis checked the MIGGS monitor where a swirling vortex began to form.

"One minute," Lo reported.

The MIGGS rumbled and howled. The walls vibrated. Standing at the MIGGS window now, Janis watched the black mist swirl around inside the gravity chamber. Like an encroaching fog, it consumed the green ceiling lights and plunged the interior into total darkness.

"This had better work," the Colonel said.

Stan huffed. "Of course it will."

"Two, one, zero," Lo said.

Everything was black. "Any second now," Stan said as the MIGGS roared and shook Tech-Com Control.

"Janis," Lo called out. "You better look at this."

"What?" Janis didn't want to leave the MIGGS window. He wanted to watch the transporter reappear.

"It's the regenerator."

Janis looked at the monitor. *ERROR* flashed across the screen. A lump formed in his throat. "What does that mean?"

"I don't know," Lo said as the Supers automatically shut down the electromagnets. Tech-Com Control stopped shaking and rumbling. Janis watched the black mist break apart and twist down the floor grates. What he didn't see made his whole body shudder. "Oh no."

"Where's the transporter?" Fallon asked.

Stan gasped. "I don't understand. It should be right there."

"We're missing something here," Janis said, glaring at Stan. "Like one transporter and three people. Where are they?"

"It doesn't make any sense." Stan went to the regenerator monitor and typed on the keyboard. "I'm telling you..." He pointed to the *X* and the *O*, which were fused together. "This thing says it has regenerated successfully."

"Obviously it's wrong," Janis said. "It's not here."

Stan frowned. "It can't be wrong." He checked a data stream readout. "The triangulator is working perfectly. See?"

"What have you guys done?" Fallon said.

Janis felt an annoying tap on his shoulder. He turned around to see Lo standing there with a dumfounded look on his face. "What is it?"

"ET phone home." Lo handed Janis the intercom mike.

"What?"

"It's Ray."

Janis keyed the mike. "Ray?"

"Somebody screwed up down there," Ray said, his agitated voice blaring through the speakers.

Janis flinched. "Is everybody all right? Lisa? Kate?"

"We're in deep shit up here."

"Where are you?"

Radio static crackled. *"According to the space probe, we're five and a half million miles from Earth. What happened to the MIGGS?"*

Stan rubbed his temple. "Five and a half million miles," he muttered, "one hundred fifty miles per second..." He started counting his fingers. "Ten hours twelve minutes, five million, five hundred thousand miles. Damn!"

"What went wrong?" Ray shouted, the intercom speakers amplifying his frustration.

Stan looked at his engineers gathered around. "You know what this means?" His team glanced back and forth at each other, sharing puzzled expressions. "The Higgs Field doesn't bend."

Ray asked, *"What did he say?"*

"The transporter regenerated via the same Higgs field," Stan said. "The same pathway back to the exact spot in space where it had degenerated from."

Janis felt a chill. "The Higgs Field didn't shift with the regenerator."

"Shift?" Ray said.

"The Earth and the sun are constantly in motion," Stan explained. "The Higgs Field isn't."

"Straight lines to infinity," Janis responded in disbelief.

"Exactly. Regeneration in the MIGGS is not possible." Stan's face turned ashen. "That means they're stuck up there."

"What did he say?" Ray asked. *"What's not possible? What's that about us being stuck up here? Janis?"*

"Take it easy," Janis said, belaying panic. "We'll figure something out."

"Stan, do something," Ray pleaded.

"I'm trying to think."

"We can't land."

"Jesus!" Fallon said. "What do you mean they can't land?"

"They'll burn up on reentry," Stan said.

A sinking feeling went through Janis's stomach. "We're not leaving them up there. They'll die."

Ray jumped in. *"Don't be talking like that, you guys. My family is up here. Do something."*

"Shut up, Ray."

Fallon groaned. "What a mess."

Janis pointed an accusatory finger at Stan. "It's your fault."

"Give me a break," Stan said. "This is all new territory for us. How were we supposed to know?"

"Tell me about the transporter," Fallon said. "If it can't land, how was NASA going to get it back to earth?"

"They never intended to bring it back down."

"But what about repairs, maintenance, that kind of thing?"

"Extended Operations," Stan said with a sudden burst of enthusiasm. "The transporter was designed for Odyssey's shuttle bay, for orbit insertion and maintenance."

The radio squelched. *"Extended Operations,"* Ray said, his voice up a notch. *"I see it right here in the flight computer."*

Fallon asked, "Are you telling me that the transporter is capable of rendezvousing with Odyssey?"

"Two hundred seventy nautical miles up," Stan

replied.

"Ray," Fallon said. "Can you acquire that orbit?"

"Can I, Stan?"

"Let's see..." Stan checked the operations protocol data readout. "Type *SHUTTLE ORBIT* into the flight computer. What does the LCD say?"

A tense moment passed. *"Initiated,"* Ray came back.

"All right," Stan said. "The sequence is preprogrammed. Press *Enter* to activate the flight path."

Radio static screeched. "But what about Odyssey?" Ray demanded.

"Leave that to me," Fallon said.

Feeling a twinge of hope, Janis asked Fallon, "What are you going to do?"

"Take Carlton up on his invitation." He looked at his watch then grabbed the ComLink from his belt. "Briggs?"

"*Yes, sir.*"

"Get me a jet to Kennedy Space Center. A fast jet."

Chapter Fifty-Two

ALARMS RANG OUT IN THE CONTROL room of NORAD, deep inside Cheyenne Mountain, Colorado. An airman stationed at one of the monitors on the console gasped. His eyes were focused on an unfamiliar blip on his radar screen, and it gave him grave reason for concern. Among the many duties carried out in this subterranean stronghold, the airman took pride in his assignment at the Space Control Center, which kept track of over 8,000 objects in orbit. However, this particular object appeared suddenly from deep space and was streaking toward earth at horrendous speed. He grabbed the microphone. "Incoming is confirmed!"

General Dowdy lumbered down the aisle, slowed by the added weight of too much Air Force food, too many beers, fat cigars, and not nearly enough exercise. "Where?"

"Sector 117, sir. It's coming in fast."

He looked over the airman's shoulder at the red blip on the monitor. "Is it a meteor?"

"Hard to tell, sir. Maybe."

"My God. Armageddon."

"It's not that big," the airman said.

"Put it on the screen," Dowdy ordered.

"Yes, sir."

The General blinked as the big screen on the front wall flickered on. For all his efforts, and those of the U.S. Space Command and the Missile Warning Center, the nation's defense condition, *DefCon*, was at level *FIVE*: peace, and it was his responsibility to keep it that way. Right now he had to make sure that was still possible.

Within seconds, a huge graphic of a cloudless earth appeared on the screen. It displayed the orbits of hundreds of satellites and thousands of pieces of space debris, some items as small as a bolt and others as big as rocket boosters that were discarded after launch. The image looked like a hive swarming with bees, total chaos at over 18,000 miles per hour. The airman and his team tracked everything up there, twenty-four/seven because, if impacted by one piece of this junk, a satellite, the space station, or even the space shuttle, would be reduced to scrap metal in an instant. Collision avoidance was Priority One.

The graphic zoomed in on Sector 117 where a blinking red dot marked the unidentified object streaking toward earth, now descending through the twenty-three thousand mile mark and traveling at tremendous speed compared to everything else up there. Dowdy felt a chill. "Where's it going to impact?"

The airman worked his keyboard. "Ah...at its present trajectory and velocity...it looks like somewhere south and west of Mexico...in seven minutes, thirty three seconds."

"That puts it in the ocean if it doesn't burn up," Dowdy said, suddenly feeling a little better about it all. He watched as the red dot bore its way through Sector 117, barreling closer and closer to earth.

"Look at that!" the airman shouted suddenly.

What Dowdy saw on the screen made every nerve in his body quiver. "That's not possible. A meteor can't change course like that. No way, unless...oh, Jesus...unless something changed its flight path intentionally." His next thought scared the hell out of him: aliens!

"It's slowing down," the airman announced. "Course correction indicates orbital insertion at 270 nautical miles." He looked up from his monitor with taut brows. "Odyssey is scheduled for that orbit in sixteen hours, ten minutes."

"Collision probability," Dowdy requested.

The airman typed, and numbers and formulas began scrolling down the screen, calculating speed, distance, bearing, and time. A red window popped up: *100%.* Then his face suddenly turned bone white as another message came up on the screen. "Oh, God."

Dowdy gulped. "What is it, airman?"

"S-sir...that thing...it's emitting radio signals...some kind of digitized code. I've never seen anything like it."

"That's no meteor," someone said. The control room erupted in a buzz of conversation. Officers and airman mingled about, their eyes on the screen and the red dot now orbiting the earth.

General Dowdy slumped in a chair at the console, his mind grappling with the possibilities of an invasion from outer space. And then he wondered what the aliens wanted with Odyssey. "Take us to *DefCon-ONE,*" he ordered.

A buzzer echoed through the control room, and red lights flashed.

He turned to his communications officer. "Get me the Pentagon."

***

In Washington, D.C., a phone rang like a child wailing for attention in the middle of the night. General Brigham rolled over and threw a pillow on his head, but the phone kept ringing.

Doris stirred next to him. "Maybe it's important, dear."

Reluctantly, he groped for the receiver. "Brigham."

"We have a problem, sir," Lieutenant Erickson said in a brass voice.

Brigham thought about hanging up on his graveyard-shift dispatcher. "Can it wait 'til tomorrow?" he grumbled.

"General Dowdy is on the line...from NORAD. He insists on talking to you right now."

"NORAD?" Propping himself on a pillow, Brigham licked his dry lips. A call this late at night from NORAD could mean only one thing: trouble. "Put him on and be sure the recorder is running."

"Right away."

The line clicked. "General Brigham?"

He yawned. "What's going on at NORAD, Dowdy?"

"We're tracking an alien spaceship in earth orbit."

As if hit with a shot of speed, Brigham's head cleared, but little spots dotted his vision. "A what?"

"A UFO."

"Don't you have anything better to do than bullshit me in the middle of the night?"

"I'm telling you, General, something came out of deep space, changed direction, and entered orbit."

"It's probably a rock."

"No rock I ever saw transmitted coded radio signals."

Brigham was having trouble taking this all in. It was too extreme, too bizarre. "Are you sure?"

"We'll not be caught snoozing here."

"Any display of aggression?"

"It's on a collision course with Odyssey."

"No shit?" Brigham looked at the clock on the nightstand. "But Odyssey is still on the pad."

"Projected collision probability is one hundred percent within three hours after launch."

"Christ! Call off the launch," Brigham ordered.

"I'll notify NASA," Dowdy replied. "In the meantime, you inform the President. Be sure he understands we're on top of this thing. SAC is on full alert, and our fighters are in the air just in case this UFO enters our airspace. I only hope our boys have a fighting chance against these aliens."

Brigham let out a grunt as PLEDG came to mind. "I've got something that'll take care of those bastards.

Keep me informed. I'll be at the Orbital Operations Center."

"Very well," Dowdy said, and the line clicked.

"Erickson?"

"Yes, sir?"

"You get all that?"

"Every word."

"I want a jet standing by at Andrews, fueled for Houston."

"And the President, sir?"

Brigham grabbed a quick breath. Hatred for the man who had backstabbed him flared in his guts. From the beginning, Star Wars had been Brigham's project. The President shouldn't have taken it away from him and humiliated him before Congress with trumped up charges of pilfering from the budget. Memories of the whole affair made his stomach sick. However, after the system had been deployed, Brigham's command was reinstated, apparently because the President couldn't find anyone else with guts enough to handle his illegal weapons system. If Congress ever found out, shit would hit the fan.

Disgusted, he was about to tell Erickson to get the President on the line when he suddenly realized the value of this turn of events. A UFO had been dropped in his hat. There had to be a way he could use it to expose the President's treachery to the whole world.

"Sir? What about the President?"

"Leave him sleep. I'll take care of this myself." Brigham hung up.

"Take care of what?" Doris said sleepily.

"Nothing to worry about, hon. I'm just going to blast some aliens out of orbit."

"How nice," she murmured. "Be careful, dear."

Chapter Fifty-Three

THE RISING SUN HUNG LOW OVER the Atlantic, and a fog bank rolled in from the ocean and lingered above the breaking waves. In the distance, Odyssey sat shrouded in haze atop launch pad 39-A. Seabirds sawed back and forth on the breeze, cawing and complaining, and marsh reeds growing in tidal pools along Banana Creek rustled from a light breeze off False Cape. The air smelled of sea brine.

Carlton loved the sounds and earthy fragrances of Florida in the morning, but the chill of this spring dawn made his arm ache, an eerie reminder of his brush with death. He rubbed the scar and put the horrid past out of his mind. Besides, the cool sand between his toes made him feel so alive. Almost every morning he took this walk on the beach, barefoot, his trousers rolled up to his knees, thankful for Bruce Fallon's bravery and thankful for another day to enjoy. And this day was forecasted to be sunny. The fog was supposed to be gone in two hours, Odyssey in six. Fueling had just begun, a three-hour process that gave Carlton time for breakfast and a stroll.

As he stooped to examine a seashell, the beeper on his belt went off. Concerned, he sprinted back to his jeep. "What is it?" he said into the radio.

"We need you back in the firing room," Mission Management Team Director Swazo said in a voice laced with anxiety.

"Is something wrong with Odyssey?"

"NORAD recommends we scrub the launch, something about a collision in orbit. You'd better check it out for yourself."

A sour feeling wracked Carlton's guts. "Be right there." He fired up the jeep and gunned the throttle, his tires slinging sand. Bouncing down the road toward the Launch Control Center, he shifted into third gear and, at the same time, caught a glint in the sky just under the rising haze. The form of an F-14 Tomcat took shape. It was approaching at high speed, its boxy air intakes and twin tails now clearly visible. This wasn't a common sight, a two-seater Navy jet flying into Kennedy Space Center. Tomcats were more at home around aircraft carriers, prowling the skies over the open seas in formations of two or four. Carlton shifted to fourth gear. Something else bothered him about this jet. He wondered why Air Traffic Control had allowed it to enter his airspace this close to launch time. The possibility of a terrorist attack on the shuttle was a concern they didn't take lightly around here. There'd better be a damn good reason for breaking the rules.

Suddenly, the sky erupted in a wail of twin turbofan engines as the F-14 screeched overhead, banked right, and leveled off for its final approach to runway three-three at the Shuttle Landing Facility. Carlton made the jeep run full throttle.

A few minutes later, he skidded to a stop in front of the Launch Control Center and shut off the engine. Two of his directors were standing at the door, Rodriguez from NTD and Swazo from MMT, their faces pinched with frustration. Swazo, middle-aged, short and stocky, rubbed the back of his neck as Rodriguez stood next to him, much taller, dark-skinned and bespectacled, with his arms crossed over his chest.

"Hurry," Swazo said.

Before Carlton made it to the top step, a wailing siren

pierced the air. He looked left in time to see a security jeep careen around the corner, throwing dust and scattering birds. That in itself didn't make him stop and stare. It was the passenger clinging to the roll cage: Colonel Bruce Fallon. The gray flight suit he wore gave Carlton reason for alarm, the F-14 coming to mind. Fallon had said he wouldn't make this launch, so why was he here? And Carlton wondered what the all-fire rush was about. His arm began to ache.

Fallon jumped from the jeep as it slid to a stop. He looked haggard, his eyes tired, face stubbly. "Carlton, hold up."

"I'm a little busy right now, Colonel."

"I've got a problem," Fallon said, rushing up the steps. "I need your help."

Swazo pulled open the door. "We've got our own problems."

"Let's take one thing at a time," Carlton said, leading Swazo, Rodriguez, and the Colonel into Launch Control. In the firing room amidst the bustle of preflight activity, they huddled under the glare of bright ceiling lights. Carlton looked over a data sheet Swazo had handed him. He couldn't believe what he was reading. "Aliens? Collision probability: 100%? What kind of joke is this?"

"Where'd you get that?" Fallon said, pointing to the printout.

"From NORAD," Swazo replied.

"I should have known." Fallon reached for the ComLink on his belt. "Briggs."

"Yes, sir."

"NORAD knows about this, and I'll bet the Pentagon has been informed. See if you can find out what General Brigham is up to."

"Right away, sir.

Carlton's mouth went dry. "What the hell's going on, Bruce? There's an alien spaceship in shuttle orbit, and you know something about it?"

"That's why I'm here," Fallon said. "It's not alien."

"According to this it is."

"It's a space transporter, one of your own, an I.S.S.T."

Carlton felt like he'd been hit with a board. "How the hell did it get up there?"

"I don't believe it." Swazo wagged a finger. "It's not our transporter. It's not possible."

"It's yours, all right," Fallon said with a frown.

Swazo leaned forward. "You'd better tell us how it got up there, Colonel."

"It's a long story."

Rodriguez balled a fist. "Regardless, we're not taking any chances with the orbiter. It's a scrub."

"Wait!" Fallon glared at the NTD director. "I've been up all night, scrunched into the cockpit of an F-14, and blasted across the country at twice the speed of sound because this is a matter of life and death. Hear me out, first."

Rodriguez shot Carlton a dagger-like glare. "Just who the hell is this guy?"

"A good friend," Carlton said, standing tall. "He—"

"I don't care if he's the goddamned President. Our job is to ensure the shuttle and crew's safety. NORAD says it's not safe, we're done. Shut it down."

"The shuttle is *not* in danger," Fallon said. "It's not on a collision course. It's a rendezvous. Your people wrote the program: *Extended Operations.* Check it out."

"How do you know about that?" Rodriguez asked, wide-eyed.

"The engineers at Solartech Labs filled me in. They've got three people up there in that contraption of yours. Odyssey is their only hope."

Carlton grimaced. "Three people? How did they get into orbit?"

Fallon raised his eyebrows. "Don't scrub the launch

and I'll tell you."

Rodriguez turned to a computer tech seated at the console. "Check the Extended Operations protocol."

The tech started typing.

Swazo cleared his throat. "What do you propose we do?" he asked Fallon.

"Change the mission assignment. Instead of the Hubble, rescue the transporter."

The ComLink buzzed and Lieutenant Briggs' voice spilled out. *"General Brigham is at the Orbital Operations Center in Houston, sir. He won't talk to me, but one of the controllers said* Pledge *went online nearly an hour ago. Then the connection went dead."*

"Damn!" Fallon turned to Carlton. "Get NORAD on the phone."

"You don't think...would Brigham...?"

"He'd blast them out of orbit without a second thought. He's got his new Star Wars weapon, and he won't hesitate to use it."

"What's his problem?" Rodriguez asked.

"He has a score to settle with the President, and I'll bet he's moving things around up there right now, planning something that will exact revenge."

"And ruin his military career?" Rodriguez said.

"He thinks he'll be a hero."

"Let's find out what he's up to." Carlton turned to his communications officer. "Get Dowdy at NORAD on the line, stat."

The computer tech looked up from his terminal. "The Colonel's right. *Extended Operations* calls for a docking maneuver, for maintenance and upgrades on the I.S.S.T. I ran the simulator at T-minus-four-hours-twenty-minutes and came up with an intercept at 1310 hours, the same time NORAD has predicted the collision."

"It's a rendezvous," Fallon said.

Carlton blinked. "Check Odyssey's mainframe for the

program executer."

The tech leaned forward. "It's already been initiated."

"Jesus."

A communications officer handed Fallon the phone. "General Dowdy, Sir."

"Hello, General," Fallon said. "Yes...a little stressed right now...of course. We need your help. Can you tell me the status of the *Pledge* satellites?"

A moment passed. Carlton thought the air in the firing room had turned ice cold.

"What's Brigham doing that for?" Fallon rocked back on his heels. "I see. How much time do we have?" He paused. "Five hours forty minutes...that'll work in our favor." Fallon thanked the General and hung up.

"What's in our favor?" Carlton asked.

"Time." Fallon handed the phone to Swazo. "A while back, Brigham moved the PLRs over Honduras. Now they're not in position to intercept the transporter. But he's moving them and re-tracking two sighting dish satellites. It's going to take a while...time we desperately need."

"How long do we have?"

"An hour and ten minutes after launch, *Pledge* will be in range of Odyssey's orbit, and Brigham will unleash Star Wars on the transporter."

"Doesn't he care about those people?"

"Dowdy told him they were aliens."

Carlton felt a twinge in his stomach. "Is that our country's official policy, to destroy visitors from other worlds? Wouldn't we try communicating with them first...? Killing them outright...it's unthinkable."

Fallon shook his head. "It has nothing to do with official policy. Brigham is running this show. If we don't do something, three people are going to die: Ray Crawford, his ex-wife Kate, and their daughter, Lisa. For God's sake, don't scrub the launch."

There was silence as Carlton shifted his eyes between

his directors and wondered what they were thinking. They'd scrubbed launches before, for the smallest of reasons. But they'd never changed a mission statement. Would his directors take Colonel Fallon's word over the recommendations of NORAD and the impending threat of a collision with aliens in orbit? Stepping forward, Carlton said, "Only our I.S.S.T could've initiated Odyssey's program executer for *Extended Operations*. It's not an alien spacecraft up there, gentlemen. I vote for the rescue."

"The press will have a field day with this," Rodriguez said.

"No doubt," Carlton replied. "The whole world is going to be watching, but look at it this way: if we succeed, we're heroes...if not, we're bums. At least we can say we tried."

"All right," Rodriguez said. "We go with the launch."

Swazo nodded.

"Then it's unanimous." Carlton felt a wave of relief. "Notify OTC and brief the crew."

"We won't need the payload specialists," Rodriguez said. "But we'll need the radio frequency so the crew can communicate with the transporter."

"It doesn't work that way," Fallon put in. "Their radio is digitally encoded. They can only communicate with Tech-Com Control in Simi Valley."

"Then how are we going to get through to them?"

Fallon held up the ComLink. "With this radio you can talk to Tech-Com Control. They, in turn, can relay the transporter."

Rodriguez frowned. "But we don't know these people, the Crawfords."

"Our crew doesn't know them either," Swazo added. "Nor their procedures."

"I can brief everyone," Fallon replied.

Carlton, thinking of a better idea, one that would solve the communications problem and give Fallon something he'd always wanted, turned to Rodriguez. "Pull the Hubble techs and suit up the Colonel."

Fallon stepped back, aghast. "I don't have the training to go up in that thing."

"You told me you wanted to fly."

"But how...?"

"A two hour briefing is all it takes. Remember, Odyssey is user-friendly. Besides, you only need to know how to do two things: use that fancy radio of yours and hang on to your ass."

Fallon's face went pale.

Rodriguez folded his arms over his chest. "And while you're getting ready, you've got some explaining to do."

Chapter Fifty-Four

COLONEL FALLON FOLLOWED THE shuttle commander and his pilot down the steps of a silver NASA van and looked up at Odyssey rising 260 feet above the dew-slicked pad. The orbiter, gleaming white in the sunshine, exhaled icy jets of vapor and creaked and groaned as it clung to its gigantic external fuel tank. With each step Fallon took toward the skeletal-steel gantry, his heart pumped dread for this incredibly dangerous thing he was about to do.

The Challenger disaster replayed in his mind, and the horrifying day over Hanoi came crashing back, too: the SAM slicing into the B-52, the ear-shattering bang, the rain of fire and debris, and the silent plunge toward earth, like Challenger.

Only an hour ago he'd climbed into this orange pressure suit, which felt familiar and even comforting. Though lighter, it was a lot like the pressure suits he, Carlton, and the bomber crew had worn over North Vietnam should a high altitude bailout have been necessary. Now he wondered if these suits could have saved the Challenger astronauts.

Stepping into Odyssey's shadow, Fallon took a deep breath. The risks were high. There were no guarantees, but he wasn't turning back. In the elevator clattering up to the white room, he took hold of his fear. The Crawfords needed his help, as Carlton did back then. Whatever was going to happen would happen, like being in the hands of God again.

"Welcome aboard." A technician, wearing a white outfit complete with shower cap, greeted them in the white room, a sterile chamber at the end of the gantry, which nestled up to the Odyssey's fuselage. The round hatch to the orbiter was open, hinged on the left with a thick round window in its center. A camera hung in one corner of the ceiling, its red LED blinking. The air smelled of disinfectant.

Fallon stood to the side and watched as an ASP, or Astronaut Support Person, assisted Commander Grant and pilot Bishop into their egress harnesses. They were fitted with parachutes and inflatable life rafts, another innovation brought on by Challenger's misfortune. Safety equipment, complete with contingency plans, were the last hope of the doomed, something to think about before total obliteration. Fallon knew and accepted a simple truth: in an emergency, something was better than nothing. Even a small chance to survive was better than no chance at all.

Finally outfitted in harness and helmet, he knelt on the boxy threshold to the round hatch, took one last look at the white room and, with his heart racing wildly, crawled into Odyssey's middeck. The bulky attire made his entrance awkward and his movements cumbersome, and as if that wasn't bad enough, the thick straps of his egress harness put undue pressure on his crotch, a condition that he hesitated to complain about.

Another ASP met him with a smile and motioned him toward the hatch that would take him up to the flight deck. Before moving on, Fallon quickly scanned the panels of switches and monitors around him: the door marked *AIRLOCK*, the galley, and what looked like sleeping compartments upended. The infinite array of computer terminals and gadgetry made him feel suddenly inept and somehow off balance. Everything was out of kilter: chairs were mounted to the wall. Floors and ceilings were in the wrong places. A sort of indoor vertigo set in.

It wasn't until he peered into the flight deck that his sense of spatial attitude came back. Sunlight beamed through six thick windows above him, and he recognized the layout of a mind-boggling cockpit nosed up in the air. The left seat was for the commander, and the right seat was the pilot's. Instrumentation, row after row of gauges and switches, knobs and levers, took up every available inch of space.

Bishop nodded from his seat on the right. An ASP waved Fallon in. With some difficulty, he managed to crawl into his designated seat behind Bishop and lay on his back with his boots up and knees bent. It was an awkward way to sit in a chair.

The ASP buckled the safety harness then hooked up hoses and wires to fittings on the pressure suit. "Now remember, at T minus 90 seconds, pull the visor down and lock it. Then switch the oxygen on, here." He pointed to a toggle valve then shut Fallon's visor. "Intercom check. Can you hear me?"

Fallon nodded.

"Commander Grant, say hello to your new passenger."

"Welcome aboard, Colonel."

"Am I an astronaut now?" Fallon asked.

"Not yet," Grant replied. "I'll let you know when you are."

Fallon gulped. "Thanks a lot."

The ASP tapped the top of Fallon's helmet. "Relax. Enjoy the ride." When he left, the hatch closed, and the cabin pressurized with a hiss.

"Colonel Fallon." Carlton's voice echoed inside his helmet.

"I hear you."

"We've established your ComLink frequency to

Solartech Labs. Janis wants a word with you now. Flip the COM-2 switch...the one on your right."

"Roger." Fallon found the switch. "Janis, you there?"

"What should I tell Ray?" Janis's voice crackled. "He's getting worried up there."

"Tell him we'll be on our way in two hours and rendezvous with him in one hour and ten minutes after liftoff. We'll reopen this ComLink when we're ready to dock."

"Good luck," Janis said.

"We're going to need it."

"Why's that?"

"Never mind." Fallon switched off COM-2. There wasn't any sense in getting everyone all worked up over General Brigham and what he was doing with PLEDG. They had enough to worry about.

***

"T minus 90 seconds," Mission Control announced.

Fallon pulled his visor down and swiveled the lock. Oxygen: *ON*. His heartbeat drummed in his ears. This was it: all or nothing.

"T minus 60 seconds."

He'd spent the last two hours jesting with the crew: two mission specialists strapped into the middeck seats, and the navigator sitting next to him. They'd sung, *Off we go into the wild blue yonder*, and told a few jokes. He even managed a thirty-minute nap while the NTD boys finished their checklists, verified weather conditions, and waited for the launch window to open. Now, every nerve in his body started to tingle.

"T minus 20 seconds."

He heard only the sound of his breathing now, faint against the background of his heartbeat. The intercom was silenced by the countdown.

"T minus 6 seconds. Main engines start."

A bit of rattling came first, a vibration, then a rumble reverberated through the cockpit as the main engines ignited and throttled up to 90 percent power. The orbiter rocked forward sharply and settled back again.

"Three-two-one."

The solid rocket boosters lit, and Odyssey lifted from the pad with a ground-shaking roar. Fallon clutched the armrests of his seat and gritted his teeth as the orbiter rose above the launch pad gantry and rolled on its back, violently climbing, shaking like a truck running on railroad ties. The compression on his chest intensified as the G-forces began building, and his ears popped. He tightened his abdomen and forced each breath, waiting for it all to end.

"Odyssey, go for throttle up."

After one and a half minutes, the solid rocket boosters separated with a sound like popping cap guns. The ride became suddenly smoother, but the G-forces kept building over the next four minutes, climbing to three Gs or ten times that of a passenger jet on takeoff. It was nothing he couldn't handle, though he felt as though the load of bricks on his chest had him permanently plastered to the back of his seat.

And something else became suddenly evident. An eerie drone came over the shuttle, replacing the once-dominate roar. Odyssey was racing its own sound now, breaking sound barriers and leaving Fallon to struggle with his breathing and listen to the intercom chatter: Bishop calling out altitudes and speeds. "Forty miles up now, Mach 4...Mach 5."

Odyssey blasted through the boundary between the atmosphere and outer space. Three minutes later and 270 nautical miles up, the engines shut off, and the vibrations stopped.

The crew cheered.

Fallon's stomach turned queasy in this unfamiliar weightless environment. Out the windows he saw the earth, bluer than any blue he'd ever seen, turning slowly under Odyssey. Africa peeked out from under bands of white clouds which stretched to the horizon, and the edge of the atmosphere changed colors from the deep blue of the ocean to a white haze to indigo and finally to the blackest black velvet of space. Then there were stars, millions of stars and galaxies stretching into infinity, glowing with a brilliance like nothing he'd ever imagined. He didn't know how, exactly, but Fallon was sure his life had just been changed forever.

"Colonel Fallon," Commander Grant said. "Now you're an astronaut."

The crew whooped and hollered.

Chapter Fifty-Five

FLOATING AROUND THE TRANSPORTER'S flight deck, Lisa passed the time doing somersaults and spins. Kate had prepared lunch in the galley, ham sandwiches and potato chips, in squeeze tubes, and now as she sat in the right seat, he could smell a fresh application of her familiar perfume. She was gazing at the view outside the windshield, her eyes scanning the heavens above, the land and sea below where a hurricane had formed in the Atlantic just west of Africa, its eye clearly visible. Now, the vast sands of the Sahara stretched out below them like a lumpy carpet as the Nile Valley and the Indian Ocean came into view. Beyond that, the twilight zone between day and night was fast approaching.

Ray settled back in his seat and watched her watch the wonders go by. It was a beautiful thing to see Kate entranced with the world. Her eyes sparkled with a new kind of joy, after all, no one had ever seen the sights they'd seen together: the Milky Way, the Green Planet, and the long-fingered aliens. Kate seemed to glow with a new outlook on life.

During the quiet times of this journey, while Lisa napped in the aft compartment, Kate had talked about her father, how he'd killed her mother and then himself, and how the horror of that tragedy drove her to the drugs and alcohol as a means to forget all life's pains. Ray felt sick as she told him the story. He'd had no idea she'd been through such hell.

Then she talked about the love she'd never had in her life, not from her foster parents, not from the men in those cheap motel rooms, and not from Willy. Ray could only shake his head, his heart aching as she told him of the torment she'd endured, until the time they met. When he came into her life, she'd clung to him for his strength and his vision of the future.

But it all became too much for her: the nightmares of her father's head exploding, the silent days that followed, and the smell of decay, all of which made sobriety a hell of its own. So she ran away, back to where she felt safe: to the chaos, the drugs, the booze, and the excuse to feel nothing at all. Kate had spilled everything, her guilt, her regret, and her remorse, a cleansing of the soul, and through it all, Ray found himself falling in love with her all over again. And now she was happy, staring out the window.

Before Janis had called with the news of Odyssey's impending launch, tension on the flight deck was unbearable. Stan's miscalculation might well have cost them their lives, but now, with the shuttle on its way, the mood onboard was light yet carried an undertone of sadness, for soon they'd be on their way back down to earth, the journey of a lifetime ended.

Kate turned away from the window and reached for his hand, smiling. "Thanks for the ride," she said. "I'm so proud of you, and proud of us. We're a family again."

"Yes we are."

"Where are you going to live, Dad?" Lisa asked in mid-tumble.

"Santa Barbara is really nice," Kate put in.

"I'll need a quiet place," Ray said. "I've got a lot of books to write."

"A celebrity in family?" Lisa replied. "How neat."

"Life is good," Ray said. And he meant it.

***

CNN carried the liftoff of Odyssey, and all the monitors in Tech-Com Control were tuned in. Janis watched the fireball blaze into the sky, the boosters fall, and three dots of light fade in the distance. Lo, Stan, and the rest of the team cheered. Then came the shocker.

Pictures of Ray, Kate, and Lisa flashed on the screen. The commentator began, "We've just learned from Kennedy Space Center that Odyssey has been charged with an unexpected rescue mission to retrieve a nuclear physicist and his family stranded in orbit. Details are sketchy at this hour, but informed sources report that Ray Crawford, his ex-wife Kate Crawford, and their daughter Lisa were part of a private space venture conducted by a research and development company in Simi Valley, California, a project which up until now had been kept secret from the world. NASA administrators agreed to change the mission statement for today's shuttle flight and have insisted that a full-scale investigation is under way.

"While our researchers probe the background of these amateur astronauts and how they got up there, space fans around the globe are watching this rescue with, what some observers have called, the same intensity as the Apollo 13 emergency."

Janis huffed. "It isn't a secret anymore."

"NASA's going to be asking a lot of questions," Stan said. "They're going to want to know how we did it. Just think, space flight without liftoff. It'll change everything."

"Imagine that," Janis said.

***

The President stalked back and forth in the Oval Office, his anger boiling to a fever pitch. "Send in the Marines," he shouted to his Secretary of Defense.

"Brigham has to be stopped before he blows the lid off this whole thing."

The Secretary leaned on the desk. "We can't invade Houston, sir. Brigham's got us by the balls."

"Shit's going to fly when the press gets wind of this." The President wrung his hands. "They'll know how we assassinated Federico Duran. Do something, for God's sake."

"Brigham's got the Orbital Operations Center locked down tight, no phones in or out, and no one's answering the emergency frequency."

The President stopped pacing in front of the windows overlooking the White House lawn and shoved his hands in his pockets. "We're in big trouble."

Shaking his head, the Secretary said, "We broke the rules, sir. We took a chance. Oh, you got Star Wars up, illegally sure, but that we can explain away. However, you told Brigham to use it against Honduras. He abused a defensive weapon, on your orders, and now he's going to show the world how you did it. Your presidency is going to end up in a heap for all your trouble."

"I'll ruin Brigham for this."

"Frankly, sir. I think he's going to be a hero. He wants revenge, and the American people want the truth. They're going to love him."

The President shivered. "He was going through SDI funds like toilet paper, robbing us blind. I had to take Star Wars away from him."

"And he's going to take the White House away from you."

A rap thumped on the door.

"Who is it?"

"Mrs. Livingston, sir."

"Come in."

The press secretary entered, her face drawn tight with worry. "The phones are lit up, sir. They want to know if the lockdown at the Orbital Operations Center and *DefCon-ONE* at NORAD have anything to do with the shuttle mission and the rescue. What do I tell them?"

The President felt a pang in his chest. And so it begins. The bloodhounds were on his trail, barking and baying. Before the end of this day there would be a call for Congressional hearings, committees and subcommittees, and lawyers looking to boost their careers with the downfall of the President. No one would care that Directive Number 119 could have ensured the safety of this nation. They'd only want his hide for the deaths of three innocent amateur astronauts. The Secretary of Defense was right. Brigham had them all by the balls.

***

"There they are," Lisa said.

The white form of Odyssey materialized out of the star-studded backdrop of space. Its cargo bay doors were wide open as it floated upside down above the blue earth, approaching in slow motion.

"Talk about a knight on a white horse," Kate said, a mix of disbelief and relief on her face. "We're going to be all right." She and Lisa embraced, their smiles bright.

The radio crackled. *"Ray?"* Janis's voice sounded like salvation.

"I'm with you," he radioed back.

"Stan needs to talk you through the docking procedure."

"Great. We're ready to go home."

"Before long you'll be sipping champagne at Kennedy Space Center," Janis said. *"You guys are heroes, I'll have you know. The whole world is watching."*

"That's a good start," Ray said. Finally, he was going to get the recognition he deserved, after all those years of obscurity. He had found and conquered the 13th Power. His name would go down in history with the other great scientists who came before him.

Stan's voice came over the radio. *"Run the D-2 program in the flight control computer."*

"I've never done this before. What if I mess up?"

"Don't worry," Stan said. *"The transporter will roll over on its back automatically, and the belly hatch will configure the docking latches. Odyssey will do the rest, just don't touch anything."*

Ray took a deep breath. "D-2 program execute. Here goes." He typed on the keyboard.

Lisa and Kate strapped themselves in.

Thrusters popped like toy cap guns, which gave the nose a shove and nudged the transporter into a roll. Odyssey crept closer, now looming over them like a mother ship, her gaping bay doors revealing the innards of the cargo hold in shadowy complexity. Ray swallowed hard as the spacecrafts floated together.

Stan came back on the radio. *"Fallon tells me the pilot will begin the docking maneuver in five minutes. He's in a big hurry for some reason."*

Ray looked out the window wondering why and saw something coming over the horizon that made every muscle in his body freeze. It was a satellite, and he'd seen it before...in the assembly room at Solartech Labs. It was a shiny titanium dish mounted to an AUX orbiter, an SDS at about his one o'clock position, and he immediately feared a PLR was somewhere nearby. That could mean only one thing: PLEDG was online, but there was no threat up here... unless...another possibility came to mind, a horrifying thought: Janis and Lo might have been right all along. This weapon of unimaginable power had ended up in the wrong hands and was about to be used as an offensive weapon...against him. Whatever the case, the sighting dish rotated toward the transporter, and Ray's pulse started racing. "Stan," he said into the radio. "Something's not right up here."

"What is it, Ray?"

"*Pledge* is sighting on us."

"How do you know that?"

"I can see it." Another SDS appeared on the left, at about the ten o'clock position, its dish rotated toward them too.

Panic gripped Ray's guts. "Stan...you'd better find out what the hell's going on...and fast."

***

Fallon's mouth went dry when Stan's voice came over COM-2. "Pledge *is sighting on the transporter.*"

"What did he mean by that?" Commander Grant asked.

"I'm not sure." The Colonel looked out the window and quickly spotted both satellite dishes hanging in the distance, one on the right, and one on the left. "Christ!" He checked his watch. *13:06*. If General Dowdy had it figured correctly, they had four minutes before alignment, five minutes left to live. "Can we dock in four minutes?" Fallon asked Bishop.

"Fifteen tops," he replied. "What's the problem?"

From a faraway point on the horizon, a thin red sighting beam shot across space, struck the SDS on the right, and angled off into the darkness. A moment later, the dish began to rotate, sweeping the beam toward the SDS on the left.

Terror took hold of Colonel Fallon. "We're too late. Brigham is going to disintegrate the transporter."

Commander Grant grabbed the controls. "My ship," he told Bishop. With a smooth swing, Odyssey moved away from the transporter.

Hesitating to radio the bad news to Stan, Colonel Fallon thought of possible solutions to this dilemma.

Perhaps the transporter could make a run for it. They could rendezvous again, somewhere south of the equator. Brigham would have to chase them around the planet. It wasn't much of a chance, but a small chance was better than no chance at all. Fallon cleared his throat. "Stan, you there?"

"What's going on?"

"I was hoping we could rescue the Crawfords before General Brigham got *Pledge* online, but he's going to disintegrate the transporter in less than three minutes."

"Why would he do that?"

"He thinks it's an alien spaceship. We had to back off...we can't risk the orbiter. Tell Ray to make a run for it."

Suddenly, the red sighting beam reflected off the SDS on the left, pivoted across space as the sighting dish rotated, and landed squarely on the transporter's nose. Fallon knew that a PLR had locked-on and would be charged to full power in sixty seconds. He turned his head away, unable to bear watching the Crawfords die.

***

Suddenly, a warning horn blared through Tech-Com Control.

"What is that?" Janis shouted.

LASER LOCK DETECTED flashed across the regenerator monitor.

"It's *Pledge*," Stan said and couldn't believe it. "General Brigham has turned Star Wars against the transporter."

"I told you that something like this could happen," Janis said.

"And I heard you," Stan replied as he disengaged the regenerator alarm. Back then, Boris, Lo, Ray, and the whole team had warned him. They all knew the horrifying downside of their technological achievements. Stan and his team of engineers had not ignored everyone's concerns.

Fallon's voice rasped over the intercom speakers. "*The transporter's not moving! Tell Ray to make a run for it.*"

"It's too late. The PLR is already locked-on."

"Then do something."

"I'm working on it," Stan said, now typing on the keyboard at Lo's terminal.

"Sixty seconds," Lo said. "The PLR is charging."

"What's going on down there?" Ray asked in a panic. *"I've got a damn sighting beam on my nose."*

"Ray," Stan said into his headset. "Some General down here thinks you guys are aliens."

"Somebody better tell him we're Americans."

"He's not taking any calls."

"Forty seconds!" Lo said.

"Then I'm going to fire up my pulse light engines and get the hell out of here."

"It won't do any good," Stan said. "You're locked-on."

"Huh?"

A screen came up on the monitor, an orange background with red letters flashing: *ARE YOU SURE YOU WANT TO DELETE THIS PROGRAM?*

"What are you doing?" Janis asked over Stan's shoulder.

"Cashing in our insurance policy." Stan hit the *ENTER* button.

***

The red sighting beam reflecting off the SDS on the left shined on the transporter, and *LASER LOCK DETECTED* paraded across the LCD on Ray's instrument panel. In thirty seconds, the PLR would be fully charged, and the General with his finger on the button could fire at will. Ray knew they were goners.

"Dad! What *is* that thing?" Lisa pointed at the red sighting beam.

Ray couldn't find the words to tell her. He took Lisa's hand, and then Kate's, and awaited the end of their lives. The technology he strove to achieve was now poised to destroy him and his family. How could he have known it would come to this?

Then he thought he should have known. Mankind's barbaric instincts, probably still lingering within DNA strands left over from his caveman days, had painted his past with blood, marred his history with misery, and foreshadowed his future with war and annihilation. *Shoot first. Ask questions later*. Mankind had a long way to go to become truly civilized. The 13th Power had taught him that much.

He squeezed Kate's hand. "I love you."

"I know."

In a flash of brilliant yellow light and white streamers, the SDS on the right suddenly exploded, hurtling pieces into space at tremendous velocity and jerking Ray upright in his seat, astounded. The SDS on the left suffered the same fiery demise. Frozen in place, Ray was unable to move, his eyes fixed on the spot where he'd last seen the SDS. It was now only a glow on his retinas. And then he started laughing, howling with glee. Lisa and Kate joined in.

"They're dying up there," Stan shouted over the radio.

"We're okay," Ray said. "How did you do that?"

"I'm an engineer," Stan replied. *"And I listen to the people I work with. You were worried that someone might misuse Star Wars, so we rigged each satellite with a self-destruct charge, just in case things got out of hand."*

"So that's what you meant when you said you hadn't

given them anything you couldn't take back."

"*We weren't about to give the Department of Defense complete control.*" The radio clicked. "*Bring them home, Colonel Fallon.*"

Ray smiled and his family mobbed him with kisses.

***

Docking took fifteen minutes, just like Bishop had said. "Houston, we have capture," he announced from Odyssey's flight deck.

"*Roger,*" the CAPCOM returned. "*Congratulations are coming in from all over the world. You guys are heroes.*"

"Just another day at the office."

Fallon floated down to middeck. The airlock hissed, pressure gauges stabilized, and the hatches came open. Lisa came through the tunnel first, and floating horizontally, worked her way along a fat air duct into Odyssey. Fallon helped steady her as Commander Grant and pilot Bishop welcomed her onboard.

Kate floated through next, smiling as their eyes met. "Hello, Colonel," she said in a soft voice. "You've no idea how glad I am to see you."

"I can imagine." Fallon took her hand. "I'm really proud of you, Kate. You did a fine job."

"I've finally got my family again."

"So I see." He passed her on to the welcoming crew.

Ray popped through the tunnel next. "Thanks for coming after us."

"You're welcome," Fallon said. "Bet you think you're going to set the scientific world on its ear with this stunt you pulled."

"You have no idea." Ray held up a CD as he floated into Odyssey. Mid-deck erupted in boisterous applause.

After pulling himself up to the flight deck, Fallon

buckled into his seat. He knew he was right about Ray and his family. What they had done, and the scientists at Solartech Labs, was nothing short of a miracle, an unprecedented achievement that would change the world.

While Fallon settled back and watched the earth go by outside his window, mission specialists went about their duties, working the robotic arm, detaching and stowing the transporter into the cargo bay, and configuring the seats for their three guests. Feeling at peace in the hands of God, he drifted into a much-deserved snooze.

***

"We're ready for reentry," Bishop said, shaking Fallon's shoulder. "Put your helmet on."

Having been ripped from a dream he could vaguely remember, Fallon rubbed sleep from his eyes, blinked a few times, then donned his helmet. He put his visor down and turned his oxygen on. "Let's go home."

Somewhere over the Pacific, flying upside down and backwards now, Odyssey shuddered as Commander Grant fired two braking boosters in the aft compartment. The burn lasted for three minutes, twenty-six seconds. Then Odyssey rolled on its belly and began the plunge back to earth.

At 17,300 miles per hour, Odyssey hit the outer atmosphere. The view out the window turned from black to yellow, then orange. Like a meteor, the shuttle ripped electrons from the rarefied gasses in the upper atmosphere and formed a plasma field around the orbiter so intense that even radio signals couldn't get through. Only static came over the speakers in Fallon's helmet. They were cut off from the world, and he felt very alone.

The shuttle shook and creaked as he felt the pull of gravity come back, the weight of his legs becoming evident again. He couldn't help but think how weightlessness had felt so natural, as though he'd returned to the womb for a short time and was now being reborn. His heart felt heavy, though, not from the weight of gravity, but because he knew he'd never go back into space again.

When the fire outside dissipated, darkness took its place, a darkness studded by twinkling stars. Somewhere over North America in the dead of night, the shuttle buffeted and boomed. "We're with you, again," Commander Grant radioed Houston.

"Roger, Odyssey. We show you right on course."

Gliding in at 12,000 miles per hour, Odyssey dropped through the atmosphere, making S turns to bleed off airspeed. Over Florida, *"Clear to land. Runway Three-Three,"* came over the radio. A few minutes later, the shuttle coasted to a ghostly touchdown, the main gear contacting the concrete with a thud, the nose gear with more of a solid bang. As the drag chute deployed, the crew and passengers cheered.

"Houston, wheels stopped."

"Welcome home, Odyssey."

Chapter Fifty-Six

THE NATION WENT CRAZY. Ray Crawford's name was plastered across the headlines of every paper in the country. He'd been to Washington D.C. for a Congressional Medal, and now he was in New York City for a tickertape parade. Big TV screens posted around Times Square replayed a video of him with Kate and Lisa on each arm as they deplaned Odyssey. His chest swelled with pride.

They were riding in a stretch Lincoln convertible with three rows of seats. Ray sat on top of the rear seatback between Kate and Lisa as confetti and streamers rained down from the skyscrapers. Cheers from the crowd echoed off canyon-like walls. He thought this was the best part about being famous.

Janis and Colonel Fallon had perched themselves atop the center seatback with Tracy in between them, waving and smiling. Lo and Boris sat in the front seat, and the driver followed four motorcycle escorts and honked the horn exuberantly.

In the car behind them, Stan Burton, Commander Grant, pilot Bishop, and the mission specialists from Odyssey waved to the crowd. Then a silver NASA van carrying Carlton, Swazo, and Rodriguez came next, and more motorcycles followed the van, their lights flashing white and blue. A marching band took up the rear, playing *God Bless America*.

The air smelled of bratwurst and sauerkraut, barbeque ribs and popcorn. Hundreds of colorful balloons drifted into the air as people, young and old, lined the sidewalks, waving American flags and clapping while the limos slowly drove by. "Now this is what I call a party," Ray said and gave Kate a nudge.

"Tonight will be even better," she said, waving to the crowd. "The Waldorf Astoria, banquet and ball. It'll be so much fun."

"NASA has gone all out for this celebration," Ray replied.

"We bought new dresses," Lisa said. "And Tracy, too."

"You're going to be beautiful." Ray waved to the masses, his heart filled with a pride he'd never known: for himself, for his family, for his country. Congress had already started impeachment hearings against the President for his unauthorized deployment and use of Star Wars. General Brigham, after his siege of the Orbital Operations Center, had surrendered to the FBI and turned witness for the prosecution.

Colonel Fallon turned around and smiled at Kate. He looked proud in his Air Force dress blues. Ray gave him a high five.

As the procession rounded a corner, a man stepped off the curb and stood apart from the crowd. Ray thought it strange that, out of so many people, he'd notice this one olive-skinned old man, but he was holding something up with his fingers, and his glaring eyes were fixed on the limo. He wasn't smiling, nor waving, just standing there statue-like dressed in all black. At first, Ray took it as a salute of some kind, but as the limo passed by the old man, Ray could see he was holding up a silver bear on a necklace, his jaw set as if in anger. Now Ray felt a chill and thought the gesture might have been meant as a curse. After all, they'd been to deep space, and some people might take that as an invasion of heaven.

Invasion. The word stuck in his mind as the limo crept along and the crowd responded with cheers. He thought the recording he'd made of the Green Planet could be construed as an invasion of privacy. Perhaps those long-fingered aliens didn't want anyone to know they were there. And what if someone like General Brigham came along, sometime in the future, and decided to send a fleet of warships into the 13th Power to invade and conquer the Green Planet? His discovery could become a means for mankind to spread homicidal madness throughout the galaxy.

And what about the religious zealots, like that old man standing in the street back there, or the other faiths on this planet? Didn't they all believe that mankind was alone in the universe, here only because one God or another had created them? If so, the revelation contained in his space probe recording could topple the beliefs of billions. Nations might rise up in arms and engulf the world in a holy war. It had happened in the past. It could happen again...and in the future, it could also mean doom for the long-fingered aliens of the Green Planet. He shivered at the thought. It seemed to him now that his discovery could do more harm than good, but there was still a way to prevent all that. Pulling Kate and Lisa closer, he said, "Promise me something."

"Sure," Kate said, still waving to the crowd.

"What is it, Dad?"

"Let's keep the Green Planet a family secret."

Kate gave him a puzzled look. "Why?"

"I'll explain later."

"But Dad, once you release that recording, you'll be more famous than anyone."

Ray shook his head. "I'm famous enough."

***

That night, the limo pulled up in front of the Waldorf Astoria. Crowds gathered around the car as if getting a mere glimpse of the amateur astronauts was a matter of life and death.

Ray fixed his tie, and as Lisa adjusted the straps on her teal satin dress, Kate checked the sheen of her red lipstick via the mirror on the mini-bar. She opened her purse. “I can still smell burnt plastic.” Out came the Enjoli.

“At least the disc is destroyed,” Ray said. He’d burned it in the hotel’s fireplace.

“I think it’s stuck to my dress.” She sprayed on extra perfume.

“Let’s go,” Lisa said. “I’m starving.”

Kate snapped her purse shut.

Satisfied they were ready, Ray signaled the chauffeur who promptly opened the car door. Chatter and cheers rose from the spectators. “There they are,” someone shouted. “We love you,” others sang out.

Ray stepped out of the car, smiling. In front of him, an aisle, cordoned off by red, white, and blue valet ropes, led to the Waldorf’s front doors. Onlookers were leaning on the ropes, waving, and some had their hands outstretched for a chance handshake or even a touch. As Kate and Lisa emerged from the car, Ray scanned the crowd. Close-up like this, he could see everyone clearly, and he focused on as many faces as he could, happily returning their smiles.

A doorman came forward and led the way. As Ray took hold of Kate’s hand and started walking down the aisle, he spotted that darkly dressed old man again, standing at the rope with the crowd hooting and howling behind him. A shiver raced up Ray’s spine as the eerie stranger again lifted the silver bear in his fingertips. Ray hustled his family along, and in passing, he tried to lock eyes with the old man, but his hard gaze was on Kate. She didn’t seem to notice him, and they made their way into the hotel without incident.

Walking through the ballroom, he looked up at the ceiling and admired the Art Deco motifs dating back to the late 1800s. Elegant coral draperies adorned the windows, and intricately carved pillars of marble reached up to the balconies. Classical music floated in the air, and the whole place smelled like fresh-baked bread.

"Ray." Janis's voice came from the bar where he stood with Tracy. She still looked a little pale and didn't seem very lively on her feet. Bullet wounds tended to slow a body down.

"You look lovely, Tracy," Kate said and kissed her cheek.

"I'm feeling much better, thank you."

Lisa gave Janis a hug. Ray waved at Lo and Boris who were smiling at him from a table across the room. A bottle of Old Crow and two glasses were sitting in front of them.

Colonel Fallon turned around on his bar stool, a cigar clenched in his teeth and a scotch and water in his hand. "Life is good," he said. "Never felt better." He clamped the cigar between his fingers. "You know, everyone on this planet should take a ride in the space shuttle. Then they'd all know how magnificent this world of ours really is, so small floating along in the black soup of space. Maybe then we'd take better care of it...and maybe each other. My God, I've never felt better." He let out a laugh and went back to his cigar.

Ray grabbed Kate around the waist. "Let's dance."

"Meet you at the table," Janis said. "Table nine."

Ray took Kate out on the dance floor. The beat of the music had livened up some, and he noticed Lisa and Janis had decided to try their luck on the dance floor, as well. Tracy seemed content to watch the goings-on from her seat at the table, smiling.

A slow waltz came next with lots of violins. Kate melted in Ray's arms. He found her scent intoxicating, her warmth exciting. Her lips brushed his neck, ever so gently, and her fingers caressed his hair. It all felt so right.

"Will you marry me again?" he asked her.

"For better or worse?"

"Let's aim more toward the better side this time, okay?"

She giggled. "Then how about 'til death do us part?"

"Is forever long enough?"

Suddenly, a shot rang out followed by the flat thump of lead slapping flesh. Kate stiffened in his arms. Men started yelling. A woman shrieked. The music stopped. Two more shots rang out. Kate shuddered and clung to Ray, her breath suddenly wheezing.

"Kate!"

Cursing echoed through the ballroom. Chairs toppled over, and dishes shattered. Panic-stricken, Ray darted his eyes around the dance floor and spotted the old man with the silver bear necklace, only this time he was wielding a snub-nosed gun.

"For my son, Willy!" The old man fired another shot.

Terror pumped through Ray's bloodstream. He wheeled Kate around, putting his back to the gunman and shielding her with his body. Colonel Fallon jumped on the assassin. The gun hit the floor.

"She killed my son," the old man shouted.

Painfully, Kate gasped. "Miguel Herrera..." She slumped in Ray's arms.

"No, Kate, no." He laid her gently on the dance floor, cradling her in his arms. Her eyes were wide open, her face wrenched with pain as blood pooled around her.

"Mother!" Lisa went down on her knees and took Kate's hand.

She looked at her daughter. "I-I love you," she said, fighting for air. Her eyes rolled slowly to Ray. "And I love you, too." She coughed. "I'm going to miss my family." Her last breath gurgled from her mouth.

"Mother!" Lisa broke into tears.

"Kate!" Ray shook her, embraced her, and bawled.

***

The Colorado sky over Flagstaff Mountain was ablaze with stars, and a nip of autumn hung in the air, crystal clear, the clearest Janis could remember. A cricket chirped from somewhere as Tracy cuddled up close to him under the blanket he'd spread out in the backyard. Her breath felt warm on his cheek, and her hand felt comforting on his chest. He stroked the wedding ring on her finger. Like in the Travis Tritt song, they'd wished for their future on a faraway star.

"Ray was up there, you know," Janis said. Even now he found it hard to believe.

"Do you think they'll be all right?" Tracy asked, playing with the buttons on his shirt.

"Someday perhaps. Ray and Lisa are strong, though losing Kate was a devastating blow."

"Poor woman."

"Her family forgave her, but her past caught up with her and made her pay dearly for the mistakes she'd made."

Tracy sniffled. "The funeral was so sad."

"I'm going to miss them." Janis once thought he'd never say those words. The 13th Power had caused them all a lot of trouble, but it was behind them now. Ray was over his obsession. He said he was going to write some books, though last Janis heard he hadn't started working on a single one of them. And he never talked about what he saw when he went into the 13th Power or what became of the recording from the space probe. He swore it was a secret he'd take to his grave.

"Maybe you should call Ray tomorrow," Tracy said, snuggling closer.

"I got a call from Stan this morning."

"I'll bet he's been busy."

"His team cut up the MIGGS for scrap, and he sold the Xenon laser to some technical institute in Southern California. Lo erased the Supers before he went home."

"Without your formulas, they can't play with the 13th Power anymore."

Janis groaned.

"And what about Boris?"

"He was last seen standing on the side of the highway, thumb out, suitcase at his heels, and a bottle of Old Crow under his jacket."

"I'm going to miss him," she said. "So what's Stan going to do now?"

"NASA offered him an engineering position at Kennedy Space Center. He'll be working on the transporter team."

"He sure was proud of that thing."

Janis sighed and scanned the heavens. "What do you suppose Ray saw up there?"

"Stars," she said and kissed him.

Next up: The 13th Power War

Then came modern man, about 20,000 years ago, and from that point on he destroyed his enemies without compassion, enslaved other races, and murdered for sport all manner of men and beasts.

In this final installment of **The 13th Power Trilogy**, the peaceful Beltzans of the green planet, 100,000 light years from earth, experience a close encounter of their own third kind. They believe a spacecraft belonging to the Tarreeda, a race of warmongers who had been banished from their planet 1000 generations ago, has entered orbit. The Tarreeda's return would mean the Beltzans' doom. However, Luthes Rez, helmsman of the Orbital Patrol Ship *Questnar* has his doubts. The Tarreeda cross is not displayed on the spacecraft's fuselage, but instead, strange symbols that mean nothing to him: *NASA – USA.* The spaceship evades capture, and the Beltzans fear a full-scale invasion in inevitable.

Janis Mackey and Tracy have been invited to NASA for a meeting with General Brigham and the unveiling of the greatest attack force ever conceived. They've built a machine capable of transporting a fleet of heavily armed Aerospace Shuttles to the green planet. Brigham needs Janis's mathematical prowess to return to the 13th Power, conquer the aliens, and steal their teleportation technology. However, Janis wants nothing to do with an intergalactic war, so Brigham arrests Tracy for her part in the previous CIA/Star Wars conspiracy that brought down the President of the United States. If Janis doesn't help, Tracy will be put to death for treason.

Ray Crawford's secret has been discovered. Aliens! Now an alcoholic recluse, he refuses to take calls from NASA until news of alien prisoners being brought back to earth drags him out of the bottle. He sets out on a mission to save the aliens who had spared his life during their previous brief close encounter in orbit around the green planet.

Though love has never come easily to Lisa, she's finally found her man. He's a quiet soul, peaceful, and a hero in his own right. However, Luthes Rez is a prisoner of war, and her father will never approve.

Meanwhile, in Ethiopia, Milton Spears, an archeologist on assignment from CU Boulder, discovers an alien truth buried on Choke Mountain for 20,000 years, a truth the government's secret *Aquarius Project* wants protected at any cost.

This is a story of mankind's treachery, the horrors of galactic war, and the only hope for peace in the universe.

About the Author

There's nothing mundane in the writing world of **Terry Wright**. Tension, conflict and suspense propel his readers through the pages as if they were on fire. Published in Science Fiction, Supernatural, and Horror, his mastery of the action thriller has also won him International acclaim as an accomplished screenplay writer. A longtime member of the Rocky Mountain Fiction Writers, he ran their annual Colorado Gold Writing Contest for five years, received their highest award for service, The Jasmine Award, and was nominated for the Writer of the Year in 2014.

Terry is a Vietnam Veteran (USAF – Red Horse - SAC), a certified pilot of light aircraft, and an avid Harley Davidson enthusiast. He's a member of the Harley Owners Group (HOG), the American Legion Post 178, and the American Legion Riders. He lives in Lakewood, Colorado, with his wife, Bobette, and their Yorkie, Taz.

Enjoy other fine short stories and novels by Terry Wright

The 13th Power Quest, Book 1 (TWB Press, 2011)
http://www.twbpress.com/the13thpowerquest.html

The 13th Power War, Book 3 (TWB Press, 2011)
http://www.twbpress.com/the13thpowerwar.html

The Grief Syndrome (TWB Press, 2011)
http://www.twbpress.com/thegriefsyndrome.html

The Duplication Factor (TWB Press, 2011)
http://www.twbpress.com/duplicationfactor.html

The Pearl of Death (TWB Press, 2013)
http://www.twbpress.com/thepearlofdeath.html

Black Jack (TWB Press, 2014)
http://www.twbpress.com/blackjack.html

Z-motors, The Job From Hell (TWB Press, 2011)
http://www.twbpress.com/zmotors.html

Street Beat (TWB Press, 2011)
http://www.twbpress.com/streetbeat.html

The Gates of Hell, Justin Graves Series (TWB Press, 2010)
http://www.twbpress.com/justingraves.html

Return me to Mistwillow – FREE (TWB Press, 2013)
http://www.twbpress.com/returnmetomistwillow.html

Wilderness Rampage (TWB Press, 2014)
http://www.twbpress.com/wildernessrampage.html

http://www.twbpress.com

www.ingramcontent.com/pod-product-compliance
Lightning Source LLC
Chambersburg PA
CBHW070800030726
47504CB00003B/633

* 9 7 8 1 9 4 4 0 4 5 2 4 1 *